D0125064

SOUTH CAROLINA BRIDES

THREE-IN-ONE COLLECTION

VICKIE MCDONOUGH

BARBOUR
PUBLISHING

© 2011 *Mutiny of the Heart* by Vicki McDonough
© 2011 *Secrets of the Heart* by Vicki McDonough
© 2011 *Dueling Hearts* by Vicki McDonough

Print ISBN 978-1-62416-735-5

eBook Editions:
Adobe Digital Edition (.epub) 978-1-62836-381-4
Kindle and MobiPocket Edition (.prc) 978-1-62836-382-1

All rights reserved. No part of this publication may be reproduced or
transmitted for commercial purposes, except for brief quotations in printed
reviews, without written permission of the publisher.

All scripture quotations are taken from the King James Version of the Bible.

This book is a work of fiction. Names, characters, places, and incidents are
either products of the author's imagination or used fictitiously. Any similarity
to actual people, organizations, and/or events is purely coincidental.

Cover design by Kirk DouPonce, DogEared Design

Published by Barbour Publishing, Inc., P.O. Box 719, Uhrichsville, Ohio 44683,
www.barbourbooks.com

*Our mission is to publish and distribute inspirational products offering exceptional
value and biblical encouragement to the masses.*

 Member of the
Evangelical Christian
Publishers Association

Printed in the United States of America.

Dear Readers,

I was born and raised in Oklahoma, a state that only celebrated its 100th birthday in 2007. When my editor asked me to consider writing a South Carolina series, I felt terribly inadequate to tackle an area with so rich a history. But as writers often do, I took a research trip. My husband and I fell in love with the Charleston area and its centuries-old homes, amazing churches, and unique historical buildings. We also visited two lovely plantations, which sparked ideas for my three-book series. I returned home with my car full of books, my camera loaded with 900+ pictures, and my mind reeling with ideas.

South Carolina Brides includes three stories about the fictional Reed family, all set in or near Charleston. *Mutiny of the Heart*, set in 1788, starts off the series with *Secrets of the Heart* following. The final book, *Dueling Hearts*, takes place in the 1880s. I hope you enjoy this collection—a century of stories set in the Old South—and fall in love with the area like I did.

Blessings,
Vickie McDonough
www.vickiemcdonough

MUTINY OF THE HEART

Chapter 1

Heather Hawthorne gazed at the monstrous homes of Charleston as another wave of doubt slammed into her with the full force of a hurricane. Was she making the right decision?

Hadn't she asked herself that question a thousand times since boarding the ship back home in Canada? Was it too late to hail the carriage driver and ask him to return them to the *Charlotte Anne* before it set sail for the Caribbean?

"Are we almost there, Aunt Heather?"

Smiling down at the lad she loved as her own, she ruffled his hair then found his cap on the seat and set it on his head. "Aye, dear one, we've nearly arrived."

Jamie furrowed his brow and leaned against her arm. "Do you think he will like me?"

Heather's heart clenched as she patted his soft cheek. "Of course he will."

Please, Lord. Let it be so. Holding the lad's hand, she watched the tall homes, and even taller palm trees, pass by. She hadn't seen the likes of such houses since her family left England and settled off the coast of Canada on Nova Scotia. Her poor cottage was probably a fraction of the size of the carriage houses that sat behind many of the giant homes. Nearly all had one- and two-story porches, or piazzas as she'd heard them called. Many of them faced the Charleston harbor, welcoming the cooling breezes of the sea. She lifted her head. Though she could not see the harbor at the moment, she could smell the salty air.

Lucas Reed was said to be one of the wealthiest shipbuilders in the area and would certainly live in one of these large homes. No sooner had the thought taken wing than the coach slowed and stopped. Heather gasped and held her hand against her chest. The imposing brick house looming above them was three stories tall. The decorative front door was sheltered by a rounded portico supported by four massive white columns. Curved stairways on either side led up to the landing. Ivy clung to the brick below the portico and crept out onto the stairs, giving the home a soft accent.

The carriage driver lowered the steps and opened the door. "The home of Mr. Lucas Reed, miss."

She accepted the hand he held out and descended the steps, turning to check on Jamie. He shrank back, staring at her with wide blue eyes. "Don't be afraid, lad. I'll be with you."

He nodded then gathered the bag that held his favorite possessions and hopped down, looking around with a crinkled brow. "Where's the house?"

The driver chuckled and motioned toward the redbrick structure. "'Tis here, boy."

"But that's a big building." Jamie tilted his head back and looked up at the portico.

"Aye, the houses here are quite large."

Now that was an understatement if there ever was one. Heather swallowed the lump in her throat. She'd gone through so much to get here, but what if the man didn't want the boy?

Lucas Reed had more money than he knew what to do with from the looks of this house, and his reputation for helping others was widely talked about—although he surely hadn't helped Jamie's mother any. She pursed her lips, trying to maintain a proper attitude. She would see that he did right by the lad, even if she had to remain in this hated country to do so.

The coachman lifted out her satchel and Jamie's smaller one. "I shall run these up the stairs for you, miss."

She smiled, found a coin in her reticule, and paid the man when he returned to the coach. "Thank you for your service."

"Should I wait for you, miss?"

"Nay." Surely Mr. Reed could provide transportation back to the docks if needed. Straightening her back and her resolve, she took Jamie's hand and climbed the stairs to the massive white door. She pounded the knocker and gazed around at the homes crowded together. How could one live with neighbors so nearby?

The door opened, and she swallowed hard. A butler studied her, gazing down her length and back up. His eyes narrowed a bit. "How can I be of service?"

"We're here to see Mr. Reed. Is he at home?"

"Hmm. . .I don't remember him having an appointment today."

"We don't have one." Heather lifted her chin at the stern man. "We've just arrived in town, and I had no chance to notify Mr. Reed in advance."

Jamie tugged her hand, shuffling his feet. "I need to use the. . .you know."

The butler backed away, holding the door open. "Step inside, miss, and I'll see if Mr. Reed is available. May I tell him the nature of your business?"

" 'Tis rather private." Heather ducked her head beneath his stern gaze. She got the impression he didn't think much of her, but he wasn't the one she was worried about. They stepped inside, and he hoisted their bags and set them in the entryway then closed the door.

"Stay here. I'll return shortly. You may leave your card in the receiving tray over there." He pointed to a long, narrow table that held a hammered silver tray with three of the four corners bent inward, then strode into the interior of the house.

She wandered over to the table, taking in the fine furnishings of the home. In the dish lay several calling cards with the owners' names on them. She had no card to leave. What would it matter anyway?

"Aunt Heather. . ."

"Hang on a bit longer, please." She stooped in front of Jamie and brushed his dark hair from his deep blue eyes. Oh, how she'd miss him. He was like a son to her, but he deserved to know his father, especially since his mother had died.

But would the father be worthy of such a fine lad?

&

Lucas Reed stood on the second-story piazza, staring at the Charleston harbor. The warm sea breeze touched his cheeks, and he lifted his head, breathing in the salty air. The morning sun glistened off the waters, causing him to squint, but even so he noticed a dolphin as it rose out of the water in a graceful arc and disappeared again.

He loved starting his mornings out here on the wide, covered porch. In fact, he just might start breaking his fast on the piazza every morning while he was in Charleston. What a perfect way to start a perfect day.

But he had business to attend to, a shipyard to oversee, and one day soon, he needed to return to the plantation and check on his servants. He donned his frock coat and took a final sip of his tea, then turned to go inside.

Langford exited the house. "There's a woman with a boy to see you, sir."

He waved his hand in dismissal. "Give them a few coins and food and send them on their way."

His butler sniffed. "Though clothed more like country folk, I do not believe they are beggars, sir. The lady mentioned traveling and that they have just arrived this morning."

Lucas searched his mind, trying to remember what ships were due into port this week. Intrigued by the mysterious visitor, he followed Langford downstairs to the foyer. A woman of modest dress stood holding a child's hand. Her woolen gown and heavy cloak hinted that she was from a cooler climate. He wondered that she wasn't sweltering under Charleston's spring warmth.

She lifted her head and followed his downward progression with something like disdain on her pretty face. Her dark brown hair was neatly tucked under her linen cap and a wide-brimmed hat. Intelligent brown eyes stared at him without the usual signs of attraction he saw gleaming in the eyes of most women he encountered, in spite of his efforts to discourage them.

Interesting.

Women often sought him out at soirees and events, but very few actually came to his home, especially without an escort. As the elder of two sons, he'd been blessed to inherit the Reed fortune, but a not-always-unpleasant side effect was that most of the town's mamas had set their caps to snare him for their daughters. And more often than not, the town's poor found their way to his door. Somehow, he believed this woman was neither.

Langford crossed to the table where visitors left their calling cards. His mouth twitched as he picked up a tattered paper the woman must have deposited in the receiving tray. "Miss Heather Hawthorne and Master Jamie." Langford turned toward the woman. "I present Mr. Lucas Reed, miss."

Heather Hawthorne. The name meant nothing to him, and he noted that the child's last name had not been mentioned. He closed the distance between him and the woman. The boy danced at her side, tugging on her hand. Lucas resisted smiling. "Langford, perhaps you could show the boy to the facilities and then see that he has a treat in the kitchen."

Miss Hawthorne's lips tightened, and she glanced down at the child as if she didn't want to turn loose of him.

Jamie leaned toward her, shaking his legs as if cold. "Please, Aunt Heather, I must go."

Miss Hawthorne nodded, and Lucas allowed a grin, taking in the boy's black hair. When the child turned his grateful blue eyes on Lucas, his heart leaped like a horse clearing a jump. Jamie smiled, revealing a twin set of dimples, and the breath whooshed out of Lucas's lungs. His mind filled with questions, but he held his tongue until Langford and the boy were gone.

"Might I offer you a seat and some refreshment, Miss Hawthorne?"

She shook her head and fanned her face. "Nay, but I thank you."

"You have an endearing boy, Miss Hawthorne." Lucas stood with his hands locked behind his back. "May I inquire as to the nature of your business?"

The woman glanced to the doorway where Langford and the boy had quit the room; then she met his gaze. "Aye, you may. I've come to deliver your son to you."

Lucas felt as if he were riding full gallop and had encountered a tree branch hard in the chest. He opened his mouth to deny the child, but the boy's piercing blue eyes, dark hair, and dimples prevented him from speaking. He'd seen the startling resemblance of a Reed male in the boy, but he knew that he couldn't have fathered a child that age. He may have been promiscuous as a young man, but since giving his heart to God seven years ago, he hadn't been with a woman. He stared at his guest, wondering what game she was about. "I can assure you, Miss Hawthorne, that boy is not mine."

Chapter 2

Heather waved her hand in front of her face as the heat of the room and the man's denial hit her full force. She took in his handsome face, black hair, and startling eyes the color of the sea. How could the arrogant rogue disallow Jamie when the boy was his miniature? Did he think she was a fortune hunter seeking to pawn off the child for the sake of a few coins? Though her heart pounded, she lifted her chin. "You are wrong, sir. Do not try to deny the lad. His face is yours."

Lucas Reed shook his head. "You are mistaken. I've never seen you before, so how could Jamie be our son? Besides, did he not call you his aunt?"

The blood rushed from her face, and she held her hand against her chest. "I never said he was mine, as much as I wish it were so. He is the son of my cousin. She is the one who assured me that Jamie was your son and made me promise to deliver him to you."

The man narrowed his eyes then waved his hand in the air. "Where is this nameless accuser? Has she not the gall to indict me to my face?"

"How dare you speak ill of the dead."

Mr. Reed's expression softened, and those startling eyes implored her to believe him, but she knew the truth. What reason could Deborah possibly have for lying about such a thing? Her cousin was amiable, genteel, and a believer in God. She would not tell a falsehood about something so important.

"I am sorry for your loss, but surely you must understand my dilemma, miss. A stranger appears at my door with a boy she claims is mine, but I know for a fact that he couldn't be."

Her irritation surged. "You must be mistaken. 'Tis a disgrace that you could father a child and not even know about it."

His cheeks actually reddened beneath his tan. He narrowed his eyes, and she could almost see the cogs in his mind turning, trying to find a way to convince her.

"What is the name of the boy's mother?"

"Deborah Farmington."

Mr. Reed blinked, and a range of emotions flooded his handsome face. If Jamie grew up to look like his father, he'd be a comely man, for certain. And if she wasn't mistaken, the man had just gone pale. "I see you recognize Deborah's name."

His stance rigid, he turned and paced away from her, as if gathering his thoughts. His long legs carried him across the wide entryway to a room that looked like a formal parlor. The exquisite furniture must have been shipped from England, or maybe even France. Her family had owned such possessions—before her father lost his fortune funding the war against the colonists. She hated being here in this country—the country responsible for her family's demise and her father's death. Her small cottage paled in comparison, and as hard as it would be to leave the lad she loved as her own, he would have a chance to get an education here and enjoy luxuries that she could never give him.

Suddenly, Mr. Reed swerved back to face her. He strode toward her then halted and shook his head. "I'll admit to knowing Miss Farmington's name, but as I said before, it is impossible that the boy is mine."

❧

For a moment, Lucas had hoped that Jamie was his, but the years didn't add up. He hadn't seen Deborah in eight years, and the boy couldn't be more than six at the most. But even more compelling was the fact that he and Deborah had never been intimate.

Miss Hawthorne's brown eyes sparked, and she rummaged around in the worn bag that dangled from her wrist. She pulled out a crinkled paper then thrust it at him. "Here, if you don't believe me, read this."

He took the paper and turned it over, noticing the Farmington seal on the back. He rubbed his thumb over the wax, traveling back to another time. A time when he still believed in love. A time before his dreams had been crushed as effectively as a spider beneath a boot heel.

He broke the seal and began reading:

My dear Lucas,
   Forgive me. I know you must be confused and most likely angry, but I implore you to accept Jamie as your own, even though you know he isn't. Surely, you can see he bears little resemblance to me, but rather has the same dark hair, remarkable blue eyes, and dimples characteristic of the Reed men. He is in fact your nephew, and Marcus's son.

Lucas sucked in a breath, drawing Miss Hawthorne's curious gaze. She obviously had no idea what message the letter held. He turned away, not wanting her to see the pain in his eyes. How could the woman he loved—the woman who was to be *his* wife—have borne a son by his brother?

His heart ached as all the memories rushed back. After a moment, he forced himself to read on:

I want you to know that I didn't go with Marcus willingly. He kidnapped me to make you suffer—to keep us from marrying. I do believe at first he saw

14

*it as a game, but then he became infatuated with me and refused to return me
to you. He hates you because you inherited your father's homes and business,
while he got almost nothing, even though he was born only a few minutes
after you.*

Lucas clutched the letter to his chest, not wanting to read what came next.
Deborah hadn't left of her own accord. He'd hoped—prayed—that had been
the case, and yet, as he thought back on things now, would it not have been
easier on her if she had left willingly rather than as a captive aboard his brother's ship? *Oh Deborah, what you must have suffered. You have no idea how long I
searched for you.*

He slowly paced the room and continued reading:

*I will admit that my heart ached for Marcus after my anger died down. He
seemed so lost and alone, even though I know much of it was his own doing.
He took me to an island in the Caribbean where he makes his home. He said
you'd know of it if you thought hard enough.*

*Marcus kept me two years, hoping I'd fall in love with him. Sad to say, I
wish I could have. He so needed someone to love him, but my heart only ever
belonged to you, Lucas.*

I longed for things that must not have been God's will.

*This next part is as difficult for me to write as it will be for you to hear.
In a drunken rage one night, Marcus came to me and begged me to tell him I
loved him. I could not.*

Lucas ran his fingers through his hair, not wanting to read what followed.
Oh Deborah.

*He took me that night. I'm sorry for the crudeness of my letter, but it is vital
that you understand—that no one ever know that Jamie is not your son, for
consider the shame that would be cast upon him if people learn he is the illegitimate son of a pirate, the Black Mark. I'm sorry for the embarrassment and
sorrows this will cause you, but for my child's sake—for the love you once held
in your heart for me—I implore you to raise Jamie as your own.*

*I am dying. I've pleaded with my cousin Heather to bring my son to you.
I pray you walk with God and that one day I will see you in heaven.*

I shall remain forever yours,
Deborah

Lucas leaned against the doorjamb, trying to grasp all the letter had said.
He clenched his fist, knowing if he ever saw his brother again, he'd flog him
within an inch of his life. He sighed and forced his hand to relax.

He'd loved his brother, but they had never been close, even though they were twins. Their father had showed his favoritism toward Lucas from the time they were small. He knew it, and Marcus knew it. As a young boy, Marcus had been content with his mother's attention—but not as he grew older and the reality of his situation sank in. He'd become increasingly disgruntled, and his behavior was abysmal.

Keeping the child could well damage Lucas's fine reputation. He considered Jamie, and his heart took wing. Could the boy be a gift from God? Lucas was being given the chance to raise Deborah's son—the boy that should have been *his* son. Keeping Jamie would change many things in Lucas's life. And what did he know about raising a child? Nothing. Yet he couldn't turn family away. Jamie was Deborah's son—and from this day forward, Jamie would become his son. He smacked the letter against his fist, his decision made, and turned to face the woman. "The boy can stay."

Relief washed over her face a moment before she buried her cheeks in her hands.

"Is that not what you want?" Lucas asked.

"Aye. But how will I ever say good-bye to him? He's such a young lad. I've tended him ever since his mother died three years ago."

Lucas jerked back as if he'd been struck. "Three years! Why did you wait so long to bring him here?"

Miss Hawthorne's cheeks matched the red of his parlor settee, and she ducked her head. "I do not have the means you do. It took me this long to raise the money for the trip, and had I not traveled with a friend of my father's, I'd not be here now."

"Why did you not write me? I could have sent the funds for passage."

She looked at him with skepticism. "I did not know how you'd receive the news and thought it better to come in person so that you could see how much Jamie resembles you."

Lucas narrowed his eyes. "And how is it you knew that when we've never met before?"

"Deborah said Jamie was the spitting image of his father."

"Indeed." Fortunately, he and his brother were identical twins. No one need ever know that Jamie wasn't his son, no matter the scourge Lucas may face among his friends and business associates for birthing an illegitimate child. For the boy's sake, he'd endure whatever came his way.

At the sound of footsteps, he turned. Jamie trotted toward him, his relief evident when he saw Miss Hawthorne. Lucas glanced at her, noting again her simple beauty. Leaving Jamie would be terribly difficult for her, he was certain. He rubbed his chin with his thumb and forefinger. And what of the boy? He'd already lost his mother. The separation from his guardian could be devastating. Lucas would need a governess to care for the boy. Turning, he watched as Miss Hawthorne bent and gave Jamie a hug. Perhaps it would work best if she'd be willing to stay on until he could hire someone permanently. That would allow Jamie time to become comfortable in his new home and with him before Miss Hawthorne left.

"Miss Abigail gave me corn pudding and a sweet roll." Jamie's eyes glowed.

"You'll have no room for your supper now," Miss Hawthorne teased. She smoothed the hair out of Jamie's eyes.

Lucas's heart swelled with love for the boy he'd just met. How was that possible? He shook his head and turned to his servant. "Langford, see that the room next to mine is made ready for Master Jamie."

Langford was a British immigrant who rarely showed emotion or expression of any kind, but at Lucas's order, the butler's gray eyes went wide. He looked from the woman to the child and back and then leaned forward. "Surely you do not mean to keep the urchin, sir."

Lucas lifted a brow, surprised that Langford would question him, especially in public. "Please do as I say. As you can well see, the boy has my blood. He is a Reed and, as such, will be living here and deserves the same respect you'd give me. Is that clear?"

Langford's lips twitched, and his eyes narrowed, as if he thought Lucas had been taken in by a pretty wench and a sad story. But he dipped his head and started up the stairs.

Jamie tugged on Miss Hawthorne's skirt. "Are you staying, too?"

She blinked her eyes and bent down, allowing Jamie to hug her neck. Patting his back, she said, "Shh. . .child, you belong with your father now."

"I don't have a father," Jamie wailed. "I want to stay with you."

"Aye, you do, and he's standing right there, waiting to get to know you."

Sniffing, Jamie turned his head but kept it resting on Miss Hawthorne's shoulder as he eyed Lucas. He offered the boy a smile and now regretted his initial harshness. But there were many who'd take advantage of his wealth, and while he didn't mind helping the poor, he wouldn't be taken in by a miscreant bent on swindling him.

Stooping down, he hoped to make himself less intimidating. "How would you like it if Miss Hawthorne were to stay awhile, too?"

A light sparked in Jamie's eyes, making Lucas want to please the boy. Jamie leaned back and gazed up at her face. "Would you, Aunt Heather? Stay here with me?"

She stood and straightened her dress then lifted a brow to Lucas.

He realized he should have asked her before getting Jamie's hopes up. "Could you stay a fortnight or so, to allow me time to find a proper governess and to give Jamie time to get to know me before you take your leave?"

Her gaze roved the house, and he wondered what she saw. She seemed uncomfortable in his home. Had she never before lived in such a setting? He tried to see the home from her eyes, but everything was so familiar that he couldn't. Once again, he realized how much God had entrusted to him, and he determined to do what he could to help others.

Miss Hawthorne glanced down at her clothing. "I would like to stay and see Jamie settled, but I don't belong here. I would embarrass you with my clothing and my lack of knowledge of American life. And I must catch the *Charlotte Anne* on her way back from the Caribbean to return home."

"Nonsense. Everyone in my employment receives the proper clothing and instruction for their position, although, I suppose you know far more about tending the boy than anyone here. I'll see to it that you have some new clothes, and perhaps you could help me interview governesses. When the time comes for you to return, I'll find a place for you on one of my ships."

"Say aye, Aunt Heather." Jamie smiled and peered up at Miss Hawthorne. "We can *both* stay."

The woman gazed up at Lucas, and he had a difficult time not fidgeting. She stared at him as if taking his measure, but finally she nodded. "Aye, we'll both stay, for the time being."

Lucas smiled, grateful the woman was willing to remain for a time for the boy's sake. Langford made his way down the stairs and stopped in front of him. "The room is being readied, sir."

"Thank you. Now, I need you to inform the upstairs maid to make ready a room near the boy's for Miss Hawthorne. She'll be staying to care for Jamie until I hire a governess."

Langford's nostrils flared, but he dipped his head. "As you wish, sir." As he retrieved their bags and turned toward the stairs again, Lucas was certain he heard the man mutter, "Highly irregular."

He resisted smiling again and shook his head. Today he'd become the father of his brother's son. Yes sir. Highly irregular.

Chapter 3

I'm starving, Aunt Heather." Jamie rubbed his stomach. "Something downstairs sure smells good."

"Aye, and we'd better get down there, or we'll not get to eat." She took her ward's hand and escorted him down the grand staircase. Last night she'd slept in a bed as big as her whole sleeping chamber back home, and it had been so soft she'd felt as if she were resting on a cloud.

"This house is bigger than any in Nova Scotia." Jamie stared wide-eyed up at the fancy ceiling with its decorative plasterwork.

"I don't know as it's bigger, but it certainly is fancier."

She stepped onto the entryway floor as Jamie leaned toward her. "Mr. Reed sure must be rich. You think he'd buy me a pony?"

"Oh Jamie. You disappoint me." Heather shook her head and stared down at him. "You should be happy that you've been united with your father and not worry about things of the world."

Jamie ducked his head and kicked the bottom step with his shoe. "Aye mum."

She tugged him close. How could she begrudge him wanting something nice? He'd had precious few things to call his own his whole life. Heather walked toward the kitchen, unsure where they would be expected to eat. She shook her head at the opulence around her. Yet as she studied the home, she realized the furniture was expensive but functional, and there seemed to be few useless extravagances and more practical items.

Her family had enjoyed wealth—not to the extreme the Reeds did, but enough that they had lived a comfortable life. At least until the colonists rose up to fight for their independence. Her father had sunk his fortune into the war efforts, but in the end, Britain lost, and the Hawthorne family had little left. Her father, born into a wealthy family, was unacquainted with poverty and all but lost his will to live, finally succumbing a year ago. For that, she'd always despise the colonists—Americans, as they now called themselves.

"Ah, there you are." Lucas Reed walked toward her, tall and straight.

Heather's mouth went dry at the fine figure he cut in his loose linen shirt, gold waistcoat, and breeches tucked into the tops of his boots. His long, black hair was neatly tied back, emphasizing his strong jawline. No wonder Deborah fell for him. Heather straightened her spine as well as her resolve. Deborah had been a much younger woman, susceptible to the fantasies of youth, when she'd given herself to Lucas Reed, but Heather would not make the same error. Above all, she wanted a man who served God, not a blackguard who'd steal a young woman's virtue and leave her to raise their child alone.

Mr. Reed stared at her for a moment, and she couldn't help squirming. She lifted a hand to tuck a wayward strand of hair behind her ear. What did he see when he looked at her? Was he appalled by her simple garment? If not for him and his kind, she'd still be back in England, enjoying her family's wealth and the privileges that came with it. She might even be married by now and have her own child.

"You must find those wool dresses dreadfully uncomfortable in the heat of the South. We need to make our first stop the dressmakers."

Heather's cheeks felt as if she'd brushed up against the flame of a candle. How dare he. "I don't believe my clothing is a proper topic of conversation."

The rogue had the gall to chuckle. "We can't have you fainting dead away from the heat, can we?"

Jamie tugged on Mr. Reed's waistcoat. "I'm hungry, sir."

Lucas squatted down. "Are you now? We should do something about that then. Come."

He took Jamie's hand, and the boy followed along, already trusting the man. Heather's heart cracked. All too soon, Jamie would become comfortable here, and she'd have to leave, never to see him again. How could she bear it?

At the doorway, Jamie looked back over his shoulder. "Come on, Aunt Heather."

She smiled, her fears tempered for the moment. Mr. Reed surprised her by sitting Jamie at the large table in the dining room. Most wealthy people relegated their young children to eating in the kitchen or the nursery. "Wouldn't you rather Jamie and I ate in the kitchen?"

"Bah! I don't cotton to family not taking meals together. I'm sure Jamie will behave himself. Won't you, boy?"

Jamie nodded then reached for a sweet roll. Heather shook her head, and the lad's eyes widened, but he lowered his hand to his lap. She sat, waiting for Mr. Reed to begin dining, but he just looked at her with those piercing eyes.

"Before meals, I like to thank the good Lord for my food. Do you mind?" he said.

She shook her head, even though she felt uncomfortable. Her father had never believed in God and had refused to allow prayers at mealtime.

"Can you bow your head, Jamie?"

"Aye sir." Jamie ducked his head, but he peered up at Heather.

"Close your eyes, son." Lucas smiled.

Son. Family. Heather's heartbeat raced at the words. Why would Lucas Reed so easily accept the child he'd adamantly denied yesterday? Until she'd given him Deborah's letter, he'd been less than convinced. She glanced down at her hands while Mr. Reed blessed the food.

When she returned home, she'd be all alone. Jamie had helped her heart, still aching from her father's death, heal with his easy smile and frequent hugs. Oh how she'd miss him. Her eyes misted, but she blinked them dry and reached for the platter of sliced ham that Mr. Reed held out to her.

"So, Jamie, tell me what you like to do." Mr. Reed spooned porridge into his bowl and then added some honey.

Jamie sat on his knees and reached for the sweet roll again. Heather decided to try a flaky bread shaped like a half-moon.

"Aunt Heather's teaching me my letters and how to read some."

Lucas nodded and smiled. "'Tis a good thing for a boy to know how to read at such a young age."

Jamie sat a bit straighter. Lucas dished up a smaller bowl of porridge and passed it to him. "What else do you do?"

Jamie's eyes lifted toward the ceiling as he contemplated the question. "I help Aunt Heather make soap."

One of Mr. Reed's brows quirked up. "Indeed."

Heather nodded, wondering what he thought of her profession. She needed some way to provide for herself and Jamie.

"Aye. Indeed," Jamie parroted. "I gather the wood for the fire."

As the meal progressed, Heather relaxed. In spite of the ire she held toward Lucas Reed for what he'd done to Deborah, she found the man likable and comfortable to be around. He didn't maintain the snobbish reserve she'd expected from someone of his stature in society and wealth.

When they were nearly finished with their meal, Langford strode in, his nose lifted high as if he were the one with all the money. "Waverly is here from the stable, sir."

"Very good." Lucas turned his gaze on Jamie. "How would you like to visit the stable and see my horses?"

Jamie bounced back up on his knees. "Truly? Aye, I would." His gaze faltered as it shifted toward Heather. "Is it all right if I go?"

She nodded. "Aye, but you should now be asking such questions of your father when he is in the room."

"But he's the one who asked *me*."

Lucas chuckled. "I did at that."

"Will you go, too?" Jamie asked her.

"I'd like to have a talk with Miss Hawthorne," Mr. Reed interjected, "if you are agreeable."

Jamie eyed them both then shrugged. "All right." Then he grinned. "I get to see the horses while you two just get to talk."

Lucas smiled, but the look he gave Heather sent a warm shiver down her back and made her think he felt he was getting the better end of the bargain.

If she didn't keep her guard up, she'd quickly be disarmed by his charm and friendliness.

"Go with Langford, and then Mr. Waverly will escort you to the stable. Be sure that you do as Waverly says, and don't get overly close to the horses. We'll be right here in this room until you return."

"Promise?"

"Jamie, you heard the man. Do not question your father." Heather knew he was afraid she'd leave while he was gone. How would he bear their permanent separation?

"Aye mum."

Mr. Reed watched with pride in his eyes as Jamie followed Langford out of the room; then he switched his unnerving gaze on her. "Would you care for more tea, Miss Hawthorne?"

Startled by his offer to serve her, she simply shook her head. Finally, she found her voice and pointed to the pastry she'd eaten. "These are quite good and so light."

"I fancy them myself. I first had one on a trip to France."

"They're delicious."

Mr. Reed nodded. "Jamie is a fine boy. You've done well with him, especially since he wasn't your own child."

Her heart clenched. Though he had complimented her, he'd only reinforced that the lad wasn't hers to keep.

"Thank you for bringing him here. I only wish I'd known about him before now." He stared into his cup, and she thought he truly meant what he'd said.

"So, how did Deborah come to live with you?"

Heather's ire returned, shoving away any compassion she might have felt for the man. "She was with child, unmarried, and too ashamed to return to her parents' home."

Mr. Reed had the good sense to wince at her intentional barb. "Yes, well, if only she had come to me, I'd have done right by her."

She wanted to ask how he could be intimate with a woman of Deborah's quality and then turn her aside like a trollop, but she couldn't voice the words. How could he dally with a woman's affections, take what he wanted, and just cast her away like bilge water? What she knew about Lucas Reed didn't match the kind, open man before her. It was as if they were two different people.

"Tell me about the Hawthornes. You have an English surname, but your Christian name is Scottish, I believe. Have you always lived in Canada?"

"Nay, not always. My mother's heritage is Scottish, but my father's is English. About four years ago, shortly after my mother died, my father and I left England and settled in Nova Scotia. He is also dead now." She left off the cause of her father's death. Though she blamed the colonists and their desire for independence from England for her family's demise, it was hardly fair to hold Mr. Reed personally to blame.

He studied her for a moment, as if deciphering the reason for her angst. He sipped his tea then set down the cup. "My family was originally from England, too, although my grandfather moved to Barbados before coming to the colonies. I've visited relatives in England and done business there but have always called America my home. Besides this house, I own a plantation called Reed Springs. I'd like to take you and Jamie there sometime soon, after I conclude my business here. I think he'd be more comfortable where he has land for running around. And before you worry about us traveling together without a chaperone, my neighbors the Madisons will journey with us. They traveled here with me a fortnight ago, and we're to return together. Also, my mother resides at the plantation."

Heather nodded. She should be amazed that the man owned another home besides this one, but she wasn't.

She'd heard that many people who lived in Charleston had second homes they went to in order to get away from the summer heat and the annoying mosquitoes and gnats that invaded the coastal regions. Suddenly, she realized he'd mentioned his mother. Heather had never considered that Jamie might have grandparents still living. How would Mrs. Reed react to Jamie? Would she embrace him as her grandson or find him a family embarrassment?

Mr. Reed steepled his fingertips. "How did Deborah die, if I may ask?"

"From an extended illness. Jamie's birth was hard on her, and she never quite regained her health." Died of a broken heart was more like it.

"I'm sorry. I wish I could have helped her."

He hung his head, and she truly believed he meant what he said. Perhaps over the years, the man had changed from the scoundrel who'd stolen Deborah's innocence. But she didn't want to feel compassion for him. She stared out a nearby window at a line of shrubs covered in brilliant pink flowers. That was something she'd noticed right off on arriving in South Carolina—the abundance of beautiful flowers. And the moss that swung from the trees like lace drying on limbs gave the place a homey feel. So different from Canada, which had barely begun to thaw.

Mr. Reed tapped his finger on the table. "What do you suppose I should look for in a governess?"

His rapid topic changes continued to take her by surprise. She dreaded some other woman taking care of Jamie, but there was no helping it. "Someone who is kind and loves children, I suppose. Someone who is patient and will be a good instructor."

"That sounds like you."

"Thank you, sir." She turned her head away as her cheeks warmed. She would have to keep her defenses raised to avoid being charmed by this rogue, and keeping Deborah in mind did just the trick. She would have to watch herself so that she, too, wasn't taken in by the beguiling Lucas Reed.

"The Madisons will arrive at ten. I thought you'd feel more comfortable having another woman along as we shop for your clothing."

"We?" She lifted a brow to him. "Do you normally purchase your servants' clothing yourself?"

He grinned wide. "No, but Jamie needs apparel better suited to our warmer climate, too, and I thought we'd go together. There are times I'll be busy with work and may not see Jamie for a while, so I'd like to spend this day getting to know him."

She nodded. "We shall be ready by ten."

Chapter 4

Heather liked Caroline Madison immediately. At Mr. Reed's introduction, the lively blond flitted away from her tall, dashing husband and came to stand before her. There were obvious questions in the woman's gaze, but she was polite enough not to voice them.

Mr. Reed introduced them all, lightly touching Jamie's shoulder when he gave the lad's name: Jamie Reed. At last, Deborah's son wore the surname that truly belonged to him.

"Welcome to Charleston, Miss Hawthorne. It's a pleasure to meet you."

Heather nodded. "And you, too."

Mrs. Madison bent toward Jamie and ruffled his hair. "And aren't you just the spitting image of your father?"

Jamie's gaze darted to his father, as if he'd never considered they might resemble each other. Mr. Reed's bright smile and sparkling eyes led her to believe he was proud of Jamie. Certainly not the reaction she'd expected from a wealthy man whose illegitimate son had suddenly invaded his life. Evidently he'd informed the Madisons of the situation before she and Jamie had come back downstairs. How had he gone about explaining the presence of a five-year-old son he'd never laid eyes on before?

"Shall we be off?" Mr. Reed reached for a tricorn hat that hung on the hall tree in the entryway and set it on his head.

"Are we to ride in a carriage, sir?"

Mr. Reed smiled down at Jamie. "No son, it's a lovely day and not far, so we shall walk."

The men took the lead with the women and Jamie following. Nearly six feet tall, Mr. Madison stood only a few inches shorter than Mr. Reed. They seemed good friends and carried on a lively conversation.

"I do have to say Lucas certainly surprised Richard and me upon our arrival when he shared his exciting news with us." Mrs. Madison glanced down at Jamie. "Besides my husband, Lucas is the most honorable man I know. I cannot believe he'd"—she leaned close to Heather's ear—"father a child and not marry the mother and raise the boy."

Heather clenched her hands together, not caring to talk about the subject. If Mrs. Madison wanted information, she'd need to direct her questions to Mr. Reed. "Have you always lived in Charleston?"

"No, I was born in Boston. My family moved here when I was only twelve.

Father wanted to get away from the cold weather, and we've lived here ever since. We do, however, visit our Boston relatives during the heat of the summer. Richard's family is from here though. He's the third generation of Madisons born in this area."

They walked several short blocks then crossed a wide street to where a number of vendors were selling their wares. All manner of food was sold in booths and shops. Jamie tugged on her skirt, and Heather looked down.

"What's she doing?" He pointed at a dark-skinned woman weaving a basket that looked to be made of straw.

"Those are sweetgrass baskets," Mrs. Madison said. "They're made from marsh grasses that are harvested along the coast."

"That's fascinating. So they braid the grasses into platters and containers?" Heather asked.

"Not braid. If you look at the unbound grass, you can see that they are just long stems that are secured together with a strip of palm leaf wrapped around them."

"The tradition of making the sweetgrass trays and baskets was brought over by slaves from Africa," Mr. Reed added.

Jamie leaned against her skirt. "Is that woman a slave?"

Heather patted his shoulder. "I don't know."

"She probably is, as are the other weavers here." Mr. Reed gazed down the street and shook his head. "I know most planters rely on slave labor, but I think owning another man is atrocious."

Heather stared at the man, surprised that he'd so openly voiced his disgust of slavery, which was a common institution in the South. She'd heard there had been slaves ever since the first ship arrived here. How did Mr. Reed run his plantation without the aid of slaves? Didn't he mention growing rice? Producing such a crop surely took numerous servants.

"You see those big platters made from grass, Jamie?" Mr. Madison said. "Those are called *fannahs*. The field workers place rice in them then toss the rice up into the air and catch it again in the fannah. The air blows away the chaff—the bad parts—and leaves the hull."

"Oh." Jamie studied the trays with woven handles on each end as if trying to visualize the process.

Mr. Reed patted Jamie's head. "You'll get to see it done when we go to the plantation."

"Can I try it?"

Mr. Reed grinned. "That's a splendid idea. You'll need to learn every aspect of plantation work if you're going to run Reed Springs one day."

"Truly?" Jamie's eyes widened as he stared up at his father.

Heather's heart jolted. Surely the man wasn't thinking in such a direction already. Why, he'd only met Jamie yesterday. She didn't want him falsely raising the lad's hopes. Someday Lucas Reed would marry. In fact, she was surprised that he didn't already have a wife, and that wife—once he did acquire one—would expect *her* son to inherit the Reed properties, not her husband's illegitimate child.

"Well, I hope for my sake that isn't anytime soon." Mr. Reed chuckled. "Are you ready to go see a couple of my ships, son?"

"Aye sir. I am."

"Might I broach a suggestion?" Mrs. Madison stepped forward. "We care as little for the roughness of the dock area as I'm sure you do for a dressmaker's shop. Why don't you menfolk visit the docks while I take Miss Hawthorne to purchase what she needs? Then we can meet up and see to Jamie's clothing."

Mr. Reed's gaze collided with Heather's, and her pulse shot forward like a startled horse. "Would that be agreeable with you?" he asked.

She nodded. "Aye. There is no sense in you men having to wait around for us." Not to mention she'd be terribly embarrassed to purchase clothing with them watching.

"So you don't mind if Jamie goes along with us?"

Her heart somersaulted at the thought of parting with the boy. "I'd thought to take him with us," she said.

"But I want to see the ships." Jamie's pleading gaze bored into hers.

She almost shook her head. Only a day ago, he'd been anxious to get off the ship that brought them to Charleston, and now he longed to see one again. Fickle boy. The truth be told, it was too soon for *her* to be separated from him. Yet he needed to gradually get used to the idea, and she needed to know she could trust Lucas Reed with Jamie's well-being. This was a perfect opportunity for a short parting. "Aye, 'tis fine with me if you go with your father, but be sure that you obey him."

"I will." Jamie bounced on his toes and clapped his hands, making his father smile.

Mr. Reed reached down and took Jamie's hand. "Shall we meet up at McCrady's at noon?"

Mrs. Madison nodded. "Noon should be perfect."

Mr. Reed grinned, warming Heather's insides. He looked down at Jamie. "Shall we be off then?"

She watched the men cross the street, and on the other side, Lucas Reed stooped down and said something to Jamie. The lad nodded, and his father hoisted him up into his arms. Jamie looped one arm around Mr. Reed's neck then turned back and grinned at Heather and waved.

"They're getting along famously, aren't they?"

"Aye." Almost too well. As much as she wanted Jamie and his father to have a good relationship, Heather dreaded seeing him distance himself from her, but it had to be. Once Mr. Reed hired another governess, she'd be on her way back to Canada.

"And it's kind of Lucas to be so concerned with your feelings."

Heather glanced sideways at the woman. "What do you mean?"

Mrs. Madison giggled and waved her hand in the air. "Nothing actually. It's just that most men in Lucas's situation wouldn't ask if it was all right with the governess to take his own son somewhere."

Heather winced. Though the words were spoken casually, she felt rightly put in her place. She may have been the one to raise Jamie and bring him here, but she was just the hired help now. Then why had Mrs. Madison taken it upon herself to escort her to the dressmaker's shop instead of letting Mr. Reed's housekeeper do that?

Two hours later, Heather's legs ached. She had stood still while the dressmaker measured her, had tried on several ready-made items that the woman had in stock, as well as stood in front of a mirror while the other two women decided which colors looked best on her. The result was two fancy silk gowns for evening wear, one green with a gold-striped petticoat and the other a lovely lavender with soft blue accents. The three day dresses made of lightweight linen would feel much more comfortable in the heat of the afternoon, but what excited Heather the most was the new drawers, chemise, stockings, and petticoats. She hadn't had any new undergarments other than those she'd sewn herself from rough fabrics since she left England. If only she didn't have to wait until the dressmaker made them. At least she'd be able to wear the one ready-made day dress that was to be delivered to Mr. Reed's house later this afternoon.

"I especially liked how you looked in that dark green gown. It goes well with your coloring." Mrs. Madison waved her lovely silk fan in front of her face. "You will love the linen fabric. It's less formal but necessary here and much cooler than wool."

Heather struggled to keep up with the taller woman's longer stride. "I think you purchased far too many outfits. I could have easily made do with less."

"Fiddlesticks. If you hadn't been so persuasive, I'd have ordered more garments. Lucas said to be sure you had all you needed."

"I'm only going to be here until he hires another governess. Perhaps if he employs someone close to me in size, she will be able to use the same clothing. I've little need of lightweight dresses in Canada."

"Who knows?" The woman waved her hand in the air and dashed across the street. Then slowing her steps, she peered over her shoulder. "Perhaps you will be here longer than you think."

Heather hurried, not wanting to be left behind. She fell in behind Mrs. Madison to allow a man and his wife to pass, then hurried back to her side. "Why do you say that?"

Mrs. Madison shrugged. "Just a hunch, my dear. You're the best person to raise Jamie. You've been with him all his life, is that not correct?"

Heather nodded. "Aye, 'tis true."

"Well, then how could another woman be better than you?"

Heather's heart soared then plummeted like a quail spooked from the grass and shot from the sky. She'd love to be there for Jamie, but how could she stay in this country she so despised? Her family had lost everything because of the colonists' bid for freedom.

She contemplated the woman's words as they continued down the street past a silver shop where fine quality cups, platters, and jewelry were displayed in a window. The hammer of a cobbler reached her ears as they walked past his open door. A young boy stood in front of a printer's shop, hawking papers. Charleston certainly was a busy place.

Could she live in this country and put aside her feelings for Jamie's sake? She'd never considered that could be an option and wasn't sure now that it was, but so far the people she'd met had been more than kind and receiving, not the rebellious troublemakers she'd half expected to encounter.

"Ah, there's McCrady's now. I hope the men are already there. I'm famished."

One thing was for certain, Heather would have to think long and hard before making a decision to stay in America—if Lucas Reed even asked her to.

વ

Lucas couldn't remember a more enjoyable morning. Jamie had tossed questions at him faster than a clipper could speed across the ocean at full sail. The boy was smart, curious, and well behaved.

"How many ships can you build in a year?" Jamie asked.

"Well now, that depends on any number of things. The weather for one. Also, the availability of skilled workmen."

"Perhaps I'll be a shipbuilder when I grow up."

Lucas caught Richard's amused glance and smiled.

"Maybe you will, son." He ruffled Jamie's hair then recaptured his hand. The child seemed to trust him totally and had expressed no fear being away from Miss Hawthorne, even though well over an hour had passed.

"I have to say, I don't believe I've seen you looking happier, Lucas, than you have today." Richard nodded.

"I am happy." Warmth flooded Lucas's chest. With Jamie's arrival, he realized how lonely he'd been. How much he'd wanted a family but had been afraid of pursuing a woman. What if his brother found out about her and decided to purloin her as he had Deborah? He clenched his fist. Marcus would have to get past him first.

"I hope you realize what a blessing from God the boy is."

Lucas relaxed his fist. "I surely do. I can't help thinking over and over how much he will change my life."

Richard cleared his throat and leaned a bit closer as they strode down the street. "I don't suppose I need to tell you that there are likely to be repercussions. While I, for one, think it's an honorable thing you've done, some people will look down on you for taking in the boy or for not marrying his mother when you learned she was with child."

Skirting a pile of manure in the street, Lucas cast his friend a quick glance. "I never knew about him until he and Miss Hawthorne arrived at my door."

"Well, it's hard to believe you didn't expect the possibility of a child when..." Richard waved his hand in the air. "You know."

Lucas clapped his hand on his friend's shoulder. "You're my closest friend, Richard, but there are things even you don't know. I'm asking you to trust me on this, and I hope I have your support whatever the result may be."

"Of course you have it, and don't feel you have to explain things to me. What man doesn't harbor a few secrets?"

"Thank you. I appreciate your friendship. Even though I've only known you a few years, I feel closer to you than many people I've known all my life."

Richard swatted a fly away from his face. "When a man becomes a believer in Christ, he becomes part of the family of God. We're more than friends; we're brothers."

Lucas smiled. It was true. He thought of his friends who were Christians and knew that he was close to them in a way he wasn't with unbelievers. Now that he was a father, he'd need to teach Jamie about the Lord. He'd better read up on what the Bible had to say about children. A verse from Proverbs popped into his mind: *"Correct thy son, and he shall give thee rest; yea, he shall give delight unto thy soul."*

His father had certainly taken pleasure in quoting verses on disciplining children, although it hadn't helped Marcus. Lucas had come to resent the quotes, too, because they often occurred before a punishment. Could that, perchance, be the reason he hadn't become a believer in God until well into his manhood?

"Fresh fish fer sale. Oysters, lobsters, and the like."

Jamie stopped and watched the near-toothless hawker. "He looks like Mr. Simons from back home."

"Does he now?" Lucas patted his son's head. How long would it take before Jamie called Charleston home?

"Aye, but Mr. Simons has teeth. Big ones."

Lucas chuckled at how Jamie widened his eyes when he'd said *big*. "And what type of work did that man do?"

Jamie shrugged. "Don't know. He just came around a lot, wanting to talk to Aunt Heather." His brow crinkled. "I don't think she liked it when he visited."

Had this Mr. Simons been a suitor? Or perhaps he'd had more nefarious ideas. Lucas hated the thought of Miss Hawthorne alone and having that man pay a visit. Why did the man not bring a chaperone if he had noble plans?

"I'm hungry. Are we about there?" Jamie rubbed his stomach.

"Yes son, it's not much farther." Maybe he should have hired a coach, but the day was fair and he'd thought the walk would be good for them all. He slowed his pace so that Jamie didn't have to work so hard to keep up.

Charleston was bustling this morning with women out shopping before the heat of the afternoon arrived. Businessmen stood chatting, while slaves and common workers hauled various items in wagons and handcarts. Lucas loved this town and hoped his son would come to feel the same way.

"Well now, are ye not a sight for sore eyes?"

Off to his right, a woman dressed in near rags pushed away from the door of a tavern. He looked around but saw no one other than himself and Richard close enough for her to be addressing. She took three quick steps and leapt in front of him so that he had to stop or knock her down. Jamie peered up at her then pinched his nose to ward off her foul odor.

"Don'tcha remember me?" She reached out and felt the edge of Lucas's frock coat with her grimy fingers. "Ye clean up quite good, ye do. 'Re ye pretending to be a gentleman?"

Richard slowed and turned, lifting his brows as if to ask, *Who's that?*

Lucas shrugged and motioned to Jamie. "Go with Richard, son, and I'll meet the two of you at McCrady's shortly. Your aunt Heather may have already arrived." He handed the boy off to Richard. "See that you obey Mr. Madison."

"Aye sir." Jamie watched over his shoulder with a worried expression as Richard led him down the street. For a child who'd not had a father until now and had lost his mother at such a young age, he was quite well behaved and compliant.

"What's the matter, dearie? Ye forget me purty face already?"

Lucas refocused on the trollop. "I've never before laid eyes on you, madam."

She swatted her hand in the air. "It's Lilly. Ye cain't forget what a fine time we had aboard yer ship, can ye?"

Lucas bristled. Until now, he'd thought she was just a beggar out to earn a coin, but she must be confusing him with his brother. When had Marcus been in Charleston? A shiver charged down his spine. He couldn't let his brother learn about Jamie.

"I fear you are mistaking me for someone else, madam."

The woman cackled, revealing yellowed teeth with a good number missing. Though filthy, she hardly looked old enough to be losing her teeth. Perhaps a few had been knocked out by less accommodating men.

"Ye cain't fool me." She leaned in closer, bringing her wretched scent along. "Ye're the Black Mark, ain'tcha?"

Lucas straightened and glanced around to see if anyone had heard the woman. "I am not. But can you tell me how long ago he was here? Is he returning?"

Her hazel eyes narrowed. "Hmm. . .I don't reckon ye're him, after all. Ye have the look and speech of a real gentleman." Her gaze softened, and she leaned against his arm. He stepped back, causing her to stumble, and he reached out to steady her.

"If ye ain't Marcus Reed, then ye must be his twin brother."

Lucas blinked, surprised at her comment. Did she mean that factually, or was she just making a random comment that he closely resembled Marcus? "Does the man you talk of have a twin?"

"He has a brother—or so says the Black Mark—but I know not if he be a twin." She peered over her shoulder to the spot where he'd last seen Jamie before he went around the corner. "But he never mentioned that brother having a son that looks just like 'im."

A fear he'd never before encountered enveloped Lucas. What if his brother learned about Jamie? Would the boy ever be safe?

He reached into his pocket and pulled out two gold coins. The woman's eyes sparked as her hand slithered out. He lifted the coins above her head. "For your silence, madam."

Her gaze narrowed but lifted toward the coins. She licked her lips and nodded. Lucas dropped the bribe into her filthy hand then hurried toward McCrady's. Paying a bribe was wrong. He knew that. But he could not let his unscrupulous brother get his hands on an innocent child.

Chapter 5

Heather watched the last vestige of Charleston disappear as the ship glided around a bend in the Ashley River. She was silly to fear venturing into the unknown again, but she couldn't shake her nervousness. Just as it had happened on the *Charlotte Anne*, civilization fell away, and she entered an unfamiliar world. She tightened her grip on Jamie's hand.

"Ow, that hurts." He tugged his hand away and stood on tiptoes to see over the ship's gunwale.

Behind them, Mr. Reed barked orders to his men. She rubbed Jamie's hair, her heart aching. This journey inland was the beginning of the end of their time together. On her return trip, she'd be alone—truly alone for the first time in her life. How could such a wee lad have been her lifeline?

"Look at that bird!" Jamie swatted her skirt with one hand and pointed toward the shoreline with his other.

Caroline Madison left her husband's side near the middle of the ship and sashayed toward them. "That's a heron. One of the larger species."

As if annoyed at them for invading his territory, the bird turned toward the ship, opened its long beak, and screeched out a call that sounded somewhere between a croak and a hack. Jamie giggled and attempted to shinny up the topsides and onto the gunwale to get a closer look. Heather grabbed him before he toppled over and into the water and hauled him back down.

"We have birds like that in Nova Scotia," he said.

"It may be from Canada. Some birds migrate down here," Caroline said. "There are many interesting creatures in the marshlands. Just mind that you don't go near the river's edge. Alligators inhabit the waters around here."

Heather's gaze snapped to Caroline's. "Are there any at Reed Springs?"

"I don't recall ever seeing one there, but take caution if you go near any of the ponds or the river."

The two men joined them. "Yes," Mr. Reed said, "we have alligators. 'Tis my greatest concern for the workers in my rice fields. That and snakes."

Heather's hand lifted to her neck. Snakes and alligators. What kind of place was Mr. Reed taking his son to?

He glanced at her and smiled.

Her stomach lurched.

"Have no fear, Miss Hawthorne. Jamie will be quite safe. It may sound as if we live in the wilderness, but I believe you will be pleasantly surprised at the quality of our plantation home."

"Yes, Reed Springs is a fine, sturdy place." Mrs. Madison said. "Amazingly, it survived our fight for independence when many of our fine homes did not. The British burned so many of them. What a dreadful shame."

Heather winced but tried to ignore the comment. Caroline did not know her past.

Jamie tugged on the bottom of Mr. Reed's frock coat. Heather reached for the boy, but his father hoisted him up in his arms. "What is it, son?"

"This ship is smaller than your other ones. Why didn't we take one of the big ones?"

"Ah, an excellent question." Mr. Reed waved his free hand toward the middle of the vessel. "This is a cutter, and the reason we're taking it is because the river is fairly shallow and the draft of a cutter is less than a ship."

"What's a draft?" Jamie stared at the man with blank eyes.

" 'Tis the vertical length of the keel."

Jamie blinked. "What's a keel?"

Mr. Madison chuckled. "You're going to have to teach the boy all about sailing vessels, Lucas."

"That is something to which I look forward." Mr. Reed smiled. "And there's no better time than the present." He turned with Jamie in his arms and walked toward the center of the cutter. "A cutter is a fore-and-aft rigged vessel with a single mast with two headsails. . . ."

"You need to speak in terms a boy can understand, Lucas. Jamie is not a sailor yet." Caroline chuckled and shook her head as father and son walked away. "I've never seen Lucas so happy. Jamie is good for him."

"I agree. For the most part, Lucas has been a somber type for as long as I've known him," Mr. Madison said.

"And how long has that been?" Heather asked, keeping her eye on Jamie and his father.

Mr. Madison looked at his wife. "What say you? Four years?"

She nodded. "We met him shortly after we bought the neighboring plantation. We call it Madison Gardens."

"Perhaps I'll get to see it before I leave," Heather said.

Caroline laid her hand on Heather's arm. "I would love that. You'll have to encourage Lucas to drive you and Amelia—that's Lucas's mother—over for tea one afternoon."

Heather couldn't help wondering how long she'd be at Reed Springs. "That sounds lovely, but I'm not sure how long it will take Mr. Reed to find a permanent governess."

"Excuse me, ladies, but I shall take my leave and join Lucas and Jamie." Mr. Madison gave a brief bow and sauntered away.

"You should probably be prepared to stay awhile. Lucas would have had far better luck at finding a governess in Charleston than he will at Reed Springs. I still think it odd that he seemed in such a hurry to return to the plantation. We weren't scheduled to leave Charleston for another week."

Heather focused again on the landscape. Mr. Reed *had* seemed quite anxious ever since the day they'd ordered clothing and had eaten at McCrady's. He'd wanted to leave that very same day, but Mr. Madison had said it would be impossible for him to go before the end of the week, and Caroline had reminded him that the clothing they'd ordered wouldn't be ready before then either. So they'd waited, but Mr. Reed hadn't seemed able to completely relax until this ship set sail. Had something happened that day?

"Perhaps he is just anxious for his mother to meet Jamie," Heather offered.

"That is probably the truth of the matter. Amelia will adore her grandson. She longs to see Lucas married and the past put behind him."

What past was she referring to? Did his mother know of his relationship with Deborah?

"Look over there." Caroline pointed to the far shore. "See that white bird?"

Heather's gaze searched the shoreline then landed on the creature. White as snow, it was. She nodded.

"It's called a snowy egret."

She studied the large bird with thin, black legs and odd yellow feet. "Why, its eyes look yellow."

"They are. Isn't that odd?"

Heather nodded and watched the bird get smaller as they moved past.

The next hour sailed by. Lucas returned with Jamie, who chattered about the various parts of the ship. Heather smiled over his head at Caroline. They returned their attention to the shoreline, playing a game of counting how many different birds they could see.

"Is that a turtle swimming over there?" Heather squinted her eyes and pointed across the sun-glistened water toward the shore.

"No!" Caroline clutched Heather's arm. "That's an alligator's head. See his wide-set eyes?"

"Where? I can't see!" Jamie tried once again to climb onto the gunwale.

Heather hauled him up into her arms, knowing she could only hold him for a few moments. When had he grown so heavy? "Right there under that branch that sticks out over the water. See it now?"

"Aye! It's so big." He put one hand on the edge of the rail and lurched forward, nearly slipping from her grasp.

Heather gasped and grabbed his pants at the waist, hauling him back. "You must be careful, lad. If you were to fall in, you might become fodder for that beast."

"Miss Hawthorne is right."

Heather jumped at the nearness of Mr. Reed's voice. She turned, and he took his son. Would he harshly scold him for his overeagerness?

Caroline left them and joined her husband, who was seated on a wooden crate, studying a paper in his hand.

"Jamie, look at me."

The lad leaned back in his father's arms and stared at him, his blue eyes filled with worry.

"You must always be careful and alert aboard ship. Accidents have killed many a good sailor. Do you understand?"

Jamie nodded his head. "Aye, aye Captain."

Heather bit back a smile at his nautical response. Mr. Reed grinned and looked at her. Something hitched inside her as they shared their delight in the lad they both cared for. She and this colonist had something very precious in common. But soon Jamie would belong only to him. Turning around, she focused on the serene setting, shoving back her melancholy thoughts. Perhaps it would have been better had she not agreed to be Jamie's temporary governess. Jamie was adapting to his father far more easily than she'd expected. Hiking her chin, she blinked back the tears burning her eyes.

Soon he wouldn't need her at all.

და

Holding his son's hand, Lucas guided him across the deck to where his first mate stood talking with the helmsman. "I thought Jamie might enjoy seeing below deck. Would you mind giving him a tour?"

The man nodded. " 'Twould be my pleasure, Captain."

Jamie glanced up. "Aren't you coming?"

"No, son. I need to keep an eye on things up here, and I want to have a word with your aunt Heather. You'll be safe, and you can return whenever you've seen all that you want to."

"All right."

Lucas watched the two go below deck then strode over to where Miss Hawthorne stood. She was a comely woman. Small in stature but like a she-bear when it came to defending her adopted cub. He liked the way her brown eyes snapped when she was upset and how she hiked that pert little nose in the air. In fact, the only thing he didn't like about her was that she planned to leave.

He hadn't been so attracted to a woman since Deborah. He should be interviewing for a governess instead of rushing back to Reed Springs, but ever since that woman confronted him near the docks, he'd felt an urgent need to get Jamie out of Charleston. He hoped the woman would keep silent. *Please, Lord.*

Lucas slowed his steps and approached from an angle, so as not to frighten Miss Hawthorne again. "So, what do you think of our fine country?"

She scowled but kept her focus somewhere other than on him. "I can't deny its rugged beauty. So many unusual birds and flowers."

"Wait until you see my mother's garden. You've not seen the likes of her flowers anywhere."

A soft smile tugged at her lips. "Sounds lovely. The growing season up north is so short that I crave things of beauty like flowers. I can see why you are fond of this region, although I don't know how you handle the abysmal heat."

"It can be hard at times, but we adapt. Evening events are held late, generally after the sun sets, and it's not uncommon to rest in the heat of the day." He boldly fingered the sleeve of her new day dress, causing her to look up at him. "We also wear clothing made of cooler fabrics. There are many things one can do."

She held his gaze uncommonly long. "You will be good to Jamie? You promise not to let anything happen to him?" She blinked her eyes then swatted at a tear. "I couldn't bear it."

He laid his hand over hers. "I'll do everything within my power to keep him safe. I already love him."

She continued to stare, as if measuring his sincerity, then nodded and tugged her hand out from under his. "And what of your mother? Will she accept an ...illegitimate child?"

Ah, so that's what bothered her. He watched the black needlerush grasses swishing in the breeze. On shore, birds chirruped a chorus, and midstream, a fish leaped out of the water and then disappeared again. "Mother will adore Jamie. Her only regret will be the same as mine—that we were unable to have him sooner."

Heather stiffened, and her chin lifted. "I thought I explained that."

"You did, and I understand, but it doesn't change the fact that we missed out on years of Jamie's growth."

"Perhaps you should have thought about that before you walked out on his mother." She hung her head, as if embarrassed by her outburst. "I wasn't sure that you'd even want him at all," she whispered so softly he barely heard her.

He heaved a sigh, wishing he could tell her the whole truth. But if Deborah hadn't, then he didn't feel he should. He still didn't know whether to tell his mother or not. She would love Jamie no matter which son sired him, but the truth was he dreaded having her think less of him—that he was capable of doing such a heinous deed.

But didn't she have the right to know?

He'd better make up his mind fast, because Madison Gardens was around the next corner, and another mile down the river, Reed Springs awaited.

Chapter 6

"Oh my goodness." Heather gazed past the dock as the ship slowly veered toward it. Her first glimpse of Reed Springs all but took her breath away. A well-used path led up to a wide, green lawn, the centerpiece of which was a three-story, redbrick house. This structure wasn't as ornate as the Charleston house, but its massive size made it every bit as daunting. The first level looked to be partially underground with windows that seemed to grow right out of the grass. A wide stairway led up to the second level, which she assumed was the main floor. On the sides of the massive white front doors were three widely spaced windows, also trimmed in white, and on the floor above were three larger windows in the center with two smaller ones on either side.

The ship bumped against the dock, and sailors cast heavy ropes to two Negroes on the wooden ramp. Lucas turned to Jamie. "Are you ready to see our other home, son?"

Jamie glanced at her then nodded. Lucas escorted Jamie down the gangplank then lifted his gaze to her. Heather's heart thumped. She didn't want to be attracted to him. She had despised him for years for neglecting Deborah and her son, but the man had already effectively disarmed her with his kindness.

He patted Jamie's shoulder. "Stay here, son, while I assist Miss Hawthorne down."

He jogged back up the gangplank then beckoned her to him with his fingers. She swallowed the sudden lump that had risen to her throat and reluctantly obeyed. She placed her hand in his, and he deftly helped her down the steep walkway. When they were on solid ground, he captured her gaze and continued to hold her hand. Her breath grew shaky under his intense stare. He grinned. The rogue knew the effect he had on her.

Scowling, she yanked her hand away, swept past him, and claimed Jamie's hand. How could Mr. Reed realize the effect he had on her when she barely recognized it herself? She tugged Jamie forward. "Come, you have a grandmother to meet."

❧

Lucas chuckled. *Feisty little thing, aren't you?* He shook his head. What had gotten into him?

Normally, he'd stay and see to the ship, but today he had highly important

38

matters to attend to. He was about to give his mother the shock of her life. Nothing could please her more than a grandchild, except perhaps to see Marcus repent of his vile ways and come to know God.

Lucas found it difficult to believe his brother could ever have a change of heart, but stranger things had happened. And last time he checked, God was still in the miracle-working business. He quickened his steps and caught up with Miss Hawthorne and Jamie. She sidled a glance at him, and he couldn't miss her apprehension. "Everything will be fine. More than fine, in fact."

As they reached the stairs, Lucas slowed his pace then stopped. He turned back to face her. "Perhaps I should inform Mother about Jamie rather than shocking her with his sudden presence."

She studied him, nibbling on her lower lip in an enticing manner, then nodded. "Aye, that is probably the wise thing to do. Jamie and I can wait here."

Lucas motioned for the servant who was carrying their satchels to step forward. "Moses, let me have those bags, and take Miss Hawthorne and Jamie to the kitchen and see that they have something to drink and something to eat if they wish."

Moses seemed reluctant to turn over the bags to Lucas, but he finally relinquished them. "Thisa way, miss."

Miss Hawthorne followed the servant around the steps to a door that led below the main stairway. She glanced up at Lucas, and he smiled, hoping to reassure her that all would be well. When she disappeared under the stairs, he hurried up to the main floor of the house. He hoped his mother wasn't resting. Now that they were home, excitement thrummed through him to reveal his news to her.

In the entry, he waited a moment for his eyes to adjust to the dimmer lighting, then searched the parlor and music room but failed to find his mother. Mouthwatering scents drifted up from the kitchen, making him wonder what was for dinner. He walked to the back of the house and finally located her in the dining room, where she had covered the table with fragrant cut flowers that she was arranging in bouquets and putting into vases.

"Lucas! Thank the good Lord you've returned." She stepped back from the table and hurried forward, worry straining her still pretty face.

"What's wrong?"

She hugged him then stepped back with her hand over her heart. "We've had some thievery."

Lucas winced. He didn't like the thought of his mother alone in this big house with just a servant or two for protection. She knew how to handle a flintlock pistol, but he didn't want her placed in the position where it was necessary to use one. "When? What did they take?"

"A hen and a few tools the first night. Then two piglets several nights later."

"Hmm...the tools rule out the thief being an animal. Perhaps we have some vagrants around. Have the field workers sighted any strangers?"

She shook her head. "Not that I know of."

"Well, worry no more. I'll see to it now that I'm here."

She hugged him again. "I missed you. How long will you be home this time?"

Rubbing his chin with his thumb and index finger, he stared at her. She looked tired. Though fifty years old, and her brown hair had not yet yielded completely to the gray, she had purple smudges under her eyes. "Are you getting enough rest?"

"Of course. Our servants are so efficient that I could rest all day if I wanted."

"But you'd never do that." He smiled. "I have a surprise for you."

She glanced past him, searching, then caught his gaze. "Where is it?"

"Downstairs."

"In the kitchen?"

"Yes. But you may want to sit down and let me explain before you run down there."

She lifted her chin. "A lady never runs."

"We shall see. Please have a seat, Mother." She did as he bid then looked up with curious, blue-gray eyes. He sucked in a deep breath and exhaled. Where to begin?

With his hands clasped behind him, he paced the length of the table and back to her. "Just over a week ago, I had two visitors. A comely woman arrived at my door with a young boy in tow, claiming he was mine."

His mother's eyes widened. "How dreadful to use a child to obtain a few coins. Did you turn them out?"

"I did not. I was intrigued with the boy. He has the look of the Reed men, Mother."

"But there are many children with dark hair and blue eyes." She squeezed the stem of a flower until it broke in half.

Lucas ran his hand through his hair. If he told her about the letter from Deborah, surely his mother would figure out what happened.

"How old was the boy?"

"He's five."

She stood and walked over to him. "Then it's impossible for the child to be yours, as much as I wish it might be so. You had already become a believer in Christ by then, and I know you'd never fall into sin in such a manner."

"Thank you, Mother." She was a wise woman, his mother. He should have known he'd have to tell her the whole truth, and perhaps that was best. "He isn't mine. The boy is Marcus's son."

Her hand flew to her chest as she gazed at him with wide eyes; then she schooled her expression. "But how could you possibly know if it's true? Anybody could show up at your door and make such a claim."

"There was a letter from the boy's mother."

"And?"

He pursed his lips and strode to the window, staring out at the green lawn. The grass had been brown when he was last here. A sudden memory of walking on that lawn with Deborah assaulted him. It pained him to think of sweet, gentle Deborah enduring what she had. He felt his mother's hand on his shoulder.

"Tell me, son."

"His mother was Deborah." The words came out on a whisper.

She turned him around, her eyes filled with compassion. "Oh Lucas. I'm so sorry." Suddenly she scowled. "How could Marcus do that to you? To Deborah? I don't want to believe him capable of such a horrible act."

"I'm sorry, Mother."

"You have nothing to be sorry for. It's not your doing."

He shook his head. "I should have searched longer for her. Looked in more places."

"No, you did far more than anyone expected. You left home, your business, and hunted for her for nearly two years. No man could have done more."

"Yet I failed."

"Shh. . .no more, I said." She patted his arm, her eyes sparking with hope. "So, it's true then? The boy is a Reed? He truly is my grandson?"

He nodded. "Jamie is his name. But there's something else. He arrived with a young woman who has raised him since Deborah died."

She gasped. "Deborah's dead?"

"Yes. Three years now. The woman's name is Miss Heather Hawthorne, and she's from Canada. Deborah told her that Jamie was *my* son."

"Why would she do such a thing?"

"To protect him. He'd be scorned all his life if people knew he was the son of the Black Mark. I've accepted Jamie as my own, and that's all anyone will ever know if I can help it."

She looked out the window, as if digesting all that he'd told her. " 'Tis a fine, honorable thing you've done, son. I know this will cause talk among our friends and neighbors and that you'll face hardship and scorn from some people because of Jamie, but I'm proud of you."

He straightened and wrapped his arm around his mother's shoulders. "Thank you. It means a lot to have your support."

She reached up and patted his cheek. "You've always had my support, son."

"There's one more thing. You need to know that Miss Hawthorne is not aware that I have a brother, much less that he's Jamie's true father."

"Don't you think she should know the truth?"

Lucas shrugged. "If Deborah wanted her to know, don't you think she would have told her?"

"I suppose she feared word getting out about Marcus."

He pursed his lips and nodded.

"We can talk more of these things later, but now, I want to see my grandson."

Without waiting for him, she lifted up her skirts and hurried toward the staircase—not running, but almost.

&

Heather surveyed the large kitchen while Jamie enjoyed a slice of bread with creamy butter and strawberry jam and a glass of milk. A soot-blackened brick hearth held a large cauldron of bubbling soup or stew. The pot hung on a long rod with a hook on the end so it could be pulled off the fire when done cooking. Two women worked in unison, one cutting biscuits and the other laying them on a baking pan.

Footsteps sounded on the inside stairwell, and an older woman with brownish-gray hair and sparkling eyes hurried down, her dress swishing. Mr. Reed's mother, Heather presumed. The woman's hungry gaze latched on to Jamie, who continued eating, oblivious that he had an audience. Mr. Reed arrived in the kitchen right after his mother. He walked around the table, and when Jamie spied him, the boy smiled.

"Come, son, let's clean you up. Your grandmother is eager to make your acquaintance." One of the servants scurried over with a damp cloth and wiped Jamie's hands and face. "Thank you, Mable."

The shorter of the two Negro women nodded, smiled, and returned to her worktable. Heather resisted shaking her head. Did Mr. Reed's kindness know no bounds?

"Jamie"—Mr. Reed motioned to his mother—"this is Amelia Reed, your grandmother. Mother, this is Jamie, my son."

The other servant peered over her shoulder with wide eyes before quickly turning around again. Mrs. Reed moved cautiously, as if Jamie were a butterfly she might startle away. "I'm so happy to meet you, Jamie, and am so glad that you've joined our family."

Jamie's gaze darted to Heather's, and she smiled and nodded. He gave a half bow and said, "I'm happy to meet you, too."

Mrs. Reed chuckled and ran her hand down his head. "You look like your father." She smiled at her son.

"Aye, that's what people keep saying." Jamie glanced down at his plate. "May I finish my bread now?"

"Certainly. Is there anything else you'd like?" Mrs. Reed pulled out a chair, never taking her eyes off her grandson.

"I think Jamie has had enough for now, but before you sit down, Mother, I'd like to introduce Miss Hawthorne." He leaned toward his mother, and spoke softly. "She raised Jamie after his mother died and is the one responsible for bringing him here. I've asked her to remain as Jamie's governess until I can hire a permanent one."

Mrs. Reed scurried toward her. "Please forgive my appalling manners, dear. I have no excuse except for being mesmerized with my grandson. I can never express my gratitude to you for all you've done."

"No thanks are needed, ma'am. Jamie is a good lad and a delight to care for. 'Tis a pleasure to meet you."

"And you. Why don't you have a seat and some refreshment? I know the trip here isn't overly long, but it's a warm day." Mrs. Reed gestured toward the table.

Heather smiled then took a seat across from Jamie while his grandmother slid in beside him. Mrs. Reed patted Jamie's shoulder and smiled. "God has surely blessed us this day."

Chapter 7

While his mother, Miss Hawthorne, and Jamie lingered over breakfast the next morning, Lucas strode out to the barn to investigate the thefts. Folks along the river were neighbors and most of them friends, with the exception of a few staunch Loyalist holdouts who were highly verbal about their beliefs and still swore their allegiance to England, but he couldn't imagine any of them resorting to stealing. He'd never had this problem before and wasn't sure how to handle the situation. Not only was he concerned for his mother's well-being, but now he had Jamie and Miss Hawthorne to worry about as well.

After watching the two ladies interact with Jamie most of yesterday, he had to admit he admired Miss Hawthorne more and more. He was certain she'd done without to provide for his son and to bring him here. Whenever he thought of hiring another woman to watch Jamie, his heart clenched. He didn't want Miss Hawthorne to go.

He inspected the well-manicured flower beds and neat hedges and nodded to a couple of servants weeding the lush spring flowers as he passed by. "Well done!"

The men smiled and nodded their thanks for his appreciation. Slavery was dreadful, and he in good conscience could not abide it. Most of the older servants remained from his father's days. Even though he'd freed them, they'd stayed on, working for room and board and a fair wage, but a few newer ones he'd purchased as slaves at public auction and then set free, only to turn around and house them and pay them a wage. The expenses cut into his profit, but he was rewarded with the workers' loyalty and appreciation. God had blessed his business, and he was able to sleep at nights, knowing he'd done right by his servants, even though some of his associates scorned him for his unconventional beliefs.

He walked into the barn, wondering where his overseer was. Breathing in the familiar scents of horses, fresh hay, and leather, he searched for one of his servants. Samuel, a master with horses, stood in a stall toward the rear of the barn, humming as he brushed Lucas's horse. When Lucas walked closer, his black gelding noticed him and stuck his head over the stall and whickered.

"Whoa, hoss," Samuel said, reaching for the animal's halter.

Lucas scratched the white diamond on the gelding's forehead. "How are you, Liberty?"

"He be just fine 'n' dandy, Missah Reed. Though I 'magine he'd like a good, long run."

"Him and me both. But first I need to know if anything has been discovered about the thief."

Samuel left the stall and shook his head. "Nah sir. Not nothin' but some footprints."

"Show me where they are."

"Well. . ." Samuel scratched his chest. "They's gone now. It done went and rained the night of that second robbery, and footprints was tracked inside the barn from all the mud, but they's good and dried up now."

Lucas scanned the barn to see if anything looked out of place. "Mother said they stole some tools."

"Just an ol' ax. I'm guessin' it was to kill that chicken they done stole."

Lucas stood with his hands on his hips, staring out the barn door. He could stand to lose a chicken to a hungry person, and even a couple of piglets, but what if the man decided he wanted a horse next time?

"Do you know where Mr. Remington is?"

"Yassah. He done went down to the fields."

Lucas didn't want to wander that far from home today in case he was needed. His mother and Jamie were getting along famously, but Miss Hawthorne seemed a bit withdrawn. Could be she was just feeling out of place or even left out since Jamie had taken so well to his grandmother's affection and pampering. If he didn't watch out, his son would soon be spoiled. Perhaps a ride out to the fields with him would be good for Jamie.

"Go ahead and saddle Liberty for me."

"You wants me to bring him up to the big house?"

"No, but thank you." Lucas studied the man who'd worked on the plantation for a good ten years. "I suppose you've heard the news that I have a son who's come to live here."

"Yassah. I think that be a blessing from God, I do."

Lucas nodded. "Me, too. If Jamie ever happens down here alone, I'd be grateful if you'd keep a good eye on him. He's not used to being around horses, and I wouldn't want anything to happen to him."

"You can count on Samuel." He smiled and nodded. "I be watchin' that boy like he's my own."

Lucas clapped the man on the shoulder. "I appreciate that, Samuel."

He started back to the house. If only things with Miss Hawthorne could go as easily as with Samuel.

❧

"I normally take a rest after luncheon, but I'm anxious to start remodeling this bedchamber for Jamie." Mrs. Reed ambled around the room. "This used to be the nursery."

Heather liked how the chamber had been refurbished and now held a double bed with a canopy and colorful floral draperies. An unusual rocking chair sat in one corner. Her gaze traveled along one arm of the chair and up and around the curved top and down to the other arm, all a single, continuous piece of wood held in place by long, decorative spindles that formed the back and sides.

Mrs. Reed lifted the edge of one drape and shook her head. "This simply will not do for a boy. I'll have to order some fabric from Charleston and have these remade."

"I'm certain Jamie won't mind things as they are now." She glanced over to where he sat in the open doorway that led to a balcony, stacking pieces of wood that looked as if they were leftover from a building project. Mrs. Reed said they used to be his father's.

What would she say if she knew her grandson had been sleeping on a simple cot, covered with ragged quilts discarded after a neighbor's fire?

Jamie was far better off here, even though he'd grow up a Canadian. He'd have family who loved him and a good education, and he'd never lack anything. He might miss her, but his grandmother and father would give him all the love he needed.

Heather should have brought him here sooner.

If only she'd had the means.

She sighed and strolled over to the door, staring out at the expansive lawn. Sculpted bushes and flower beds ran all along the front of the house, adding color and loveliness to the brick and wrought iron.

"Well, there's nothing more to be done in here until I order some new things. Would you two care for a stroll in the garden before the temperatures warm too much?"

Heather spun around. "Aye. That would be lovely. I've been wanting to see your pretty flowers up close."

The older woman smiled. "Wonderful. I do so enjoy them, but I much prefer to have someone else with me. And before you get your hopes up, some flowers are blooming, but it's still early, so many varieties have yet to open their faces to the sun."

Heather wondered if Mrs. Reed was lonely. Living so far from Charleston, she was all but isolated here for much of the time. She would certainly enjoy having her grandson's company.

Mrs. Reed reached out a hand to Jamie. "Come, Jamie, shall we take a walk?"

He eyed the wood pieces he'd stacked in a tall tower as if he wasn't quite ready to leave them; then he glanced at Heather.

"Those will be here when we return," she said. "You may play with them again later."

Looking a bit disappointed, Jamie stood and took his grandmother's hand.

He'd always been a sweet, compliant child and rarely complained or pitched a fit. Until now, she'd assumed he had inherited such traits from his mother, but having met Mr. Reed and his mother, she was no longer so certain. Both Reeds seemed to be good-natured people with big hearts. Guilt nibbled at her for thinking so badly of them all these years. But if Mr. Reed was as good a man as he seemed, how could he have done such a deed to Deborah?

As Mrs. Reed led Jamie from the room, he reached out and took Heather's hand, too. She smiled down at him, receiving a grin from him in return. Perhaps he did still need her.

They ambled through the wide hall with its decorative ceiling, soft bluish-green walls the color of the sea, and furniture so shiny that she could see her reflection. Two chairs upholstered in ivory-colored brocade sat in a corner alcove with a potted palm tree about Jamie's height situated between them.

At the front door, Mrs. Reed took a straw hat off a hall tree and handed Heather's to her. Once outside, they descended the front stairs into the warm sunshine. Mr. Reed met them as they reached the ground.

"Off on an outing, I presume?" he asked.

"No son. We're simply out to take a walk in the gardens."

He eyed Heather. What could he want with her? Had he already hired a governess? She swallowed hard. Jamie was adapting well, but would he be bereft once she left? Her heart ached at the thought of causing him pain.

"I wonder if I might have a chat with Miss Hawthorne."

Mrs. Reed glanced back at her and smiled. "I suppose you should ask her. Jamie and I can stroll the garden and hunt for butterflies and bees."

Jamie scowled. "I don't like bees. They sting."

Mrs. Reed hugged the boy. "Then we shall see how many different butterflies we can find. All right?"

He nodded and waved at Heather.

"Oh my. A carriage is coming." Mrs. Reed stared down the long lane. A fine coach drawn by a pair of matched gray horses emerged from the tree line and rolled past a creek with an arched walking bridge and a pond with a white gazebo partially covered with ivy.

"Are you expecting guests, Mother?"

Mrs. Reed shook her head. "I've no idea who that could be."

Heather didn't know whether to snatch up Jamie and run back inside or stay. How would Mr. Reed explain his son—and was he ready to do so?

He stared at the carriage for a moment then turned back to his mother. "Isn't that the Duponts' carriage? I recognize the horses."

Mrs. Reed gasped and held a hand to her mouth. "What day is this?"

He lifted one dark brow. "Saturday. Why?"

"Oh dear. I'd forgotten that Gwenda and Hilary were coming to tea. They were not supposed to be here until four though. Surely it can't be that late."

She glanced at the sun. "I wonder why they are so early." Mrs. Reed squeezed her forehead. "I'm not even certain if there's anything ready to serve them."

"I'm sure there is something. Mable always has goodies of some sort available." Mr. Reed dusted the sleeves of his white shirt and tugged on the bottom of his waistcoat. "I need to fetch my frock coat. I'm not in the proper dress to receive guests."

"Would you like me to go and check with Mable about refreshments?" Heather offered.

Relief softened Mrs. Reed's face. "Oh, would you, dear?"

"I'd be happy to."

"And could you please find Mrs. Overton and have her locate Elijah, my manservant? Have him run up to my room and get my tan frock and bring it to me?" Mr. Reed's expression looked hopeful.

"Aye. My pleasure."

"Take Jamie with you." Mr. Reed reached for his son's hand and smiled. "Go inside with Miss Hawthorne, and perhaps Mable will have a treat for you."

Heather returned to the house with Jamie in tow. Had his father purposely sent them both away? Was he ashamed of Jamie?

She hurried through the house, searching for the housekeeper, but had no luck finding her. Even though she'd offered her assistance, she couldn't help feeling as if Mr. Reed hadn't wanted the guests to meet Jamie. She shook her head, scolding herself for her negative thinking. Perhaps he simply wanted to prepare them first. When she didn't find the housekeeper, she scurried downstairs to the kitchen with Jamie following. Should she return out front after finding out if there were any cakes to serve with the tea?

Mable was alone today, but she smiled as they entered. "They's that fine, young gent'aman."

Jamie smiled. "Father said I might have a treat."

"Did he now?"

"Indeed." Jamie climbed onto a chair at the worktable. "What kind of treats you got?"

"Have, Jamie. What kind of treats do you have?" Heather smoothed his hair and tucked in his shirt.

"That's what I said."

Mable giggled. "I has some scones and strawberries or some o' them little cakes you'uns had yesterday at tea."

"Mmm, I want the cakes." Jamie bounced on the chair.

"Before you give him that, I need to inform you that Mrs. Reed has guests who are just arriving."

Mable nodded and stirred something in a pot over the fire. A delicious scent filled the air. "Mmm-huh. She done told me last week that they's a'comin'. But I thought they was comin' later in the afternoon."

"I think they were supposed to, but they're here now. Mrs. Reed said something about them being early."

"Humph. That Miss Hilary, she likes to make a scene. She gots her cap set for Mr. Lucas if you ask me." Mable brought over a plate with two small cakes and set them before Jamie.

Heather's heart skipped a few beats. Miss Dupont had designs on Mr. Reed? What would that mean for Jamie? What did it mean for her?

Heather's hands tightened on the back of Jamie's chair. If Mr. Reed were to marry, his new wife might be cruel to Jamie or send him away altogether once she had her own children.

Heavy footsteps and a metallic jingling sounded on the stairs, and a flash of black skirt showed as the housekeeper stepped into the room. "We've guests. Make haste, Mable."

The cook set a teapot onto the fire. "The wata' is heatin' and the scones is made."

"Ah, very good." Mrs. Overton's shoulders lowered as she relaxed.

Heather approached the housekeeper. "Mr. Reed asked me to have you find Elijah and have him collect Mr. Reed's tan frock coat from his bedchamber and take it to him. He was outside in front of the house a few moments ago."

"Ach! That man. Don't know why he can't take his coat when he leaves the house." The tall, thin woman spun around, and hiking up her skirt, dashed up the stairs. The clinking of the numerous keys hanging from her chatelaine could be heard until she reached the second floor.

Mable shook her head. "That woman, she's more flighty than a nest of spooked pheasants." She shook her head and laid a half dozen scones on an etched silver tray. She removed a shiny silver teapot from a shelf and set it on the table.

Heather giggled at the woman's bluster. She'd been around a few slaves, and the servants at Reed Springs were little like them. Slaves tended to keep their heads down and never looked a white man in the eye or sassed him. The servants here had more spunk and seemed happy and content. Just one more thing that elevated Lucas Reed in her mind.

Chapter 8

Lucas slipped his arms into his coat and straightened it just as the carriage made its final turn. "Elijah, please inform Mrs. Overton that we'll take refreshments in the parlor as soon as our guests are settled."

"I'll see to it, sir."

"Thank you." He nodded.

His mother leaned toward him. "What do we tell them about Jamie?"

A myriad of thoughts raced through his mind. Hilary Dupont was the last person he'd expected to see today. The pretty but chatty woman had long ago set her cap for him, even though he'd offered no encouragement. He hadn't been interested in making a match with a woman since he'd lost Deborah. But if he was being completely honest, of late his desire to settle down had been stirred up by a shy northerner. What he needed to figure out was if that desire was birthed from gratitude because Miss Hawthorne had brought Jamie to him—or if it was the woman herself who intrigued him.

He refocused on the carriage as it slowed. He'd hoped for a week alone with his mother before he had to introduce Jamie to any friends or neighbors. If Hilary knew, it wouldn't be long before everyone along the Ashley River did, and guests would be arriving in droves to hear how it all had come about.

Sooner or later, everyone would know anyway. Wouldn't it be better if he was the one who first delivered the news to Hilary? At least there'd be less spurious blather that way.

The carriage rolled to a halt, and Lucas stiffened his spine. He could only pray for a brief visit. Normally, he'd offer his greetings and take his leave after a short while, but with Jamie here, he didn't want to leave his mother at the mercy of the two Dupont women, who would pry and prod until they'd revealed every sordid detail. He loved his mother, but she could never keep a secret. The last thing he wanted was for people to know Jamie was Deborah's child. Or Marcus's.

He opened the carriage door and forced a smile. "Good afternoon, ladies."

"Why Mr. Reed, what a lovely surprise to see you." Hilary smiled and reached for his hand, and he helped her disembark. Her silver and lavender skirts rustled as she stepped as close as her petticoats would allow. An overpowering floral scent permeated the air, putting him in mind of a walking lilac bush.

"I thought you weren't expected to return until next week." She batted her thick lashes. The beguiling look in her unusual, near-violet eyes made him wonder if she'd known he was home and that was why she was here now. Had word already gotten out about Jamie?

"I decided to return sooner than planned," he said.

Hilary's mother was just as bold in her stare. Both women had made it clear that they intended to see Hilary married to him, but he'd rather be keelhauled. Still, he would be the polite host and hope they'd soon lose interest in making him their quest and focus on some other prey.

"Welcome." His mother stepped forward. "It's so good to see you both. Shall we go inside where it's cooler?"

Mrs. Dupont nodded and fluttered her fan. "Dreadfully hot for so early in the day, is it not? You needn't have waited outside for us, Amelia."

"Oh, but I was about to take a stroll in the garden with—"

"Mother, perhaps the conversation could wait until we're inside and we've made our guests comfortable?" Lucas despised interrupting her, but he wanted control of any talk of Jamie. He offered his arm to both older women, helping them up the stairs and effectively holding Hilary at bay.

"Of course," his mother responded. "Do let us retire from this heat."

In the parlor, Mrs. Dupont sat on the sofa while Hilary situated herself on the narrower canapé, leaving room on the end, no doubt, for him. Resisting Hilary's unspoken invitation, he strode to the fireplace and rested his elbow on the mantel.

"How is the shipping business these days?" Mrs. Dupont asked.

"Fine. We've been blessed with clear weather for the past few weeks and have accomplished much." He bided his time until the chitchat died away. Suddenly, he straightened. Would knowing about Jamie dissuade Hilary from her mission to ensnare him as her husband?

If it did, then he was correct about the woman. But if not. . .

"And how is Howard these days?" his mother asked.

Mrs. Dupont pursed her lips. "Oh, you know men and their politics. He's working hard to see that South Carolina ratifies the Constitution. He's certain it will be the demise of us all if we don't. They need a majority of nine colonies, you know."

His mother waved her hand in the air. "I know nothing of such things. I leave all that to Lucas." She glanced at him and lifted her brows, as if asking, *When?*

He knew how eager she was to share Jamie with her friends. There was no point in delaying things. It would go as it would go, but he had the distinct feeling that neither of the Dupont women would take the surprise of his son well. He pushed away from the wall. Hilary smiled and scooted her skirts closer to her in an open invitation for him to sit beside her. Mrs. Overton strolled in, carrying the teapot, followed by Mable, who held a tray of scones.

"Mrs. Overton, where are Miss Hawthorne and Jamie?" Lucas asked.

"In the kitchen, sir. Shall I send them up?"

Lucas nodded. "Please do."

Hilary turned curious eyes upon him, as did her mother. When the servants left, he cleared his throat and plunged forward. "I had a rather startling surprise arrive while I was last in Charleston. A woman came to my door with a young boy in tow."

Hilary cast an odd glance at her mother, while his mother sat on the edge of her seat, obviously anxious.

"As it turns out, the boy is a Reed. I received documentation proving it, and I've claimed him as my son."

Hilary gasped and bounced up, her silk skirts swishing. "But—but you can't. I mean how can you possibly be certain the child is yours?"

"Just wait until you see him, and you'll understand. Jamie is a miniature of his father." His mother's warm smile revealed the love she already felt for her grandson.

Hilary flitted to the doorway and back. "You must be wrong."

"There is no doubt in my mind."

She flicked open a fan that hung by a cord around her wrist and waved it vigorously in front of her reddened face. "Who is the mother? Why have we not heard about this—this child before now?"

"Because I did not know about him until just last week."

Mrs. Dupont's fan snapped open and joined her daughter's, flapping like a pair of hummingbird wings. "This is highly irregular, Lucas. Why are you willing to take in the urchin when you weren't married to his mother?" Her cheeks paled suddenly. "You *weren't* married, were you?"

Lucas straightened, and his eyes narrowed. This woman would rather he fathered an illegitimate child than have married the boy's mother? He knew the Duponts were shallow, but he never expected them to be so coldhearted toward a child.

"Of course he wasn't married." His mother twisted her hands in her lap. "Oh dear, that didn't sound quite right. Lucas is a different man than he was when he was younger. We've all made mistakes in the past."

Lucas paced across the room then realized that brought him closer to Miss Dupont, so he strode to the front window and looked out. "Thank you, Mother, for defending me, but it isn't necessary, and Jamie is not a mistake."

A very unladylike snort erupted from Hilary's direction. "You will have a difficult time finding a woman to marry if you take in that—"

Lucas spun around and cut off her last word with a glare.

"Now, Hilary," Mrs. Dupont said. "Let's not make a mountain out of a molehill. Do come sit down."

The young woman returned his stare with her nose in the air. With a flick of her hand, she closed the fan, sashayed back to the canapé, and gracefully lowered herself onto the cushions. "When will we meet this *boy*?"

He cared not for her snide tone. How could he ever have looked twice at this woman? Aye, she was lovely on the outside, but she was like a potato whose perfect outward appearance hid a black and rotted interior. So different from Miss Hawthorne, whose love and devotion for a child that wasn't hers compelled her to travel more than a thousand miles to bring him to his father. "Any moment now. I asked the housekeeper to send him and Miss Hawthorne up."

"And just who is this Miss Hawthorne?" Mrs. Dupont asked.

Lucas straightened under her glare. "She's the woman who brought my son to me in Charleston."

Hilary narrowed her eyes at him. "How can you be certain *she* isn't the child's real mother and just trying to make a quick buck by pawning her illegitimate child off on you?"

ta

Heather held on to Jamie's shoulder, refusing to let him enter the parlor until the negative remarks died down. How could these women consider themselves friends and ask such atrocious questions? Why, it almost sounded like a wife quizzing her husband about his illegitimate son. But what gave them that right? Did Mr. Reed have an understanding with Miss Dupont?

Her heart twisted. Why should she care if he had given his affections to another woman? He was perfectly within his rights to do so. She was only concerned for Jamie.

"I have a letter from his mother stating the facts. I'll not have you slander Miss Hawthorne's reputation. She's a kind, generous woman."

"Indeed."

Though Heather couldn't see who spoke last, she thought the voice sounded as if it may have belonged to the younger woman.

"Have you considered how taking in this child might damage your reputation?"

Heather nearly gasped. She had wondered the same thing after she'd gotten to know Mr. Reed better, but for a guest in his home—especially a female guest—to voice such a thing. . .why, it simply wasn't done.

"My son is more important to me than my reputation."

Jamie glanced up at her and grinned. She cupped his cheek with her hand and smiled back, sincerely hoping he didn't fully understand the nature of the conversation.

"Without a good reputation, what future will your son have?"

Heather was certain Mr. Reed must have some kind of relationship with these women for them to speak so candidly.

A long moment of silence reigned, and Jamie started fidgeting. Could he sense the tension in the room?

"I shall go see what's keeping them."

Heather stiffened as Mr. Reed strode out of the parlor and all but collided with her. His gaze captured hers, asking how much she'd heard. His lips pursed, and she wondered if he was upset with her for eavesdropping or angered by the Duponts' bluntness. She leaned toward him. "We were waiting for. . .um. . .the heat of the conversation to die down."

He stared for a moment then nodded. "I'm sorry you had to hear all that." He squatted down in front of Jamie. "Ready to meet some of our neighbors and my mother's friends?"

Jamie nodded and released her hand.

His mother's friends. Not his? "I shall wait here until you're finished with him." Heather glanced around for a place to sit.

"No, I want you to come, too."

He held her gaze again. Her heart thudded hard. "Why do you need *me?*"

"I could use your support." He transferred Jamie's hand to his right hand and held out his elbow.

Heather stared at it, warmed and surprised by his offer to escort her when she was but a servant. She shook her head. "It wouldn't be right for me to enter on your arm, although I thank you for the offer. I'm a servant, and we don't want to give your neighbors the wrong idea."

His lips tightened, and a bit of the light drained from his eyes, but he nodded. "We shall talk about that later."

He led Jamie into the parlor, but Heather halted in the doorway. What was there to talk about?

Two finely dressed women sat stiff and unwelcoming. Their eyes latched onto Jamie. The young woman's gaze jerked up to inspect Heather. She was a beautiful woman with blond hair the color of flax piled atop her head in a becoming manner and unusual eyes that looked deep blue with a touch of purple. Perhaps her lovely lavender dress was reflected in her eyes. Everything about this woman spoke of wealth and quality. Even Heather's new day dress paled in comparison to Miss Dupont's. She shifted her feet, uncomfortable with the young woman's stare. Why should this stranger be so interested in her?

The older woman wore a day dress of pale blue that complimented her medium brown hair and blue eyes. She continued to watch Jamie, although rather than pleased with the boy, she looked. . .saddened. Had Jamie's arrival spoiled her plans for her daughter?

Mrs. Reed patted the sofa. "Jamie, come and sit by me. Miss Hawthorne, won't you have a seat? I want to introduce you to our neighbors to the northwest, the Duponts. Gwenda and Hilary live at the Magnolia Mist plantation."

Heather perched on the edge of the nearest chair and received their cold stares without flinching.

"Miss Hawthorne was so kind to bring Jamie to us. I can't tell you how wonderful it is to have a grandson. I feel as if I'm in the springtime of my life again." She kissed Jamie's head. He stared into his lap, his cheeks turning crimson. "He's such a dear boy, and can't you see how much he resembles his father?"

"Indeed." Miss Dupont flipped open a lavender fan that matched her dress and waved it in front of her face. "Do you plan to reside long at Reed Springs, Miss Hawthorne?"

Before she could answer, Mr. Reed said, "That remains unsettled. I've asked Miss Hawthorne to stay and serve as Jamie's governess to ease his transition into our family."

"I see." Miss Dupont's lips looked as if she'd sucked on a lemon. "And where do you hail from, Miss Hawthorne?"

"England, originally." Heather was purposely vague.

"So, where do your loyalties lie? With England or America?"

Heather didn't miss the woman's challenge, but she wasn't going to fall into her trap. She lifted her chin. "With Jamie."

A small smile lifted one corner of Miss Dupont's mouth as if saying *touché*. "But surely you must have strong ties to England."

She shook her head, realizing the truth. England meant little to her now. Everything she cared about was here. "Not any longer."

Mrs. Dupont turned her attention to Jamie. "So, what do you think about your new home?"

Jamie shrugged and toed the carpet with his shoe. He wasn't one to be shy with family, but he generally became quiet around strangers.

"Have you started learning your letters? Do you enjoy walking on stilts? Surely there's something special you enjoy."

He glanced at Heather then his father. "Papa's going to teach me to ride, and he showed me where he builds ships."

Heather's heart lurched. She watched Mr. Reed to see his reaction to being called *Papa* for the first time.

He blinked his eyes several times and actually looked stunned just before he regained his composure. "That's right, I plan to teach him to ride."

"He's too young for that, Lucas." His mother gazed up, concern tightening her lips.

"I beg to differ, Mother, but he is not. I've been riding since I was three."

She shook her head. "I didn't like your father putting you tiny boys on those big horses. I was so afraid you'd fall off and get hurt."

Mr. Reed smiled. "We did a time or two until we learned to hold on."

His mother shook her head. "Men and their ideas. It's a wonder that any child lives long enough to grow up."

"I'm sure he will do fine," said Mrs. Dupont. "Boys adapt to physical activities far more quickly and easily than girls."

"Really, Mother, a girl could learn to ride just as easily as a boy if she had the proper instruction." Miss Dupont patted her hair and smiled. "I was wondering, Lucas, if I might have a moment of your time to discuss an important matter."

A muscle twitched in his jaw as he coolly stared at her. The difference in their behavior confused Heather. Miss Dupont referred to Mr. Reed by his Christian name and seemed highly familiar with him, while he was more reserved, tense, and withdrawn. "I suppose that can be arranged. We can step into the music room if you'd like."

She arose, regal like a princess, and strutted toward him with a beguiling smile on her face. Glaring at Heather, she looped her arm through Mr. Reed's without his offering it to her, then tugged him out of the room. At the doorway, he stopped suddenly. "Miss Hawthorne, would you be so kind as to serve as chaperone?"

Heather's mouth went dry. She was glad to see the snippety woman leave the room, and she had no desire to follow them—although she was uncomfortable with the two of them being alone together. What if Miss Dupont said something about Jamie? She rose.

Jamie shot to his feet, a hopeful gleam in his eyes. "Might I come, too, Aunt Heather?"

"You must ask your grandmother."

He spun to face her. "May I go?"

Mrs. Reed smiled and laid her hand against his cheek. "I don't suppose an active boy like you wants to listen to two old women's prattle. You run along, and I shall see you later."

"Really, Lucas, I wanted to speak to you in private."

"Perhaps a walk in the garden would work better," he said. "That way Miss Hawthorne and Jamie can chaperone us from afar."

"I hardly think it's necessary for those two to oversee us. It's not as if I intend to take liberties with you."

Mr. Reed narrowed his eyes then lifted one brow as if remembering a time Miss Dupont had done that very thing. Heather couldn't help wondering if the woman *had* pressed her interest on him at one time or another. He moved a step ahead of Heather and glanced back over his shoulder at her, his expression imploring her to follow. She wanted to go along as little as Miss Dupont desired her to, but if her presence made Mr. Reed more comfortable, she'd go. Taking Jamie's hand, she followed them to the door. Just before she went outside, she heard Mrs. Dupont say, "Really, Amelia. You must get rid of that girl as soon as possible. As far-fetched as it sounds, she's turning Lucas's eye away from Hilary, and we can't. . ."

She closed the door, not hearing the final words. Surely the woman was mistaken. Mr. Reed had never shown the slightest interest in her. He was simply being kind because that was his nature. Yet didn't his gaze linger a bit longer than was necessary at times? And his hands had prolonged contact when he'd helped her down from the ship the day they arrived. Why would he take a second look at her—an *Englishwoman* with no dowry—when he could have the lovely Miss Dupont by his side?

What stuff and nonsense.

Chapter 9

Lucas escorted Miss Dupont down the front stairs and into the garden. A variety of flowers had already opened up and filled the air with their sweet scent. Butterflies flitted from bloom to bloom, peaceful and quiet, soothing his irritation. He'd known some of his friends and acquaintances would question if he was doing the right thing by taking in Jamie, but his heart indeed confirmed that he was. He'd already grown to love the boy.

Hilary glanced over her shoulder, staring back at Miss Hawthorne and Jamie, where they lingered at the beginning of the garden. She edged closer to him. "Really, Lucas, I don't see why you had to insist we have a chaperone."

"We wouldn't want tongues wagging now, would we?"

"Just what do you think will happen when word gets out about that boy living here? Why couldn't you board him in some school and provide for him that way? Why is it necessary to bring him into your home?"

He stopped and turned to face her, causing her to release his arm. "Because he's a Reed."

"He's a—"

"Hold your tongue, woman. That's my son you're referring to." Lucas had never held a special interest for Miss Dupont, other than to admire her beauty, as did every other man she encountered. He thought her a silly girl, somewhat younger than he, and found her efforts to snag him for a husband humorous. Until today, he hadn't realized what a vixen she was.

She stomped her foot. "I won't let that...that...*boy* come between us. When we marry, *our* children will be your rightful heirs, not that—"

Lucas held up his hand. "You forget yourself, madam. How is it you remember me proposing when I have not done so?"

Her eyes turned pleading, and her cheeks a bright red. She stuck out her lower lip in a pout that he assumed other men found enchanting, but the effort was wasted on him. "Everyone knows we have an understanding."

He quirked a brow. "Everyone but me, it would seem. I never said or did anything that should lead you to believe I wanted to marry you. I don't know that I'll ever marry."

She clutched his arm. "But you must. You can't leave all your wealth for that scoundrel brother of yours to inherit. I could give you a son, many rightful sons. Don't you know that I love you?"

Lucas heaved a sigh. He'd never been quite sure if Hilary Dupont was an innocent, spoiled woman or if she was crafty and sly. At the social events he'd attended, he noticed she often used her beauty and flirtatious ways to get the man she had designs on to lavish his attentions on her. He'd never succumbed to her childish games, but had she somehow gotten the impression that he had? *Heavenly Father, how do I get out of this without wounding her deeply?*

He cleared his throat. "I ask your forgiveness if I gave you the wrong impression, Miss Dupont. I never committed to marry you and am sorry if I did anything that implied I wanted to. I'm sure in time you will find a worthier man on whom to bestow your devotion."

Her blue eyes flashed. "Surely you know our mothers have had an arrangement since we were children. Everyone expects that we will marry."

He shook his head, more than a little confused. "How is it everyone but me understands this?"

"Because you're a stubborn buffoon who can't appreciate the woman right in front of your eyes."

Not true. His gaze darted to Miss Hawthorne. Now *there* was a woman he appreciated. From her sweet nature to her love for Jamie to her intriguing brown eyes.

"Not *her*. I meant me. How can you prefer that English trollop over a woman of my standing? How do you know the boy isn't really hers and she's just trying to pawn him off as yours to worm her way into your money box? All because he has the same coloring as you?"

Lucas stepped back as if slapped. "Woman, you forget yourself. Do not impose on my hospitality by slandering the very woman who had the gumption to travel a thousand miles to bring Jamie to me. I'll not have you belittle her."

"Humph!" Miss Dupont flung her head sideways, lifting her chin. "I see. Well, I shan't waste anymore time in a place where I'm not welcome. I shall turn my attentions elsewhere, and I shall see that my father no longer does business with you."

She swirled around and marched away, her lavender skirts swaying back and forth like a bell. As she passed a rosebush, a gust of warm wind blew, snagging the fabric. She halted, shrieked a noise that put Lucas in mind of a pig squeal, and yanked her skirt. A ripping sound made her gasp. She flung a wounded look his way then stomped toward the garden entrance.

Miss Hawthorne noted her coming and moved Jamie to her other side and out of her way. Hilary halted, said something that made Miss Hawthorne go pale, then stomped up the stairs and back into the house.

Miss Hawthorne cast a glance at him, said something to Jamie, then dashed off toward the pond. His son strolled toward him, looking concerned.

What in the world had that woman said?

&.

Heather had never before been so insulted. A hussy, indeed. And the word Miss Dupont had called Jamie—why she'd never heard a woman utter such vile accusations. What had Mr. Reed said to cause that woman to turn fangs on her?

She marched toward the pond and past it to the charming arched bridge that spanned the wide creek, trying to shake her irritation and embarrassment. Atop the bridge, she halted, staring into the water. Recent flower blossoms, which had yielded to new spring leaves, floated along on the slow current, stealing away some of her anger. A turtle sitting on a rock near the shore basked in the warm sunlight. Being able to walk around outside in April without a cloak was a delight. If only she could enjoy it.

She heaved a heavy sigh. Clearly that woman thought Heather was Jamie's mother and that she was lying about Lucas being the father. Miss Dupont said she was a swindler, stealing from the Reeds. Tears formed in Heather's eyes, blurring the lovely view, but she blinked them away.

That woman had no idea how much it had cost her to bring Jamie here. He was the only person she had left in her life. Her mother was gone, and now her father. Without Jamie, she'd be alone. Completely alone.

She sucked in a sob. She couldn't—she wouldn't—think about that now.

Jamie was still a part of her life for the time being, and she'd enjoy every moment.

In the back of her mind, a voice whispered, *He could have been yours alone if you hadn't been so honorable. His father never would have known about him. You could have kept him.*

She swatted the air, chasing away a mosquito and her wayward thoughts. Too late for such shameful regrets. Jamie would have a better life here, and hers would be better just knowing he was well cared for and loved.

If only there was someone who loved *her*.

She stood for a while, enjoying the beauty of the serene setting and allowing the peacefulness to calm her worries. The trees swayed on the light breeze, flies buzzed past her, flowers of red, purple, white, and yellow dotted the shore like an artist's palette. Birds peeped above her head, and across the bank about fifteen feet downstream, a huge spider had spun a massive web that stretched between two trees and glimmered in the sunlight.

All she had to do was not think of the day she and Jamie would be parted, and she could bear it.

Footsteps echoed beside her on the bridge, but she kept her focus forward. She wanted to be alone, but she was shirking her duties. If she didn't tend Jamie, some other servant would have to abandon her own duties to watch him.

Mr. Reed stopped beside her. His large hands grasped the top of the bridge, and he stared out at the water as she did. "It's beautiful here this time of year, is it not?"

She held her tongue, halfway afraid of what she might say. At least he hadn't come here to scold her.

He heaved a loud sigh and hung his head. "For whatever Miss Dupont said to you, I sincerely apologize."

"'Tis not your place to express regret on her part."

"No, but she is our guest and had no right spewing her anger on you."

Again, Heather wondered what had passed between the two to make the woman lash out as she had. Could they have had a lover's quarrel? Had the woman said something as vile about Jamie to Mr. Reed as she'd spoken to her?

He glanced over his shoulder and back in the direction of the house. Anyone looking out the front parlor window could surely see them together. He straightened and pointed to the far side of the bridge. "Have you ever ventured down that path?"

"Nay." She shook her head. "After your mention of alligators, I was afraid to take Jamie anywhere near the wooded areas or ponds."

"Would you walk with me? I have some things to discuss with you."

She glanced up. Had he already found a replacement for her? Had he changed his mind about keeping Jamie in the face of his friend's outburst?

She was half afraid to agree, but she had no choice. For now, he was her employer. "Aye," she all but whispered.

He smiled and held out his elbow. "Shall we?"

She hesitated touching him. If doing so affected her as much as his smile, she was in big trouble. She couldn't afford to harbor feelings for her employer.

Still, he might be offended if she refused his escort, and spurned men often heaped their anger on the women who rebuffed them.

His dark brows rose, and his friendly blue eyes glimmered with humor. "Really, Miss Hawthorne, is it such a difficult decision to accept my arm?"

Smiling inwardly at his chivalry, she forced her hand around his warm, well-muscled arm. It was not the limb of a man from the city.

They walked along in silence, and a warm shiver wiggled down her spine when he didn't force her to talk. Birds chirped in the trees above them, and spots of sunlight broke through the heavy canopy of leaves, dappling the ground. The well-used dirt path wound through a grove of trees lining the creek, then opened up to a fenced pasture where more than a dozen horses grazed. Several foals frolicked in the knee-high grasses, kicking their awkward legs and chasing each other, while others nestled in the tall grasses, sleeping next to their grazing mothers. Nearby, a solid brown foal with a fuzzy black mane and tail nursed while its patient mother dozed. Heather's cheeks flamed, and she tried not to watch. As a young girl, she'd often slipped down to her father's stables to see the young horses come springtime, but viewing such with a gentleman present...

Thankfully, Mr. Reed continued to meander down the path without commenting. As they neared the end of the fence, he finally stopped and released her. She leaned against the wooden rails and continued to watch the horses, the birds, the flowers. Anything but him.

She held tight to the weathered wood, hoping to stem her nervousness. Her feelings were changing. She'd come to America a staunch British Loyalist who despised the colonists for what they'd done, but she realized now they were just people fighting for what they felt was rightfully theirs. She could understand why they wanted freedom from a ruler an ocean away who didn't understand the plight they faced in this wild land. And if she faced the truth, America's War for Independence wasn't responsible for her father losing his wealth as much as was his lust for gambling. She didn't want to believe him capable of such a deed, so she had blamed the faceless colonists.

But now they had faces—and names.

Mr. Reed paced the grass beside her with his hands locked behind his back. Whatever he wanted to talk to her about must be difficult. Why else would he be so anxious? She swallowed hard, hoping he wouldn't send her packing.

He cleared his throat. "Again, I want to express my apologies for Miss Dupont's lack of self-control. You don't need to tell me what she said. I could see that it bothered you immensely. She can be. . .um. . .overly feisty at times."

"Don't you mean rude?" Too late, she realized she'd voiced the words out loud.

He chuckled. "That, too." He stopped beside her and leaned his hip against a fence rail, staring in her direction.

She glanced sideways at him, caught his intense gaze, then smiled and looked away. *Oh my.* Did he have any idea how he affected her?

She tightened her grip on the fence, wincing as a splinter from the dried wood pricked her hand. She simply must put a stop to such nonsensical thoughts.

"I was wondering. . ."

She peered sideways, watching him fidget. Why was he nervous?

Chapter 10

Heather held her breath. The next words he uttered could mean joy or utter sadness.

"I mean," Mr. Reed said, "would you consider staying longer? I haven't had a chance to interview anyone for the governess position, and now that we're here at the plantation, I don't anticipate being able to easily interview prospects. I just think it would be best for Jamie if you could stay longer." He ran his hands through his thick, black hair and heaved another deep sigh, as if the words rushing out of him had left him breathless.

Heather's pulse increased. She could have more time with Jamie.

But then it skidded to a halt. Wouldn't that make the separation harder for him in the long run?

"Miss Hawthorne—Heather—please look at me."

Startled by his use of her Christian name, she turned toward him. His lovely eyes roved her face, making it hard for her to breathe. He tucked a strand of hair behind her ear.

"Can you deny that there is something growing between us?"

He felt it, too? She wasn't just imagining the impossible or letting her emotions run wild? She tried to swallow, but her throat felt too dry.

"I know this is an awkward situation, but I want you to know that I've not felt a thing for another woman since I lost Deborah—not until you burst into my life."

"But what of Miss Dupont? She seems to believe that you and she have an understanding."

He harrumphed and crossed his arms. "She is mistaken. I've never given her reason to assume such a thing and told her so not half an hour ago."

He cared nothing for Miss Dupont? A smile tickled her lips, and she ducked her head, ashamed at her unbridled joy.

"So, my question remains: Do you have any interest in staying longer not just for Jamie's sake, but to see if this"—he waved his hand in the air—"attraction, or whatever it is we are sensing, has any merit?"

She wanted to give free rein to her excitement, but common sense pulled back on the lines. He was as much a nobleman as you'd find in this new country, so why would he be infatuated with a poor soap maker?

Somehow, even though it might break her heart, she had to make him see reason. "I fear you've already weakened your standing among your friends and associates by agreeing to raise Jamie. How would they feel if you were to associate with a British citizen?"

He shrugged. "I have done far worse, I can assure you. And if I recall, you're now a Canadian." An enticing smirk danced on his lips.

"You may call a mule a horse, but that doesn't make it so."

"Bah! Do not belittle yourself like that." He stepped closer. "When I look at you, I see a lovely woman with beguiling brown eyes, who left her home and ventured on a long, dangerous journey to unite a young boy with his family. You're sweet and generous, and it would be my honor to have you walk at my side."

"You're too kind, sir." Tears stung her eyes as she stared at the tiny white flowers at their feet. No man had ever stood up for her, not even her father. She didn't deserve someone like Mr. Reed, not that he'd offered marriage, but she knew if they started on this course that well could be where it led. A thought burst into her mind. If she married Mr. Reed, she would be Jamie's mother!

But she couldn't do that—marry the father for the lad's sake.

Something suddenly shoved her hard in the back, forcing her forward and against Mr. Reed. His arms encircled her, and he chuckled. "It seems someone else took offense to your mule reference."

She glanced over her shoulder into a horse's muzzle. The animal blew warm breath against her face and pulled its head back to its side of the fence. She squealed and buried her cheek against her employer's waistcoat. His torso vibrated with his laughter. Realizing the impropriety of where she stood, she pushed against his chest, but the hands clutched behind her back refused to yield.

"You have not yet answered me." His eyes blazed like blue fire.

Oh, could this really be happening to her? Was he simply toying with her?

"I see a battle going on in that pretty head of yours. Have I made a dreadful assumption?" His smile disappeared, and he let go so fast she stumbled. "Do you feel nothing for me?"

"Nay."

He scowled, disappointment clouding his eyes.

"I mean nay to the first question."

He blinked, relaxing his stance. "Which question was that?"

"I, too, have felt an. . .attraction. . .to you." Her cheeks flamed. Never had she talked with a man in such a manner. "I would like to stay. . .to see what happens."

His wide smile was her reward. He ran a finger down her cheek, his eyes filling with tenderness.

"Fate has blessed me this day," she said.

He shook his head. "Not fate. God is the one who preordained it all."

She frowned. "God has never been so inclined to bless me before. I fear He has all but turned His back on me."

"I believed that once, too. After I lost Deborah, I tried to drown out my sorrows with ale, but it never worked. I'd sober up then try it all over again. I couldn't understand why God would allow something to happen to such a gentle soul like Deborah. Until you arrived, I never knew if she'd decided marriage to me was too unbearable and ran away, or if something more nefarious had happened to her." He shook his head. "I'd be lying if I said I understand it all now, but I'm beginning to see God had a greater plan."

"Why would He allow Deborah to suffer so? After Jamie was born, she was so weak and fragile that she could hardly hold and enjoy him."

He ran his hand down the back of her head, sending delicious chills up and down her spine. "I don't know. But I can tell you that after searching for her for almost two years and not finding even a hint of where she might be, I finally reached the keel—my lowest point. A kind clergyman found me passed out in a filthy alley in Boston, took me in, and poured God's Word into me instead of ale. He helped me to see that I was a sinner loved by God but in need of repentance, just like the rest of mankind. The day I gave my heart to God, everything changed. I became a new man."

Heather pondered his words. Her mother had been a devout believer in God but her father was not. After her mother died, her father never let her attend church again.

"Come, we should be getting back." He took her hand, guiding her onto the path. "As much as I wish it wasn't so, I've guests to attend, and I'm sure Jamie thinks we've abandoned him by now."

She felt almost as if they were a couple, but she didn't dare get her hopes up. What if Mr. Reed grew tired of her? Would he cast her aside?

She realized just how little she actually knew about the man. But one thing she was certain of, though he'd once been a rogue, Lucas Reed was now an honorable man. He'd certainly done right by his son.

"Do you suppose you could call me Lucas when we're alone?"

She stopped, surprised by his soft-spoken request. "You're my employer. It would hardly seem proper."

"Heather, I'd like to be a lot more than just your employer. Would it help if I were to fire you and allow you to remain here as a guest of the family?"

A smile tugged at her lips. "Nay. That isn't necessary."

He ran his knuckle across her cheek. "I love your name."

A breath caught in her throat. "Thank you."

"When we're alone, will you please call me by my Christian name?"

She ducked her head, still unsure.

With one long finger under her chin, he lifted it so that she had to look at him. "Please?"

With a resolved sigh, she nodded. "Aye. . .Lucas."

His whole face lit up with his wide grin. Curving her hand around his arm, he led her back toward the bridge, whistling a jolly tune.

&

"You sure seem happy this morning, Lucas. Almost giddy, if you ask me, especially considering what happened yesterday."

"I do feel quite well today." Lucas glanced across the breakfast table and met his mother's curious gaze. "I'm sorry for upsetting your friends, Mother, but Miss Dupont needed to know that I'm not the man for her."

His mother stirred her tea. "I suppose I've known for a long while that you only look upon her as a neighbor and possibly a friend."

He lifted a brow. Hilary surely would no longer consider him a friend. He couldn't help wondering what kind of backlash he'd receive from rejecting her affections. The Dupont women had wide circles of influence. Well, no matter. His affections lay elsewhere, so there was nothing to be done about it. He slathered twice as much jam as normal on his bread in his effort not to look at Heather. Keeping his attraction to her under control in front of his astute mother would be difficult, but he must give Heather as much time as she needed to get to know him—and to fall in love. For he had little doubt that's where their relationship was headed.

"And what do you plan to do today, young man?"

While his mother's gaze was directed at Jamie, he peeked at Heather and winked. Her eyes widened, and her cheeks turned bright red. He bit back a grin. Teasing her and flirting would be enjoyable.

"I hope Papa will take me riding." Jamie peered at him, looking shy, but Lucas was glad his son felt bold enough to express himself. The boy was gradually coming out of the cocoon that he'd been wrapped up in living alone with Heather.

"I imagine that could be arranged, son. But first, finish your breakfast. A man needs a full stomach to work all morning."

Jamie frowned and stared at his porridge. Did he not like the food?

"That's a splendid idea," his mother said. "Heather and I will busy ourselves with redoing Jamie's room and making a list of the supplies we'll need to purchase to finish the project."

Heather sat quietly to his left, sipping her tea. She spoke little during mealtimes, and he wondered if she still felt odd partaking with the family. If he had things his way, he'd keep her close for the rest of their lives.

A quick rap sounded at the back door. Mrs. Overton entered the dining room shortly afterward with Samuel following. The horseman had removed his hat, revealing curly black hair tinged with gray, and he crinkled the brim in his hand. Something had happened.

Lucas stood and crossed the room into the hall, where they could talk and not be overheard. "What is it?"

Samuel followed. He glanced at the family through the doorway then leaned in close and whispered, "We's had us another robbery."

Lucas sighed. "What did they take this time?"

Samuel scratched his ear. "Well now, that be the odd thing. All's they stole was a feed bucket and an ol' horse blanket."

Lucas excused himself and strode to the barn, with Samuel hurrying to keep up. Three thefts in eight days meant the robber was getting comfortable—bolder—and had to be somewhere close by. How long before he decided to break into the house—or until someone got hurt?

In the barn, he surveyed the tack room, looking for anything amiss. "Everything here seems in order. Why would someone risk capture just to steal a bucket and blanket?" It made no sense.

"Just downright foolhardiness if'n you asks me." Samuel shrugged and picked up an embroidered handkerchief. "Found this wheres the blanket was."

The linsey-woolsey fabric had neat but almost childlike stitching around the outer edge. Had the thief accidentally dropped this? Left it as payment for what he took? Lucas shook his head. A wooden pail was easy enough to make if you had the skill, and the blanket wasn't overly expensive, but both were worth far more than a simple handkerchief. Something had to be done to stop the thefts.

He set the handkerchief on a high shelf. "Leave that there, and don't let anyone else touch it. Send Julius up to the house with horses for him and me. I'll send him to Ben Ellison's house with a note, asking Ben to bring his hunting dogs. Perhaps we can use the cloth to track the thief."

"That's a right good idea. I'll go fetch him."

While Samuel searched for Julius, Lucas hurried back to the house to prepare a note requesting Ben's help. Then he'd ride over to Madison Gardens and see if Richard had encountered the thief or could help in the search.

In his office, he quickly penned the note to Ben, melted some wax over the raw edge of the paper, and stamped the Reed seal into it.

A knock sounded outside his open door, and his mother stood in the hall holding a vase of flowers. She smiled and entered the room. "I brought something to brighten up your work area."

He stood. "This dull place could use something lively."

She set the vase on the back of his desk, and the scent of candle wax faded against the fragrance of the flowers. His mother's silver and blue day dress looked beautiful and blended well with her eyes. "Is something wrong? I couldn't hear your conversation with Samuel, but you both looked worried."

Lucas blew out a heavy breath. "There's been another theft."

His mother laid a hand across her chest. "Oh my. Was anything valuable taken?"

"That's the odd thing. This thief only takes small things, and one or two at a time. A hen, a bucket, a horse blanket. I can't make any sense of it."

"Hmm. . .sounds like things a person might need to survive." Her eyes widened. "You don't suppose it's a runaway slave, do you?"

He laid a hand on her shoulder, hoping to reassure her. "I sincerely doubt it. I thought that at first, but I can't see a slave staying this long. He'd want to get as far away from his owner as possible."

"Perhaps he feels safe here, knowing that you don't own slaves."

Lucas pursed his lips and shook his head. "I just can't see it. A runaway is still his owner's property and wouldn't be any safer here than somewhere else. As much as I despise slavery, it is legal, and I'd be breaking the law to harbor someone else's slave."

His mother narrowed her eyes and stared at him. "It wouldn't be the first time you've broken the law for a good cause."

He turned and strode to the open doors leading onto the balcony. Across the shaded lawn, he could see Heather and Jamie seated on a quilt in the shelter of a massive live oak in the far corner of the garden. Shrubs in full bloom framed the area in pink, white, and lavender flowers. Such a lovely sight warred with the memories swirling in his mind. "Those days are behind me, Mother. Besides, I was young and headstrong then, determined to free our country from Britain's stronghold. Being a privateer with the blessings of the Patriot government was a way to help the war efforts and to hinder the supply line to the British troops."

His mother crossed the room in a swish of skirts and stood beside him. "You say those days are behind you, yet you refuse to sail your ships except for the trip to Charleston and back. I never understood that."

He clenched his jaw as the memories continued to assail him. "I did things that I'm not proud of. We took lives for the sake of food and ammunition."

"It was war, son. During such dire times, men are often forced to do things beyond what they feel capable of doing."

"That doesn't change the fact of what I did. Sacrificing my love of sailing on the open sea is my penance to God."

"Lucas, Lucas. You know God has forgiven you. When you became a believer, you repented of your sins, and the blood of Christ washed you clean. You're a new creation. The past has been made pure, and you no longer need to be chained to it."

"I know, Mother, and I believe what you say. But I made an oath to God, and I'll not break it."

She sighed. "I fear one day you will be required to—and then what?"

Lucas shrugged. "I hope that day never comes." He turned to face her. "In the meantime, I'm sending a rider to Ben Ellison's to see if he can come and bring his tracking dogs. I'm off to the Madisons' to recruit Richard's assistance.

I mean to catch the thief this day."

"Do invite Caroline to come and stay with us if Richard agrees to help you."

He nodded. "That's a brilliant idea, Mother. Heath—uh. . .Miss Hawthorne and she seemed to get along well in Charleston."

She eyed him with the precision of a hawk high up in the sky watching a poor mouse; then she glanced across the garden to where Heather and Jamie sat. She'd noticed his faux pas, no doubt, and where his gaze had been focused.

He cleared his throat. "I must be off. I want this thief caught before dark. Please see to it that Miss Hawthorne and Jamie stay within sight of the house today."

Without waiting for a response, he strode past his desk, snatched up the letter to Ben Ellison, and stormed from the room. He'd encouraged Heather to keep their budding relationship a secret, but he was afraid he'd just let the cat out of the bag.

Chapter 11

Tired of reading several chapters aloud, Heather closed the book. "What did you think about Robinson Crusoe making friends with Friday?"

Jamie sat on the corner of a blanket shredding a leaf that he'd plucked from a nearby shrub. "I'm glad he didn't have to be alone no more."

" 'Tis *anymore*, Jamie, not *no more*." She smiled. "I am also happy he found a friend." If things went well between her and Lucas, perhaps she wouldn't have to live alone, either. She'd lain awake much of the night, reliving their walk and Lucas's surprising revelation. That he could care for her was almost beyond hope. Had their attraction to each other blossomed because of their common love for Jamie?

Yawning, she noticed Jamie had risen and was creeping toward a bush covered in a blanket of fat white flowers. This garden was an Eden. She couldn't look at the brilliant, flower-covered bushes or breathe in their sweet scent enough. Mrs. Reed had told her that soon the flowers would fade and fall off, and the plants wouldn't bloom again until next spring.

Where would she be then?

A bird suddenly darted out of the bush and flew past Jamie's head. He jumped then glanced at her, grinning. The brown bird with red highlights glided over to a vivid purple shrub and alighted.

"Jamie, if you'll be quiet and watch, there's a fine possibility that you'll see that bird's mate. It will be a bright red."

He lifted his gaze and looked up into the huge tree above them then scanned the garden. The female chirped, and Heather smiled. It almost sounded as if the bird was rapidly repeating, "Here, kitty, kitty, kitty."

Jamie hunkered down and tiptoed toward the female. Heather knew she should scold him for scaring the birds, but the warmth of the day and her lack of sleep made her listless. She understood why many southerners took a rest midday.

She yawned and closed her eyes for a moment, listening to the birdcall and Jamie's soft giggling. If she and Lucas were to marry, Jamie would one day be a big brother to their children. He would like that and be a good one. . . .

Heather felt the sudden sensation of falling into a dark cavern and jerked awake. It took a moment for her to realize she'd been dozing. Stretching, she yawned and looked around. She was outside—not in her bed? Oh yes, she'd been reading to Jamie.

She bolted upright. Where was Jamie? How long had she slept?

Peering up at the sun, she realized that she must have dozed for close to an hour. Panic shot through her like a musket ball. Had Jamie gone inside? Had he wandered off?

"Jamie! Where are you, lad?" She stood and scanned the gardens but didn't see him. "Jamie?"

Her heart throbbing, she picked up the book and quilt and rushed back into the house. Surely he was eating a treat in the kitchen or with his father or grandmother. *Please be there.*

Scolding herself for being so lax, she entered the house and deposited the book and blanket on a bench just inside the back door. She burst into the kitchen.

Mable's startled gaze lifted from her task of slicing a hunk of meat. "Land sakes, you done frightened a dozen years offa me."

"Have you seen Jamie?" Heather frantically searched the kitchen.

"No miss. Not since breakfast. Did you lose him?"

"I'm sure he must be upstairs. I'll check there." How could she tell the woman that she had indeed lost him? How could she bear it if anything happened to him?

She hurried up the steps then quickly looked in each room, and all but collided with Mrs. Reed as she exited the library, book in hand.

"Oh my dear, what's the big rush?" Mrs. Reed smiled, blue eyes shining.

Heather looked past her, hoping against hope that Jamie was with his grandmother. Tears burned her eyes when she didn't locate him.

Mrs. Reed's smiled faded. "What is it?"

Heather grimaced and broke her gaze. "I was reading to Jamie—and drifted asleep. He was in the garden, watching some birds." She gasped a sob. "Now I can't find him."

Mrs. Reed pulled her into her arms and patted her back. "Now, now, he can't have gone far. We'll gather up the servants and find him quickly." She set her book on a hall table, guided Heather into the parlor, and tugged on a bell pull.

"I feel dreadful." Heather collapsed onto a chair. "Mr. Reed will never trust me with his son again."

"Don't fret so, my dear. I raised two boys and know how they can go wandering off."

Two boys? Lucas had never mentioned a brother. Had he died in childhood? Could he have wandered off like Jamie and never come back? Unshed tears stung her eyes. "Oh, I should never have fallen asleep. I had some things on my mind and didn't rest well last night."

Mrs. Reed stared at her with a knowing look. A tiny smile tugged at the corner of her lips. Had Lucas told his mother about them after requesting her silence?

"Do you suppose Jamie could be with his father?" Heather asked.

Mrs. Reed shook her head. "No, Lucas rode over to the Madisons' a short while ago. I suspect he'll be back soon with them in tow. Let's see if we can't locate Jamie before they return."

Mrs. Overton hurried into the room, the jingling keys on her chatelaine heralding her arrival. "You rang for me, ma'am?"

"Aye, Jamie has gone missing, and we need to find him quickly. Please assemble as many servants as you can to join us in the search."

Mrs. Overton nodded and sped from the room.

"Now, I will thoroughly search the house, and why don't you look farther outside?" She patted Heather's hand. "We will find the boy. The good Lord wouldn't send him this far to us and let something happen to him."

"I wish I had your faith."

"You can, dear. All you must do is repent of your sins and believe that Jesus is the Son of God and that He died for you. Trusting God during difficult times can be quite reassuring."

Heather nodded, wondering if that was why Mrs. Reed seemed so calm in the face of such a calamity. She rose, anxious to continue her search. "I'll check the outbuildings, garden, and"—she swallowed hard—"down by the pond and the river."

"You know how much Jamie loves the horses. Why don't you start with the barn? Then I can have the servants search around the water." Her smiled wobbled, revealing that she wasn't quite as composed as she portrayed.

"Aye, Mrs. Reed."

"Won't you please call me Amelia?"

Heather offered a weak smile and a brief nod and hurried from the room. Why hadn't she thought of the barn? Jamie frequently asked his father to take him to see the horses or to go for a ride. She all but jogged the distance to the stable. When she stepped inside, it took a moment for her eyes to adjust to the dimmer lighting. She lifted a hand to her nose, blocking the odor of horses and hay. Dust motes drifted lazily on the sunlight shining in the open doors and windows. A horse whickered at her, but there was no sign of Jamie.

She stood still, trying to listen in the quiet over the thrumming of her heart. Could he be hiding? If he was and he saw her, she was certain he'd start giggling. When she heard nothing, she called to him, "Jamie, are you here? Please come out."

After a few moments, she hurried to the far side of the barn. Jamie had thoroughly enjoyed the tour of the servants' outbuildings when they'd taken a walk down that way one morning. Perhaps he'd gone to watch the candlemaker who had so fascinated him or to play with some of the servants' younger children that two older women cared for while their parents worked.

Sweat streamed down her spine as she quickened her pace. The servants' village came into view. She received odd looks from the servants when she peeked into the weaving and sewing houses, the candle- and soap makers' cabin, and the dye house. Her hands shook, and she battled tears. Where could he have gone?

Two large black men walked toward her. She recognized one of them as the man who often worked in the barn. She picked up her skirt and hurried toward him. "Please, sir, have you seen Jamie?"

The taller man's dark eyes widened. "That boy, he be missin'?"

"Yes. I can't find him anywhere." Tears coursed down her cheeks, but she cared little. Her life was over if anything happened to Jamie.

"I'm Samuel, and this here be Abraham. We's gonna help you find that boy."

Heather reached out and grabbed the man's calloused hands. "Oh thank you so much."

"You go gather ever'body and ask if they done seen Master Jamie." Samuel nodded to Abraham, who took off jogging toward the nearest building. He picked up a mallet and whacked a circle of tin hanging from a cord. A loud *bong* filled the air, and men and women poured from the buildings, gathering together.

"Why don't you go back to the big house? We'll find that boy."

"Perhaps he went to play with the other children."

Samuel gently turned her toward the house. "We'll check there. You go keep Miz Reed comp'ny."

Heather nodded and wandered back to the house. Her feet felt as if she were wearing lead shoes. Never in the years she'd cared for Jamie had she ever let him out of her sight until coming to Charleston. What if. . .

All manner of heinous thoughts assaulted her. She lifted her hands to her face and sobbed. "Oh God, please watch over him. I'll do anything You want if You'll let us find Jamie, safe and sound."

The thud of quickly moving hooves drew near, then stopped. Leather creaked. "Heather, what's the matter? Why are you crying?"

Her tears flowed faster at the sound of Lucas's voice, and she couldn't bear to look at him. "I've lost Jamie."

His arms encircled her. "Shh. . .tell me what happened."

She longed to nuzzle against his chest and stay there, but she couldn't. She didn't deserve to. What would happen to Lucas if he lost his son when he'd barely gotten to know the lad? "I—I was reading to him—and I fell asleep."

"I see. Where have you looked for him?"

At the clipped tone of his voice, she stepped out of his arms, and her cheeks warmed when she realized Richard Madison was also present atop his horse. "Your mother is searching the house. I checked the barn and the servants' work houses. Samuel has gathered the servants, and they are also searching."

Heather's chin wobbled, but she stayed her tears.

Lucas lifted his tricorn and ran his hand through his black hair. "Has anyone checked near the river or ponds? You know how Jamie likes searching for tadpoles."

She turned toward the river and noticed a trio of men headed toward the dock. "They're checking now."

"How long has he been missing?"

"I don't know." Heather winced. "Perhaps an hour."

"Go stay with Mother. We will find him."

Lucas mounted, and he and Richard Madison rode at a gallop toward the servants' quarters. Heather forced her feet to move toward the house. In spite of the warm sun beaming down on her, a cold shiver made her cross her arms. If anything happened to Jamie, Lucas would forever blame her.

❧

Lucas shot one prayer after another toward heaven, but a sense of dread still clung to him like barnacles on a ship's hull. How could Heather have been so careless? Where would Jamie go if given his freedom to explore without an adult along? What if the thief had found Jamie and done him harm or held him for ransom?

Lucas rode his horse to the barn and tugged Liberty to a stop just outside the doors. "Samuel!"

Richard followed, his eyes filled with compassion. "I'm sorry about this, Lucas. We'll find him."

Lucas nodded. When his servant didn't answer, he spun his horse around and trotted him alongside the creek. Surely Jamie wouldn't venture near the water after being warned about alligators.

A motion drew Lucas's gaze toward the road leading to the house. A wagon with a saddled horse tied behind it rolled toward him. "Good. Ben Ellison is here."

When he'd sent someone for Ben, he surely never expected he'd have to use the dogs to find Jamie. "Richard, could you ride up to the house and ask Heather for something Jamie has worn recently? We can use it so Ben's dogs can catch his scent."

Richard nodded and rode off, while Lucas trotted Liberty forward to meet Ben. Two brown-and-white hound dogs jumped up on the back of the wagon's bench seat and bayed a greeting.

"I'm mighty obliged to you for coming so quickly," Lucas said.

"Happy to do it." Ben smiled. His curly gray hair stuck out from under his hat in ringlets. His fuzzy eyebrows and beard were still a dark brown that matched his friendly eyes. Ben was a neighbor who always came if called on. "If you have a thief here, he just might hit my place or my daughter's next. It's best we see to this problem before someone gets hurt."

Lucas clenched his jaw, not quite ready to tell his neighbor about Jamie, but there was nothing to be done about it. He needed Ben's help. While they waited for Richard to return, Lucas explained about Jamie and how he was missing.

Ben scratched his beard. "That's a shame that you just found your boy and now he's gone off somewhere. But my Lolly and Molly will find him." The dogs whimpered and wagged their tails at the sound of their names. Ben jumped down to the ground then motioned for the dogs to do the same. He untied his horse from the back of the wagon and walked toward Lucas.

Richard galloped back with the shirt Jamie had worn yesterday in his hand. He gave it to Ben. The dogs began baying again, as if sensing the chase that was soon to ensue.

"Where was the boy last seen?" Ben asked.

"In the gardens." Lucas pointed toward the house.

"That's where we'll start." Ben mounted, and they rode to the area in the garden where Heather said she had been reading to Jamie. Ben slid off his horse then called his dogs and held the shirt for them to sniff. Tails wagged and the dogs yipped, their eyes riveted on their owner. He waved a hand in the air. "Search, Lolly. Search, Molly."

The dogs ran from tree to shrub to grassy alcove. One of them bayed. The other dog joined in, and both bolted out of the garden toward the barn. They stopped and sniffed around a bush a short distance from the barn then dashed off in the direction of the pond. Ben jumped back on his horse. "They've got the scent!"

All three horses jumped the low hedge and galloped after the dogs, which were already nearing the arched bridge. Lucas's heart throbbed in time with Liberty's hoofbeats. "Please, Father, keep Jamie safe. Watch over him."

Chapter 12

Heather paced in front of the parlor window. The men had followed the howling dogs across the creek and into the trees on the far side. What could have compelled Jamie to venture in that direction? Had he gone to the creek in search of tadpoles? Had he chased a bird so far that he'd gotten lost?

"Heather, please come and sit down." Amelia patted the sofa beside where she sat. "Caroline and I would like to pray together for Jamie."

"It will give us something more constructive to do than worrying." Caroline Madison smiled. "And it's the best way we can help. The Scriptures say, 'For where two or three are gathered together in my name, there am I in the midst of them.'"

Twisting her hands, Heather glanced at the two women. "I prayed earlier—when I was looking for Jamie." She blinked back the tears burning her eyes. "I told God I'd do anything for Him if He saved Jamie."

Amelia rose and came to Heather then took her hand. She gently led her to the sofa and pressed down on her shoulders until she sat. Amelia resumed her seat. "God doesn't bargain for our love and obedience. He loves us freely and longs for us to love Him in return. He will protect Jamie because He loves him far more than we ever could. He loves us so much that He allowed His own precious Son, Jesus, to die for our sins."

Heather had never heard the Bible message explained in such simple terms before. She listened, wondering again how Amelia could remain so calm in the face of her grandson's disappearance. Her heart longed for that peace—to know God. To have Someone she could talk to when she was alone. Someone to comfort her in troubling times such as this one. "What do I have to do then to become a child of God?"

Amelia's warm smile chased away some of Heather's anxiety. "The Scriptures say to believe on the Lord Jesus Christ and you shall be saved. We are also instructed to repent of our sins."

Heather glanced at Caroline, who smiled and nodded her agreement. "It's that simple."

She stared out the window, longing for peace. Most of her life had been spent in turmoil. Her mother had lost several babies then finally died giving birth to another child who failed to survive. Her father had disappeared for months at a time, leaving her in the care of a coldhearted governess. When he was home, he drank until he could no longer function. Then just when she came of age and hoped she might find a decent man to marry and give her some stability, her father had lost their home by gambling and had hauled her off to the Nova Scotia wilderness. Deborah had been her only close companion until she died, and then a year ago, Heather's father passed away, leaving only Jamie and a few neighbors, none of whom she was close to.

She heaved a heavy sigh. If God could fill the emptiness in her heart, then she welcomed Him. She looked at Amelia and nodded. "How do I ask Him?"

Amelia took hold of her hands. "Just what I said before. Talk to God, either out loud or in your head. Tell Him that you believe that Jesus Christ is His Son and that He died to save you from sin."

Bowing her head, Heather focused her attention on her sins. She hadn't been a naughty child, but surely she'd done many things that were wrong in God's eyes. She couldn't bear to say the words out loud, so she prayed in her mind. *Dear God, I do believe in Jesus, Your Son, and I thank You that He died for me. I'm truly sorry for the bad things I've done, whether intentionally or not. Forgive me for losing Jamie.*

The weight of that thought caught in her throat, making it hard to breathe. But she pressed on, determined to make peace with God. *Thank You for saving me. And please, Lord, show Lucas where Jamie is.*

She sat with her head bowed for a while longer. She wasn't sure, but it felt as if the strain of the day lessened. Finally, she peered up, catching both women eyeing her with open curiosity. "I did it."

A breath whooshed out of Amelia, warming Heather's face. She cupped Heather's cheek. "Wonderful."

Caroline reached out and bridged the gap between them, touching Heather's arm. "I'm so happy for you. The angels in heaven are rejoicing this day."

"I hope the angels are helping look for Jamie." Heather ducked her head and picked a seedpod off her skirt.

Both Amelia and Caroline chuckled. "I'm sure they are," Amelia said. "Now, would you like to join Caroline and me in prayer for Jamie?"

"Aye. I would." Heather closed her eyes, feeling a unity with God she'd never before encountered. Her chest warmed as Amelia pleaded out loud for Jamie's safe return. Heather felt as if God granted her the assurance that the lad would be home soon. One thing was for certain—she was not the same woman she'd been this morning. God had washed her clean—white as snow.

⁊⁊

That evening as the sun began to set, Heather lit several lanterns and hung them on the front porch to help Lucas find his way back home. Amelia did the same upstairs and placed them in the windows, while Caroline helped Mable in the kitchen. With the light fading, the men would soon cease their search. Jamie would be frightened and alone all night. "Please, Father. Bring them home. All of them."

Heather opened the door to go inside when she heard a dog bark. She spun around and hurried to the railing, searching the twilight. Large, dark shapes emerged from the trees and plodded toward her. Lucas!

She snatched up a lantern and scurried down the stairs. One horse broke into a gallop and closed the distance. Lucas stared down at her, looking tired and revealing nothing in his expression. But where was Jamie?

Her heart near shattering, she gazed at the silhouettes of the other horses but couldn't make out if he was on one of them. Then she looked up at Lucas again and noticed the little hands on his waist. "Jamie!"

"Aunt Heather!"

Lucas slid Jamie around and lowered him to the ground. Heather nearly dropped the lantern in her effort to grab hold of the lad. "Oh Jamie. You scared half my life off of me."

He hugged her neck so hard she could barely breathe. She squeezed him back, relishing the scent that was only his.

"Ow. That hurts."

Reluctantly, she released him. "Where were you? Why did you run off?"

"I didn't. I was chasing that bird. Then I saw a squirrel and chased it. It went up a tree. So I decided to go in the barn and see the horses."

"You know you're not supposed to go there alone."

He shrugged and glanced up at his father. Lucas dismounted but didn't add anything.

"I didn't. I saw a lad sneak out of the barn carrying the blanket Samuel puts on Papa's horse. He didn't see me because I hid behind a bush."

Heather clutched her chest. Jamie had encountered the thief?

"I followed to see where he took the blanket. I thought he must be the thief Papa was looking for."

"Oh Jamie, don't you know how dangerous that was? What if that lad had hurt you?"

The dogs scurried over then flopped down in the grass near Jamie, their pink tongues hanging limp from the side of their mouths. They looked well satisfied. The other two horses stopped just past Lucas's, and the men dismounted. Richard walked into the circle of light, carrying a sleeping young lass with matted brown hair and a filthy dress. The poor thing was barefoot. Ben joined them, leading a dirty lad who looked about ten years old. His tattered clothing was a grimy gray. His shoulder-length blond hair was ratted and held pieces of hay, and listless green eyes peered at her. She glanced at Lucas.

"We need to get these children cleaned up so they can eat," he said. "We're all starving."

Quick footsteps sounded in the darkness, and Samuel appeared. "Praise be to God. You's found him."

Lucas nodded. "Yes, thanks to the good Lord's guidance and Ben's dogs." He handed his horse's reins to Samuel. "Could you also see to the other horses?"

"Yassah. Don't you worry. I's a gonna take good care of 'em." He gathered up the reins and led the three horses away.

Jamie tugged her arm. "I haven't eaten since breakfast."

"And whose fault is that?" She was so relieved to have him back that her worry turned to irritation.

"Jamie knows it was wrong to run off after Kit." Lucas rubbed the lad's hair.

"I was just trying to protect our stuff, Papa."

"I know, and I appreciate that, but next time come and find me or one of the other men. Run on along now. Your grandmother will be anxious to see you."

Jamie trotted off toward the big house, but when he reached the stairs, he turned back toward them and waved. Richard and Ben followed along with the two children in tow. Heather, not ready to be separated from Jamie again, started to follow, but Lucas grabbed her arm.

"Wait."

She turned to face him. Was he going to discharge her now? Did he despise her for falling asleep and allowing Jamie to wander off? And where did he find those children? "Who is Kit?"

Lucas sighed, his warm breath touching her face. "He's the boy. The girl is Janey, his sister."

Her heart ached for the ragamuffins. "Where did you find them?"

"They'd set up camp about a half mile from here in a group of trees near the creek. I'm surprised the field workers never saw them since they walk past those trees every day on their way to the rice fields and back."

"But where did they come from?" Heather relaxed now that Lucas wasn't snipping at her as he'd done earlier in the day.

"Charleston. Their father was a sailor who died at sea. Their mother—" Lucas stared up at the sky. "She became a dock strumpet after her husband's death. She couldn't feed her children, so she started taking in men. One of them killed her, and Kit took his sister and ran away, fearing for their lives. Somehow they stowed away on a vessel bound inland. Kit's been stealing things just so they can survive."

"Those poor children." In spite of the lad endangering Jamie, she couldn't help feeling sympathy for him and his sister.

A horse whinnied off in the distance, and a warm gust of wind caused the lantern to flicker and go out. Heather held her skirts down. One might even call their environment romantic, if there weren't so many unknowns. "So how did you find the children?"

"The dogs led us to Jamie—and he was with them, trying to talk them into returning here with him."

Heather smiled. That was her lad—kind and generous, just like his father.

She swallowed hard. Did Lucas still care for her? Losing a man's only son could cause some men to become fighting mad. Lucas seemed overly quiet and hadn't said anything except to answer her questions. "Well. . .I suppose I should get inside and help get the children cleaned up. Whatever will you do with them?"

"They have no family. Richard seems to think Caroline will be agreeable to taking them in. They've wanted children for a long while but haven't had any."

"That would be nice. She would make a wonderful mother." She started to turn away but couldn't. "I'm so sorry, Lucas. I didn't sleep well last night—I know it's not a decent excuse. I fell asleep when I should have been watching Jamie." Her lower lip trembled. "I don't know how I would have survived if something had happened to him."

"I know. I felt the same." He exhaled another sigh. "I'm sorry I was so short with you. When you said Jamie was missing, I didn't. . .know how to bear it. I'll admit I was upset with you, but I was wrong." He stepped closer and found her hands in the dark. "I was a young boy once, and I know how often I tried to sneak away from my governess. Will you forgive me?"

Heather closed her eyes, not believing what she was hearing. He wasn't going to turn her out. He wanted *her* to forgive *him*. "I'm the one who needs *your* forgiveness."

"Then shall we agree to forgive one another?" His voice took on a husky tone.

"Aye," she whispered. "I. . .um. . .asked God to save me today and prayed with your mother and Caroline for you to find Jamie."

He ran his hand down the side of her head. "I can't tell you how happy that makes me. My relationship with God is the only thing I place above family."

She longed to be a part of that family but was afraid to hope. Too many things in her life hadn't gone as planned. "You're a good man, Lucas."

"Would you run screaming to the house if I were to kiss you?"

Heather giggled at the silly picture that popped into her mind. "Nay, I would not."

He drew his hand to her face. Her breath quickened.

"I don't know how I survived all these years without Jamie and you in my life. Do you understand, Heather? I fear I am falling in love with you."

Tears stung her eyes for the hundredth time that day. "I feared you'd release me."

"Never." He cleared his throat. "I mean, only if you wish to be released."

She shook her head. He lowered his face, and his lips met hers. She clutched his arms tightly; then he drew her to him, deepening the kiss. It was everything she'd dreamed of and more, but it was over far too soon.

He pressed his forehead against hers. "Is our relationship advancing too quickly for you? I'll be thirty in a few weeks, and I'm ready to move on with my life. Deborah will always hold a place in my heart, but that's in the past. I want you to be my future."

Heather leaned her head against his chest and wrapped her arms around his waist. He smelled manly—of the outdoors. "I care for you, too, Lucas. I've never been close to a man before."

He leaned back as if to look in her face. The lights from the house faintly illuminated his surprised expression. Then he grinned. "You mean I'm the only man you've ever kissed?"

"You don't have to say it as if you're so proud. I had Jamie to care for and never found a man that interested me."

His grin widened. "Until now."

"Aye."

He cupped his hands around her face. "Good. I like that." He kissed her again, their lips and their breath melding together. After he placed another quick peck on her lips, he stepped back. "I suppose we should go in. Mother will call out the militia if we don't return soon."

"I imagine she would." Heather took his arm.

Lucas bent and retrieved the lantern then escorted her to the house. Excitement pulsed through her.

Jamie was safe.

God had redeemed her, and she was falling in love.

This miserable day had turned out surprisingly well.

Chapter 13

After depositing Jamie into Samuel's care, Heather hurried back to the house. While he was occupied with his riding lesson, she was determined to share her idea with Lucas. She'd hoped to have a surprise party, but with Lucas's birthday just two weeks away, she'd need his help and his mother's to pull off such a large event.

Hurrying up the steep stairs to the back door, she considered how much had changed since she'd first come to Charleston. Jamie and his father were getting along as if Lucas had raised him from birth. Such a feat could only be the hand of God.

Her heart warmed at thoughts of her heavenly Father and how He'd come into her heart so recently. Her whole outlook on life had changed. She now had hope, where before she had only an abysmal future. Her relationship with Lucas had continued to grow, and she might soon find herself married. A smile tugged at her lips at the thought of being Lucas Reed's wife. And, too, she'd never have to leave Jamie. He'd be her son, just as she'd dreamed. Afraid to allow her hopes to soar too high, she pulled them back. From now on, she would leave her future to God.

She searched the downstairs rooms then headed upstairs when she didn't find Lucas. He was probably in his office, as he was most early afternoons. Her footsteps echoed through the open upstairs parlor where guests were generally entertained. She could hold the party here, but Amelia thought it best to have it at the Charleston home so the majority of the guests would have less of a distance to travel.

Lucas wasn't in his office, but rather leaning against a pillar on the veranda reading a book. She smiled at the picture he made. Tall, handsome, engaged in a mental activity instead of the physical ones in which he so often participated— the ones that had shaped his well-formed muscles and broad shoulders. She wondered at how she had ever despised this man. But she hadn't truly known him then.

The warm breeze ruffled her skirts, drawing Lucas's gaze from his book. The smile he sent her stirred her senses and made her want to rush into his arms. Instead, she forced her feet to take small, feminine steps. Lucas straightened and tucked the book under his arm.

"To what do I owe the pleasure of this unexpected meeting?"

Heather giggled. "You just saw me at luncheon, less than an hour ago."

He placed a hand over his heart. "But it seems as if years have passed."

"You goose."

He faked a wince. "Oh, the lady maligns me when, in fact, my heart doth take wing whene'er I see her. If that makes me a goose, then yes, I am one." He bowed and pretended to tip a hat, which he wasn't wearing. "Goose Reed at your service, miss."

Laughing, Heather shook her head and stared out at the beautiful river scene. Spanish moss hung from the trees, dancing in the breeze like fine lace on a lady's gown. Moss covered the top of the water, making it a bright green. Though just midspring, countless flowers bloomed in the cultured garden.

Lucas moved beside her, his shoulder touching hers. "It's a lovely sight, is it not?"

"Aye." She nodded.

He turned to face her and lifted his hand to her cheek. His eyes glowed with love—for her. She still had a hard time grasping that thought, with her coming from a Loyalist family and his being American patriots.

"All of this pales in comparison to you."

Her breath caught in her throat.

He smiled, making her stomach feel as if butterflies were doing a winged battle in it. "I thought my chance for love had passed me by, but then you and Jamie came into my life. How did I ever live without you?"

Heather hated the doubt that crept in and spoiled the moment, but she still couldn't help wondering if his love for her was tied to Jamie. He'd have never met her if not for the boy, yet she wanted him to love her for who she was, not because she brought his son to him. Until she knew for sure, she couldn't allow him to kiss her again. She wouldn't share her affections with any man but the one meant to be her husband. She forced herself to face the garden again. "I can see why you prefer to stay here instead of in Charleston."

He scowled. "You don't like our Charleston home?"

"What?" Her gaze darted to his. Had she offended him? "Aye, I do, but I so love the serenity here, and you don't see your closest neighbors when you're on your porch."

He chuckled. "There is that, though I do miss the ocean when I'm here."

"Your mother said you used to sail frequently but that you no longer do. Can I ask why not?"

His jaw tightened, and all merriment fled. He remained silent so long that she thought he might not answer. "It's not something I often talk about, but you'll find out sooner or later if you remain here for long. I'd just as soon you heard the truth from me."

Heather turned to face him, concerned with the serious tone in his voice. Perhaps she shouldn't have asked, but she longed to know everything about the man she was quickly growing to love.

He pursed his lips and drew in a deep breath. "I do fear, though, that the fondness you've developed for me will flee when you learn the truth."

"I sincerely doubt that. A relationship that's worth its salt must be built on truth and not secrets."

"You're right." He gestured to a chair behind her. "Would you care to sit?"

Heather shook her head. "I'm fine. Thank you."

"I suppose I should start telling you about Marcus."

"Who is Marcus?"

⁂

Lucas loathed mentioning his brother's name. He couldn't tell Heather the whole truth—that Marcus was really Jamie's father—but she deserved to know most of the story. He faced her again, seeing the curiosity gleaming in her lovely eyes. "Marcus is my brother. My twin brother."

Her mouth formed an O, but she remained silent.

"He was born just a few minutes after me, but you know the traditions of England and of the father passing down his holdings to his eldest son. We may have lived in America, and my father's family in Barbados, but Father was still English, through and through.

"As a boy, Marcus was happy and content with our mother's love and attention, but as we grew older, he became aware of how our father favored me." Lucas clenched his jaw. He'd have gladly shared the family wealth with his brother, but his father wouldn't hear of it. "When Marcus realized that he could never compete for our father's love or his blessing, he began rebelling. He started drinking at a young age and causing all sorts of trouble. Mother tried to keep him reined in, but her love wasn't enough anymore."

Heather laid her hand on his arm. "I'm sorry, Lucas. I understand. My father didn't have a son, and if he had retained his wealth, it would have gone to my cousin rather than to me."

He nodded, glad she understood the situation at least partially. He took her hand and continued. "Marcus and I had a falling out, and then he left. I haven't seen him in nearly a decade." Close to eight years, he wanted to tell her, but then she might piece things together.

"It must be difficult being separated from your only sibling. I have none, so I can't imagine what that feels like."

"It does bother me, but Marcus caused so much trouble I actually felt relieved that he was gone." But fiercely angered that he took Deborah with him.

"Thank you for telling me. Your mother mentioned having two sons, but I never asked her about that."

He appreciated that his mother left the decision up to him as to how much to tell Heather about Marcus. As much as he'd like to end the conversation about his past, he had to tell Heather about his time in the navy, and he dreaded doing so for fear she'd no longer want to have anything to do with him.

"Nothing you've said so far could change how I feel for you. Did you think my affections were so shallow?"

Lucas gritted his teeth, wishing he didn't have to continue. "You've not heard all. During the Revolution, I served the colonies as a privateer. I would sometimes raid British ships and steal their cargo."

Heather's eyes went wide, and her struggle was evident.

Please, heavenly Father, don't let me lose her over this.

"A British seventy-four-gun man-of-war could hurl tons of hot iron with a few of her broadsides, but she wasn't much use when she ran aground. I captained a sleek Chesapeake Bay schooner, armed with a handful of six-pounder cannons. We'd run the blockade, easily outsailing Britain's larger ships, and slip away to the West Indies to trade tobacco for gunpowder and cash or credit to support the Revolution."

Heather's hands gripped the porch railing, but she didn't comment.

"We were fighting for our freedom."

"Was it so terrible being a British colony?"

"We were heavily taxed but had no say in how things were run here. We were under the authority of a ruler who lived across the ocean, one who cared little about what happened here, save to extract burdensome taxes from us." He turned her to face him. "We've set up our own government and laws that will benefit the people of this great land. We're free now. Do you know how that feels?"

She shook her head. "I don't suppose I do."

"What I did still haunts me, even though the deeds were done under the guise of war. After I became a Christian, I gave up sailing, though I love it. I build ships, but I haven't sailed on the open seas since the war ended." He heaved a sigh, glad to have told her about his past. It would be up to her whether she found it within herself to forgive him for the deeds perpetrated against her countrymen or if she left at first light.

❧

Heather's heart ached from the heavy burden that Lucas had heaped on her. She ought to be livid that he'd fought against Britain and possibly her own father, but that was all in the past. What bothered her most was how his own heart must hurt over his estrangement from his brother.

"So, do you hate me now?" Lucas asked.

"Nay, even though a part of me says I should."

His tight expression relaxed, and he blew out a breath.

"But there's something I don't understand. You told me that God loves us and forgives past sins once we've confessed them, and I believe that now, so why do you feel you have to give penance by giving up sailing?"

He shrugged. "I just do. It's difficult for someone else to understand."

She shook her head and ran her hand down his arm. "I think you're wrong,

Lucas. If you're forgiven, God wouldn't expect you to endure penance. The blood of Christ has set us free."

His brows dipped down. "You don't understand. It's not just the war; it's Marcus, too. I should have done more to keep him here." He waved his hand in the air. "I didn't ask for all of this. I'd have gladly shared it with him. I just had to wait until after my father died, because he was so set against it. Once the estate and business became mine, I was free to do with them as I wished. But Marcus couldn't wait. He wanted things when he wanted them. Even—"

She gazed up at him. "Even what?"

He turned his back to her. "Nothing. I was afraid explaining all this would drive you away. I don't expect you to understand." He walked inside then spun back around. "And please forget this nonsense about having a party for me. It isn't necessary."

She opened her mouth to call to him as he strode away, but she remained quiet instead. If anything, she was the one who should be upset. Imagine kind-hearted, generous Lucas a privateer. A warrior fighting for his freedom against an overwhelmingly strong opponent. Nobody expected the colonists to win the war, but they had by their grit and determination.

Had God been on *their* side all along?

Chapter 14

Heather stared at her list of things to do before the night of Lucas's birthday party and heaved a sigh. How would she accomplish it all? Footsteps drew her away from her task. Amelia glided into the room, her face glowing from her afternoon rest. "How are things progressing, my dear?"

"I fear I may have overestimated my abilities."

"Pshaw." Amelia waved her hand in the air. "It's a simple thing to organize a gathering. Make a list of food, and I'll see to it that Miss Haversham, our housekeeper in Charleston, gets it. She will arrange everything."

"It doesn't seem fair to ask her to take on such a big event."

"Nonsense. It's part of her duties. The Reeds have entertained far too little. Lucas has no desire to plan such events, and I confess that my heart hasn't been in it either."

"Am I wrong to want to do this?" Heather leaned her cheek against her hand.

Amelia rested her palm on Heather's arm. "No dear. It's a fine thing you want to do and will be good for Lucas. Besides, it will be the perfect time to make an announcement about Jamie."

Heather smiled. "I want to thank you and Lucas for so willingly accepting Jamie into your family. I know it can't have been easy for either of you."

Amelia glanced around the parlor. "Where is my grandson?"

"Lucas took him riding. They're on a quest to find an alligator."

Amelia chuckled. "Boys will be boys." She sobered and gazed into Heather's eyes. "I should be thanking *you* for bringing Jamie to us. That boy has given me new life. I'd given up hope on Lucas marrying and becoming a father. Jamie is a wonderful boy."

"I think of all the wasted time I put in worrying about bringing him to you. I wish I could have done it sooner. I wish Deborah would have had the nerve to face Lucas once she learned she was with child."

Amelia pursed her lips and looked away. "Lucas loved her so much. He would have welcomed her return. But life for her would have been difficult with people knowing she'd borne a child out of wedlock. I can understand why she chose to stay away."

"What of her parents? I don't believe she ever told them of Jamie."

"I don't know. All I heard was that they returned to England after spending much of their wealth and several years searching for her."

"'Tis sad they couldn't have enjoyed Jamie while he was so young."

Amelia tapped the table. "Perhaps I should write to them. They should know they have a grandson."

Heather straightened, doubt niggling at her. "But what if they decide to seek custody?"

"Hmm...I can see where that could be an issue. Perhaps Lucas should have some kind of legal document proving Jamie is his son. I do believe the law holds that a child first belongs to his father."

"Aye. 'Tis a wise idea. I can testify that Deborah admitted Lucas is Jamie's father. And Lucas has that letter from her. That could be entered in as evidence."

"I'm not sure that would be helpful." Amelia rose suddenly and tugged on a long narrow tapestry that rang a bell in the kitchen. "Some tea would taste good right about now."

"Aye, it would." She glanced down at her list of party guests. "Will the Charleston house be too crowded if we invite twenty people?"

"No, I don't think so. Besides the dining room and the great room, we can use the piazza. We should be able to easily handle that number."

"Here's the list of names you gave me. Is there anyone we should add before we issue the invitations?"

Amelia quickly read down the page. The maid walked up to the table and waited. "I suppose there are always others to invite, but I don't want Lucas to feel overwhelmed. He's not one for crowds." She looked up. "Oh Talia, would you please bring tea and biscuits for Miss Hawthorne and me?"

"Aye ma'am." The maid scurried from the room, her feet tapping across the wooden floor.

"Lucas asked me to cease plans for the party," Heather said. "Do you think we should?"

Amelia shook her head. "No, it will be good for him. You're good for him."

Heather's cheeks warmed. She flashed an embarrassed smile and looked away. "I'm not so sure of that."

Lucas's mother leaned forward, resting her arms on the table. "I am. For so long, Lucas has been caught up in his work. He not only oversees the ship-building enterprise, but it's nothing for him to actually get out there and work on a ship himself. Many of our stature looked down on him for doing such menial labor."

"But you don't?" Heather could easily see Lucas hanging from a rope, sanding wood or hammering the side of a vessel.

"No, I think it's admirable that he wants to experience every facet of the business. I believe it helps him to better understand the complete workings."

"You're an unusual woman, Amelia."

She cocked her head and smiled. "Thank you, dear. We have too many close-minded people in Charleston. God would have us look at things from different vantage points. Take slavery, for instance. It's an abysmal, degrading venture." She shook her head and pressed her lips together. "I've heard of planters who have broken up slave families. Separated husbands from wives, children from parents. I fear God will punish us one day for mistreating His people so."

" 'Tis refreshing to hear someone from the South speak in such a manner. How do your neighbors tolerate your attitude?"

Amelia rose and walked to the open double doors and stared out at the garden. "We have enemies, certainly, but there are others who believe as we do yet simply can't afford to free their slaves and in turn pay them a wage."

Heather stood and crossed the room to stand beside Amelia. "Well, I for one admire you for not keeping slaves." She shivered as a thought raced across her mind. If she left and returned to Canada, she would know just what it was like to be separated from the child she loved.

"I know of a nice string quartet we could hire to play for the party. Would you like that?"

Heather nodded. "Aye, but I do feel odd that the party was my suggestion and you're having to pay for it all."

Amelia wrapped an arm around Heather. "Lucas is my son. I should have been the one to think of the party, and I thank you for your suggestion. It's a grand idea. If only..."

"Are you thinking of Marcus?"

Amelia's eyes widened. "You know of him?"

"Lucas told me yesterday. I can't imagine how much it must hurt you to never see him."

She shrugged and faced the garden. "Let's walk while we're waiting for the tea."

Amelia took Heather's arm and led her outside and downstairs. The fragrant scent of roses and a myriad of other colorful flowers filled her senses. Yellow butterflies flitted from flower to flower, sampling the sweet nectar. Wisteria clung to a wooden archway, its flowers looking like fresh grapes ripe for the picking. What must it be like to enjoy such beauty almost year-round? The South was growing on her, although she could well do without the heat.

"Marcus was always a morose child who grew into a cranky, discontented young man. Lucas, on the other hand, was a pleasant boy, obedient and eager to please. I tried to give Marcus what he needed. From the time they were born, Cedric lavished praise on Lucas and all but ignored his other son. Dreadful shame, it was. Marcus's jealousy grew until it couldn't be contained."

Heather patted Amelia's arm. "How difficult that must have been for all of you."

"If only Cedric had loved Marcus as he did Lucas, I believe things would have turned out all right. I think Lucas has been hurt the most by all of this. His heart is tender, even now, and it crushed him when Marcus left and—"

Heather had the distinct feeling that Amelia had just censured what she was about to say, but she shrugged off the thought. Of course there were things Amelia couldn't tell her.

"I wish he'd return to us, but sad to say, I don't believe I shall ever see him again." She leaned in close. "There's talk that he's a pirate. It grieves me so to think such a thing of my own son."

Heather shook her head, amazed that twin brothers could turn out so different. If Marcus was truly as wicked as Lucas was good, she hoped their paths never crossed.

❧

Heather opened the door of Jamie's bedchamber and peered down the hallway at the growing crowd in the second-floor great room. Soft music drifted toward her, along with the chatter of voices. She should go back, but she felt so out of place among Lucas's friends and associates.

"When do I get to go to the party?"

Heather closed the door and smiled at Jamie. "Soon. When your father is ready." She stooped down, her blue taffeta silk skirts rustling, and smoothed Jamie's collar. He looked striking with his dark hair and vivid blue eyes in his new, white cotton suit, though the ruffled collar and cuffs were a bit too fancy for a lad, in her opinion. "You look mighty handsome."

"Will I get to eat?"

She blew out a breath. "You can't fool me. I know that you've already eaten."

He leaned against her. "Please, can't I have at least one sweet?"

"We shall see. It's close to your bedtime." She smoothed down his hair where it stood on end. "Do you understand the importance of tonight?"

He nodded.

"Tonight your father is announcing to his close friends that he has a son."

"Why don't they already know that?"

"They may." And she was sure they did and were filled with questions about where said lad had come from. "You are to smile but not talk. Do you understand?"

Jamie nodded again. "These shoes hurt my feet."

"Well, you shan't be wearing them all that long. Try to act like a gentleman. And if anyone asks about your mother, please don't say anything. Especially don't tell them her name."

"Why not?" Innocent blue eyes stared up at her.

How did she explain that Lucas wanted to protect Deborah? To not sully her family name? "Because your father wishes it to remain a secret."

Jamie's brow wrinkled, and he stared up at the ceiling as if thinking deeply.

"What did my mother look like?"

"Oh dear lad." She pulled him against her skirts, just as a knock sounded at the door. He was only two when his mother died. How could he remember what Deborah looked like when her image was fading even from Heather's mind? "We should talk more about her, but not tonight." She pulled open the door and revealed the footman.

"Mr. Reed is ready for you and the boy, miss."

"Thank you. We shall be there directly." She shut the door and turned back to Jamie. "Are you ready?"

He nodded and hurried to her side, taking her hand.

"Mind your manners. This is a very important evening for your father and your grandmother. You don't want to embarrass them."

"Aye mum."

Heather's heart pounded as she made her way down the hall. What would Lucas's guests think of his son? Would they reject him? Cast crude comments his way? Eye him with disdain? *Please, Lord, no.*

Chapter 15

Lucas's gaze shifted toward Heather the moment she entered the room. The footman rang a bell for attention, and when the room quieted, he announced, "Miss Heather Hawthorne and Master Jamie."

Whispers resounded in speculation as Lucas strode forward to meet his son and the woman who'd stolen his heart. His mother joined them, coming from the other side of the room. Heather looked enchanting in her pale blue gown and with her hair curled, and Jamie looked like a miniature of Lucas. No one would doubt their relationship, though he was sure they'd question where the boy had been the past five years.

He reached down and lifted Jamie into his arms. It wouldn't be too many more years and the boy would be too old to carry on occasion. If only Heather had brought him to Charleston sooner. But tonight was not for regrets. He patted his son's back and turned to the crowd.

"Honored guests, I thank you for coming to celebrate my birthday this night. I, more than anyone, have cause to celebrate, and not because I've reached the ripe old age of thirty."

Chuckles filled the room.

"Aye, you're nigh on ancient." Richard Madison grinned. "Before long, you'll be losing your teeth and finding gray hairs."

Lucas smiled at his friend's jesting. "Better gray hair than none."

The room filled with laughter.

Lucas cleared his throat. "I suppose you're wondering about this fine boy, here." He glanced at Heather, and her smile gave him the courage to continue. Some of the people in this room may choose to no longer associate with him once they knew about Jamie. "A few weeks ago, Miss Hawthorne appeared on my doorstep with young Jamie in tow. I didn't want to listen when she claimed he was my son—"

A unified gasp circled the room.

Lucas held up his hand. "But a letter she had in her possession confirmed that Jamie is a Reed. I've had formal papers drawn up to make everything official, and I now present to you, Master James Reed."

The Madisons led the applause and cheers. Jamie smiled and studied the crowd, but Lucas's stomach churned. He'd been careful not to lie to his friends about Jamie, but how would he respond when people asked about his son's mother?

92

"Can I have a sweet now?" Jamie asked.

Lucas smiled and glanced at Heather. She lifted one shoulder as if to say it was his decision.

"We've already finished dining," his mother said, "but perhaps the maid could take you to the kitchen for a treat. I imagine there's still some pumpkin pudding left."

Jamie licked his lips and turned to Heather. "May I go now?"

"Do you not wish for him to stay a few moments?" Heather asked.

Lucas shook his head. "I wanted to introduce him tonight, but a fine party is no place for a child to linger, even one as well behaved as Jamie."

"Then I'll take him down for his treat and put him to bed afterward."

"You should stay," Lucas's mother insisted. "Talia can tend to Jamie."

Lucas knew his mother was trying to keep Heather here so people would associate them as a couple. Too bad they couldn't have made an announcement of their own tonight. He never thought it possible he'd again desire to marry, but he longed to make Heather his wife.

She took Jamie from him. "'Tis no problem. Jamie will go to sleep easier if I see to him."

"Be sure you return. You promised me a dance tonight."

Heather's cheeks turned crimson. Her wide eyes gleamed, and she tipped her head in the slightest of nods. He watched her scurry away with his son, his heart swelling with pride for both of them.

A hand clamped hard on his shoulder, drawing his attention back to his guests.

"I say, you sure surprised us, old man." Ferrill Whitmore's keen gaze bore into him. "How is it you managed to father a child and didn't know about it until now?"

"Simple. The boy's mother chose to keep him a secret."

"Then why send him to you after all these years?" Whitmore twisted the end of his mustache as other guests crowded around, also eager to know more about Jamie, if their curious expressions were any indication.

"She died and left instructions for Miss Hawthorne to bring Jamie to me."

"Sorry for your loss. I mean, I suppose it's that."

"A good woman died, Ferrill. It is a loss."

"Humph! She couldn't have been too good or she wouldn't have—"

Lucas closed the few feet between him and Mr. Whitmore. "Say no more, sir. You're talking about the mother of my son. I'll admit the situation is less than ideal, but I'll not have you slandering Jamie's mother."

Ferrill's left eye twitched, and his warm breath touched Lucas's face. Finally, the man nodded.

Lucas lifted his chin and faced his guests. "What happened in the past matters not. Jamie is my son. He is an innocent child, and I hope that you will all treat him with the courtesy that befits my station in this community."

Heads nodded, and he caught his mother's proud gaze. His heart warmed at her affirmation. Releasing a pent-up breath, he realized things had gone better than he'd expected. Yes, his life was close to perfect now that Jamie and Heather had entered it. Nothing could change that.

The music started again, and one by one, couples began dancing. Lucas waited for more questions, but none came. He thought about Heather returning and dancing with him.

"You've a right to be smiling, son. That went better than I expected." His mother hugged his arm.

"I'll admit it's a relief that people know about Jamie."

"Well, well, you have a party and don't even invite your own brother."

His mother gasped and spun around. "Marcus!"

Heart racing, Lucas glanced up at the sound of his brother's voice. Had Marcus heard the announcement? Had he overheard the talk about Jamie's mother?

Above all things, Marcus could never know that he'd fathered a son.

His mother hurried to her estranged son. "Welcome home, Marcus."

His twin stared down at their mother, and his hard expression softened for a moment. "Mother, 'tis good to see you're still alive and well."

Tears ran down her cheeks. "My heart has ached for you. Have you returned to us for good?"

Marcus shook his head, sending his long, untamed hair flying over his shoulders. "Nay. I know not why I've returned, but I can see life has continued without me."

Lucas glanced around the room. His friends hovered along the walls, whispering and staring. Women dressed in their colorful gowns huddled near their husbands; some looked worried, others curious. Someone uttered the word *pirate*.

Catching Richard's concerned gaze, he nudged his head toward the door, and his friend nodded. Lucas wanted these people out of here in case his brother came with the intent of causing trouble.

"Mother, if you'll please see to our guests, I'll talk with Marcus."

"But so much time has passed since I last saw him." She cast a longing gaze at her younger son. "Please don't leave. I so want to sit and talk with you. Where have you been all these years?"

Marcus winced. Doffing his tricorn, he bowed, as if to cover up his discomfort. Lucas watched him, his gaze sharp and senses on alert. So the rogue still had a soft spot for their mother. Perhaps all was not lost if the man wasn't completely hardened. But with the many crimes his brother had purportedly committed against ships in the Caribbean, it was foolish to think he could ever live a normal life.

" 'Twas good to see you again, Mother. It warms my heart to know you are well. But I shan't tarry. 'Tis time I was taking my leave."

"But you only just arrived." She clutched her hands to her bosom, a mother aching for a lost child. Seeing Marcus again would only cause her more pain.

"Mother, see to our guests, *please*," Lucas said. She cast another emotion-filled glance at Marcus then turned and glided from the room, her guests following.

Lucas faced his brother. "So, why have you come now?"

Marcus's lips tilted in a cocky smirk, but his hand rested on the hilt of his sword. "I've come to wish you happy birthday, brother."

Lucas sincerely doubted that was the truth, but he chose to be cordial even though all his senses warned him to be on guard. "How have you been?"

Surprise entered Marcus's hard, blue eyes before he schooled his expression. "The life of a pirate is always daring. Looting, plundering, and the like. I've amassed quite a fortune, brother. Perhaps I'm ready to settle down and start a family like you have."

Lucas winced. So he knew about Heather and Jamie.

Marcus's face twisted into a vile grin. "Quite a lovely wench you've wedded and bedded."

"We're not talking about her." He had to steer the conversation in another direction before his brother deciphered the truth. "It's never too late to change, Marcus. Give your heart to God and seek His forgiveness."

His brother snorted, strode across the room, and swigged down a glass of punch. He grimaced and wiped his sleeve across his arm. "What, no ale?"

"I no longer drink spirits."

"You've gone soft, brother. That's what a woman will do to you."

Lucas stepped through the door Marcus opened. "Tell me what happened to Deborah. What did you do to *her*? Is she still alive?" He knew the truth, but it was good that his brother didn't know that.

"I see how much you loved her. How old is your son? Five? Six? Did you wait a whole month before finding another skirt to warm your bed?"

Lucas strode forward, his fist clenching and unclenching. "I searched for Deborah nigh on two years. I loved her with all my heart, but you stole her from me."

Marcus heaved a laugh. "Brother, brother, the wench loved me, not you."

Lucas lifted his chin. "I'm the one she was going to marry."

All manner of emotions crossed his brother's tanned face, but his eyes smoldered like blue fire. "Aye, well, 'tis all in the past now, is it not?"

In Lucas's mind, Deborah's abduction had happened only days ago. "What did you do with her?"

His brother shrugged and took on a bored look. "I grew tired of her sniffling and begging to return to you. I let her off ship along the coast of Canada, where she said she had relatives."

"Why did you not bring her back here?"

"She did not wish to return."

And Lucas knew why. Even though she'd been the victim of a kidnapping, people would still look down on her for spending years aboard a pirate ship and birthing the captain's illegitimate son.

"Do you have any idea how much her parents suffered? She was their only child."

Marcus lifted his hand and glanced at his dirty fingernails. "My goal was to hurt you, not them."

"You succeeded."

Marcus studied him and then grinned. "Good."

Lucas had to try to find a way to reach his brother. He might not get another chance. "Why do you hate me so? It's not my fault I was born first."

"Nay, but you *were* and thus received all our father had to give. His wealth, his admiration, even his love—at least what love he was capable of giving."

Lucas walked over to his brother. "And I'd have shared it all with you."

Marcus snorted a laugh. "I can't imagine why. I would not have assigned even the smallest parcel to you, had it been within my power."

"I'm not you, brother. Family means more to me than wealth."

"Ha! Easy for a man to say who has more wealth than he knows what to do with. Try livin' in poverty on the streets and see if you feel the same."

"I'm sorry, Marcus. I never wanted this."

His brother's gaze hardened. "And therein lies the rub. You never wanted our father's wealth, but you received it, while I ached for it but got nothing."

"I'm sorry."

"Keep your apologies. I don't want them. 'Twas a mistake to return here." Marcus turned on his heel and strode toward the stairs, boots clicking on the tile and loose shirt fluttering, looking every bit the heinous pirate he was. Lucas surmised he should be thankful that he'd survived the confrontation unscathed. He shook his head. "Lord, turn my brother's heart. Help him to find You and gain freedom from his sin and misery."

He wanted nothing more than to hold Heather and Jamie close. But he still had guests, and protocol dictated that he see to them first. Quitting the room, he heard the buzz of conversation and hurried downstairs. It looked as if most of the guests had fled for the safety of their homes. He cringed, knowing the Reeds would be the talk of the town as one guest after another gossiped about how his pirate brother had disrupted his party. He jogged down the last of the stairs, glad he was in time to bid farewell to the Madisons.

Richard followed his progress down with a worried gaze. "So, you're still alive."

Lucas grinned. "For the time being."

"What did he want—if I might be so bold as to ask?"

Lucas shrugged and put an arm around his mother, drawing her close. He noticed the tears gleaming in her eyes, but she'd held them back for the sake of her guests. She leaned her head against his chest and sniffled.

"Would you like me to have your housekeeper fix you some tea?" Caroline offered.

His mother shook her head. "Thank you, but I'm feeling quite tired and plan to retire soon."

Lucas gently squeezed his mother's shoulders. It would have been better for her if Marcus had never come. He'd only upset their mother, and now she'd most likely spiral off in an emotional ride of "if only she'd done more" or "if only she'd stood up to their father for the way he ignored Marcus." Lucas sighed, hating that she'd question herself. She'd been a kind, loving mother to both of them and didn't deserve Marcus's scorn.

Richard's brows drew together, and the look he gave Lucas set him on edge. "This is probably ridiculous, but I just had a thought. You don't suppose your brother saw you and Heather together around town or heard that you were growing fond of her? What if—"

Richard's eyes grew wide, and Lucas deciphered his thoughts.

Heather.

A pain like the blade of a hard-thrust sword ramming into his heart gripped Lucas. What if Marcus had learned that he had fallen in love again? What if his brother had come to steal Heather away as he had Deborah?

"No! Not again." He quickly set his mother aside and took the stairs three at a time. He couldn't lose Heather before he'd even told her of the depth of his love.

☙

"I like that pun'kin pudding. Could I have some more tomorrow?" Jamie licked his lips as Heather tugged off his shoes.

"We shall see. Perhaps if there is some remaining. It was tasty with the cinnamon sprinkled on top."

"I liked how it squished between my teeth."

Heather smiled, took Jamie's nightshirt from the wardrobe, and shook it open. A movement near the balcony caught her attention, and she saw Lucas leaning against the doorway, staring at her. He must have come across the piazza to bid Jamie goodnight. Her heart taking wing, she started toward him, but the coldness in his gaze stopped her. Why would he have such animosity for her all of a sudden? Had she done something wrong downstairs?

"Who's that?" Jamie asked as he leaned against her.

"Why, 'tis your father, silly lad."

"Uh-unh. That's not Papa."

Heather looked at the man again, and he pushed away from the door and sauntered out of the shadows toward her. In the light of the room, she realized Jamie was right. This man had a ruffian's look. His hair was longer and his beard unshaven. He wore his linen shirt loose and stained. His short pants stopped just below the knee, as sailors often wore. Where Lucas's eyes burned with intelligence and excitement, this man's smoldered like dark coals. Aye, they were twins, identical in many ways, but so different. Where Lucas emanated kindness and goodness, this man stank of evil. How could two brothers be so different?

"You've a bright son there." The man pulled his wide-brimmed hat off his head and bowed. "Allow me to introduce meself. I'm Marcus Reed, better known as the Black Mark."

Heather's heart jolted. Here she was alone with a vile pirate and no weapon with which to protect Jamie. She tucked him behind her. "What do you want? You've no business here."

Standing with his hands loosely on his hips, he grinned. "Ah, but you're wrong there. 'Tis me birthday, and I've come for the celebration."

"The party is not in this room, sir. I'm just putting the lad to bed."

"Aye, but what interests me *is* up here. So my brother has a son." The man cocked his head as he stared past her. "The boy has the look of a Reed, does he not?"

Heather's mind raced. What should she do? Should she scream for help? Was the man merely curious and wanting to see his nephew? His sinister tone set her nerves on edge.

"Come hither, boy. Let your uncle have a good look at you."

Jamie huddled behind her, as if he, too, sensed something wasn't right.

"Please, sir, can it not wait until tomorrow? Jamie has stayed up far past his bedtime in order to be presented at the party."

The man shook his head and took a step toward her. "I'll not be here on the morrow. I've found what I came for."

Heather lifted her chin. "And what is that?"

The rogue grinned and ran his gaze down her body, making her feel dirty. Making her want to run and find Lucas.

"Your son doesn't resemble you in the least. How long have you been married to that blackguard brother of mine?"

The insolent cad. "Mr. Reed and I aren't married. I'm Jamie's governess."

The man muttered something she couldn't make out and ran his hand over the dark stubble on his chin. "If only I'd had a comely wench like you for a governess, I might not have turned out to be a cutthroat pirate."

Heather placed her hand over her throat and swallowed hard. "You're a pirate by choice."

The man leaped forward, grabbing the front of her dress. "You know nothing about me, missy. Because I had the misfortune to be born minutes after my brother"—he spat on the floor—"Lucas inherited all of our father's wealth while I got nothing."

Heather knew a man like this would take advantage of a weak woman, so her best hope was to face him head-on and not let him know her legs were trembling so hard she felt certain they'd give out any moment. "I'm sure Lucas would be happy to share with you if you were to cease your pirating and return home. Your mother misses you."

He snorted a scoffing laugh.

"Aunt Heather? I'm scared." Jamie clutched the back of her skirt.

"Ach, boy." The pirate glared at him. "Reed men aren't frightened of anything. Quit hiding behind those petticoats and prove you have a backbone."

Heather shoved the pirate, and he took a step back, grabbing her arm with one hand. "Jamie, quick, run to your father."

"Stand fast, boy!" A chink of steel on steel filled the room as Marcus Reed drew his sword.

"Nay! Jamie, run!"

Heather saw the man's fist only a second before it smashed into her head. She plunged into a realm of pain and darkness.

Chapter 16

Lucas charged into Heather's bedchamber, his heart nearly breaking in two when he found it empty. Pushing through the door into Jamie's connecting room, his frantic gaze took in the empty chamber. Lucas hurried to the piazza, searching in all directions. His hands raked through his hair, pulling it loose from its tie. He staggered back into the room and collapsed onto the bed.

"No! Please, God. No."

He couldn't lose Heather.

He couldn't lose his son.

"God, help me."

A moan sounded behind the open door to the piazza, and he bolted up, wishing he had a sword. His eyes landed on a pair of shapely ankles and Heather's gown. Relief washed over him like the warm sun after a turbulent storm. He knelt down beside her.

"Are you hurt, my love?"

Heather moaned and reached for her head. A stream of blood flowed from a swollen cut on her forehead and ran down her cheek. Her eyes suddenly widened, and she lurched to her feet and staggered through the room. She grabbed his arm, her distressed gaze searched his. "Jamie. Please tell me he didn't take Jamie."

A deep chasm opened up in Lucas's chest where his heart had been. He didn't have to reach the house to know that Jamie wasn't there. Nothing could hurt him more than losing his son—and Marcus knew that.

"Oh Jamie." Heather's sobs filled the room. Lucas drew her against his chest and closed his eyes.

"You've got to go after him."

He thought of his oath to God never to sail again. How could he break such a devout promise to his heavenly Father?

Yet he could not allow his brother to get away with Jamie. The poor boy must be frightened out of his wits. Like a pendulum, Lucas's thoughts swung from one point to another and back. He had to go after Jamie. He couldn't break his word. He had to save his son.

Heather released him and stepped back, staring at him with an incredulous gaze. "Lucas, you've got to go—before they reach open seas. Each moment you waste in indecision allows them to get farther away. You've got to rescue Jamie."

"I can't. Don't you understand? I did things almost as vile as my brother, all in the name of my country. I promised God I'd never sail again."

Heather stared at him as if he'd turned green and lost all of his hair. "God would never hold you to such an oath. 'Tis all your own doing." She grabbed his arms and shook him, her brown eyes wide. "You've got to save your son."

A war raged within him. "If I fail to keep my promise to God, what kind of man would I be?"

Richard burst into the room holding Lucas's sword in the air like an avenging angel. When he saw Heather, his relief was evident.

She rushed to his side. "Please, sir, take me to the docks. We've got to rescue Jamie."

Richard's confused gaze dashed to Lucas and back. "Marcus has the boy?"

"Aye, and Lucas refuses to go after him because of his *precious* oath." She spat the words as if spewing a foul substance from her mouth.

"What does she mean?" Richard asked.

Lucas gazed up at the ceiling where the light from the wall sconces danced like sails in the wind. He rubbed the back of his neck, feeling ripped apart by his indecision. He'd changed from the carousing youth he'd been and given his heart to God, but now when he needed Him most, he felt betrayed. "God, how could You have let this happen again?"

" 'Twas not the hand of God that did this vile deed, but the evil of man," Richard said. "Don't be doubting your faith, Lucas, for you'll need it more than ever if you hope to track down your brother."

"But what about my pledge? I gave up sailing as penance because of all that I did before and during the Revolution."

Richard shook his head. "Lucas, you're my best friend, but that's just plain fanatical. God has forgiven you, and you don't need to punish yourself that way. God doesn't ask it of you. But He does expect a father to protect his children, and you've got a son who needs you. You're the only one who can save him. Just think how Marcus will warp his mind if you do nothing."

Lucas listened to his friend's earnest words and saw hope burn away the anger in Heather's eyes. He walked outside to the piazza railing and stared up at the ebony sky. Was it true? Had he needlessly punished himself all these years?

When he couldn't find Deborah, he'd given up on sailing. Perhaps he'd made that oath because he'd so miserably failed. His ship hadn't carried him to his beloved, so had he just walked away from it all and used God as a convenient excuse?

He heaved a heavy sigh. God was love. Forgiveness. He wouldn't take away something Lucas loved as punishment. If Lucas believed that, he was equating God with Marcus. And there was nothing in the least about God that was similar to his brother. He tightened his grip on the railing as he thought of Jamie. How dreadfully frightened the boy must be. He would expect his father to rescue him.

Hope rose in Lucas's heart like a ship on a swell. He pounded his hand against the wooden rail, knowing what he had to do. Straightening his body and his resolve, he spun around and marched into the room, taking his sword from Richard. He clapped his friend's shoulder. "Thank you for setting me straight. You're a good man."

"So, you're going after them?" his friend asked.

"Yes."

Heather sucked in a gasp, rushed forward, and fell against his chest. "Oh, praise be to God. Thank you, Lucas."

Heedless of Richard's presence, he held her tight with one arm, keeping the sword well away from her. He kissed her hard, showing her the depth of his love. When he pulled back, a grin tugged at his lips at her shocked expression. "Pray for me, beloved. Pray that I find them fast and return with our son."

"Aye, pray I will, but you're not going without me."

❧

Heather held tight to the gunwale as Lucas's ship glided across the open seas. The scent of salt tickled her nose, and the brisk wind pulled her hair loose from its bindings. High above her, sails snapped.

Once they'd set sail, Heather's heart sunk like a ship torn asunder at the magnitude of the task before them. How did one find a single vessel on such a vast sea, especially in the dark of night? Why, they could sail right past another ship and not even know it. She shivered as the cool breeze tugged at her clothing, damp from the sea spray.

"You should try to get some sleep." Lucas joined her at the railing.

She shook her head. "I can't. I'm too worried about Jamie. I keep wondering if he's scared. Has he been mistreated? Is he locked away below ship in a dark hole?"

She turned to face Lucas, her heart aching with such a fathomless pain that she didn't know if she could survive it. "What if he hurts Jamie?"

Lucas brushed tendrils of loose hair from her face. "I don't think he will. He'll gain nothing by doing that."

"What did he hope to gain by taking him?"

Lucas stared out at the black sea. "At first, I thought he'd taken you."

" 'Tis my fault he took Jamie." Heather fidgeted with the edge of her cuff.

He took hold of her shoulders. "No. It is not."

Heather nodded, tears making her eyes gleam in the moonlight. "Aye, but it is. I told Jamie to run and get you while I tried to keep your brother away from him. Perhaps if I hadn't done that, he would have taken me instead of Jamie."

"Shh, enough of that."

Lucas pulled her into his arms and pressed her head against his chest. Her chill fled at the warmth of his body.

"My brother is a brigand. A scoundrel. He takes pleasure in hurting me, but I don't think he'd do damage to a child."

"But how will we ever find them?"

"Things are not as bad as they seem. There are only a handful of places a rogue like my brother can make port without the authorities coming for him."

Heather leaned back and gazed up at him. "But what about you? After fighting the British like you did, surely you must also be a wanted man."

He didn't answer for a while. "There's truth in what you say."

"If you are captured on the open seas, you'll be taken back to England. I've put you in danger by insisting you go after Jamie."

He ran his finger across her cheek, sending delicious chills down her spine. "I would have gone after him anyway. I was foolish to hesitate and think I was breaking my vow. I know more than most how big God's arms are and how much He forgives."

Even with God's help, Heather didn't see how it was possible to lose a child and ever get over it. She felt as if she'd die if they didn't find Jamie. Tears stung her eyes, and a sob slipped out as she fell back into Lucas's arm. "He's so little. So alone."

Lucas laid his cheek atop her head. "He's not alone. God is with him."

Her tears overcame her, and she wept against Lucas's chest. What if they never found him?

They stood together, Lucas with his feet braced apart to stand steady on the rising and dipping ship, and she in the shelter of his arms. She recalled how he'd called her *beloved* back at the Charleston house. Was that just a slip of the tongue during an emotional time?

After a while, he loosened his hold on her a fraction. "Heather, there's something I want to tell you."

She leaned back against the side of the ship and gazed up at him. She could barely make out one side of his face where the moon illuminated it, while the other side remained dark. Just like the two brothers. Twins, carried together in the womb, born on the same day, but one was kindhearted and honest, while the other was a blackguard with no heart at all.

Lucas heaved a deep breath and took hold of her hand. "It's hard to believe how much things can change in a few short weeks. A month ago, I didn't know you or Jamie. Then you both sailed into my lonely life and made my world whole again." He cupped his hand around her cheek. "I don't want you to leave. Ever."

Heather's heart flip-flopped, but she was afraid to hope that he cared for her as much as she did him.

"I love you, Heather. Can you find it in your heart to marry a brigand like me and put me out of my misery?"

Her cheeks lifted in a smile, and joy flooded her like a rogue wave in a squall. "Aye. I'd love nothing more."

He pulled her to him and lifted her up at the same time, and his lips collided with hers. His were warm, demanding but gentle, and all her fears and worries fled. After a few moments, he set her down but held her close. "I love you so much. I never expected to find love again."

That thought sobered her, stealing her delight. Who had he loved? Surely not Miss Dupont? He'd told Heather that he had no feelings for the woman. And if he had loved before, why had he never married?

Lucas pressed his hand against her head and held her close. "You should rest. It's a good thing you've agreed to marry me, because your reputation will have flown south after you set sail alone with just my crew and me."

He said the words in jest, but she couldn't help thinking of her cousin. Had Lucas promised her the world then taken her virginity and left her alone to raise their son?

Heather shook her head. Lucas may have been reckless in his youth, but he wasn't like that now. Where were all these doubts coming from? "I am tired. All the excitement of the party and the tragedy afterward has worn me out."

"Then I shall escort you to my cabin so you can retire." He took her arm and tugged gently, but she didn't release the railing.

"Why am I going to *your* cabin and not one of my own?"

Lucas waved his hand in the air. "This is a cargo vessel, not a passenger ship. My cabin is the only one suitable for a lady. There's a lock on the door you're free to use."

The recent joy of the night fled at the slight bite in his voice. Had she offended him?

"Come. You're safe here. There's nothing to fear from me or my crew."

She allowed him to lead her toward his cabin, hating her doubts. Just when she thought her life was about to change, she couldn't rid her mind of all that Deborah had suffered at the hands of the man they'd both fallen in love with.

I'm sorry, cousin, for loving the man who caused you so much pain. Am I making a dreadful mistake? Has he truly changed, or am I living an illusion?

Chapter 17

Hands behind his back, Lucas paced the deck of the *Victory*. A week had passed, and he still hadn't located his brother. *Think! Where could Marcus have gone?*

He knew his brother, and Marcus would want him to give chase. It was all a game to him. Take what Lucas loved, because that was the only way to truly hurt him. First, it had been the woman he'd planned on marrying, and now, Jamie.

Could Marcus have guessed that Jamie was his own son? Did he know that Deborah had borne him a child?

Lucas strode to the bow and stared out over the glistening blue sea as the schooner glided swiftly across the waters. The scents of salt, pitch, and oakum filled his nostrils, and he breathed deeply. Oh, how he'd missed sailing. What a fool he'd been to believe that God would expect him to forsake something he loved so much. Lifting his face, he stared up at the brilliant sky. "Forgive me, Lord, for believing a lie. Perhaps I was merely punishing myself, when You'd already freely given Your Son to die for me. Please, Lord, grant me favor. Show me where Jamie is."

His clothing fluttered in the stiff breeze, and behind him, sailors lifted their voices in a jolly time, but jolly was not a word that described his mood. With all but the topsails unfurled, they traveled at a quick speed. Yet they still hadn't caught up with Marcus. He pounded on the gunwale. "Where are you, brother?"

Thoughts of Jamie assaulted his mind, causing him to rest little at night. He ached to protect the boy. To hold him in his arms again. To laugh at something Jamie said.

In a matter of days, he'd lost his heart to his nephew.

His son.

And also to a pretty, brown-eyed wench who wore her heart on her sleeve. He'd asked her to marry him, yet he saw the doubts in her eyes. What put them there? Had he ever given her reason to question his sincerity? To fear him?

His grip tightened on the gunwale. Maybe he should tell her the whole truth even though Deborah had pleaded with him in her letter not to let anyone know that Jamie wasn't his son. But shouldn't Heather know?

He was surprised that Deborah had never told her cousin the truth about

Jamie's father. Yet she'd done it to protect her son. The child of a pirate would have little chance to live a normal life. A decent life.

And what if Marcus ever learned he'd fathered a son? He would have done exactly what he did: He would have come and taken Jamie.

Lucas had to believe that the boy's kidnapping was a sudden impulse. How could Marcus possibly have learned about Jamie?

Lucas suddenly remembered the trollop in Charleston who'd thought he was Marcus. She'd seen him with Jamie and had commented about the boy. Had the woman relayed the encounter to Marcus, even after Lucas had paid for her silence?

Without a doubt, that was more than likely.

But the biggest question of all remained unanswered: Where was Marcus?

Lucas searched his mind again, thinking of all the places he'd traveled with his father as an older youth. They'd sailed the Caribbean, searching for ports where they could purchase tropical fruit and other goods to import to the colonies. It was during those days that his love for sailing blossomed.

Marcus had joined them only on two occasions. Their father had succumbed to Marcus's pleas to take him and Lucas on their journeys. His father hadn't wanted Marcus along, partly because he caused trouble but also because he wouldn't inherit any of the Reed holdings and hadn't needed to learn the shipping business as Lucas had.

He thought about the time when they visited Virgin Gorda, one of the larger of the Virgin Islands. Gigantic boulders littered the shores in an area known as the Baths. He and his brother had climbed the enormous stones said to be remnants of a volcanic eruption. Lucas smiled at the memory of chasing Marcus and hiding among the boulders. It was one of the fondest memories he had of his childhood.

Lucas rubbed his arm—the one he'd broken on that trip. He'd climbed upon the largest boulders, yelling that he was the king of the island. Marcus had taken that as a challenge, shinnied up the same boulder, and promptly shoved Lucas off. The next thing he remembered was being back on board his father's ship with a head injury and a broken arm. That trip was the last one their father allowed Marcus to go on.

A sudden gust of wind yanked Lucas from his memory. His gaze roved up the mast, to the sails, and back to the deck. Men faithfully tended their duties, needing little assistance from him.

His thoughts drifted back to Virgin Gorda. Marcus had boasted that he'd return to the island again, and Lucas felt certain he had. Maybe one day he could take Jamie to see the large stones. But first he had to find him.

A flame of a thought burned into his mind, flickered, and then exploded as if someone had set fire to a barrel of gunpowder. Of course. Virgin Gorda. That's where Marcus had gone.

He spun around. "Helmsman! Change course. Southeast by forty degrees."

Lucas crossed the deck, searching for his first mate. "Unfurl the topsails, Mr. Burton."

"Aye, aye Captain. Unfurl the topsails!"

Sailors scurried up the ratlines like monkeys on a jungle vine. Lucas strode to the quarterdeck and stood with his face to the wind. For the first time in a week, he felt sure of his course.

❧

Heather tugged on the last of her petticoats then looked in the small oval mirror that hung on the wall next to a map of the Atlantic. The swelling had gone down, but an ugly bruise remained where that nasty pirate had hit her. Picking up her horn combs, she held one in her hand and shoved the other into her hair, hoping to keep the stiff winds from flinging it in all directions. She smoothed down her hair then lifted the other comb. The ship suddenly canted to the right, throwing her off balance. The comb slipped from her hand as she was thrown backward into a chair. She grasped for a hold, but her hand slipped, and she was tossed to the floor.

Her arm collided with the hard wood, and a sharp pain stabbed her elbow. She clutched it and groaned. "What in the world?"

She wrestled her skirts and managed to gain her footing again. After locating her lost comb, she pushed it into her hair, effectively pulling the wayward tresses out of her face. Glancing in the mirror again, she noticed her cheeks looked pale in the dim light, so she pinched them then spun around. Something was happening. She could sense it. A change was in the air.

She exited the cabin and climbed the stairs to the deck. Squinting against the bright sunlight, she held her hand over her eyes and searched for Lucas. In the week that had passed since their last kiss, he'd been concerned for her welfare, but he hadn't touched her other than to escort her around the deck. Had he seen the apprehension in her gaze?

How could she love a man and also doubt his sincerity?

Her gaze landed on Lucas's broad shoulders, and her heart leaped. He stood so tall, erect, with his feet spread to balance his stance. He pointed aloft and said something to a sailor standing nearby. The small man scurried up the network of braided ropes and climbed into the crow's nest. Heather laid a hand over her heart. Did these sailors have no fear?

Lucas turned, his gaze landing on her, and he smiled. He strode toward her, setting her pulse dancing with each step he took. She longed to toss her doubts overboard and fall into his arms, but she restrained herself.

"My dear lady, how do you fare this morning?" He smiled, but his lovely eyes held apprehension.

Again her heart frolicked like a child skipping through wildflowers, and she despised herself for causing him worry. A smile tugged at her lips. "I am well.

Thank you. I felt the ship veer in a different direction. Am I correct?"

"Yes." He grinned, and this time his eyes sparkled. "I remembered a place my father took Marcus and me when we were only boys of twelve years. I feel certain that's where we'll find him and Jamie."

Heather grasped his arm. "Truly? I do hope you are correct. My heart aches for him."

Lucas stepped closer, holding her hand in his. "We will find them. The good Lord is on our side, and I fully believe He reminded me of Virgin Gorda."

Heather's brows lifted. " 'Tis an odd name. What kind of place is this?"

Leading her around the deck, he explained about the island and its huge boulders.

"But what does Virgin Gorda mean?"

Lucas chuckled, drawing her gaze. She loved seeing him cast aside his worries.

"Legend says that the island was discovered by Christopher Columbus and that he named it Virgin Gorda because the land resembled a fat woman lying on her side."

"How peculiar."

"True, but the island is as they say. You will see when we arrive."

She swallowed hard. "Do you really think we'll find Jamie and your brother there?"

He nodded, his dark hair falling over his eyes. She longed to reach up and brush it back but, instead, clasped her hands in front of her. "I do. I've prayed all week and believe God brought that memory to mind so that I'd go there."

"I've prayed, too. More than I have about anything."

Lucas rested his hands lightly on her shoulders. "We will find them. I won't stop searching until I do."

"I don't know how to thank you. Jamie is like my own son."

He brushed the back of his fingers across her cheek, a longing gaze filling his eyes. "He *is* my son. I won't stop searching until I find him."

Heather smiled up at him. What would life be like as his wife?

She couldn't deny that she cared for him. Even loved him.

But would her doubts ruin any chance they might have for a happy marriage?

Lucas smiled and leaned down, kissing her forehead. "Let us see what we can find for you to eat. It's time you broke your fast."

One thing for certain, she would marry Lucas. After first losing Jamie back at Reed Springs and now being away from him this long, torturous week, she could not bear to be parted from him again.

Chapter 18

At sundown two days later, the *Victory* drifted into a cove. They carefully maneuvered around huge boulders that hid the bay from the sight of anyone sailing past the island. Closer to shore, yet a safe distance away, Lucas recognized his brother's ship floating on the still waters.

"Lower all sails, and tell the men to keep silent," Lucas told his first mate in a loud whisper. He stared at the lights of the campfire on the beach and knew Marcus and his men couldn't see them where they hid behind a wall of giant boulders. In the distance, he could hear the revelry of pirates as they drank their ale, played games of chance, and challenged one another to fights. With God's blessing, he hoped they could sneak ashore and steal Jamie back without anyone getting hurt.

"What is yer plan, Captain?" Mr. Burton asked.

"We'll wait until they are further into their ale and then attack them."

"Forgive me for questioning you, sir, but don't you think it would be better to locate the boy first? What if he's on their ship?"

Lucas rubbed his chin and considered his first mate's words. "You're right. If we attack the men on the beach and Jamie is still on the ship, someone might harm him when they hear the ruckus. Perhaps we should send a couple of men to scour the ship and see if Jamie is there first."

Mr. Burton nodded. "A grand idea, although it could take awhile to search the whole ship."

"We have all night. Send Mr. White and Mr. Henning. They're our best swimmers and are less likely to be noticed than a rowboat. Be sure to instill in them the importance of keeping quiet. And bring me my spyglass."

"Aye, aye Captain."

The man quietly strode off. Lucas focused on the dancing blaze across the bay. *Keep Jamie safe, Lord, until I can rescue him.*

Marcus wouldn't willingly let the boy go, but would he harm Jamie to keep Lucas from getting the child back?

His brother had harmed an innocent woman—done the worst thing imaginable—but had he gone so far off the deep end that he would hurt a child?

He'd told Heather no, but now he wasn't certain. Marcus wanted Lucas to pay for the way their father had treated him. And he *had* paid—he had suffered Deborah's loss. The pain from that horrific event still haunted his sleep

109

on occasion. He should have searched longer for her. Should have found her and brought her home.

He had failed Deborah.

But he would not fail his son.

❧

Heather's knees ached from being bent in prayer on the hard floor for so long. Even her skirts no longer seemed to cushion them. She rose and walked over to the porthole and peered out. She could see nothing in the inky blackness, only her reflection staring back. Somehow it made her feel not so alone. The steady rolling of the ship had stopped, and she'd heard the splash of the anchor earlier. They had arrived at the islands, but she feared going outside. What if Marcus's ship wasn't there? What then?

A soft knock sounded on the door, and she rushed to answer it. Lucas's face appeared in the darkness as the light from her lantern illuminated it. His gaze darted past her to the light. He took her hand, led her to the bed, and lifted her onto it.

Heather laid a hand over her pounding heart. What was happening? She opened her mouth, but he held two fingers over her lips, then turned and extinguished both lanterns. The room plunged into deep darkness.

Lucas's footsteps crossed assuredly toward her. She scooted back farther onto the bed until her back hit the wall.

"All lights must remain out. We've arrived at the island, and a ship is here. We must stay dark and silent so my brother doesn't discover our arrival. I've sent some men to search his ship."

"How long will it take?"

"I don't know. Most of the ship's crew is on the beach from the sound of things, so I'm hoping that my men can handle any left on board."

"Do you think they will find Jamie?" She heard a rustling, and then his hand found hers, warming her and driving away her fears.

"If he's on board, my men will find him. If he isn't, we will sneak off ship and try to find him on the island."

Heather clenched his hand, knowing the danger he'd be in. She realized in that moment that she'd miss Lucas as much as Jamie if anything should happen to him. "I desperately want Jamie back, but I don't want you to get hurt."

He pulled her forward until she slid off the bed and stood in front of him. His hand found her cheek. "Shh, I will be fine. Don't worry."

"But you don't know how far your brother will go. What if he orders his men to kill you?"

He heaved a heavy sigh laced with the scent of coffee, warming her face. "I don't believe he will. Marcus is like a disobedient child who causes a ruckus but then wants to be loved afterward. I think he's in pain, and I long to help him. If he'll only let me."

Heather laid her hand on his chest. "Be careful. I saw the hatred in his eyes. He had no qualms about knocking me to the floor."

"God will be with us. Try to sleep and not worry."

"I cannot sleep, knowing all that could happen tonight."

"As you wish, but I must ask you to remain in your quarters. Darkness covers the ship, and you could get hurt if you wander about. Please stay in your bed. I will come to you as soon as I have news."

She clutched his shirt in her tight grasp. "Promise?"

"Yes," he whispered. "I promise."

He stood in the darkness, his hand to her face. His thumb caressed her cheek, and she longed to turn and kiss his palm. But such an action seemed too forward.

She'd had a full week with nothing to do but walk the deck, pray, and read the Bible in Lucas's chamber. She'd realized that she'd been letting her doubts rule her. Lucas had done naught to earn such misgivings. He captained his ship efficiently, and even when she'd seen a man mishandle a sail, causing it to tear and have to be repaired, Lucas gently reprimanded him and encouraged him to be more careful in the future. She was certain other captains would have severely punished the man for damaging something as vital to everyone's survival as a sail.

Lucas remained kind; he took time to visit with her and never once behaved in a dishonorable fashion, even when he walked her to the cabin door each evening. He'd never lied to her as far as she knew but took special efforts to keep her informed. She'd been foolish to let her doubts steal her future with Lucas. She'd never find another man as good as he.

His other hand touched her cheek. "I'm going to kiss you, my dear, unless you object."

With her heart thundering in her ears, she shook her head. His mouth found hers, and she received his kiss, letting him know that her heart belonged to him. Her hands slid up his chest, and she wrapped them around his neck. He teased her mouth with his, nipping her lower lip, then returning for a full kiss. After what seemed mere seconds, he pulled back then drew her to his chest, nearly crushing her in a fierce hug. His rapid heartbeat pounded in her ears. "Do you have any idea how much I love you?"

"Aye, I believe so."

"I'd love nothing more than to stand here and kiss you all night, but alas, that isn't the wise choice." His voice sounded husky, as breathless as she felt. He lifted her onto the bed again. "Stay here tonight, but lock the door after I leave. I can't keep my mind on finding Jamie if I have to worry about something happening to you."

"All right. I shall stay here and pray. But please let me know if you discover anything."

He kissed her cheek and stepped back. "I will."

Quickly, he crossed the room and exited, shutting the door behind him. Heather slid off the bed, felt her way across the cabin, and held out her hands, carefully searching for the door and then the lock. She finally found and secured it and made her way back to the bed.

The inky black of the room pressed in on her. Getting up on her knees, she reached for the porthole over the bed, wrestled with the latch, and finally got it to unlock and open. A warm breeze, salty with the scent of the sea, drifted in, bringing with it the sound of revelry. Men laughed, and raucous cheers sounded in the distance. She swallowed hard. What would happen to her if Marcus won the battle?

"Please, Lord, keep Lucas safe, and show him where Jamie is."

Lucas paced the deck of the *Victory*, pausing every few minutes to lift his spyglass and search the dark water between the ships. He rechecked the position of the waxing crescent moon, a mere sliver of light. Several hours had passed, and yet he'd heard not a sound from the direction of his brother's ship. Either his men hadn't made the swim successfully or they'd boarded and secured the ship and were searching it even now.

"Help them find the boy, Lord," he muttered softly. Lifting the spyglass, he searched the shore near the campfire. The loud ruckus had softened, and he suspected that many of his brother's men were passed out in a drunken stupor by now. He could make out the reclining bodies of only a half dozen men around the fire. Where were the others? Sleeping outside the circle of light?

A gentle splash sounded to his left. His hand flew to his cutlass, and he cautiously gazed over the side.

"H'lo the ship," a loud whisper pierced the silence.

"That you, Henning?"

"Aye Captain."

"What of the boy?" Lucas tossed down a coil of rope, making sure one end was securely attached.

"We have him, sir."

"Thank the good Lord." Lucas glanced up at the ebony sky and nodded his gratitude toward the heavens.

"Grab hold of me neck, Jamie, lad. Keep silent like I told ye to, and don't let go." Mr. Henning prepared to climb up the side of the ship.

Excitement surged through Lucas as he peered down at the three silhouettes in the stolen rowboat—two large and one small. His son was being returned. He tapped his palms on the gunwale, wanting—needing—to hold Jamie in his arms again. "Hurry, man."

A grunt sounded below; then the rope jiggled and a scraping along the side of the ship grew nearer. Mr. Henning's head appeared over the side, a wide grin on his face. "We did it, Captain."

Jamie peeked up with wide eyes. "Papa?"

Lucas lifted the boy off his mate's shoulders, while two sailors hoisted Mr. Henning aboard ship. "Are you hurt, son?"

Jamie shook his head but his grip on Lucas's shoulders tightened. "Nay, but I was scared."

Lucas winced at the thought of the poor boy, alone and frightened. "Didn't you know that I'd come for you?"

"I prayed you would."

"That's a good boy. God showed me where to find you." He squeezed his son in a fierce hug, pleased that Jamie kept his voice low. Lucas's heart felt whole again. How was it possible to love Jamie so much in such a short time?

"That pirate looks just like you; did you know that?"

"Yes, he's my twin brother."

Jamie rubbed his eyes. "But he's mean. He's not nice like you are."

"Well, let's hope you don't have to see him again."

"Are we going home?" Jamie yawned. "Is Aunt Heather here?"

"She is, and she'll be wanting to see you." Lucas turned back to his men. "How many are aboard my brother's ship, Mr. Henning?"

"Only two, sir. Mr. White and I managed to conk them out. Then we tied them up and gagged them whilst we searched the ship. Found the boy and made haste to return to the *Victory*. What say ye now? Do we go ashore and battle the rest of them scallywags?"

Lucas stared at the shore. He wanted to deal with his brother, but part of him wanted to take Heather and Jamie and flee. If he did, would they ever be safe? Would the threat of Marcus returning and taking Jamie again always hang over their heads?

He had to deal with his brother. "Mr. White, take Jamie to Miss Hawthorne in my cabin and stand guard outside the door until I return."

"Aye, aye Captain." He reached for Jamie, and the boy went, but he cast a longing gaze at Lucas.

Suddenly the sound of metal clanked against the wooden deck. Lucas turned toward the noise.

"Pirates!" a sailor yelled.

Lucas spun back to Mr. White. "Go! Guard them with your life."

The sailor nodded and hurried across the deck with Jamie in his arms. Lucas's sword made a *ching* as it slid from the scabbard. Pirates spilled over the starboard side of the *Victory* with war cries spewing from their mouths. His men were well-trained and fought back, man-to-man. Metal clanged against metal.

Lucas lifted his sword and fended off a pirate who looked unsteady on his feet. The man lurched sideways, took three quick steps, and fell overboard.

Lucas could only hope the rest of his brother's men were as far into their cups as that fellow.

The roar of men filled the night air as Lucas searched for his brother. Mr. Henning had his hands full with a black-haired pirate. Lucas knocked the rogue on the head with the pommel of his sword, and the man dropped to the deck. Mr. Henning nodded his thanks, wiped the sweat from his brow with his sleeve, then turned to engage another brigand.

A shout rang up, and the fighting slowed. Once again someone yelled to cease fighting, and slowly the pirates backed away from Lucas's men. His gaze finally located his brother, and his heart dropped to his feet.

"No! Do not harm the boy," he cried, crossing the deck in wide strides. Mr. White lay unmoving on the deck, his forehead bloody. The sight of Marcus with his knife at Jamie's throat chilled Lucas to the bone.

"Move! Get out of my way!" With a lantern in one hand, Heather squeezed between two sailors and gawked at the scene. Her eyes widened when they landed on Jamie. "Nay!"

Lucas motioned to Mr. Burton to keep Heather out of the way. The first mate took the lantern from her and handed it to another sailor then grabbed Heather around the waist with one thick arm. She pounded his forearm and kicked her feet in her effort to get free.

"Aunt Heather," Jamie wailed.

"Well, if this ain't a perfect picnic." Marcus sneered at Lucas. "You thought you could sneak in and take the boy back without me noticing?"

"Out of my way." Lucas pushed through the crowd as another lantern flamed to life. "Your quarrel is with me, brother. Don't hide behind the boy."

Marcus lifted his chin and glared back. "You'd like me to turn loose of him, wouldn't you?"

"Of course. I'll not lie. Set him free and fight me."

Marcus lifted the knife closer to Jamie's throat, and the boy whimpered. "Take another step closer, and I'll kill your son, brother."

Chapter 19

"Nay!" Heather screamed and fought the man who held her tight in his beefy grasp. Her heart pounded so hard she thought it would burst from her chest. She looked at Lucas, but his gaze was directed at his brother.

Two more lanterns were lit, illuminating the ragtag group in a spooky glow. It seemed as if all on deck held their breath. Heather didn't want to believe that Lucas's brother could harm Jamie. *Please, Lord. Spare him.*

"There's something you should know, Marcus." Lucas cast a glance at Heather, and her heart jolted at the intensity of his gaze. He turned back to his brother. "Jamie is *your* son, not mine."

Heather blinked, trying to comprehend what he'd said. How could that be possible? Deborah would never associate with a pirate.

Was Lucas simply lying to his brother to save Jamie? Or had he been deceiving *her* all this time?

Marcus's expression went white; then it hardened. "Ah, so you'd try to trick me, would you?"

"No." Lucas closed the distance until he was just a half dozen feet from Marcus. "Jamie is your son. Deborah is his mother."

The knife lowered, and Marcus turned Jamie around and stared into the boy's face.

"Think about it," Lucas reasoned. "Jamie is five. You last saw Deborah six years ago. If you look into your heart, you know I'm telling the truth."

Marcus ran his hand through Jamie's hair, a look of acceptance on his face. Suddenly, he pushed the boy to the side, drew his sword, and pointed it at Lucas. "You stole everything from me, even Deborah. I loved her as I've never loved another woman, but she never cared for me. It was you she cried for at night. And now you mean to have my son?

"Nay! I won't allow it." Marcus lunged forward.

Lucas swerved sideways, dodging his brother's thrust.

"Captain!"

Lucas turned, and one of his men tossed him a sword. He lifted the blade and prepared for the next assault. "I don't want to hurt you, Marcus. Things don't have to be like this. I never wanted them to be."

Marcus regained his balance and held out his sword, waving it in the air. "Aye, it does. You've ruined my life, and I mean to see an end to yours."

In two quick steps, Marcus attacked. Swords clanged, metal against metal.

"Please, let me go." Heather kicked her captor hard and pinched the forearm locked so tight around her waist that she could hardly breathe.

Mr. Burton grunted and carried her forward, as if to better see the fight. Heather frantically searched for Jamie, all the while praying for Lucas. Swords clanged, and cheers filled the air, but she couldn't see the two she loved most in this world. Marcus had held the lad a moment ago, but where was he now? The arm around her waist loosened, and Heather took full advantage and went limp. She slipped right through the man's arm and rolled away. She quickly untangled her skirts and stood. Mr. Burton, so engaged in his captain's battle, never noticed she'd gained her freedom.

Heather rushed behind the sailors, searching for Jamie. She pushed past a smelly man and looked everywhere.

"Aunt Heather!" Jamie squeezed out from between a barrel and the hull of the ship and stood.

She rushed forward and hoisted him in her arms, while sailors and pirates alike cheered on their captains. "Are you hurt?"

He shook his head and clutched her forearms tightly, tears swimming in his eyes. Heather carried him to the quarterdeck steps and helped him up. From her higher vantage point, she could see the two brothers—identical in features but so different in all other ways—battling for their lives. She cuddled Jamie and watched the melee as sword banged against sword. Brother fought brother.

What would happen to her and Jamie if Lucas didn't survive?

"Please, Father, give Lucas the victory."

Marcus stumbled backward and fell against the mainmast. He stood as if dazed. Lucas waited, not attacking. She wanted to urge him on, to have him seize the opportunity, but she couldn't ask him to kill his own brother, even though she doubted Marcus would have any misgivings about doing so to Lucas.

Marcus stood and charged his twin with a loud roar. Lucas leapt backward, tripped on a pirate's outstretched foot, and fell to the deck.

The pirates cheered.

Heather gasped.

She wanted to turn her head, but the scene below held her captive. She held Jamie's face against her side, not wanting him to witness the heinous duel. "Save Lucas, Lord."

Sneering, Marcus sauntered forward, keeping his sword on his brother. "Methinks I'll enjoy living in that fine house of yours and raising my son in it. Tell me. Where *is* Deborah?"

Lucas wiped his sleeve across his bloody mouth. He tried to rise, but a pirate's boot to his shoulder held him down. "Dead," he yelled. "She died far away from everyone she loved because she was too ashamed to return home after you were done with her. God forgive you for what you did."

A vile laugh filled the air, sending chills up Heather's spine. "Somebody help him," she screamed.

Marcus glanced up at her, grinning. "That wench of yours will do fine to replace Deborah in my bed and to raise the boy."

Lucas struggled again to rise. "She'll never be yours."

Marcus pointed his blade at Lucas's heart. "Aye, brother, she shall."

A movement below caught Heather's eye. Mr. White lurched to his feet, swiped the blood from his brow, then lifted his arm over his shoulder and swiftly drew it forward. A knife glimmered in the light as it flew toward the pirate. Marcus bellowed and clutched his chest. A unified gasp rang out from the crowd as he stumbled backward and fell to the deck. Lucas jumped up and hurried to his brother's side. He knelt beside Marcus and reached for the knife penetrating his brother's chest, then pulled his hands back without touching it.

Heather held her breath, afraid to believe they might yet be saved and at the same time sorry that Lucas had to witness his brother's suffering. All was quiet, as if each man held his breath.

"I forgive you for all you've done. Call out to God, Marcus. It's not too late for you to be saved."

The pirate chuckled then coughed. "I've no need for God in life or death. You win, brother."

"No. . .please, ask God to forgive your sins. Life doesn't end here. There's an eternity with God that remains if you'll only call on Him." Lucas grasped his brother's shoulders.

"Nay. I will not." Marcus's limp hand fell from his chest onto the deck.

Heather grieved for Lucas and the pain she knew he was enduring, but she couldn't help being relieved that his pirate brother was no longer a threat.

Lucas knelt with his hand against his forehead. She longed to go to him, to comfort him, but feared another fight might break out. She had to keep Jamie safe.

Grumbling arose from the crowd. A pirate shoved a sailor. Lucas shot to his feet. "There'll be no more fighting this day. My brother's men are free to return to the island."

"What of our ship?" a large man called out.

"Your ship will be torched, but you may live—as long as you throw down your swords. There's produce and wild game a'plenty on this island to feed you for a long while."

Heather watched Lucas's men as they kept their swords trained on the pirates. In spite of their grumbling, one by one Marcus's men dropped their weapons, clambered over the side of the ship, and disappeared. She blew out a deep breath as the last one jumped off the gunwale.

With the danger over, she felt as if she might collapse. She ruffled Jamie's hair. "We should get you to bed, lad."

"I want to see Papa—I'm hungry."

Smiling, she took his hand and led him toward the stairs. "Let's see if we can find you a bite to eat."

Lucas took the steps to the quarterdeck, two at a time, his relief evident when he saw them both safe. He took her in his arms, crushing her to him. Heather longed to hug him back, but she couldn't get over the fact that he'd lied to her. She pushed away from him. The light from the lantern below cast a flickering glow on the side of his face. Lucas gave her a quizzical stare.

"Is what you said true? Is Jamie your brother's son?"

Lucas glanced down at Jamie then picked him up. "Can this not wait?"

"Nay. Have you been lying to me all this time?"

Lucas closed his eyes and inhaled deeply. He strode to the stairway. "Mr. Henning, come up here."

The tall, lanky man hurried to do the captain's bidding. "Aye sir."

"Take Jamie to my cabin."

The boy locked his arms around Lucas's neck. "Nay, I want to stay with you."

Lucas patted the lad's back. "Did I not hear you say you were hungry?"

"Aye." Jamie nodded.

"Then go with Mr. Henning. He will find you a bite to eat, and Heather and I will be down shortly."

Jamie glanced back and forth between them. "Promise?"

"Most certainly." Lucas nodded. "I will be down to tuck you into bed, just like I do when we're at home."

"All right." Jamie allowed Lucas to pass him to the sailor, and Heather watched them descend the stairs, not yet ready to see him go.

Lucas remained silent until they heard the door below close. "It was Deborah's wish that no one know. That's what she wrote in her letter."

Anger blazed through Heather at her cousin's betrayal. She had tended Deborah, cared for Jamie, and even risked her own life and Jamie's to bring him to Charleston. No wonder Lucas hadn't accepted the boy at first glance. He wasn't Jamie's father, after all. She pounded her fist against Lucas's chest, releasing her fear, anger, and hurt. "Don't you think I had a right to know the truth?"

"If Deborah had wanted you to know, she would have told you. She was only trying to protect her son." Lucas grabbed her wrists and held them.

"And what was I doing? I've raised him as my own all these years. Scrimped and saved to bring him here to you, when you're not even his true father."

"You think that matters to me? Did I not take him in as my own even though I faced ridicule and my family name was threatened by the gossip of an illegitimate son?"

Heather jerked away, turned her back to him, and strode to the side of the ship. She couldn't explain why she felt as if she'd been betrayed. Wouldn't she have cared for Jamie even if she'd known the truth?

She shivered, thinking what her cousin must have gone through in the hands of that pirate. Had he taken her by force? Or had she succumbed to his wiles and given herself freely?

Either way, Jamie was the son of a vile pirate. No wonder Deborah wanted everyone to think that Lucas was the father. But had she considered what it would cost him?

She heard his footsteps drawing closer and stiffened. He laid his hands on her shoulders. "You have a right to be angry. But I was only honoring Deborah's wishes. At the time, I didn't know that you'd be here long term or that I'd fall in love with you. Try to understand, Heather."

She hung her head, ashamed at her outburst. All he was doing was protecting Deborah and her son. Tonight's tension and Lucas's near death had paralyzed her, and then to learn the truth in such a horrible way. . .

She'd lashed out at him because of her fear. "I'm sorry."

He turned her around but just stood there, not touching her. "I never wanted to hurt you. I only told Marcus the truth to save Jamie. I was afraid he'd kill him just to get back at me."

"I feared the same. I do believe he meant to." Heather shook her head. "How could two brothers be so different?"

Lucas took hold of her hands. "I don't blame Marcus. Our father's favoritism drove a wedge of anger and bitterness in my brother and warped his mind. Nothing I did helped. I only made things worse by trying to be the peacemaker."

Heather squeezed his hand. "It's not your fault. Marcus made his own decisions. There are many younger sons of wealthy men who've made something good of their lives. Marcus could have done the same, but he chose not to." She wanted to tell him that she was sorry for his brother's death, but she couldn't voice the words, knowing they weren't completely true. She *was* sorry though that Lucas was grieving and that she'd vented her anger toward him. Stepping forward, she wrapped her arms around his waist and laid her head on his chest.

His arms encircled her. "If only he had repented. . ."

"Shh. . .you did all that you could."

Footsteps sounded behind them, but Lucas didn't release her. A man cleared his throat. "We await your orders, Captain."

"Send three men over to my brother's ship. Have them set free the men they tied up and let them swim ashore; then set the vessel afire."

"But what of the bounty aboard, sir? Mr. Henning mentioned a wealth of treasure was stowed below."

Lucas let go of her and turned to face his first mate. "I want nothing to do with stolen wares, Mr. Burton. Prepare to set sail at first light. And see to it that the men keep watch in case my brother's men decide to try and retake the ship."

"Aye, aye Captain." Mr. Burton cast an odd glance at Lucas, and Heather wondered if he expected to get keelhauled for allowing her to escape. Then he spun on his heel and strode away.

Lucas wrapped his arm around Heather's shoulders, and they stood facing the island. The sliver of moon prepared to sink below the horizon. A warm breeze tugged at Heather's hair and teased her skirts. After all that had happened tonight, she was almost afraid to feel. To hope for a future with Lucas.

"I need to spend some time in prayer. I wanted to run my sword through my own brother when he talked about making you his."

She felt him shudder. "Cease your worries. He can harm us no more."

Lucas lifted a hand to her cheek then ran his thumb over her lip, sending delicious chills racing through her. "You're skin is so soft. I love your brown eyes." His hand brushed over her hair. "And your hair is so lovely. You've a kind, generous heart. There's nothing about you I don't love."

Tears stung her eyes to think she had been ready to walk away from their relationship a few minutes ago. When she'd first brought Jamie to Charleston, she'd never expected to fall in love. She lifted her hand to Lucas's bristly jaw. "I feel the same way. I can hardly wait to awaken each morning, just to see your sky blue eyes, to listen to your voice. I'm sorry for getting upset."

Lucas chuckled. "I've no doubt that there will be many other times that I shall upset you, but with love and God's help, we can just as quickly set aside our differences and make up."

"Aye," she whispered.

He lowered his face until she felt his breath mingle with hers. "I believe my heart mutinied the day I first laid eyes on you. I mean to make you my wife, Heather Hawthorne. Have you any qualms almost that?"

She smiled and shook her head. "Nay. None at all."

His lips met hers, and Heather knew she'd discovered where she was meant to be. She never dreamed she'd find happiness in the land that had warred against her homeland and ultimately caused her father to give up on living.

But God moved in mysterious ways, and He'd certainly worked a miracle for her.

SECRETS OF THE HEART

Chapter 1

Near Charleston, South Carolina
1810

The hairs on the back of Cooper Reed's neck stood on end. He peered over his shoulder and reined his tired horse to a stop, straining to hear the sound he'd heard a moment ago. Nothing moved in the woods behind him. Nothing but the trees dancing in the light spring breeze. The wind swished through pine branches above, and a waxwing whistled from a nearby bush. Overhead, a hawk screeched. Cooper glanced up at the bird soaring high in the sky, without a care in the world. He heaved a sigh and pulled his gaze back to the trail. Had he finally lost the men pursuing him?

Coop's horse jerked its head up, ears flicked forward, and stared back the way they'd just come. The animal snorted and pranced sideways. A shiver charged down Coop's spine. A tree limb snapped, intruding on the peaceful scene, and hoofbeats pounded toward him.

He reined his horse around and slapped the leather against his mount's shoulder. "He-yah!" The animal leaped forward, in spite of its exhaustion, and stretched to a gallop. Coop's hand went instinctively to the pouch tucked into his waistband—the pouch that held his precious cargo. He had to see it safely to his father.

"Halt, or suffer the consequences!" a shout heralded behind him.

He hunkered over his mount's neck, knowing that stopping most likely meant death. A shot rang out. He ducked, and the lead ball whizzed past his ear. Soon he'd be on Reed land. He had to reach home. He had to reveal the traitor among his father's friends.

Up ahead, Coop could see the open fields of Reed Springs. Not a soul was in sight. Perhaps he should have headed to the Madisons. They were his parents' best friends and closest neighbors. Though he hadn't seen them in years, he could get help there, but seeking their assistance could endanger them, and he couldn't risk that. He urged his horse to run faster.

Shooting a man on horseback was difficult, but once he reached the fields, he'd be a clear target, without the cover of the trees. His heartbeat kept time with his mount's thundering hooves. He needed to get rid of his cargo. If those men caught him, they would find it, and he'd have no proof to back up his accusations.

His mind raced for a solution, and suddenly he knew the answer. He lifted his gaze, searching the edge of the approaching tree line and found the exact spot where he, Jamie, and Michael Madison had hidden when they were hunting deer. The logs they'd piled up had grayed and partially collapsed, but the shadowy interior would be the perfect hiding place. He yanked the leather pouch from his waistband and flung it sideways, praying his pursuers didn't notice. All the times he'd played there as a boy, he never once considered it might one day harbor a dreadful secret.

His horse plunged out of the trees. Down the hill and up ahead, the cotton field spread far and wide. Coop's mount flicked his ears forward, slowing his pace as they raced down the steep hill, toward the quickly approaching creek that separated the field from the woodlands.

"C'mon, boy." Cooper hoped the horse could keep going. Just another half mile or so, and he'd be home. Safe.

Another shot blasted behind him. The horse squealed, staggered, and fell to his knees. Coop flew over the animal's neck, and his head and shoulder collided with the hard ground. He rolled over and over, pain surging through his body. Finally he stilled at the edge of the creek, and water seeped into his pants. He blinked open his eyes. His horse, blood seeping from his left thigh, plummeted toward him. Coop lifted his arm as the horse rolled over him.

❧

"Are you actually going to marry a man you hardly know?"

Hannah glanced at her friend sitting next to her in the buggy. "How many times are you going to ask me that, Ruthie?"

"Until you get some sense. This isn't the dark ages, you know." Ruthie Sutherland shook her head, tucked up a strand of light brown hair that had come loose, then redid the tie of her straw hat.

"No, but parents do still arrange marriages. Sometimes." Hannah shoved down a niggle of doubt. "Besides, Jamie has always been kind and treated me respectfully. He's a handsome man with his black hair and blue eyes."

"Whatever became of that brother of his? Wasn't he lost at sea or something? What was his name?"

"Cooper. That's such a sad situation." Even though she hadn't seen Cooper Reed in many years, Hannah's heart ached at the pain his disappearance had cost the Reed family. "Jamie was devastated that they couldn't locate his brother on their trip to England."

"Un-huh, he sure 'nough was." Chesny, Hannah's former nanny and now lady's maid, nodded. "Those brothers was closer than a flea on a hound dog."

"Didn't he quit school and run off or something?"

Hannah shook her head. "I don't think that's true. Something more nefarious must have happened, I'm sure of it. Coop was a good boy, just like Jamie.

Oh, he was a bit more independent and feisty, but he deeply loved his family. He'd never go off and not leave word."

"Somethin' bad done happened to that boy."

"I certainly hope not," Hannah said. "The Reeds sent word that they had found no clue as to what happened to him. They extended their time in England but are now returning because of the wedding."

"At least the Reeds are wealthy. And if that other son doesn't return, you'll be all the richer." Ruthie fanned her face with her hand, not looking the least bit sorry for her coldhearted words.

"Ruthie! What a horrible thing to say." Hannah could hardly believe some of the things that fell from her friend's lips. "I pray every night that Cooper will be found and returned to his family unharmed."

"You probably wouldn't even recognize the man if he passed you on the street. How long has he been away?"

"More than seven years. He served aboard one of his father's ships before finally deciding to attend college in England. He was your age—sixteen—I believe, when he left." Hannah pressed a fold of her apron with her fingers. What could have befallen Cooper Reed? The family had not received a request for ransom, so a kidnapping had been ruled out. Had Coop lost his temper and gotten in a fight and killed? It was all such a mystery and cast a pall on her wedding plans, but she would cancel them in a moment's notice if it meant Coop's safe return. *Please, Lord. Return him to his family. Keep Cooper safe until that day. And please comfort the Reeds and give them hope.*

"Well, at least the Reeds have this big plantation and that shipping business and exquisite house in Charleston. Oh!" Ruthie gasped and turned in the seat. "If you live in town, we can see each other every day."

Hannah glanced across the seat and caught her former nanny's gaze. Chesny rolled her dark eyes and adjusted her colorful head wrap. Hannah bit back a grin and tried to act more enthusiastic than she felt. Ruthie was a dear friend, but she was several years younger and of an outgoing nature that grated on Hannah's nerves after spending two weeks together. She searched her mind for a truthful response. "That would be nice, but I plan to live on the plantation most of the time."

"Oh pooh." Ruthie fell back against the seat, her arms crossed. "Why ever would you want to live out here? There's nothing but dirt and—and—cotton."

Staring out at the fields, Hannah tried to see the plantation from her friend's eyes. The cotton seedlings were only a half-foot tall, their green shoots waving a greeting on the warm breeze. On the other side of the buggy, abundant trees and tall grasses hugged the Ashley River that started at the Charleston Harbor and flowed miles inland. The fresh air filled her nostrils, so vastly different from the stench of Charleston on a hot day.

Ruthie nudged her with her elbow. "Well, don't you have anything to say?"

"I love it out here. It's so peaceful, and you don't have neighbors peering out their windows at you when you're sitting on your piazza."

"You're daft. That's all there is to it. Why your parents didn't make you go to school in town, I'll never know. I suppose I'll have to satisfy myself by continuing to make these treks to Madison Gardens—or rather Reed Springs—even after you are married."

Hannah shrugged. "Last I heard, Lucas Reed was going to continue searching for Cooper. Jamie will be overseeing Reed Shipping, so I'm sure we'll get to town quite often."

Ruthie smiled, contented at last. Hannah turned her attention to the tall home belonging to the Reed family as it came into view. The three-story, red-brick house rose up majestically against the bright blue sky. The wide white porch and well-manicured garden welcomed visitors. Though the structure wasn't as ornate as the Reed's Charleston house, it was much roomier.

Hannah had looked forward to being mistress of the house for as long as she could remember, and her mother had prepared her since she was young. Heather Reed and Caroline Madison had cooked up the marriage between her and Jamie shortly after her birth. Jamie always enjoyed playing with her when they were young, and as she grew, she took pleasure in seeing him whenever the family visited. Their marrying had started out as a joke among their parents, but somewhere along her childhood, the idea had taken root and grown and had become something to be expected one day.

But now that the day of her wedding was less than a month away, doubts assailed her continually. Was she making a big mistake in marrying Jamie Reed?

Chapter 2

Simeon, their driver, helped the women from the buggy, then led the horses toward the back of the barn where he always parked the buggy whenever they visited Reed Springs. Hannah patted her pocket, checking to be sure the treat she'd brought for Honey was still there.

"So, what are we doing today?" Ruthie asked.

"I thought we'd air out the upstairs bedrooms, then make sure that all the linens are clean and everything's ready for the Reeds' return." Hannah waved at the west end of the house. "Let's start there. It will be cooler now than it will be this afternoon."

Chesny carried the basket that held their lunch. "I'll go on inside, Miss Hannah, and see if Maisy and Leta are he'pin' us today."

Hannah nodded. "I'll be right there as soon as I give Honey the treat I brought her."

Chesny chuckled and shook her head. "You and that ol' hoss."

"Why do you always have to visit that horse?" Ruthie crossed her arms. "And why do you let your slave tell you what she's going to do? You know you have to use a strict hand on them or they'll—"

Hannah held up her palm. "Our Negroes are not slaves; they're employees. You know that."

"I may know it but I don't have to like it. Why, it's just plain absurd—paying those people a wage. What do they need money for?"

"You sound like your father."

Ruthie hiked her chin. "So?"

Hannah shook her head. "Nothing. Do you want to go with me to the barn and see Honey?"

"Eww. No. I'd rather do menial labor inside than visit a smelly barn." Ruthie swirled around and stomped away.

Hannah sighed. She couldn't help thinking about what Chesny sometimes murmured when visitors were particularly peevish. *Fish and guests, they both stink after three days.*

Hannah smiled and walked toward the barn. Having guests visit the plantation and stay for an extended time was common, but she was always a bit relieved when they finally left and things could get back to normal. She pulled open the barn door, noting that the latch had not been fastened. "Israel, are you in there?"

127

When the Reed Springs caretaker didn't respond, she stepped inside and looked around. Dust motes floated on fingers of sunlight that poked through the cracks in the old building. Ruthie said the barn stank, but Hannah found the scent of hay and horses comforting. She'd always loved venturing out to the barn, both here and at home.

Most times when she arrived at Reed Springs, the caretaker was present. She even brought him a treat on occasion. "Israel?"

Honey lifted her head over the stall gate and nickered. Hannah lifted the skirt of her high-waisted day dress and crossed the hard-packed dirt floor to her destination. "Good morning, girl. How are you today?"

Honey bobbed her head as if to say she was fine. Hannah loved the brown mare, which she'd ridden with the Reed boys and her brother when she was small. "How's your leg today? Huh? Still bothering you?"

The horse stretched her neck and blew against Hannah's skirt. She giggled. "Ah, you found your treat, huh?"

She inserted her hand into the slit in the side of her gown, fished two big carrot chunks out of the pocket she had tied around her waist, then held them out to the horse. Honey's big lips lapped up the treat, tickling Hannah's hand. She giggled, then noticed the horse slobber on her hand. "Ruthie would scold me for certain if she saw this."

Hannah hunted around for a piece of burlap or cloth on which to clean off her hand. She pursed her lips at not finding what she needed. Hay would have to do. She crossed over to the pile of fresh hay that Israel must have forked from the overhead loft, and her shoe smacked into something hard. She looked down. Her gaze landed on a boot—with a leg attached.

The skin on Hannah's face tightened, and her heartbeat galloped like a horse running a race. The boot moved, and Hannah leaped backward, tripping on her skirt. She fell flat on her backside on the hard ground, never taking her eyes off the boot.

Suddenly, the whole pile of hay moved and a second boot slid out from under the pile. Who was under there—and how could they breathe?

The mound of hay moved again, and a ghastly moan ascended from it. Hannah forgot her bruised backside. Rolling over onto her hands and knees, she scrambled across the filthy barn floor, her gaze searching for anything she could use as a weapon. She spied an old ax handle leaning against the wall and grabbed it, then used it to help her stand. She spun back around, holding the weapon above one shoulder.

She struggled to swallow the burning sensation in her throat. The rapid pounding of her heart kept time with her staccato breathing. In the shadows, two black boots now protruded from under the edge of the hay, along with a man's muddy trousers. That man had been there the whole time she was feeding Honey.

One of the boots shifted again, and a second moan caused the hairs on the back of her neck to stand up. She glanced at the door, knowing the smart thing would be to run back to the other women, but could she be putting them in danger? Mustering her courage, Hannah crept toward the lumpy pile of hay, keeping the handle ready in case it was needed.

Oh Lord, please help me. I don't know if I could whack a living person, even to protect myself.

Before she lost her nerve, she nudged one of the boots with the toe of her shoe. The stranger rewarded her with another groan and a raspy cough. Hannah took a shuddering breath and backed away. Maybe she should go find Israel.

But curiosity overpowered her fear. With white-knuckled hands, she clutched the ax handle and used the end to flip hay off the person. The long, lean form of a dark-haired man appeared.

She poked him in the shoulder with the handle. "Mister, are you awake?"

When he didn't respond, she knelt down to get a closer look. A thick trail of dried blood ran from his nose to his bloodied and bruised lips. Hannah took a deep breath and mentally steadied her trembling hands. She reached forward, lifted a wad of hay off the top half of the stranger's face, and tossed the debris aside. To her surprise, she discovered a young man who looked to be only slightly older than herself.

"That's a nasty gash you've got over your eye," she whispered. "You won't be seeing out of it until that swelling goes down." Hannah shook her head. The man needed help, not an inventory of his wounds. She stood and turned her back to the man, lifted her skirt, and quickly untied the double pocket from around her waist. The linen fabric would serve well as a bandage until she could get the stranger to the house.

"I'm going to wrap your head wound now." She doubted he could hear her, but maybe the tone of her voice would somehow comfort him. She brushed aside most of his dark brown hair, which was littered with pieces of grass. Then she folded the fabric, placed one pocket over the lump on his forehead, wrapped the tie around his head, and secured it.

She sat back, ready to go get Chesny, but then decided she'd better check for broken bones before they moved the man. Wasn't that what her father said to do when Michael had fallen from a tree and injured himself? Thankfully, her brother had only bruises and scrapes. She reached toward the stranger's leg, pausing in a moment of uncertainty, then gently ran her hands down the length of it, checking for swelling. A breath of relief slipped from her lips at finding none.

She ran her hand along his firm shoulder then cut a path down his forearm to his wrist. Her hand lingered a moment on his warm, calloused palm. She lifted his arm, turning it over to examine his dirty, scraped knuckles. It was a strong, tanned hand, accustomed to hard work.

"What in the world happened to you? If you were in a fight, I certainly hope you were on the right side of the law." She laid his hand down to his side and leaned over the stranger's chest to check his other arm. As she reached out, he erupted in a coughing spasm and drew up his right leg. Hannah jerked her arm back, but the man's knee rammed into her shoulder, throwing her off balance. Unable to stop her momentum, the full weight of her body landed hard across his solid chest.

"Aahhh, you t–trying to k–kill me?" the man cried in a hoarse voice. Fast as lightning, his left hand snaked out, grabbing her upper arm. He pushed her body off his.

Hannah screamed. She struggled to free her arm, but the man's rock-hard grasp didn't yield. The strength in his bruised body amazed her. She cast a glance at the ax handle, which lay just out of reach.

Swallowing with difficulty, she found her voice and stopped struggling. "You'd b–better let me go, if you know what's good for you." She hoped she sounded braver than she felt. Could the stranger hear her pounding heart, racing like a ship in a stiff wind?

The man stared at her, his dark eyebrows furrowed into a single brow. With short, choppy breaths, he fought for air. Hannah squirmed against his hold as he watched her with his open eye.

Why hadn't she thought about him possibly having broken ribs? Knowing she caused him such discomfort when she fell on him concerned her nearly as much as the fact that he still held her captive.

After a moment, his tense expression eased, and he relaxed. She caught herself licking her lips as she watched him try to wet his dry, cracked lips with his tongue.

"W–water," he croaked as he released her.

Hannah rubbed her aching arm. She doubted the man meant to hurt her, but she would carry the bruises he'd surely inflicted for a long while. As her fear ebbed, she eyed the man with growing compassion. He must be in terrible pain. She stood, looking for the bucket of water Israel generally kept handy.

"Don't go. I w–won't hurt you. Need water, p–please." He reached toward the bandage on his forehead with his filthy hand.

Hannah grabbed his arm and pulled it back down. "Don't touch that. I put a bandage on your head wound. Just hold on a bit, and I'll be back shortly with some water."

She located the bucket in the corner and carried the dipper back to the stranger. He attempted to push up on one elbow but then sucked in a sudden gasp as pain etched his face. He pressed his hand to his side.

"Here, let me help you." Taking care not to spill the water, Hannah stooped down and slipped her hand behind his head, lifting it just enough that he could slurp up the water.

He grunted and laid his head down. His lips tightened into a thin white line, and he scrunched his eyes shut. "Who are y–you?"

"My name is Hannah Madison, and my family lives on the neighboring plantation, just over a mile away. Who are you, and what are you doing here, might I ask?"

The man stared up at her with a dazed look. He pressed his fingertips against the uninjured side of his brow. "I—I don't know."

"What do you mean?"

He squeezed his forehead. Pain and confusion engulfed his battered face. "Don't know how I got here. Can't remember."

Chapter 3

Hannah stepped back and narrowed her eyes. Could he be telling the truth? Perhaps he was a thief hiding from pursuers. Or a servant who'd suffered a beating at the hand of the man he worked for and then run away. But his confusion didn't look faked.

A Bible story her mother had once read during evening devotions blazed across her mind like a wildfire. The Good Samaritan helped the wounded man on the side of the road. Hannah had few opportunities to help others outside of those living on her family's plantation. This was her chance to put those biblical truths into action.

"Do you know where you are?"

The man looked around again. For the first time, a hint of a smile tugged at his puffy lips. "Looks rather a lot like a barn, best I can tell with one eye." Then the smile disappeared, and a scowl replaced it. Glancing down, he grabbed a wad of hay off his shirt and tossed it aside. "Daft, is it not? A grown man who doesn't even know where he is."

"I'm sure it will all come back to you. It looks as if you took a hard blow to the head, and I've heard that can cause a person to be disoriented."

He stared at her a brief moment, then turned his face away. The man's helplessness and confusion obviously embarrassed him. His calloused hands and muscular frame proved he was a man accustomed to taking care of himself. What could have happened to him?

"Shhh. Don't fret," she whispered, hoping to reassure him. "I need to get some help, then get you inside the house and clean up your injuries. There's dirt and pieces of hay in your wounds. You might even need some suturing to close up that nasty gash on your head."

He looked at her again. "I don't fret."

Hannah's lips twitched. Men and their need to appear strong. Her father and brother acted the same. "Ah, my mistake. But at least you remembered that." She stood and stepped back. "A big, strong man like you doesn't need any help, right?"

"That's not what I said."

She spun around. He may not want her help, but he needed it. And she needed to find Israel.

"Wait! You're not leaving me here, are you?" he whispered.

Remorse twisted in her stomach at causing him distress. She shouldn't have poked fun at him. She faced him again. "Tell me, what's your name?"

The man pressed on the bandage covering his right brow and gazed up at her with his uninjured eye. Hannah's heart lurched at the panic and vulnerability in his expression. His hoarse whisper broke the silence. "I—I can't remember."

"You can't remember your own name?" She reached out to comfort him.

He shook his head. Utter despair encompassed his battered face.

&

"I declare, you have all the luck. Imagine finding such a finely built man in a barn." Ruthie stamped her foot and crossed her arms. "Why couldn't this have happened when I first arrived instead of the day before I return home?"

Hannah and Ruthie stood outside the closed bedroom door while Israel and Chesny washed the stranger and helped him into an old nightshirt that had belonged to Mr. Reed. They had wrapped his chest before moving him, but even with help, the long walk from the barn had exhausted the man.

"Who do you suppose he is?"

Hannah shrugged. "I don't know. He can't remember his name or how he got to the barn."

Ruthie's hazel eyes widened, and she clapped her hands. "I do love a good mystery." She tapped her index finger on her lips. "Perhaps he's the son of a king, traveling to meet his princess and was attacked and the treasure stolen." She gasped. "Oh, what if the ruffians kidnapped the princess?"

Hannah smiled and shook her head. "That's some imagination you have."

"Ooo, no, what if he is the kidnapper and has hidden away the princess for a ransom? Why, she could be locked away somewhere all alone."

Hannah sighed. "Or perhaps he's just a man traveling on business."

"Then how did he get all beat up?"

The door opened, and they both stepped back. Hannah's gaze shot past Chesny to the stranger. "How is he?"

She shook her head. "Not so good. Someone done beat him up real bad."

"You just have them wimmenfolk fetch me if'n you needs anythin'." Israel told the stranger; then he backed away from the bed.

When Israel stepped out of the room, Hannah motioned him to follow, and she walked the short hall to the upstairs sitting room. She glanced at Chesny and Israel. "Have either of you seen that man before?"

Israel shook his head. "No, Miz Hannah. I never did."

Chesny didn't respond for a moment. "I thought maybe there was somethin' familiar about that boy, but I dunno. He just too busted up to tell."

Hannah glanced back toward the stranger's door where Ruthie stood, peering in. Perhaps in the better light of the house she might recognize the man, although he hadn't seemed at all familiar before.

Maisy plodded up the stairs, carrying a cream-colored pitcher with blue flowers on it. "Where y'all want this here water?"

Hannah pointed the way. "Maisy, did you find any bandages?"

"No, Miz Hannah, but Leta, she be lookin' in some other places."

Hannah nodded. "All right. Bring them up as soon as you locate them—and some medicinal salve, if you have any."

"Yes'm." Maisy disappeared into the bedroom.

"Chesny, would you please set some water to boil and see if there's any fresh meat we can stew to make some broth?"

"I can go an' catch a chick'n," Israel offered.

Hannah nodded. "That would be nice. Thank you." She spun around to head into the bedroom when a hand on her arm stopped her.

"Just where you be goin', Miz Hannah?" Chesny stared at her with brows lifted.

"Why, to doctor my patient of course."

"I'll help her," Ruthie added.

"Un-uh, t'ain't proper." Shaking her head, Chesny shoved her hands to her hips.

Hannah lifted her chin. "And why not? Mama often doctors our family and workers who get hurt. It's one of the duties of the plantation's mistress."

"You ain't the mistress of *this* house yet, and besides, yo' mama, she be a married woman."

Hannah blushed, wondering just what Chesny thought she would do. "There's nothing improper about it. The man is completely covered with a nightshirt and a sheet. You and Israel have taken care of his ribs. I just plan to tend the wounds on his face."

"And I'm going to help her," Ruthie stated again, as if no one had heard her before. She crossed the hall and stood beside Hannah and joined her in staring at Chesny.

The older woman shook her head and trod toward the stairs. "It just ain't right, if'n you asks me, but them girls, they ain't askin'. They's just tellin'."

Israel nodded and followed Hannah's maid down the stairs.

Ruthie leaned toward her and grinned. "You told her. I didn't think you had it in you." She sashayed toward the bedroom door with the long skirt of her high-waisted gown flowing behind her.

Chesny stopped on the stairs, and Israel almost smacked into her. She glanced back at Hannah. "I'm'a goin' to the kitchen like you done asked, but then I'm'a comin' back to that man's room. It just ain't proper fo' two wimmen to be alone with him."

Hannah wasn't sure what had gotten into her, but she didn't like upsetting Chesny. She rarely butted heads with the older woman, who had been her nanny since she was a young girl but now was more of a friend and confidante. It was an odd relationship for the daughter of a plantation owner and a black servant, but she didn't want it to be any other way. She'd grown up despising slavery. Her family and the Reeds were among the few plantation owners who paid their Negro workers a wage. They were employees, not slaves. She just had to overlook Chesny's bossiness at times. The woman was only watching out for her.

A pretty lady strolled into the room—no, not a lady, but rather an adolescent not more than fifteen or sixteen, he'd guess. He looked past her, hoping the other woman would return—the one who'd found him in the barn.

The girl looked at him and grimaced. She twisted her lips, then spun away and busied herself with opening a window. He sighed and turned his face toward the wall. What must he look like to repulse her so?

From the waist up, every part of him ached. He could only take slow and shallow breaths or risk stabbing pains in his side. His head pounded, and his face felt like mush. What had happened to him?

Why couldn't he remember anything further back than awakening in that barn? Who was he? Where had he come from?

He clenched a wad of the fresh-smelling sheet in his hand. Efforts to remember only brought sharp pains to his head. Perhaps the woman—Hannah Madison—was correct. Time would heal him. He had to believe that. He couldn't live in this fog forever.

A gentle touch on the top of his hand drew his gaze. Ah, Miss Madison—or perhaps it was *Mrs.* Madison—had returned.

"Are you in pain?"

He shook his head, then grimaced. Vision blurred, and his head felt as if a horse had sat on it.

She patted his hand. "Try to relax and rest. I'm going to clean up your wounds; then we'll leave you alone so you can sleep. Later, we'll have some broth for you."

"Broth—that's a weak soup, is it not?"

She nodded.

"Why is it I can remember something as trivial as broth but not more important issues like who I am?" He hated the confusion fogging his mind and this feeling of helplessness. He couldn't even sit up without assistance.

"It is an odd thing, but I trust that God will restore your health and your memories."

God. He hadn't thought about God since coming to. He laid his head back and stared out the window at the soft blue sky, not all that certain what he believed about the Creator. Perhaps God would be merciful and do as the kind woman said and restore him.

Unless, of course, God was punishing him for some horrible deed he had done.

Chapter 4

Hannah moistened the cloth, then gently wiped the dried blood from the stranger's face. She removed the bandage from the wound above his eye, examined the injury, then laid her hand on the man's forearm. "This might hurt a bit."

He breathed out a slow sigh, then nodded.

Hannah worked carefully, dampening the wounded area. After a few moments, the blood softened, and she pulled a lock of dark hair out of the gash on the stranger's eyebrow.

"*Owww!* Take it easy!" The man grabbed her wrist again. Hannah stared down at him with her brows lifted, and he quickly released her.

"I'm sorry that hurt. Just hold still a bit longer and I'll be finished." She remoistened the cloth. With one hand, she held the man's stubbly chin, and with the other, she carefully wiped the remaining blood off his nose and lips.

She glanced up and discovered his intense gaze on her face, mere inches away from his. His good eye—a grayish blue—studied her, and his warm breath tickled her cheek. The intensity in his stare made her hand shake. She straightened, keeping her features composed. Tearing her gaze away from his, she focused on cleaning his lips. They'd be nice lips when they healed.

Hannah sucked in a gasp. Where in the world had that thought come from? It was hardly a decent thought for a woman preparing to be married.

Ruthie stepped away from the window across the room. "How can you stand to do such a menial, disgusting task? Why not let your Negro do it?"

How could Ruthie be so insensitive? "I'm merely offering Christian charity by tending this man's wounds. Would you have me ignore his pain because the task is unpleasant?"

"I would have you back at your house sipping tea in the parlor if it was up to me. I'm going downstairs. It stinks in here."

Stunned, Hannah watched her friend flounce from the room. Ruthie was immature, but she'd never known her to be so cruel and uncaring, except where slaves were concerned—and that strong opinion had been expertly cultivated by her outspoken father. Hannah had worked hard to get her friend to see Negroes as real people with emotions, but Ruthie only thought of them as property. Such a sad thing for people to be so heartless where others were concerned.

Something brushed the back of Hannah's hand, and she glanced down. The man's fingers were just inches from hers.

"Could I have some more water, please?"

"Certainly." Hannah poured fresh water from the pitcher into a glass Maisy had brought up earlier. He lifted his head and rested his palm against the back of her hand, warming it. Hannah's heart thumped hard as she stared at his hand on hers. Finally, he lay back.

"I need to know what happened to me."

"Can you remember anything about that? Did you take a fall off your horse, or perhaps you met up with some scoundrels who robbed and beat you?"

"No. . .uh, I don't know—" He coughed and grabbed his chest.

"Shh, there now," she said, patting his shoulder. "We can talk about this later. Right now, you need to rest."

Hannah pulled her arm away and poured a generous amount of water on a clean cloth. Folding it, she placed it over the man's eye. "Hold that right there. The coolness of the water will help the swelling to go down."

She started to walk away, but the stranger reached out and grabbed her wrist. He groaned from the effort. "I'm not always this helpless."

"I'm sure you aren't." She glanced at his wide shoulders and strong hands, then pulled her gaze away from her shameless study. Her cheeks warmed. "Get some sleep now, and we'll figure out everything else later. I'm so sorry this happened to you. I remember when one of our workers found two white men stealing from our barn. The thieves attacked Jasper when he tried to stop them. One man hit him in the head with a shovel and left him for dead. His head had been badly injured, and I thought for sure he would die. For weeks, he didn't know a single one of us, not even his wife and children."

"That would be rough. I don't think I have children." He gazed up at the ceiling as if thinking deeply. "Surely I'd remember if I did."

"I would hope so. You'll be encouraged to know our worker's memory came back after a few weeks. Yours will, too, I would imagine. Just give it some time. In the meantime, you can stay here, and we'll take good care of you until you're up and about again."

"Thank you. I do appreciate your kindness."

Hannah smiled and nodded, then backed away. Already he'd closed his eyes and looked more relaxed. She turned and came to a halt when she saw Chesny standing just inside the door.

"I done brung up them bandages and the salve. Maisy and Leta are fixin' to pluck that chick'n Israel done killed. They'll make chick'n soup that we'all kin eat."

"That sounds nice. I'll go check on Ruthie. She seems more out of sorts than normal."

Chesny snorted. "That girl, she always got a beehive under her skirts."

"I suspect, she's probably just upset at returning home tomorrow. She won't admit it, but she likes being at Madison Gardens."

"Humph. I sure cain't tell by how she acts." Chesny leaned toward Hannah and nudged her chin toward the bed. "That stranger, he be a learned man."

Hannah turned back to her patient. Now that she thought about it, he didn't have the dialect of a common-born man. She wasn't certain, but she thought she'd detected a faint English accent.

Her eyes widened. What if he was an Englishman come to stir up trouble? Talk about there being another war with England ran rampant these days. What if he was a spy?

≈

"What do you mean you lost him?"

Sam smoothed his bushy mustache and cast a wary glance toward the man he knew only as Boss. Average in height, with a belly resembling a pregnant woman's late in her term, Boss preferred telling others what to do rather than doing things himself. Boss only answered to one man, and Sam had no idea who that was, but as long as he was paid for his work, he didn't care.

"Jeeter was a bit rough on the kid," Sam said. "When he wouldn't talk, Jeeter punched him in the face and kicked him in the side a couple times."

"He didn't feel nuthin'. He was already mostly dead from that fall off his horse." Jeeter said, spewing a stream of tobacco spit on the ground, mere inches from Boss's dusty boots.

Boss jumped back four inches, almost too much for his rotund frame. "Jeeter, you idiot."

Sam stifled the laugh rising up within. Boss reminded him of a chicken with clipped wings as his beefy arms flapped and he wrestled to regain his footing.

"You spit on my new boots, and I'll knock the tar out of you. I didn't want that kid killed, at least not until I found who he told what to. Mr. S. won't be happy about this." Boss removed his hat and smoothed out his thinning strands of hair in a futile attempt to cover his balding head. Cramming his hat back on, he turned to Sam. "Did you search him?"

"Yeah, Boss." Sam studied the dust on his own boots to avoid Boss's scrutinizing gaze. "We went clean through his clothes and the saddlebags of that horse he stole. There wasn't nuthin' there," he muttered, twisting the end of his bushy mustache.

"You sure you got the right kid?" Boss asked.

"Well, I reckon," Jeeter scratched his chest. "We found him at a tavern in Charleston not long after he jumped ship. Would'a caught him then if he hadn't seen us come in the door. He climbed on the nearest table and jumped out a window. Was down the road and nearly out of sight on that stolen horse before we could get out the door."

"Don't you keep those shanghaied sailors locked up when you make port?" Boss yanked off his hat again and slapped it against his leg. A small cloud of dust floated down to the ground. "I still don't see how he got away once you caught him."

"It took most of the day to catch up with him, and we only did then because his horse gave out. The kid was out cold all evening, so we bedded down for the night. Jeeter was on watch, but he must'a nodded off." Sam glanced at the scrawny little sailor. He was nothing but an old fool as far as Sam was concerned. There was no reason for him to be so rough on the boy, but he'd taken an immediate disliking to Cooper Reed the day he was brought aboard ship.

"I did not fall asleep." Jeeter puffed up his chest, his black eyes flaming.

"Wasn't the kid tied up?" Boss asked.

"He was knocked senseless. Kicked in the head by his horse, from the looks of it. There weren't no reason to tie him up." Jeeter curled his lip, crossed his arms over his chest.

"I told you to tie him up anyway, whil'st I got the firewood." Sam wasn't about to take the blame for something Jeeter had failed to do.

"You two wretched good-fer-nuthin's. You sound like a couple of kids arguin'. I should'a gone myself. Now, what am I gonna tell Mr. S.? If that kid tells anyone what he knows, we're all gonna be dead, Mr. S. will see to that. His business—and his good name—are on the line."

"The kid couldn't have got far. We scared his horse off so he was on foot, and bad as he was hurtin', he's gotta to be around here close by."

"Pack up then," Boss ordered. "We gotta find him."

❧

"Miz Hannah, somebody be comin'." Simeon slowed the buggy and glanced back over his shoulder.

Hannah lifted the large brim of her straw hat and gazed across the meadow. Squinting from the glare of the brilliant morning sun, she lifted her hand to block the light. A tall, thin man rode toward them. His thick, droopy mustache touched the bottom of his chin. His musket was drawn and rested across his lap. Hannah glanced at Chesny, seated across from her, gave her maid a brief nod, then focused her gaze on the stranger.

When the buggy stopped, two more men rode out of the trees in their direction. Hannah wished now that she'd taken her brother up on his offer to escort her to Reed Springs this morning, but with her father in Charleston, along with her mother, Michael was needed at home to oversee things. "Drive on, Simeon."

The smaller man kicked his horse, trotted over, and stopped in front of the buggy.

"Now just hold on there, ma'am. We don't mean you no harm. Just need some information."

Hannah eyed the heavyset man who'd spoken, wondering how he'd ever managed to get on his horse. The poor animal would be swayback before the year's end, for sure. She plastered a charitable smile on her face and struggled to keep her voice steady. "What kind of information do you gentlemen need?"

"Who are you? Start with that," the fat man ordered.

Hannah stood, hoping the benefit of height would make her seem less vulnerable, and it put her closer to the muff pistol hiding under Chesny's apron, should she need it. "My name's Hannah Madison, and this is my father's land." She narrowed her eyes and glared at the third man positioned in front of the matched black geldings that pulled her buggy.

"My, my, Boss, we got us Richard Madison's girl." The small man's leering gaze roved down Hannah's body and back up.

She crossed her arms over her chest and swallowed. *Keep us safe, Lord.*

"Shut up, you fool." The man called Boss stared at her. "Look, Miss Madison. We just want to know if you've seen a stranger 'bout your age, riding a dun gelding around these parts. We've got some business to take care of with him. That's all."

"Uh. . .no. You three gentlemen are the only folks I've seen since we left home." It was true, she reasoned. She hadn't seen her stranger today—and he definitely wouldn't be riding with all his injuries. Not yet anyway. "We don't usually see too many folks way out here. 'Course we do see a trapper and an old Indian ever so often. Oh, and once in a great while, a traveling man comes past our home and sells his wares to my mother. Life on these big plantations can be lonely." Of course, not too lonely when Ruthie had just boarded a ship back to Charleston less than an hour earlier.

Hannah smiled and casually smoothed out her dress, hoping to come across like an overly friendly neighbor. While her outer demeanor remained calm, her insides were treacherously close to giving her away. Could it be possible that these three men had attacked her stranger? What could these ruffians want with him? He had nothing—no possessions of any kind that Hannah had noticed. Not even a horse or a change of clothing.

The big man snorted and rolled his eyes at the other two men. "Missy, all we want to know is if you've seen a dark-haired kid riding a big dun."

"I've already answered that, haven't I? Excuse me, gentlemen, but I'm expected somewhere soon. I can assure you that I haven't seen the man you're searching for, riding a horse or not. In fact, you're the only people I've seen riding today."

Hannah forced herself to look from man to man. Both the mustached man and the smaller one looked ready to agree, but Boss scowled at her. She kept a smile on her lips and steadily held his gaze, though she wanted nothing more than to race away like the wind.

Finally, he grunted, "I guess you don't know nothin'. We'd best be gettin' along."

"Good day, gentlemen." Hannah flashed them what she hoped was a charming smile. She sat down and eyed Chesny. The woman lifted a corner of her apron, revealing the walnut stock of the flintlock pistol Hannah's father had insisted she learn to use and carry with her whenever she left home. This was the first time she had come close to possibly needing it. But then, what good would one gun have been against three? She blew out a heavy sigh. Perhaps she should let Michael escort her to the Reeds from now on.

Chapter 5

Hannah could barely wait to get to Reed Springs to see how her stranger had fared overnight. *Dear Lord, please let him be all right.* "Them men's lookin' fo' that stranger you done got stowed up at the Reeds, ain't they?"

Hannah stared at Chesny. The dark-skinned woman was beginning to age. More gray than black hair peeked out from her head wrap, and small wrinkles were etched in the corners of her eyes and around her mouth. She boldly held Hannah's gaze, unlike most Negroes. Hannah nodded.

"I wonder what that young feller done to rile them so."

"I don't know, but nothing could deserve such a beating. I do believe they aim to kill him." Hannah wrung her hands. "We can't let them find him, and if they're of a mind to search the Reeds' house, none of the servants would be able to stop them."

Chesny leaned forward just as Simeon pulled the buggy to a stop in front of the Reed Springs main house. "We needs to put him in the hidey hole."

Hannah jumped up and hugged her maid. "Perfect! Why didn't I think of that?"

"Because you ain't played in that place in years."

Hannah climbed down. "I'll go and check on our patient, and you can see what state the secret room is in."

Chesny clambered out of the buggy backward. On the ground, she straightened her dress and head wrap, then followed Hannah inside and up the stairs.

Hannah glanced back over her shoulder. "Why aren't you checking on the room?"

"I ain't leavin' you and that feller all alone together."

Hannah reached the landing, shaking her head. "What's he going to do? He's stuck in bed and needs help so much as to sit up."

"He be in bed—in a nightshirt, no less. Just ain't proper for you two youngun's to be alone in a bedroom."

Hannah knew Chesny was only watching out for her and doing as Hannah's mother would do if she were here. She took a breath, then tiptoed into the room. She stopped next to the bed and watched her stranger's chest rise and fall with his steady breathing. He'd shaven—or been shaved. His wounded eye was as large as a goose egg and colored an angry black and purple. His lips

142

were still swollen, and the bandage on his head needed changing.

She turned and tiptoed back to Chesny. "See, he's asleep, so you can go ahead and check out the secret room."

Chesny crossed her arms over her ample bosom. "I ain't goin' nowheres—leastwise not unless you go, too."

Hannah rolled her eyes and strode from the room. Downstairs in the dining room, she stopped in front of a sideboard that ofttimes when she visited as a child with her parents had been covered with food. Her hand grazed across the smooth wood of the elegantly carved sideboard, and for a moment she lost herself in the memories.

Those had been enjoyable times when she'd played with the Reed children. She'd been the youngest child. Jamie and Cooper were both older than her and Michael, though Coop was only three years her senior.

She glanced around, making sure no one other than Chesny saw her; then she crossed the room to a pantry that sat between the dining room and the stairs to the kitchen on the first floor. She reached her hand behind a large crock and found the lever that opened the door of the secret room.

She pushed on a wide board, and the door swung back. The opening was much smaller than she remembered. Glancing behind her, she caught Chesny's eye. "Do Maisy and Leta know about this room?"

Chesny nodded. "They do."

"We're going to need a lantern." Hannah studied the opening. Her stranger would have to turn sideways to get in. She hoped moving him again wouldn't be a mistake.

But then, she could hardly take a chance that those men might find him and finish the job she was certain they had started.

Back upstairs, she studied the sleeping man. His politeness and gentleness in the face of so much pain impressed her. She wondered if he had a family who worried about him. A mother and father. A special lady friend or wife. Suddenly it dawned on her there was something else she could do to help this stranger in need. She could pray.

She bowed her head. "Dear Lord, why would anyone want to hurt this man? I know a blow to the head and broken ribs can be serious. Please watch over him and heal his body. Give me wisdom to know how to treat his wounds, and if those men are after him, Lord, please don't let them find him."

❧

He awoke to the sound of ripping fabric. The young woman—Miss Madison—stood at his feet, tearing a large piece of cloth into smaller pieces.

"You came back." He smiled, stinging his lips.

"Did you think I'd forget about you?"

He shrugged. "Where is your friend?"

"She left this morning on her father's vessel, bound for Charleston."

"Ah well, I'm glad you're here and not her."

Miss Madison's brows lifted as if in chastisement. She turned away, but not before he caught the tiniest of smiles teasing the corners of her lips. She walked to the window and stared out. "You should not say such things."

"Why not? I'm simply speaking the truth. Your friend was obviously put off being in the same room with me, where you graciously tended my wounds with care even though you could have easily assigned one of your servants to do the task." If anyone had ever touched him so tenderly, he couldn't remember. He winced. What a shame it would be to forget something like that.

What else was he not remembering?

He stared up at the ceiling, searching the vast emptiness of his mind. How could he have lived to be a grown man but not know anything of his past?

Miss Madison's servant bustled through the door, carrying a tray. The scent of eggs and ham drifted toward him. His stomach hollered for attention. He attempted to sit up, but a sharp pain in his side shoved him back to the bed. He sucked in a ragged breath.

Miss Madison rushed to his bedside. "What's wrong?"

"Nothing."

The servant stepped to her side and scowled. "You should'a waited on me, Miz Hannah."

He eyed the woman and her servant. It seemed odd for the black woman to be talking to her mistress in such a manner, but it didn't seem to bother Miss Madison.

"Don't you think we should move him before he eats?" Miss Madison glanced at her servant.

"Move me?"

"We. . .uh. . .had an encounter with some ruffians this morning." Miss Madison wrung her hands together, her pretty face puckered with worry. "They were looking for a man who resembled you."

"Me?" Who would be after him? What had he done? He pressed his palms against his forehead. Why couldn't he remember?

Miss Madison gently pulled his hand down. "Don't fret. It won't help things."

He glared up at her. "How would you feel if you knew nothing about who you were, not even your name? I don't know if I have a family who's worried about me or if I'm totally alone in the world. And now you say someone may be hunting for me. I may be putting you in danger by simply being in your home." He blew out a frustrated breath.

"We're prepared for that. There's a special hiding place in this home, and that's where we're moving you."

"But first, you needs to eat up and get some strength in them legs of yo's." The Negro woman set the food tray on a nearby table that held a lamp.

"Do you think you can sit up if we help you?" Miss Madison smiled, her beautiful blue eyes lighting up, and he felt he could do just about anything to make her grin again. He nodded.

"Wonderful. Chesny, if you'll reach across the bed and take hold of his right hand, I'll help lift his shoulders. Maybe we won't put too much pressure on his ribs that way."

The servant eyed him and looked as if she would argue with her mistress, but then she reached across the bed and held out her hand. Miss Madison bent down and slid an arm behind his shoulders. In spite of the older woman watching him like a mother bear, he tilted his head slightly and sniffed Miss Madison's sweet scent. Would her skin be as soft to touch as it looked?

A yank on his arm brought him back to his senses. He glanced up to meet Chesny's narrowed gaze. "You'd best hurry and eat 'fo' them men come for you."

"Are you ready?" Miss Madison's cheek was pleasingly close to his, but this time he kept his head properly facing forward.

"Yes ma'am."

"All right then. Just take it carefully. I don't want to hurt you any more than you have already been."

Bracing for the unwanted pain he knew was coming, he took as deep a breath as was possible with his chest tied up tighter than a woman's corset. With a heave, he hoisted himself up, with one lady pushing and the other pulling. Every little movement sent pain resonating from his head to his toes. No, come to think of it, his toes were about the only part of his body that didn't hurt.

He finally sat up with his legs hanging off the side of the bed. Fighting the dizziness that made the room tilt on its axis, he closed his eyes and leaned forward. Miss Madison's firm grip on his shoulder offered him support as he struggled to regain his balance. He concentrated on a mental picture of Miss Madison's golden hair and kind blue eyes. After a few moments, he opened his eyes. The room slowly came back into focus.

The woman's steadying hand remained on his shoulder. "Are you all right now? If I let go, you won't fall, will you?"

"He ain't gonna fall, not so long as I's got ahold of him."

The servant released his hand but stood so close he could have leaned against her for support if he was of a mind to. But he wasn't. Now if that had been Miss Madison. . .

"I'm fine." He spat out the words a bit harsher than he'd planned.

"If'n you's so fine, then haul yo'self over to that table and start eatin'."

He glanced at the servant's stern glare with his one good eye and couldn't help smiling. She sure was cocky for a slave, but he liked her for it and for her protectiveness where Miss Madison was concerned. "Yes ma'am. I'll do that, just as soon as my head stops spinning like the wheel of a ship that's lost its helmsman in a storm."

Much to his surprise, the woman's features softened. "You ketch a lot more flies with molasses than you does with vinegar."

Miss Madison pulled the chair out from under the small table and hurried back to his side. "Do you think you've sailed on a ship before? It sure sounds like you know something about them from the analogy you used."

He stared up at her, searching the shadowy recesses of his mind. Did he know something about ships? If he did, his mind was keeping it a secret. He shrugged one shoulder. "Wish I knew."

Her bright expression dimmed. He hated disappointing her. "Well, you'll remember one of these days. I'm certain."

For now, he'd have to rely on her faith that he'd get better, because he had little of his own.

He stood and was surprised to see that the pain in his side was less severe. The scent of the food drew him to the table. He picked up the plate and stood at the window, shoveling in the delicious meal. He could almost feel the strength returning to his body.

He stared down at the manicured gardens, laden with color. Beyond them stretched a wide green lawn with a creek off to the right and a white gazebo. "You certainly have a nice home here."

"It's not actually my home. I live at Madison Gardens, which is the nearest plantation. The Reed family lives here. They've been gone for a while but will be returning soon. I'm overseeing the cleanup here. I want to make sure everything is in order when the family comes back. They suffered a tragedy of late."

He swallowed the bite of biscuit covered in sweet, creamy butter; then he took a swig of his coffee and glanced at her. "I'm sorry."

She smiled up at him, her eyes sad. He wondered what had happened but didn't feel it was his place to ask. He scraped the plate and shoved the last bite into his mouth. How long had it been since he'd tasted anything so good? "My compliments to the cook."

Chesny nodded. "I'll let Leta know you enjoyed her cookin'."

"So, where's this clandestine room?" He didn't like the idea of hiding, but if keeping his presence secret would ensure the women's safety, he'd cooperate.

"Downstairs. If you're ready, we'll help you."

"I think I can get there on my own. Just show me the way."

Chesny picked up the tray of food and carried it toward the door. She shook her head, cast a glance back at him, and he thought he heard her mutter something about stubborn men. Alone again with Miss Madison, he gazed down at her. Wispy curls as golden as corn silk. Deep blue eyes that rivaled the color of the ocean on a sunny day. And skin so creamy that his fingers ached to touch it.

She nibbled on her lower lip in an intriguing manner that stirred his senses. He swallowed hard.

"Are you certain you're up to walking on your own?"

He was most likely a fool to refuse her assistance, knowing that meant he could put his arm around her and hold her close to his side, but he wanted her to see him as a man and not just her patient. "I'll be fine."

"All right, but if you start getting faint, let me know, and I'll help you."

He was getting weaker already, but he wasn't sure if it was from being on his feet so soon after receiving his wounds or because of her nearness. He nodded, pushed away from the wall, and walked across the room. His head swirled, and the doorway blurred into two. He grabbed hold of the doorframe to steady himself.

Miss Madison hurried to his side. "Do you need to sit for a moment?"

He shook his head, immediately sorry. Summoning up all the strength left in his body, he held one arm against his side and angled for the stairway across the wide parlor. He made it to the railing and gazed down the cavern of steps. The wide opening darkened then came back into focus. His breakfast threatened to escape from his belly.

Miss Madison stepped to his side. "If you don't mind, I'd feel better helping you downstairs. Head wounds like yours can cause dizziness, and the last thing you need is to stumble and fall down the stairs."

As much as he hated admitting it, he needed her help. And since he did, he might as well enjoy the moment. He nodded. She paused and stared up at him, as if unsure now about touching him.

He offered a smile to calm her nerves. "It's all right. I don't bite—at least I don't believe I do."

She grinned and stepped closer. "I'm glad to know that. I was very worried."

She placed her arm around his waist and his arm encircled her shoulders, which seemed far too thin to support his weight. He leaned against the stair railing as much as possible, and with her next to him, the journey down was not all unpleasant.

But when she showed him the door to the secret room, he balked. The small, dark opening reminded him of another place he'd been, but he couldn't quite grab hold of the image in his mind. All he knew was that it wasn't a good place. And it had rats. He pressed his hand on the doorframe and refused to go farther. "I—I can't go in there."

Miss Madison gazed up at him, her chin almost resting against his chest. "Why not? It's just a room. The opening is a bit dark, but there's a lantern once you get around the corner."

His whole body trembled. The memory screamed for release, but the door of his mind kept it locked away. Maybe one day soon he'd locate the key. He closed his eyes. If he remained outside of the room and those men came, he—and the women—could get hurt. He was in no shape to protect them, other than to point a flintlock at someone. The best thing he could do was disappear—and going into the room was his only option for the moment. *Help me, Lord.*

"It's all right. I'll stay with you until you're comfortable. It's really a nice-sized room."

He huffed out a laugh. "It's idiotic, is it not? A man afraid of the dark."

"No, it's not." She tightened her grip around his waist. "You don't know the source of your fear. I'm sure there's a perfectly logical reason you don't want to go in there."

Perhaps she was right. But even if she was, he needed to conquer his fear and face the room.

A loud pounding on the front door made Miss Madison jump. Her eyes widened. "What if it's those men?"

He clenched his jaw and stared into the shadows. A ghost of light danced at the edge of the darkness. He would concentrate on that—reaching the light. Forcing one foot forward, he heard quick footsteps behind him.

"Git yo'self in that room and shut the door. I'll go see who's making all that ruckus out front." Chesny scurried behind him and Miss Madison.

With each shaky step he took into the room, the light grew stronger. He turned the corner and discovered a stairway that led down to a room about six feet long and four feet wide. He swallowed back the bile burning his throat. Smaller than he'd hoped for, but at least the bright lantern illuminated the area with flickers of dancing light on the walls and ceiling.

A narrow cot lined one wall. A table holding the lantern and a pitcher of water and two chairs filled the other wall. A shelf on the far end held a half dozen books and some jars of food. He made for the nearest chair and collapsed into it. He already missed the warmth of the sun shining in the window.

Miss Madison hurried away and shut the door. He thought she'd locked him in, but then he heard the rustle of her dress, and relief washed over him. He could face this if he wasn't alone. But he'd been alone for a long while now, hadn't he?

"Don't look so glum." She squeezed past him and sat in the other chair. "Maybe once those men stop by and don't find you, they'll move on."

He shook his head. "We can't take that chance. I sense they *are* after me, as you said, but I have no clue as to why."

He leaned his elbows on the table and rested his head in his hands. Suddenly, it dawned on him that he'd asked God's help to face his fears. Perhaps God would also heal his mind.

Chapter 6

One man held his shoulders while another man kicked him, over and over, yelling something about some papers. The vision of a woman and man, their faces hidden by shadows, floated across the dark chasm of his mind. There was something familiar about them, and he reached out. Just when they drew close enough that he could almost see their faces, they drifted away again.

Food now. A platter heaping with fried chicken glided into the space the couple had vacated. No. Maybe he actually smelled *real* food. The fogginess of sleep ebbed, but he couldn't quite tell if he was awake or dreaming. He blinked his heavy eyelids and forced them to stay open. Flickers of light sashayed across the walls and low ceiling. His eyes closed again.

A low, rumbling snarl forced its way into his stupor. Suddenly he jerked wide awake and focused on the teeth of a wolf-like creature, standing at the bottom of the stairs. Ignoring the pain clawing at his chest, he scrambled back against the far wall, distancing himself from the creature's hair-raising growl. He blinked again. Was this real or just another nightmare?

Someone at the table moved, and he realized Hannah was still there. She set aside something she was stitching and reached out and tapped the dreadful creature on its snout, effectively silencing it.

"I'm sorry that Buster frightened you. He wandered over from Madison Gardens. One of our workers came over to check on us, and I thought it was a good idea for you to meet him with me present. He can be quite nasty if he happens to cross your path and he doesn't know you." She reached her hand toward him. "If you feed Buster this bit of meat, he'll take a shine to you. His bark is much worse than his bite."

"I don't believe that for a moment." He studied the somewhat calmer beast, then glanced back at Hannah's face. Her warm smile encouraged him. With more than a little trepidation, he took the chunk of chicken from her hand, just as the beast growled again.

"Hush, Buster. This man's our friend. This is Adam."

He jerked his gaze back to Miss Madison. "Adam? That's my name? How did you discover it?"

"I didn't. I made it up. I decided that we need to have something to call you." Her cheeks turned deep red in the glow of the lantern, and she shrugged. "Since you're the first man, except for Israel and Simeon, of course, to come to

149

Reed Springs in ages, and it seems you may have a broken rib or two, I figured it's a good name for you. You do know the first man mentioned in God's Holy Book was named Adam, don't you?"

He nodded his head. The name sounded familiar even though he couldn't remember the story. "I suppose Adam works all right, at least until I remember my real name."

Adam pushed against the wall and managed to sit up. "Come here, Buster." He held the meat out to the beast, wondering if he'd have all his fingers afterward. Based on the stature of the beast standing at the foot of the bed, he felt he had every right to be a bit nervous, but the last thing he wanted was for Hannah to think he was lily-livered.

Adam—the name was growing on him—leaned forward, holding out the meat. The wolf-like animal's gray-and-black head popped up, and he snarled a low, menacing growl. Adam held his breath while the big dog crept toward him. The vicious-looking snout sniffed his hand. Grayish-black ears twitched forward and back, and beady onyx eyes stared him down. Sweat trickled down Adam's temple, but he didn't move an inch. The brute's wet nose touched his hand, and sharp yellow teeth clicked together as the dog cocked its head and snatched the morsel away. Buster gave Adam a final sniff, turned, and trod back up the steps.

"Guess I passed muster, huh?"

"That wasn't so bad, was it?"

He stared at her but didn't comment. Anything he said would make him sound less masculine.

"Do you feel like eating something yourself?"

He reached up, wiping the drops of sweat from his temple. He hoped she hadn't noticed his discomfort. "I swear I've been dreaming about fried chicken. I can even smell it."

Hannah's gentle laughter rippled through the small room. "You're smelling chicken all right, but it's soup, not fried. It's been there on your table for fifteen minutes while I went back upstairs for some blankets. Do you feel like sitting at the table for a while?"

Adam nodded and pushed up from the bed. The simple effort of moving sent daggers of pain radiating throughout his head and chest, but once he was upright, the pain lessened. Leaning back against the wall, he studied Hannah as she scooped up a spoon of soup and held it out to him. His lips tugged into a smile. "If I'd have known I was going to be spoon-fed by such a lovely lady, I'd have stayed abed."

She smiled and lowered her eyes and the spoon. "My apologies. I don't want to baby you, but I also don't want you overdoing things and being sorry later."

He lowered himself into the chair, taking care to keep his torso rigid. He breathed in the delicious scent of the chicken soup, but it was the bowl that snagged his attention the most. Running his finger around the indigo-and-white, rope-like scroll, he grasped at ethereal memories drifting through the haze of his mind. He picked up the bowl and cocked his head, studying the small red flowers clustered against a bed of green leaves.

Hannah leaned forward. The glow of the lantern was reflected in her blue eyes—eyes as deep a blue as the indigo design on the bowl. "Do you recognize that pattern?"

He scrunched his eyes together, grappling for a hold. The memory was there, but the fingers of his mind couldn't latch on to it. Sighing, he set the bowl down. "Perhaps." He flung his hand in the air. "I don't know. I thought it seemed familiar."

Hannah reached across the narrow table. "You realize you've seen this design somewhere, but just can't remember where. That tells me the memories are there and will be revealed soon, but you've got to allow your wounds time to heal." She pulled back her hand and touched the plate holding a half dozen slices of bread. "This is an English pattern that's been in the Reed family for generations. Do you think you might have been in England before?"

He shrugged. "Who knows? I could have been anywhere, for all I know." Hating the self-pity in his voice, he grabbed a slice of bread and dunked it into the soup. The amazing flavors of the soft bread and salty soup teased his tongue. It had been a long time since he'd eaten food this fresh.

The food was delicious, and he devoured it, but what he enjoyed most was the close-up view of his rescuer. Tight spirals of blond hair hung down the sides of Hannah's face where they'd pulled loose from her mobcap. Shorter wisps curled across her forehead in an enticing manner. He wanted to reach out and touch one, but he kept his hands flat against the table.

A sudden thought drew his gaze back to the last of his food. *Do I have a woman somewhere waiting for me to return?*

❧

Hannah sat stiffly in the chair, trying not to stare at her patient. Last night, she had dreamed about him. And today, she kept getting the feeling she'd seen him before. But was that simply because she was getting more familiar with him?

He would be a handsome man when his wounds healed. His injured eye was slightly open today, but it was still purple. The cut on his lip looked better, but more bruises had appeared on his face. He sure didn't complain much. If Michael were in his shoes, he'd be soaking up the pampering and demanding more.

Though she knew little about Adam, she liked him for some reason she couldn't explain.

Footsteps sounded, and then Chesny stopped on the landing. "That boy down there behavin' hisself?"

"Yes ma'am. I am. And thanks for this delicious food. I'm going to be spoiled with all this caring attention I'm getting." He held up his cup of coffee as if in toast to Chesny.

"Ah, you do go on. If'n you needs mo' food, I can fetch you some." Chesny scooted sideways between the table and the cot. She gathered the empty dishes. "You want some mo' soup?"

Adam leaned back stiffly in the chair and patted his stomach. "No thank you, but it was most tasty."

Chesny beamed. "I like a man that know what's good and is grateful fo' it." She trod back up the stairs, humming a tune.

Adam leaned forward. "Why is she leaving us alone?"

Hannah had wondered the same thing. "I don't know except that she must not see you as a threat any longer."

"Good." He tapped the table. "I'm not a danger to any of you. You said this is not your home." Adam swiped his hand through the air. "So tell me about where you do live. It must be nearby since you can go back and forth daily."

"It is. Just a little over a mile. I live on a plantation called Madison Gardens with my parents, Richard and Caroline Madison, and my older brother, Michael. We also have a home in Charleston, where my father has an import/export business, although I tend to stay at the plantation far more than I do the town house."

"Why is that? Seems like a pretty, young woman would want to be closer to her friends and closer to town events like parties and concerts."

Hannah shook her head. "I've always loved living on the estate. Town is noisy and it smells. I do enjoy a party now and then, but not several in a single week like people often have in Charleston."

He nodded. Hannah wondered if he had been to Charleston and knew what she meant, but she kept quiet. If he didn't remember, she didn't want to bring that to mind again. She couldn't imagine how horrible it must be to not remember your family or friends.

"So what's this place? Why do you come here since you don't live here?"

"The barn I found you in belongs to my parents' oldest and dearest friends. Lucas and Heather Reed had two sons that were somewhat close in age to Michael and me. Jamie is older than Cooper by six years, Cooper is just a year older than Michael, and three years older than me." But there were things she couldn't say. Didn't want to say. Such as explaining that Jamie was her fiancé. Or that Cooper was probably dead by now. Still, there were happier times she could tell about. "I remember their dark hair and mischievous grins."

"So are they living in Charleston now?"

Hannah's heart leaped. "Uh. . .no. They're on a trip to England."

Adam scowled and looked lost in thought. What did a person with no memories think about?

"England sounds very familiar. I surely must have been there a time or two."

"It sounds to me like you have a bit of an English accent."

His gaze snapped up and caught hers. "Truly? Do you think so?"

"Perhaps a little, but I doubt that you're from there or your accent would be thicker. With all the tensions between England and America now, it's probably a good thing if you aren't."

He drummed his fingertips on the table and yawned. "What tensions?"

Hannah pressed her lips together, unsure just how much to say. What if he turned out to be a British spy, after all? Could she be endangering her family by talking about the struggles their young nation was still having with England?

She stared at him and somehow deep within knew he could be trusted. She couldn't have explained it to anyone, but she just knew. "There's talk that there may be another war between England and America."

"*Another* war?" His perplexed expression tugged at her heart, but suddenly his countenance brightened. "Yes. We did fight a war—for our independence. Isn't that correct?"

She nodded and smiled. "Yes. And there are Englishmen who still think it a travesty that the lowly colonists were able to defeat mighty Britain." She stood and paced the small area, nearly touching him as she passed by. She'd listened to her father and his friends debate the pros and cons of another conflict with England numerous times.

"England is refusing to trade with American shippers. But the worst thing is that, because Britain lost so many young men during the years of the Revolution and then still others who abdicated to America, they are short sailors for their own ships. They are capturing *our* ships and forcing *our* sailors into service for the king. It's atrocious."

She paced to the stairs and turned back. Adam's elbows rested on the table and his fingers were forked through his dark hair. He glanced up, and all the color had run from his face. She hurried to his side. "I think you need to lie down."

"No." He shot out of the chair then grimaced and grabbed his side. "I—I think I may have been on one of those ships."

She opened her mouth to question him, but a scream upstairs silenced her. She spun around and hurried to the top of the stairs. Adam was right behind her. Hannah lifted her foot to step out of the room, but Adam yanked her back against him and closed the door, leaving only an inch open.

She turned in his arms, ready to scold him. Something was going on, and the servants needed her.

The light from the room illuminated one side of his face, and he held a finger to his lips. "Shh. . ."

Hannah forced herself to stand still and listen, but all she heard was the sound of her pounding heart. Adam's hand still rested across her mouth, but gently, not hurting. His hand was warm against her lips.

A deep voice growled. Glass shattered. Hannah jumped. Adam slid his arm from her mouth, wrapped it around her shoulders, and pulled her against his chest.

She could no longer breathe. Never had she been held in such a manner by a man, other than by her father.

"Where is he? And where is that pretty lady?"

"Nowheres, suh."

Hannah recognized Leta's terrified voice.

Another crash of glass rent the air. "Don't lie to me. Where is that Madison gal? I seen her come over in that buggy this morning."

"I—I don't know, suh. I think she done returned back to her home, I th–think."

"Check the other rooms."

Hannah stiffened at the sound of Boss's voice. Heavy footsteps thudded across the floor in different directions. So, they'd actually come, and if she hadn't moved Adam to the secret room, they would have found him. *Thank You, Lord, for protecting Adam. Please keep the others safe, too.*

Adam quietly closed the door the rest of the way, plunging them into darkness. His warm breath tickled her cheek.

She stepped back, but her spine connected with the wall.

"Let's stay right here. We don't want to chance the stairs squeaking and giving us away." His soft whispers teased her ear, sending her stomach into spasms.

"I—"

"Shhh. . .no talking." Adam's hand found her mouth again, but instead of covering it, he ran his finger across her lower lip, effectively stealing away her breath, her thoughts, and any words she might utter. Her heart thrummed in a way it never had when Jamie was near. He was always gentle and considerate, but he'd never touched her in such a provocative manner, as if she were someone special. He'd never even kissed her. Yes, he was a good friend, but was friendship enough to build a marriage on?

Chapter 7

Buster's low-pitched growl yanked Hannah back to the events at hand. Footsteps came in their direction, and a man cried out. Buster's fierce snarls nearly drowned out the man's frantic howls. She wanted to jerk open the door and help her dog, but she didn't dare. Surely the men would leave if they didn't find what they wanted.

A gun exploded on the other side of the wall, and Hannah jumped. Buster yelped; then things grew eerily quiet. Adam tightened his grip around her, as if cradling her from the danger. Tears stung her eyes. Had they shot her dog?

Scuffling sounded just outside the hidden door. She wanted to run out and check on Chesny and the other workers. She wanted to see if Buster was hurt and needed tending. She wanted to stay just where she was, nestled in Adam's arms.

Thumps and thuds echoed from the other side of the wall. Someone muttered a curse. For long minutes all she heard was the sound of Adam's breath, his heartbeat, and a ringing in her ears from straining to hear what was happening outside their cocoon.

She prayed for each of the workers and for Buster. *Don't let those men harm them.*

Adam's grip on her lessened, and he backed down the first step, putting a gap between them. She touched her warm cheeks, suddenly embarrassed by her behavior. What was she doing clinging to Adam like that?

She crossed her arms. Yes, she'd been afraid. All her life she'd lived a quiet, fairly sheltered life and had never encountered bad men bent on hurting someone before. Both her parents were loving, kindhearted people. She wished her father or Michael had been present to chase those men away, but she would have to be the strong one today if things had gone bad on the other side of the wall. One day soon she'd be mistress of this plantation, and she had to have gumption and grit to keep it running. Things wouldn't always go smoothly.

She stiffened at the sound of hurried footsteps. The door rattled, and Adam reached out and squeezed her hand, then stepped up in front of her. She peered around his arm. Either they were caught or someone had come to inform them of the situation.

Chesny appeared as the door fell back. "Is you two all right in here?"

"Us?" Hannah shoved Adam back against the wall and squeezed past him.

"Is everyone safe? Is Buster hurt bad?"

"We's all fine. Israel took that beast of yo's out to the barn. He was winged, but not too bad. Them men's gone, so you can come out if'n you wants."

Hannah slipped past Chesny. Spots of blood still pooled on the wooden floor. She glanced at her maid.

"Some of that belongs to that dog and some of it to the scoundrel he bit." She looked up at Adam. "They's looking fo' you, from the sound of it. What'd you do?"

Adam glanced past her to Hannah and leaned against the doorjamb. He looked exhausted. "I wish I knew."

"Where's Maisy and Leta?" Hannah asked.

"Maisy's upstairs straightening what them men messed up when they's searching fo' him. Leta's out helpin' Israel."

"I need to check on Buster. Could you clean this up?" Hannah motioned to the blood.

Chesny nodded. "That's just what I was fixin' to do." She bustled to the back of the house and disappeared around the corner.

Hannah stepped closer to Adam. "You should go lie down and rest."

"I should do something to help."

She shook her head. "It's too soon. You took a fierce clobbering, and you need to regain your strength. Besides, those men might still be keeping watch on the house. If they see you outside or through one of the windows, they'll come back, and next time they might not let you live." She didn't want to mention that the men might also not be too happy that Chesny and the others had lied to them.

Adam blew out a heavy sigh. "All right, but when I'm better, I want to do something around here to help out. I'm used to pulling my own weight—not taking charity."

Hannah lifted her chin. "It's not charity to save a man's life."

"I just don't like hiding behind a bunch of women's skirts or being in that cave." He motioned toward the secret room.

"Well, those *skirts* and that *cave* may have just saved your life for a second time."

He held her gaze for a long moment, then turned and ambled back down the stairs. She watched for a moment and shut the door. She supposed she wouldn't like being stuck in the hole alone either, but he could at least show a little gratitude.

She spun away, determined to check on her dog and put the mysterious stranger from her mind, but with each step she took, his scent traveled with her. The feel of his arms around her warmed her from the inside out. Would hugging Jamie feel as. . .wonderful?

As much as she wished it were so, she didn't think it would.

Adam trod down the stairs, back into his dark pit. The dank, dreary hole reminded him of another place—not a good place—but he couldn't latch on to where that place was. Weary beyond belief, he stopped at the table and downed the last of the chilled coffee. He set the mug down and started to turn away when Hannah's stitching caught his eye.

He swiped his hands on his pants, then picked up the ecru fabric and held it up to the light. The sampler had an intricate, scrolling, ivy and floral border on three sides. At the bottom was a house resembling the three-story, redbrick home he was staying in, surrounded by trees and more flowers. Could the houses be one and the same?

Above the house, Hannah had expertly stitched a Bible verse: "IF A MAN SAY, I LOVE GOD, AND HATETH HIS BROTHER, HE IS A LIAR: FOR HE THAT LOVETH NOT HIS BROTHER WHOM HE HATH SEEN, HOW CAN HE LOVE GOD WHOM HE HATH NOT SEEN?" I JOHN 4:20.

Below the verse in larger cursive letters was the saying, NEXT TO GOD, FAMILY IS. . .

He blew out a breath and set the unfinished stitchwork on the table. Whom was she making the sampler for? Her parents? A friend who was getting married?

Holding his side, he slowly lowered himself to the cot and lay down. With his arm behind his head, he closed his eyes. He ought to be helping set things in order upstairs, but the truth of the matter was he felt like an eighty-year-old man. His head pounded in a steady rhythm. He pressed his fingertips into the indentation just above his neck and massaged it, receiving some relief. He yawned.

NEXT TO GOD, FAMILY IS. . .

What?

Next to God, family is. . .

Most important.

Adam's eyes shot open. Next to God, family is most important.

How could he possibly know what Hannah's sampler would say? Was his mind just searching for words that fit? If so, why had those particular ones come to mind?

He had heard them before. He knew them in the core of his being. Adam thumped his chest. He didn't know his real name or where he was from. He didn't know who his parents were or if he was married, but in his heart, he knew those words.

"Next to God, family is most important."

Hannah walked toward the barn, struggling to get her wayward thoughts under control, and concentrated on thinking positive things about Jamie.

The Reed boys had been good friends as children. She'd played more with Cooper because he was closer to Michael and her in age, but she would soon be marrying Jamie.

She hadn't seen him since he was home for Christmas. He'd gone back to Charleston, to his work at the Reed shipping yard, with the promise to return a few weeks before the wedding, but when word came that Cooper was missing, they hopped one of his father's clipper ships and went to England. Would Jamie return in time or would the wedding have to be postponed?

She couldn't help wondering how England's embargo against American products had hurt his business. She supposed he could still build ships, but fewer people would want to purchase them if they were unable to sail them without fear of them being confiscated by His Majesty's navy.

A high-pitched whine drew her back to the task at hand. She slipped through the open barn door and searched for Israel. Maisy stood leaning against one of the stalls, and she found Israel on his knees, stitching up Buster's hip. The dog gazed up with pain-filled eyes and whined. Hannah hurried to his side.

"Don't you be movin' none, dog. I know it hurts," Israel said.

"Oh you poor thing." Hannah dropped down into the straw, heedless of her dress.

Maisy straightened. "Oh Miz Hannah, let me fetch you a blanket to sit on."

She waved her hand. "Thank you, but I'm fine. Buster may have well saved some of our lives today. The least I can do is comfort him."

"You's a good woman. Dat Jamie lad is lucky to be marryin' you."

Hannah forced a smile. "Thank you."

Ever since she was little, her mother had planned for her to marry Jamie. Arranged marriages were a tradition among her mother's ancestors, so her mother had said. Why had Hannah never questioned her upcoming marriage before Adam came along?

She heaved a sigh, and Buster licked her hand. She smiled, petting the dog's head. Wistful thinking wouldn't change anything. Jamie was coming back soon, and they'd be getting married. He was a good man who would provide for her well, and he had a strong belief in God.

Israel snipped the silk thread and sat back. He patted Buster's side, then reached for a bottle of whiskey and poured some over the wound. Buster yelped and snapped at the man, but then the dog licked Israel's hand.

The caretaker chuckled. "Dat dog, he knows I'ma just tryin' to help him."

Israel stood and pressed his hand to his back. "He be fine in a few days, Miz Hannah."

"Thank you so much for tending to him."

Israel nodded, then shuffled to the stall gate. He glanced at Maisy. "Could you give me and Miz Hannah a minute alone?"

Maisy's gaze shot to Hannah, but she nodded and hurried from the barn. Hannah patted Buster's head again and stood. "Is something wrong?"

Israel rubbed his chin and rocked from foot to foot. The man had worked on the Reeds' estate for as long as she could remember. That the Reeds left him in charge when they were gone spoke a lot about the quiet man's character.

"Meb'be it's just an ol' black man's foolishness, but they's somethin' familiar about dat patient of yours. I keep gettin' a feeling in my gut dat I's seen him 'afore."

Hannah rushed forward. "Me, too! But I can't for the life of me figure out who he is. Do you think he did something bad since those men are after him?"

Israel looked deep in thought for a moment, then shook his head. "No, Miz Hannah. I don't. Dem men's what came after him is bad men, so that says to me our stranger, he must be a good man."

Hannah leaned her arms on the stall gate. "But what if he was part of their gang and stole from them? That could be why they're after him. Or perhaps he was a witness to a crime."

Her thoughts ran rampant again. She didn't want to think badly of Adam, but she had to keep her mind open to all possibilities.

Instantly, shame surged through her. How could she think badly of a man who was so gentle and polite? A man who stirred her and made her dream things an engaged woman had no business dreaming?

Israel shrugged. "I'll keep a'thinkin' on it, and meb'be it'll come to me."

Hannah peeked back at Buster. The dog was asleep with his head across his paws. "Please, Lord, heal Buster."

She closed the gate, hoping to keep the dog corralled long enough that he'd heal well; then she strode out of the barn.

She peered up at the beautiful blue sky. Soft clouds floated like tufts of cotton in the air at harvesttime. How could things be so peaceful after the morning's events?

Her feet headed for the house, but at the last minute, she turned and walked out to the garden. Spring flowers in a multitude of colors surrounded her and teased her nose with their sweet scents as she strolled the stone path. Her eyes gravitated to her favorites—the azaleas in pink, red, and white blossoms that covered their shrubs at the far end of the garden; an arched trellis blanketed with wisteria, the vivid purple clusters of flowers hanging from the arch reminding her of grapes. She sat on the bench under the arch and breathed in a deep breath.

She arranged her skirts to cover her ankles and peered up at the sky again through the canopy of flowers. Yellow butterflies flittered around the spectacular blooms. "What do I do, Lord? Why am I suddenly questioning my marriage to Jamie when I've never done so before?"

Her thoughts shot to Adam. Could God have sent him there to show her that her feelings could be so easily swayed? Was she a wanton woman to be engaged to one man and attracted to another?

She buried her face in her hands. "I don't know what to do, Lord. Reveal Your will to me. Please, Lord."

Chapter 8

"King me!" Hannah ordered, unable to hold back a victorious grin. "That's two kings for me and only one for you." Perhaps two days of playing checkers with Adam had finally improved her ability.

He grinned. "I'm not too worried. You don't exactly have an intimidating record so far. What is it? Twelve to nothing, I believe?"

Hannah glanced across the table. The smug, lopsided smile gracing Adam's face only heightened her desire to win this game. "I do believe it's your turn, *sir*."

After a few moments of studying the board for her next move, Hannah began to wonder why Adam was taking so long to make his. Usually he moved his man right on the heels of hers. She looked up to find him staring at her, and her heart turned a flip. Adam's compelling gaze captured hers.

"Do you have any idea how beautiful your eyes are?" he said, after a moment.

Hannah blinked. She opened her mouth to respond, but her shocked brain refused to communicate with her mouth. Like a driver who'd lost hold of the reins and let the horses run free, she struggled to regain control of her addled brain.

Adam glanced down, and his hand snaked out, obviously taking full advantage of her bewilderment. *Plop! Plop! Plop!* He jumped three of her men, including one of her kings. A triumphant gleam danced in his good eye. "Not too shabby for a one-eyed sick man. Huh?"

"You beast!" Hannah smacked the table, causing the remaining pieces to dance in place on the board. "No fair distracting me. Perhaps I should blacken your other eye so I'll have a fairer advantage." Hannah leaned back in her chair and crossed her arms to avoid the temptation. Losing so many games to him brought out a competitive side of her she never knew existed—and she didn't like it.

"Aw, come on, Miss Madison, you don't really think I'm a beast, do you? I can't help it if I'm a good draughts player." Amusement flickered in the gaze that met hers. After a moment, Adam's grin faded as he reached behind his neck and rubbed it. He twisted his head from side to side as if he were trying to shake out the kinks.

Hannah's eyes narrowed, and she wondered if this was another ploy to distract her. She enjoyed sparring with Adam as much as he seemed to enjoy it. She pushed her last king forward and Adam immediately countered.

Placing her elbow on the table, she leaned her cheek against her palm.

"Why is it you're so good at checkers, anyway?"

"Well, that's the strange thing. I can remember how to play draughts, but I can't tell you where I learned to play the game or who I played with before."

"And why do you call it *draughts*? Isn't that what the game is called in England?"

He glanced up and to the side, a movement she knew meant he was trying to remember something. He winced and ducked his head, then began massaging his forehead with his fingertips. Leaning forward with his elbows resting on the table, Adam laid his face in his hands.

"Are you still getting headaches?"

"Yeah, but mostly only when I try hard to remember things."

"Don't worry about it, Adam. I'm sure it will all come back in God's timing." She couldn't imagine what it would feel like to be totally alone, dependent on strangers, and unable to remember her family or where her home was. Family was so important, especially when you lived on an isolated plantation. How could she bear it if she couldn't see her family frequently. The only time she was separated from them was when her parents went to Charleston and she chose to stay at home on the plantation.

Perhaps that's why she accepted marriage to Jamie so easily. At least she'd always be close to home.

Not so good of a reason to get married. She stood, and Adam shot up from his chair. Hannah walked around the table, stopping beside him. "Whenever Michael or I have a headache, we massage one another's necks. May I try and see if it will help your headache?"

He stared down, his eyes holding a special look that he reserved only for her. As usual, it stole her breath away. He stared at her for a moment, then nodded and sat down again. He laid his face against his arm on the table. Hannah gently kneaded her fingertips into his shoulders and then up the back of his neck for a few minutes. "Perhaps we should call it quits for a while? What do you think?"

"Aw, you're just afraid you're going to lose—again."

She smiled at the playful tease in his voice.

"I'm worried that you're overdoin' it. You should be resting more." She continued to massage his neck and solid shoulders. Her fingers splayed through the long, dark hair draping his neck. *Such nice thick hair he has.*

"I'm tired of resting. I need to be up and moving around. Two days of being in bed is making me stiff."

"I have an idea. Why don't you lie down and rest your head a bit, and I'll read another chapter of *Robinson Crusoe*. And if you behave, perhaps I could ask Israel to take you outside for a short walk after the sun sets. How does that sound?"

Hannah stopped rubbing as Adam lifted his head and turned around in his chair to look at her. Grimacing, he grabbed his side and turned back around.

"Careful now. You shouldn't be twisting your body like that until your ribs heal."

Adam used both hands to slowly push himself up. He exhaled a loud breath. "I feel like an old man."

You sure don't look like an old man, she wanted to say, but she kept silent. "Uh—you'll be feeling better in a few more days." She reached out to help him back to the cot and looked up into his face. His tender expression took her breath away, and she thought her knees would surely give out any second.

He turned toward her and slowly reached out, cupping her cheek with his hand. If she had a breath left before, it was definitely gone now. "Hannah, I can't say I'm thankful for the attack on me, but I did meet you as a result of it, and for that, I'll be forever grateful. You've been such an encouragement to me. You know you saved my life, most likely."

Hannah stood mesmerized. He'd never used her Christian name before, and she loved the sound of it on his lips. Adam's gaze roamed her face, and she felt her cheeks flame when it rested on her lips. Goodness! He looked as if he wanted to kiss her. What would she do if he did? *Oh dear Lord, I actually think I want him to. Forgive me, Father.*

Guilt instantly assailed her, and a heaviness centered in her chest. She broke his gaze and ducked her head. *How can I be standing here wishing Adam would kiss me when I know good and well that I'm going to be married to another man soon? It's just plain improper.* No wonder Chesny didn't want them to be alone.

She opened her eyes in time to catch a brief look of disappointment flash across Adam's face. A solemn mask of reserve replaced the tenderness that had just permeated it. He ran his fingers along her jaw, and his hand dropped listlessly to his side. Hannah felt as if he'd read her thoughts. Somehow she had to tread very carefully until Adam was well enough to leave. She couldn't lose her heart to this man who'd already become her closest friend. The thought of him one day walking out of her life for good brought her more than a small measure of anxiety.

"I'll take you up on that reading, if you don't mind." Adam walked over to the cot and slowly sat down. He let out a deep sigh and leaned back against the wall with his eyes closed.

Hannah watched him for a moment, wondering what was going through his mind. Did he interpret her distancing herself from him as not caring?

She moved over to the table and turned up the lamp. The dimmer lighting was all right for playing a board game, but not for reading. She glanced up the stairs, wondering what time it was. It wouldn't be good to head for home after darkness set in. Things would be much easier if Chesny would allow her to stay the night at Reed Springs while she cared for Adam, but the woman flat refused to budge on that issue.

Hannah tugged the book off the shelf on the wall and sat in the chair Adam had vacated. She would read quickly.

Adam reached up to touch his ear, which he was certain must be beet red. *What a fool I am! I actually wanted to kiss Hannah.*

He knew she was only doing her Christian duty to aid a stranger in need. Yet he couldn't deny his overwhelming attraction to her. Was it wrong for him to be so drawn to her? She was compassionate, gentle, and pretty. But he was fooling himself to believe a woman like her could actually fall for a man who didn't even know his own name.

Wrestling with his confusion, his heart wrenched at the memory of Hannah's expression moments earlier. Her fingers biting into his neck, massaging the tenseness out, had felt like a little piece of heaven. She had encouraged him and looked as if she couldn't tear her eyes away from his. He mistakenly thought she actually wanted him to kiss her. Then suddenly, a look of sheer panic engulfed her face. Women were so hard to decipher.

Adam jumped at the sound of the book slamming shut. With remorse, he realized he hadn't heard a single word Hannah had just read.

"Sorry. I didn't mean to startle you. Were you sleeping?"

"No, just resting."

"It's time I was going. We need to get home before the sun sets."

"What about the walk you promised me? I could do with a heavy dose of sunshine. Besides Maisy or Israel, you're the only other living creature I see all day. You also said you'd tell me about your family and your plantation."

Hannah laid the book on the table and smoothed her skirt. "I suppose I could be persuaded to stay a short while longer. What is it you want to know about my family?"

"I don't know." Adam rubbed his hand along his whiskery chin, creating a bristly noise. "Umm, how long have you lived on. . .what is it called?"

She smiled, and a butterfly danced in Adam's belly. "Madison Gardens. I guess you'd have to say I've lived there my whole life, except for our regular treks to Charleston. I was born on the plantation."

"Guess it's in your blood then. You just have one brother and no sisters?"

"No, actually I also have an older brother and sister, Kit and Jane. My father and Lucas Reed found them in the woods before Michael was born and adopted them. Jane's married, and Kit is off sailing on one of our father's ships, so Michael is the only one still at home. He's a great brother—don't take me wrong. I love him, but he's such a tease."

"Must be nice to have such a large family. Didn't you mention being friends with the people who live here?"

Hannah nodded. "Jamie and Cooper Reed. Our families visited one another quite often when I was young. We still do, in fact."

Jamie. That name sounded strangely familiar. "I remember you told me about them the other day, when you were doctoring me, I believe." He reached up and tugged on the bandage around his head.

"They're the family who used to live here. Jamie, the oldest son, and Kit were always playin' tricks on Coop, Michael, and me. It used to make me so mad."

Adam's eyes narrowed. *Jamie.* She'd mentioned that name several times now, and he'd begun to notice an odd look in her expression that wasn't there when she talked about the others. Was there more to their relationship than just friendship? He definitely needed to pry more information out of her concerning this Jamie fellow.

Adam sat up. "So, tell me more about Jamie and—what's his brother's name?"

"Jamie and Cooper. I played with them from the time I could sit up. But like I said, Michael and I mostly played with Cooper and helped him with his chores."

"So you never ran around with Jamie?"

Hannah gave him a curious stare. "Well, certainly. From the stories my parents tell, Jamie was quite enamored with me when I was younger and would carry me around. Our families did many things together, for one reason or another, mainly because they're our closest neighbors." She cocked her head. "Why did you want to know?"

"Just curious, I suppose." He felt the need to change the subject before his curiosity got him in trouble. "Have your parents always lived here?" He flicked a fly off his leg. "Surely, you get together with your other neighbors at times. Don't you?" The fly buzzed his face. He swatted his hand in the air to shoo it away and inwardly sighed when it flew up the stairway. "Why is your slave so bossy?"

Hannah straightened; her lips puckered. "Slavery is abominable. The Madisons do not own slaves, and neither do the Reeds. Our workers are employees who are paid a salary and treated as all humans deserve to be."

He held up one palm. "My apologies. I wasn't aware of that, but it is an admirable stand to take, and one I'm sure is not overly popular among most Southerners."

She deflated as quickly as a hen drenched in a downpour. Hannah sighed. "That's true, and probably the reason I don't have more friends."

"Is that partly the reason you stay on the plantation when most women your age would much prefer to be in Charleston?"

She ducked her head and nodded. "Partly, I suppose. Some people can be so unkind. But I do prefer the country life much more than city life." She folded up her stitching and placed it in the cloth bag that she carried it in, looking a bit forlorn.

Touched by the loneliness in her eyes, Adam carefully scooted to the edge of the cot and sat with his elbows on his knees. His hands, clasped together, were mere inches away from hers. "Have you never had any close friends other than the Reeds?"

"No, not really." Hannah shook her head. "I used to spend a lot of time around the barn and watch the men train the new horses, but Dad made me quit after I got older. He said it wasn't proper for a young lady to be spending so much time with so many males."

"Sounds like a wise man."

Hannah looked over at him as if she were checking to see if he were teasing. He held her gaze steadily without flinching.

"I have some friends like Ruthie—the girl who was here the day we found you—but they all live in Charleston. Occasionally one of them will come and stay a week or two, but most find it boring here." She smiled sweetly; then her gaze darted away.

Adam's heart was touched by her vulnerability. She was so cheerful most of the time that he hadn't stopped to consider she might have problems of her own. He'd been so caught up in his own pain that he hadn't thought about hers. Reaching out, he laid his hand over hers and gave it a gentle squeeze. "It must get lonely sometimes."

"Oh, I don't know." Her brave smile didn't reach her eyes. "It's all I've ever known. I remember being lonely whenever Jamie and Cooper left with their parents to go to Charleston. My father ofttimes traveled with them." She offered him a benign smile. "But I wouldn't trade my life for city life, even if I had hundreds of friends. I love horses and all kinds of animals. I wish I had the freedom to hop in a saddle and ride astride like a man." Her cheeks turned a becoming red. She pulled her hands from his and fiddled with the string of her bag. "There are times I wish I'd been born a boy."

Adam wondered if the subject made her nervous because she was babbling again. "I'm certainly glad you weren't. You're way too pretty to be a boy." Adam couldn't hold back his grin when she blushed again.

"Would you kindly stop saying that?"

"What? That you're pretty? No, I can't, because it's the truth."

Hannah, discomfort written all over her face, jumped to her feet, her chair banging against the wall. "I think I'll be going now and just leave you to yourself."

The cot creaked as Adam slowly stood up. "Hannah, are you mad at me?"

Her head hung down, and she shook it slowly.

"Hannah," he pleaded.

When she didn't look at him, he reached out with two fingers and tilted her head up. "Hannah, you're beautiful, inside and out, and you deserve to have someone tell you that. You shouldn't be embarrassed about the way God made you. But if it makes you uncomfortable, I'll try to keep my opinion to myself. Though it might be hard to do." He smiled, hoping to reassure her. "Please, let me be your friend."

With a hesitant smile, Hannah glanced up at him. "We *are* friends."

"Good." He grinned and reached his hand out to her. "How about that walk?"

Timidly, Hannah slipped her small hand into his. "All right, but there's only time for a short one. I don't want you to be overdoin' it, and Chesny will grumble all the way home if we don't set out before dark."

They ambled through the house, and he stopped on more than one occasion to inspect something that seemed familiar. Even the floor plan felt recognizable. Had he been in this home before?

He spied an open set of double doors and hurried across the room. He had a need to inhale some fresh air. Stepping into the sunlight that shone in the entryway, he lifted up his face, allowing the fingers of warmth to caress it. Good thing he'd come up when he had or the sun would have sunk below the horizon. "I smell the flowers from the garden."

Hannah stopped beside him. "You shouldn't be standing out in the open. What if those men are keeping watch? They could see you."

He wanted to say he didn't care. But he did. If those men saw him and came here again, they might hurt the women for harboring him. In the condition he was in, he wouldn't be able to fend off one man, let alone three. He heaved a sigh and stepped back into the shadows of the house. At least he was out of that dungeon.

"Fine. Allow me a few minutes to escort a lovely lady around the house; then I'll head back to my cage." He held out his elbow to her.

She slipped her arm through and walked beside him. "It really isn't a cage, you know. It's meant to protect you."

"I know, but I'd rather be back in that room where I can see the sky out the window and enjoy the light."

She patted his arm. "It's just for a little while. Israel is keeping watch around here and has the field workers also keeping an eye open for the men. Hopefully if they come back, we'll get some warning."

Adam noticed a picture of a ship and crossed the room. He stood, hands behind his back, and gazed at it. "That's a fine schooner there."

Hannah stared at him for a moment. "How do you know it's a schooner?"

He pointed to the sails. "A schooner has two or more masts with sails fore and aft."

"I know what a schooner is, but how is it you know?"

He turned to face her. "I've sailed on one before—with my father."

Hannah clutched his arm. "You remember your father? What's his name?"

Hope poured through his chest as he caught on to her meaning. He'd remembered something of his childhood. He closed his eyes—willing—struggling to grasp hold of the image of a tall man. . .just out of reach. A sharp pain speared his head, and he scowled.

"Stop, Adam. The memories seem to return when you're relaxed, not when you're fighting for them."

She was right, but he was so close. He almost saw his father's image, but his family name remained as elusive as his chances at winning Hannah's heart.

Chapter 9

Arms crossed against his chest, one foot resting over the other, Adam relaxed against a huge live oak. The warmth filling him wasn't from finally being out in the bright sunshine, but it came from watching Hannah toss pebbles into the creek that flowed a good distance from the house. Four days had passed, and with no sign of the motley trio that had been searching for him, Hannah had relaxed her stance on keeping him hidden.

Buster splashed in the shallow water, still limping, but getting better each day. He and the dog had made friends, much to his relief.

Hannah cupped her hands into the water and splashed the dog. Adam smiled, surprised at how much he enjoyed her company. In the span of a few short days, they had become close friends. Whenever he was alone in the pit, his thoughts focused on two things: regaining his memory—and Hannah.

His head itched and he reached up, vigorously scratching it. He looked longingly at the water, wondering if there was some way he could bend over enough to wash his hair. Hannah turned and waved at him. Jerking his hand from his head, he waved back, hoping she hadn't seen his uncouth scratching. He lifted his shirt and took a whiff, shamed by his filthy appearance. He had crawled through the dirt, buried himself under hay on the barn floor, and gone days—maybe weeks—without a bath. How could Hannah stand to get within ten feet of him?

She tossed him an I-know-something-you-don't-know smile and walked over to a bag she'd brought with her. Adam watched her slip her hand in, remove something, and turn quickly around, hiding the item behind her back. She walked toward him, her perfect pink lips curled into a bright smile.

"I have a surprise for you." Her teasing expression melted away, and her eyes widened.

"What?" He asked, looking over his shoulder to see if someone was behind him.

"Uh. . .your eyes."

"What about them?" Adam grimaced, looking away, knowing his appearance was appalling. He'd gazed at his reflection in a mirror in the parlor several times the past few days. His injured eye had progressed through a colorful metamorphosis from red to purple and black and was now starting to turn a nauseating greenish-yellow. It gaped open slightly, and he could just barely see out of it. "Looks awful, doesn't it?"

"Uh. . .no. They're so. . .blue."

"Blue?" That was one color he'd missed in the mirror.

"Aye," Hannah said, her face beet red. "And such a beautiful shade of blue."

"So, my eyes are blue. . .and black and green and purple." He chuckled. "They're more colorful than my vivid personality."

Hannah giggled, but her cheeks flamed, and she ducked her head. "It's just that in the dimness of the secret room, I'd never noticed you had such blue eyes. They. . .um. . .always looked darker."

Adam grinned. It pleased him immensely that Hannah was so mesmerized with the color of his eyes. "I guess that's understandable, especially since you've only seen one of them for the most part."

"Your eyes remind me of the Reed men. All of them have beautiful blue eyes."

His smile dimmed. He didn't want Hannah admiring any other men's features. Kicking a stone, he frowned. He despised the jealousy coursing through him. He'd been reading the Bible Hannah had left downstairs and knew that such a trait wasn't pleasing to God.

"Don't you want to know what your surprise is?"

Adam couldn't imagine what she was holding behind her back. He hoped it was one of those delicious apple pastries she'd brought him the day before.

She walked right up to him and looked him straight in the face. "It's time you got rid of that shaggy stuff on your chin. You're starting to look like Buster." She giggled.

Adam's heart nearly jumped out of his chest when Hannah reached up and ruffled his whiskers. She pulled her hidden hand from behind her back and held up a razor, a horn bowl, and a bar of lathering soap. "So, is it a good surprise?"

Still reeling from her touch, he smiled and nodded. Hannah grabbed his shirtsleeve, dragging him toward the creek. He followed along compliantly, shaking his head and chuckling to himself. *I'm as willing as a calf being led to the slaughtering block.*

"Sit down on that boulder and hold on to the razor. I'll get the soap good and wet."

Adam sat down, rubbing his whiskers. It would feel good to be clean-shaven again. He tried to think if he preferred a beard or not. Nothing came to mind, only the inky darkness that persisted whenever he tried to remember. He sighed in frustration, humbled by being so dependent on a snippet of a woman. Looking down at his calloused hands, he wondered what kind of work had earned him those battle scars. How could a man simply forget everything about himself?

At the sound of Hannah's approach, he looked up. Her hands were covered with a mound of sudsy lather. Her twinkling eyes and mischievous grin set his crazy heart racing again.

"It's difficult to decide where to put this. Your whole body could do with a good scrubbing."

Adam's ears warmed at her comment. He grappled for a response, but none came.

Totally oblivious to how her words embarrassed him, Hannah walked up to him and smiled. Without hesitation, gentle hands smoothed the lather around his cheeks and under his chin. His eyes closed, savoring the moment. He could get used to this treatment quite easily. His eyes popped back open when he felt Hannah tugging on the razor in his hand. When he didn't let go, she looked at him, blue eyes wide open, brows raised in a question. Such beautiful eyes. He loved the way the indigo ring encircled the lighter shade around her pupil.

Adam gripped the razor tighter. "I can shave myself," he said, a bit gruffer than he meant to be. He didn't want Hannah to think he was totally helpless.

"So you can." Relinquishing her soapy hold on the razor, Hannah turned and headed back toward the creek. She stooped down, rinsed her hands, and filled a cup with water. Adam watched her, feeling remorse over his brusqueness.

He flipped the razor open and slid the sharp blade along his jaw and down to his chin, the bristly sound bringing with it a memory he couldn't quite grasp hold of. Hannah returned to his side with the tin cup filled with water, and he dipped in the razor and took another swipe. After several minutes of scraping and dipping, he had a freshly shaved face again. He ambled over to the creek and stiffly stooped down. Careful to not twist his midsection, he dipped the razor in the creek. He dried the razor on his trousers, flipped it shut, and scooped up a handful of water, rinsing the lather residue off his face.

He stood at Hannah's approach. She handed him a towel and he dried his face, conscious of Hannah's appraising gaze.

"You look much nicer without all that hair on your face." She took the edge of the cloth and reached up, wiping his lip and the bottom of his chin. "Blood. You cut yourself a little bit." Hannah stuck the towel in his face as if to prove her point.

He snatched the towel and dabbed at his lip. He must have gotten a bit too close to his wound.

Hannah stepped back a few steps, putting her hands on her hips and looked up at his head. Her mouth twitched, and she looked as if she were chewing on the inside of her cheek. Golden brows furrowed and then rose as a blaze ignited in her eyes.

Adam sighed, realizing she had just formulated another one of her plans. "What now?" he asked, though not completely sure if he wanted to know the answer.

"Don't think I haven't seen you scratching your head. I would imagine you'd like to wash it?"

"I'd love to, but I don't see how I can since I can't bend over yet."

Taking the razor from him and stuffing it in her pocket, Hannah grabbed his arm and pulled him back toward the boulder. "I have an idea," she said. "Sit yourself down on this rock. No, wait!"

Hannah ran over to her buggy, put the shaving supplies in the back, and yanked off the old quilt that lay on the seat. Adam watched with skepticism as she spread out the blanket on the large, flat boulder, which jutted out over the water.

"Lie down here with your head toward the water."

"You're planning on washing my hair?"

"Yes."

"No ma'am, you are not." Adam stood his ground, glaring at her. Enough was enough.

"Surely you're not afraid to have your hair washed, are you?" Hannah turned and looked directly at him.

Adam followed the track of her gaze. Jerking his hand down to his side, he realized he was scratching his head again. Against his will, his mouth turned up in an embarrassed grin.

"Hannah, it just doesn't seem proper for you to wash my hair."

"It ain't proper." Chesny stood just inside the tree line, hands on her hips, her lips twisted to the side. "And if'n she do, I'll tan her backside."

Hannah flung her hands out to her sides. "It's just hair. I washed Michael's a time or two when he broke his hand. Adam's not in any shape to be washing it himself." She spun to face him. "And besides, you're miserable. You can hardly keep your hands off your head because it's itchin' so badly."

"It can wait."

"See! It's itching now, is it not?"

Adam yanked his hand back down to his side, chastised that she caught him scratching again. "Oh all right. But you're not washing it." He cast Chesny a pleading glance.

The older woman nodded. "I don't mind helpin'." She motioned to a nearby boulder. "Sit yo'self down there and let me take off that bandage."

He did as ordered, and Hannah marched off and dropped onto a blanket she'd brought for them to picnic on. He couldn't help grinning at her indignation. He knew she had a good heart and just wanted to help him feel better, but there was an appealing innocence about her that caused her to not make the wisest of choices at times. Perhaps that came into play when she found him in the barn. He imagined most young women would have rushed off out of fear or fainted, but not Hannah. She had boldly tended to him, and he admired her for it. But she needed to learn that some lines couldn't be crossed.

"Hmph. That there wound is lookin' good. Don't see as why you need a bandage any mo'." Chesny tossed it aside and pushed up her sleeves. "Get yo'self up on that flat rock and lay back."

Again, he obeyed like a boy and lay down on the sun-warmed stone, listening to the trickling water below. Crickets, locusts, frogs, and birds joined together in an entertaining chorus. The warm spring breeze flittered through the emerald canopy of trees overhead, rustling peacefully.

Adam closed his eyes as Chesny scrubbed his head, and he pretended that Hannah was actually tending to him. Everything about Hannah was kind and gentle, unlike Chesny. He'd be lucky if he wasn't bald by the time she was done with his hair. He smiled and refocused on Hannah. He feared he was falling in love with her. But what could a nameless stranger possibly offer a girl like her?

All he knew about himself was that he was used to working hard. The idleness of the past week was making him antsy. He needed to be working—doing something productive. And now he knew for certain that he'd sailed before. Little things kept creeping back into his mind—of climbing the ratlines and staring out at nothing but brilliant blue water as far as the eye could see. And the wind constantly tugging at his clothing and hair, and the fresh scent of the ocean. But the truly important things like who he was and where he'd come from were still a blur in his mind. If only he could remember everything.

"You's done, boy. I had to use that there shavin' soap on yo' hair." Chesny splashed a few more handfuls of water on his head. "You can get up now."

Hannah smiled and stood. "Doesn't that feel so much better?"

He nodded, relishing in feeling halfway clean again. Water ran down the back of his shirt, saturating it and the wrap on his chest. Suddenly there was a loud crack above his head, and he glanced up. Something long and dark fell. It landed right beside him on the boulder.

Hannah squealed. "Snake! Adam, there's a snake on the other side of you."

He didn't take time to think. Bringing his arms protectively across his chest, he flipped onto his left side, and quickly rolled over twice until he dropped to the ground, landing on his knees. With the grace of a grandpa, he scrambled to his feet and grabbed Chesny's hand. He pulled her over to the blanket where Hannah still bounced on her toes, and turned to see where the snake had gone.

He blinked his eyes to make sure he wasn't seeing things. His lips pursed, and he pressed his hand to his aching side. *I don't believe this.*

On the boulder lay not a snake, but a gnarly, grayish-brown tree branch.

A very unladylike snort erupted from Hannah's mouth, and Adam turned around to see what was wrong. She stood with her lips pulled tightly together, mirth filling her eyes. No longer able to hold back, she burst into laughter, bending over at the waist. Chesny's chuckles rumbled and bounced her shoulders.

Adam realized he had been the brunt of Hannah's childish prank. Was it similar to the kind that Jamie fellow and his brother had played on her? He grabbed hold of his side, still stinging from the sudden exertion. He didn't know whether to be mad or not.

Fighting back another snicker, Hannah looked up at him, semirepentant. "I couldn't help it, Adam. I'm sorry."

"Yes, I can see. You can hardly stop laughing you're so sorry."

Hannah bit her lip until it turned white.

"Go ahead and cackle before you bite a hole in your lip." Adam leaned over and knocked the dirt off his pants and draped his right arm across his chest.

Hannah sobered immediately. "I truly hope I didn't hurt you."

Chesny walked to the boulder and picked up her scattered supplies, still snickering.

Adam scowled, turned away, and walked back toward the water.

Hannah walked up behind him. She tugged on his sleeve, and he turned to face her.

"Adam, please don't be mad. I was just teasing. I'm truly sorry."

The penitent look on her pretty face and in her watery, blue eyes cut him to the core. He reached out and cupped her velvety cheek with his hand. "I can't stay mad at you, even if I try."

Hannah laid her hands on his arm. "That was a stupid thing I did. I could have caused you more pain. I didn't think about it, I just did it. Being impulsive has always been a problem for me." She ripped her eyes away from his and looked down.

"Like when you found a beat-up stranger in a barn and rescued him?"

Hannah looked up at him, her gaze framed by thick lashes. A small, embarrassed grin flittered on her lips.

His heart did a flip-flop, and he knew in that moment he'd completely lost his heart to the beautiful, young woman.

She reached out and grabbed his hand, then pulled him over to the boulder and picked up the quilt. Handing it to him, she looped her arm through his and propelled him to a grassy spot. Suddenly, she stopped in midstride, and he worked hard not to run into her. She turned to face him. "Oh, here's another present."

He looked down at the comb in her hand and couldn't resist teasing her this time. He bent over at the waist and put his hands on his knees, aiming his head toward her. When she didn't move, he peeked up at her and grinned. "So, you gonna comb my hair for me, or do you think I can do it myself?"

Her nostrils flared, and he thought for a moment she was going to punch him. As she stood there appraising his head, an embarrassed grin tugged at her appealing lips, and she held out the comb. "Touché."

He took the comb but claimed her hand with it. His thumb glided over her soft skin, and she gazed up at him, her mouth slightly open. He swallowed hard, peeking over his shoulder to see where Chesny was, and she stood there staring at him with her arms crossed and brows raised. He cleared his throat and dropped Hannah's hand.

"It's time to eat our lunch," she said, disappointment evident in her voice. Grabbing one edge of the blanket, she pulled it under the shade of a big oak. Then she knelt down and started removing things from the basket she'd brought.

Adam pulled the comb through his hair, hoping to make himself more presentable. She pulled one thing after another from the basket until she'd spread a fabulous array of food before them.

"I hope you like cold chicken."

"Mmm, love it!" Adam laid the comb on the blanket and turned to find Chesny. "Are you joining us?"

She strolled over to him and glanced down. "I reckon it's safe for you two to eat alone. Just don't go lettin' her talk you into takin' no bath." The twinkle in her eye belied the serious tone of her voice. "I be back in a bit with Israel and some fresh clothes; then we'll tend to that task."

He nodded but looked away, uncomfortable with such talk in front of Hannah. Chesny walked to the tree line, turned back, and wagged her finger at him. He knew she was entrusting Hannah to his care, and it meant a lot that she would trust him.

"Look, Adam. I brought cheese, applesauce, biscuits, and blackberry tarts."

He sat and took the chicken thigh she held out to him. "I think I'm in heaven. Great food and beautiful company, what more could a man ask for?"

A name. My own name. The ever-present thought intruded on his happiness. Hannah's smile faded at his audible sigh. "What's wrong?"

He shrugged. "I just wish I could remember something about myself. It's so frustrating not being able to." He stared out across the water to the trees on the far bank.

Hannah touched his arm. "I'm prayin' for you, Adam. It will all come back one of these days. We just have to be patient. Besides, even if you did remember, you're not ready to travel yet."

Adam rubbed the back of his neck. He could travel if he had to, but where would his memories take him? To a family in another place? To a job? Across the ocean to England?

One thing he did know: Regaining his memory would most likely take him away from Hannah. That was something he didn't mind postponing.

Chapter 10

Hannah watched the different expressions dancing across Adam's face. What could he be thinking? It must be so hard not knowing who he was.

Realizing she was staring at Adam's striking blue eyes, she looked away. Today was the first time she'd seen him in the full light of day. His eyes were bluer than the clear Carolina sky. . .and there was something—something vaguely familiar about them. The contrast of his long black lashes, which any woman would love to have, framing his azure eyes against his handsome, tanned face was more enticing than a sapphire pendant. Adam's hair, she had discovered, was inky black, not dark brown, as she'd first thought. Hannah ducked her head when she felt her cheeks flame. Her feelings for Adam ran far deeper than was proper for a woman promised in marriage to another man. Was it merely because of the bond created from her saving his life, or because he'd been so dependent on her, or was there more depth to her attraction?

"How do you manage to spend so much time away from your home without anyone missing you?" Adam leaned back on his hands. His long legs stretched out in front of him, hanging off the edge of the blanket.

"My parents have gone to Charleston on business," Hannah said, thankful for the distraction from her errant thoughts. "The Reeds are returning home after a long while away, so I'm seeing that everything here is clean and in order. Michael is busy with the spring planting and doesn't care what I do as long as his meals are seen to."

"That's quite kind of you to take on the task of preparing this plantation house for its owners. When you marry, your future husband will certainly be blessed having such a lovely and capable woman overseeing his home."

The skin on Hannah's face tightened. She hadn't mentioned to Adam that she was to marry Jamie. Had one of the servants told him, or was he speaking in generic terms?

When he didn't question her, she assumed the latter. The longer she was around Adam, the less appealing marriage to Jamie sounded. What would Jamie expect of her? That was something she'd never considered before. Would he expect her to stick to the house and do all the domestic chores her mother did? Would he want her to travel to Charleston every time he went? Most likely he would. Her days of living mainly on the plantation could be numbered. She plucked a tiny flower and twirled it in her fingers. The truth was she knew very little about Jamie Reed other than that he was handsome and kind.

I wonder what Adam would expect of his wife. Just the thought sent her cheeks flaming again.

"So what can you do besides clean, tend the wounded, and stitch samplers?"

Hannah sat up straighter. "I can cook as well as any of the servants—my mother made sure of that. I'm an expert seamstress and have sewn clothes for our workers' children. I know how to keep books and can play the harpsichord quite well. I don't mind at all tending the plantation, but I can't say I enjoy city life all that much."

"I don't blame you for not wanting to leave. This place is beautiful—and so peaceful." He smiled at her, his eyes warm. "So how about another piece of that delicious chicken you spent all morning cooking?"

She handed him another thigh and took special delight at how he seemed to enjoy her cooking. He picked up the last of the chicken bones from his plate and tossed them in the bushes. "So what would you expect in a wife?"

He shrugged. "The same thing as most men, I suppose. That she be sweet and loving, a good cook, capable of caring for the home and any children we had. I also think it's important that she be a godly woman. I've been reading the Bible and am certain that I believed in God before."

Adam's wife will be a fortunate woman. Hannah leaned back on her hands and stared at the puffy, white clouds overhead and listened to his mellow voice. It lulled her into a relaxed, peaceful state. Her mind drifted, and she wondered what Adam's children would look like. She envisioned cute, tiny versions of him with dark hair and remarkably blue eyes. She watched the children playing in the dirt. Three, no, four of them, two boys and two girls. One little girl with curly blond hair toddled over to Hannah, reaching short, pudgy arms up to her. Hannah smiled and looked down into the child's sweet face. A pair of bright blue eyes stared lovingly back—eyes the same color as Adam's. She sucked in a sharp breath.

Shaken from her daydream, her gaze darted over to him. He licked his fingers and stared at her with a strange expression. Hannah knew he couldn't read her thoughts, but somehow she wondered if he knew she'd been thinking of children—their children. She jumped up and jogged over to the creek. Stooping down, she rinsed the chicken grease off her hands.

I feel as if I've betrayed Jamie. Oh God, how can I be promised to Jamie Reed in marriage and dare think about being Adam's wife and having his children? It's so wrong. Lord, my whole life long I've heard Mama's plans about me marrying Jamie when I'm grown. I never questioned them before, so why am I now? Why did I have to find Adam? Why now, when Jamie will be returning soon? Maybe it was a mistake to take care of Adam as I have.

Instantly, she felt condemnation for her thoughts. If she hadn't found him, he'd most likely be dead by now. The thought of Adam lying cold and dead on the Reeds' barn floor chilled her. Hannah crossed her forearms and rubbed the goose bumps that had suddenly popped up. In a few short days, Adam had become her best friend.

What should I do, Lord? I can't help the way I feel about him. I like everything about him. I hardly even know Jamie anymore. Please, God, couldn't You work a miracle for me?

"Hannah, are you all right?" Adam had walked up behind her, and she hadn't even realized it. She stood, drying her hands on her skirt, but she didn't turn to him.

What could she say when her emotions were so raw? Adam's fingers came to rest on her shoulders, gently kneading away the tension. "I'm sorry if I said something that upset you."

"It's not you," was all she managed to squeak out.

He stepped beside her, keeping his left arm draped loosely around her shoulders. Why did that feel so right? When she leaned her head against his shoulder, he tightened his grip. She wasn't sure how long they stood there in the quiet setting, serenaded by nature's symphony. The gently moving stream rippled along, birds of all sorts chirped their cheerful songs, while unseen insects hummed their tunes. Hannah appreciated that Adam didn't press her for more information. She just enjoyed the moment. . .because she knew it wouldn't last.

❧

Hannah rocked in one of the four old wooden rockers on the front porch of her family's home.

The barn in the distance stood out as a black silhouette against the evening sky, blazing with the brilliant pinks, oranges, and deep purples of the setting sun. Staring at the beautiful scene, Hannah raised the cup warming her hands and sipped the hot tea. The events of the past few days flashed through her mind as she rubbed the back of her neck with her free hand.

Even though Adam was doing much better, leaving him each evening was getting harder. He had been a model patient. He'd stayed in the cramped little bed without complaining and allowed her to care for him. She smiled as she remembered the conversations they'd had about her family, the checkers games he'd trumped her at, and the times he'd rested while she'd read to him from the Bible or a novel from her father's library. She had faithfully brought him his meals, and he'd rewarded her with his heart-stopping smile.

Hannah looked heavenward and sighed. *Heavenly Father, I'm losing my heart to Adam. He's so easy to talk to. So funny. So patient with my feeble attempts at doctoring. The way he looks at me—as if I'm the most precious thing in all of America—sends shivers through my body. I don't care what his past is or who his*

178

family is. Oh, what am I going to do?

She stared up at the few stars bright enough to be seen in the twilight. Why had she always gone along with her mother's plan for her to marry Jamie? Maybe because she liked him? But if the truth be known, she had always liked Cooper better. Cooper had been her buddy. He'd even written to her many times during the long years he'd been away, but Jamie had only written her a brief note a few times recently.

Hannah sighed and sipped her tea. She'd kept up with Jamie through the letters her mama had received from Heather Reed and with visits when she was home at Reed Springs. Once she had even asked her mother why she had to marry Jamie instead of Cooper. Mama's response was, "He's the oldest, and the oldest marries first." Hannah let the comment resting on the tip of her tongue slide off unsaid. *If the oldest is supposed to get married first, then why do I have to get married before Michael?*

Wasn't there a story in the Bible like that? Who was it? Joseph? No, it was Jacob. Jacob traveled to the land of his forefathers in search of a woman to marry. He found Rachel and fell in love. But after Jacob had worked for seven years for her hand in marriage, Rachel's father tricked Jacob, and he ended up marrying Rachel's older sister, Leah. Laban had insisted Leah must marry first since she was the oldest.

Rachel must have been heartbroken to have her sister marry her beau. Hannah shook her head. Too bad Jane hadn't married Jamie, then maybe she and Adam would have a chance at a life together.

Rather than dwelling on things beyond her control, Hannah shifted her focus to a happy memory. A smile tilted her lips as she remembered Cooper's youthful gallantry. On the day he left to go to sea as a cabin boy on one of his father's ships, Cooper had handed her a wilted daisy and told her that he would marry her when he grew up if Jamie didn't want to. They had been best friends. Why was it that the people she grew closest to were the ones to leave? First Cooper left—and now he'd never return—and it was only a matter of time until Adam was well enough to move on, too.

The door banged as Chesny walked out onto the porch. Hannah turned her face away and wiped the tears stinging her eyes. Chesny dropped down in the rocker next to hers.

"Tomorrow is the day yo' mama say we oughta take her weddin' dress out of the trunk. The Reeds, they be back soon and yo' mama say they want to have the weddin' right away. With a few adjus'ments, that gown should fit you jes' fine."

Hannah blew out a loud breath.

"Somethin' wrong?" Chesny's chair creaked a steady rhythm as she moved back and forth.

"What if—what if—"

"You ain't havin' second thoughts, are you?"

Hannah huffed out a laugh. "Second and thirds and fourths."

Chesny's chair halted, and she turned toward Hannah. "When'd that start?"

"I don't know. Before Adam came, if that's what you're wondering."

"Humph. I'ma thinkin' that boy is a big part of yo' doubts."

She leaned forward and put her face in her hands. "I don't know what to do. If I don't go through with the wedding, I'll disappoint everyone—Mama, Heather, Jamie—and they're already distraught over Cooper's disappearance."

Chesny patted her back. "Now, now, it ain't all that bad."

"Yes, it is."

"What you need to do is pray about this and talk to the good Lord. He wouldn't have you marry a man that you'd be miser'ble with."

Wiping her face, Hannah sat up. "You're right. I do need to pray more." She'd been so tired each night that she'd almost fallen asleep at supper, and in the mornings, she'd been so anxious to get over to Reed Springs to see how Adam had fared that she hadn't had her normal prayer and Bible reading time in the mornings. That needed to change. She could hardly expect God to speak to her if she wasn't seeking Him each day.

Chapter 11

Hannah pushed open the door to the secret room, her other hand pressed against her stomach, trying to squelch the tingly sensation. She felt as if a passel of lightning bugs danced in her stomach. In her devotional time this morning, she had spent a half hour in prayer, and her desire to see Adam again hadn't lessened one iota, not even after she pleaded with God to remove the desire if it wasn't His will.

When Adam didn't respond, she knocked harder and walked halfway down the stairs. Israel had said Adam hadn't slept well the night before, so perhaps he'd fallen asleep after breakfast. "Adam, are you awake?"

When no answer came and her eyes had adjusted to the dim lighting, she continued down the stairs, her excitement waning, replaced by concern. Had yesterday's outing been too much too soon?

Adam lay scrunched up on the narrow cot, a pile of quilts on the floor. She picked up the covers and laid one over him, then folded the rest and set them on the table. He stirred slightly but didn't awaken. She retrieved his cup from the table, filled it with water from the pitcher, and set it down again.

She had worried about him all night. He had been holding his side ever since she played that snake joke on him. That had been such a foolish act on her part, and she sorely regretted it. She allowed herself a moment to study his sleeping form. His large frame was much too big for the cot. Over six feet tall, he towered over her by a half foot. She remembered the day she'd massaged his neck and shoulders. His build was lean but muscular, the kind of muscles earned by hard work—and that work must have been done outside, for no man with a desk job would have such sun-kissed skin. She touched her warm cheeks, remembering the pleasantness of his strong arms around her that day the three men came to the house.

Would she feel the same inner delight if Jamie held her? She wished he was still in England—and that thought took her by surprise. When had she started dreading Jamie's return to Reed Springs? She dropped onto one of the chairs and propped her chin up with her hand. Dare she call off the wedding? Her mother and Heather Reed would be so disappointed. And what about Jamie? Did he truly want to marry her?

He was twenty-nine now and surely ready to marry and start a family. She would be hard-pressed to find a man as good and responsible as he. And he was a godly man. But was he the right man?

Adam murmured something unintelligible in his sleep, drawing her gaze to his face. The bruises and cuts were pressed against the bed, leaving his handsome side showing. His chin was fresh-shaven and his hair gleamed like a raven's wing from yesterday's scrubbing. He was a fine-looking man with eyes that reached clear to her soul, but that wasn't what drew her to him. He needed her—and a part of her needed him. She loved his quiet, teasing nature and ached for him to be reunited with his memories.

Reaching down, ever so gently, she brushed a lock of dark hair away from his face. The lantern light danced against his cheek. She stood next to him, admiring his tanned face and his thick, ebony lashes that lay in a half moon against his cheek. Hannah's gaze wandered down to his healed lips.

Adam jerked his head sideways and moaned. "No, not again." He rolled onto his back, his head tossing to one side and then the other. "Won't tell you where it is."

Hannah leaned forward to hear better. He suddenly cast the quilt aside and sat up, and his rock-hard grasp clamped onto her wrist. Stunned, she yelped and attempted to jerk away, but instead of getting free, he pulled her toward him, and she fell across his lap.

With her cheek pressed hard against Adam's stomach, held there by his strong arm, she gazed up at him with fear in her heart for the first time since she'd discovered him in the barn. The disheveled mess of his long, dark hair added to his frightening countenance. The relentless pounding of her heart abruptly stopped at the angry glint in his eyes and snarl on his lips.

۞

Adam held tight to the man who had attacked him. The relentless trio had chased him all the way from Charleston. They meant to take him back—or worse. He had to get away—had some vital information they wanted. He fought the fog threatening to suck him under and forced his eyes open. What he saw drove away all hint of sleepiness. Hannah was crushed against him, held there by his iron-hard grasp. "Hannah?"

"Y—yes, it's m—me."

"My apologies. I didn't realize it was you." He blinked his eyes and squeezed his forehead, trying to understand what was real and what he'd dreamed. "I thought those men were attacking me."

"I can assure you, I have no plans to harm you."

Regret washed over him as he realized he still held her in his tight grip. He gazed down at her and brushed her hair back from her forehead. A smile tugged at his lips. "The thought of you attacking me isn't altogether unpleasant."

For nearly a week, he'd wondered what her hair would feel like. He must have knocked off the linen cap she wore when cleaning. Hannah's wavy mass of hair filled his lap and flowed over the side of the cot. He pick up a strand of pure gold and rubbed it between his fingers. "So soft. So lovely."

He could feel her fervent heartbeat pounding against his thigh.

He loved her. He was certain.

Had he ever been in love before?

I wish I could remember. But surely if I had ever felt like this, I would not have forgotten about it.

Filled with remorse for scaring her half out of her wits, Adam scanned Hannah's lovely face. It no longer held any fear, but rather something else: trust and—affection. This lovely, innocent young woman had stolen his heart in a matter of days. He pulled her into his arms, and with a groan of pent-up longing, he held her close against his chest.

20

Hannah wrapped her arms around Adam's waist, carefully avoiding his cracked ribs. She relished the security of his strong arms around her again. With a mind-opening revelation, she realized what she'd been feeling for this man whom she knew nothing of a few days ago, must be love. She'd read the Song of Solomon and talked to her friends about falling in love, but never dreamed it could happen to her.

When Adam released her slightly, Hannah stared up at him, biting her lip to stop its trembling. Though he no longer held her imprisoned within his powerful grasp, the expression on his handsome face held her captive. Hannah couldn't hold back the contented sigh that slipped out. The crooked grin on Adam's lips made her smile.

"Hannah, my angel, do you know what I'm thinking?"

Slowly, she shook her head, mesmerized by his compelling gaze.

"I'm thinking I want to kiss you." He brushed her cheek with the back of his fingers. "Would that be all right with you?"

Surely, one kiss couldn't hurt anything, could it? After a moment's hesitation, she nodded. Hannah licked her lips in anticipation of her first kiss. Her throat thickened, and she held her breath when Adam leaned toward her. She stretched her arms around his neck and ran her fingers through the dark hair hanging past his collar as he placed an achingly sweet kiss on her lips. His warm lips lingered. When she responded with enthusiasm the kiss turned a corner from sweet to intense.

Adam groaned, whether in pain or emotion, she didn't know. Suddenly, he pulled away and set her roughly on the ground. Hannah blinked and stared up at him. Confusing thoughts swarmed her mind. *What did I do wrong?*

"I'm sorry." He leaned back against the wall and forked his hair back from his face.

"Why?" she whispered, completely bewildered.

"Hannah, you shouldn't be here alone with me like this."

"I don't understand. You wouldn't hurt me, would you?"

"No. Not in the sense you mean." Adam smacked his fist against the cot. "I don't trust the way I'm feeling right now, and besides, you don't know a thing about me. I may be a highwayman, an escaped convict—or something worse."

"No." Hannah shook her head. "There's a gentleness in you, and I'm sure you'd never do anything against the law or anything to hurt me."

"No matter—the sooner I find out who I really am and get out of here, the better it will be for you."

Hannah pushed to her feet and nailed him with an angry look as she grappled for a response. She blinked, trying desperately to hold back her tears. *How could he think of leaving when he has just turned my world upside down with one kiss?*

As she opened her mouth to snap at him, she heard Chesny's call. Ducking her head to hide the tears streaming down her cheeks, she turned and fled. For once, she had to get away from this perplexing man.

≈

Hannah pounded the bread dough with all her might. *What did I do wrong? Was my kiss so bad?* She punched and rolled and beat the dough some more.

"That bread'll be hard as a stone if'n you don't stop beatin' it." Chesny stared at her with her hands on her hips.

Could Adam have disliked my kiss so much that it repulsed him? His kiss was wonderful—she sighed and slapped the dough again—*until he dumped me on the floor. I just don't understand.*

"What's got into you, child?"

"Did you love Peter when you two got married?"

Chesny's eyes widened. "Well, 'course I did, or I wouldn't have married him. Why're you askin' me such a thing?"

"I guess I've been thinking of marrying Jamie. I don't even know him anymore. He's been working in Charleston for so many years and rarely returns to Reed Springs."

"That Jamie, he's a good boy and he'll take good care of you."

Not wanting to get flour in her hair, Hannah used her forearm to push some wayward tendrils of hair from her face. "How long did you know Peter before you knew you loved him?"

"Don't rightly know. We didn't see each other often, what with him workin' the fields and me in the house." Chesny's lips lifted in a soft smile. She reached up and patted her hair as if preparing to see her husband, who'd been dead four years.

"It all started with a look. That Pete, he would stare at me likes I was somethin' special. I grew to look fo'ward to seein' him of a evening. I grew to respect Peter, 'cause he was a hard worker and took good care of his mammy. Eventually that respect bloomed into affection and affection grew into love. One day I realized I was in love with that tall buck, and we jumped the broom."

Hannah watched Chesny staring off as if seeing her beloved again. She and

Peter were married ten years before he got hurt in an accident and died the next day. She could still remember crying because her nanny was so sad for so long—but at least she got to marry the man she loved.

"But what if I never learn to love Jamie? Maybe Jamie won't even like me. He probably prefers city women now to the backward daughter of a planter."

"What's bringin' on all these strange ideas, girl?" Chesny picked up a paring knife and began to cut up some strawberries. "Don't you fret now. Jamie, he always was a handsome boy, and he come from a good family. Everythin'll work out fine, you'll see."

Hannah tore the dough in half and patted one part into a loaf and placed it in the pan.

"You had a fondness for that boy when you was young. You'll rekindle that attraction once you spend time with him again."

"I had a fondness for *both* Jamie and Cooper as boys. I felt like I'd lost two brothers when they rode out of my life." Hannah stared at Chesny. "That's how I think of Jamie, as another brother. Marrying him would be like marrying Michael." Hannah shivered at the thought.

Chesny put her hands on her waist, scrunched her eyebrows together, and pursed her lips. "Miz Hannah, let's have none of that silly talk. Mastah Jamie is not yo' brother. He will be yo' husband. Yo' mama has her heart set on that."

"But she said the oldest should marry first, and she hasn't found anyone for Michael, and he's older than me. Besides, this is America. Arranged marriages aren't so common here." She tried to calm her steadily rising volume. "What if I don't want to marry Jamie?"

"And who else would you be wantin' to marry?" Chesny straightened her spine and narrowed her eyelids. "Certainly not that Adam. Or meb'be you'd prefer yo' parents marry you off to one of them ol' widow men from town? One with a whole brood of child'en already?"

Hannah felt the color drain from her face. She knew the truth. There *were* plenty of men in the town who would be thrilled to marry a young woman from a prominent family like hers.

"I heard yo' daddy tell yo' mama that he done had more than a few inquiries from interested gentlemen." Chesny's expression softened. "You don't like livin' in town all the time, and if'n you marry Jamie, you might not have to, bein's as he's so understandin' and all."

Hannah felt sure she'd die if she had to spend the rest of her life in town—never able to walk in the gardens or ride across the open fields in her buggy, unable to visit her favorite thinking spot down by the creek. She had to tell Chesny what was on her heart. "I. . .I'm just not sure that the good Lord wants me to marry Jamie Reed."

"Well then, you'd better pray hard that He be speakin' to yo' mama and yo' daddy and tell them the same thing. The Bible says that child'en are to honor and obey their parents."

"Oh, it's hopeless! They'll never understand," Hannah cried. She turned and ran out the door. Its slam echoed behind her as she raced toward the barn and the comfort of the animals.

Chapter 12

Adam paced the length of the small *dungeon* and back. Pausing for a moment, he peeked up the stairway, but there was no sign of Hannah. She must have fled back to the safety of her home, or else she was working in some obscure region of the Reed house, because she hadn't been back to see him all day.

His stomach rumbled, once again notifying him that he had missed lunch. How could he eat when he'd done such a foolish thing? "I never should have kissed Hannah. I barely know her." The memory of her warm kisses and the feelings they stirred within him, irritated him. He turned and kicked one of the table legs, sending his mug of water tumbling to the dirt floor.

If he truly loved her as he believed he did, the best thing he could do was to stay away from her. Adam tiptoed up the stairs and peeked into the dining room. Seeing no sign of anyone and sick of being cooped up, he left the confines of the secret room and headed for the nearest door. The woods and water called to him. As deeply as his bound-up chest would allow, he breathed in the fresh spring air. Once in the shelter of the trees, he paced back and forth, trying to sort out his emotions.

Why can't I remember who I am? How can I have such strong feelings for a woman I've just met? Why did I have to hurt her like that? He felt like he'd been gut shot at the hurt and confusion in Hannah's blue eyes, as she sat on the floor where he'd dropped her after their wonderful kiss.

He knew she was attracted to him. He could tell by the way she looked at him and how she responded to his kiss. "Show me what to do, Lord. Don't let there be anything in my past that could hurt Hannah."

Adam stopped pacing and looked up through the trees to the bright blue sky. It suddenly dawned on him that he'd been praying. It had been such a natural thing to do. Hour after hour of Bible reading had solidified any doubts that he believed in God. Talking to God seemed so right that he knew he was a believer. A warm peace filled his whole being.

Behind Adam, a twig snapped. The nearby bushes rustled with movement, and he froze. He had the unnerving feeling he was being watched.

Then Hannah stepped out from behind a huge tree.

"Hannah." He offered a smile, but the apology stuck in his throat.

She returned his smile with a feeble one and kept her head down. She wrung her hands together.

He walked to her and took hold of her hands, but she didn't look up. He'd really hurt her by his actions. He felt lower than a worm. "I. . .uh. . .feel bad that I kissed you this morning."

She sighed and batted her lashes as if she had dust in them.

When she didn't look up, he cradled her cheeks and lifted her face. The unshed tears shining in her eyes rent his heart. "I apologize."

"Shh," came her soft response. "It's not as if you didn't ask permission."

"Tell me what's wrong."

She shrugged and lowered her gaze.

Tiny chills raced up Adam's spine. Hannah's head nearly rested against his chest. He fought the urge to wrap her in his embrace. Wisps of her hair tickled his chin. Adam couldn't breathe, but he was sure the snug binding around his chest was not the reason.

Hannah finally looked up. Their faces were inches apart, and Adam could feel her warm breath on his face. She blushed and started to back away, but he reached behind her with one arm and pulled her close again. "Did anyone ever tell you that you're an angel?"

A melancholy smile danced on Hannah's lips. "Just you."

"Guess I did, didn't I?"

"Yes."

Adam ran the back of his fingers down her cheek. "Well, it's true."

"I doubt if my mother would agree. I've caused her more than her share of worries over the years, and I'm sure Michael thinks I'm more devil than angel."

"You've earned the title by rescuing me."

Adam continued to hold her gaze. He wished more than anything that he could spend the rest of his life right here. Long tendrils of Hannah's hair curled playfully around her face. He wanted to kiss her again. The audible grumble in his stomach brought just the diversion he needed.

Hannah's lips twitched. "You wouldn't be hungry, perchance?"

He patted his stomach. "My angel deserted me at lunchtime, and I didn't have much of an appetite."

Hannah pushed out of his embrace. "I'm sorry."

"You have nothing to be sorry about. I chased you away. I never should have kissed you like I did."

Her head hung down again. "It wasn't your kiss that caused me not to come back," she whispered softly.

"Then what did?"

When she didn't respond, Adam reached out and touched her shoulder. "What is it, Hannah? What upset you?"

"Umm. . .I don't know." She shrugged.

Adam tightened his grip on her shoulders. "Come on, tell me what's the matter."

Her brows dipped down, and her nostrils flared. "Fine, then. After you kissed me, you threw me on the floor like I was poison. You couldn't get away fast enough." She looked up, tears flooding her eyes and running down her cheeks. "What did I do wrong?"

He caressed her shoulders. "Oh angel. *You* didn't do anything. It was me."

"You?" Her innocence and trust wrenched his insides worse than the beating had. She had no idea what she did to him.

"Hannah, I didn't want our kiss to end. It was something so special," he said, caressing her cheeks. "I guess it scared me when I realized that I've come to care so deeply for you so fast. I don't want to hurt you, and I sure didn't mean to upset you. Please, forgive me."

"Let's not talk about it anymore." Hannah shook her head, and they shared a smile. "I feel the same way."

"All right, we won't mention it again then." He pulled her to him and wrapped his arms around her, resting his chin against her hair as Hannah's arms encircled his waist.

All too soon, the grumbling in his stomach became too much to ignore. Hannah started giggling against his chest, and Adam found himself laughing, too.

"If the stomach is the way to a man's heart, I guess I had better get busy and feed you."

❧

Hannah wiped the porcelain statue with the dustcloth, while her thoughts wandered back to a Bible verse she had read just that morning: *"Trust in the Lord with all thine heart; and lean not unto thine own understanding. In all thy ways acknowledge him, and he shall direct thy paths."*

I'm trying not to lean on my own understanding, but it's so hard, Lord. I don't understand what's happening between Adam and me. Why did You bring him into my life? Why did I have to fall in love with him? What do I do about Jamie? I don't want to hurt or embarrass him, but how can I marry him when I care so much for Adam? Show me a way out of marrying Jamie, if it's possible. Please.

Hannah sighed and set the statue down. She knew in her heart God was directing her to tell Adam about Jamie, but so far she hadn't been able to bring herself to do so. She didn't want to lose him when she had just found him.

"You sure ain't very good comp'ny today." Chesny fluffed up a pillow on Lucas and Heather Reed's bed, then flipped the quilt over it.

"I'm sorry. Just a lot of things on my mind, I suppose." Hannah swiped the thin layer of dust off a side table with her rag.

"Meb'be it's time you wrote yo' mama a letter and told her what all you been a thinkin'."

Hannah's gaze darted to Chesny. "I can't do that. She'd never understand."

"Meb'be she understand mo' than you give her credit fo'." Chesny shrugged.

"I'ma goin' back down to the kitchen and he'p Leta with supper."

Hannah knew what would happen if she wrote to her mother. Caroline Madison would be on the first ship inland. Perhaps she would have better success writing to her father. He always was softhearted where his daughter was concerned. And what about the Reeds? Could she actually break off the wedding, which would most likely cause them distress, when they were still searching for Cooper and hadn't accepted that he was probably dead?

She pressed her hand to her heart, hoping that wasn't the case. Perhaps Cooper had left college early for some reason and set sail for home. Perhaps the ship had sunk in a storm, but Coop had survived and was stranded on a tropical island like Robinson Crusoe. Or perhaps his ship's captain had changed their course and set sail for a distant land. There could be a myriad of reasons why Coop had gone missing, but she refused to believe that the fun-loving youth she had been so close to was dead.

She glanced around the room to see what else needed attending. A desk sat in the corner, ready for its owner to return. She knew there was paper in the drawer, but could she actually write a letter? What could she say? "Dear Father, I can't marry Jamie because I've fallen in love with a man who doesn't know his name."

She heaved a sigh. It sounded so absurd. And though she would be happy—relieved—to have the truth come to light, everyone she knew would be disappointed. Jamie would be hurt. But wouldn't he be hurt even more in the long run if she married him, knowing she could never love him as he deserved to be loved?

A board in the floor creaked, and she spun around, one hand splayed across her chest. Her eyes widened and her mouth dropped open but nothing came out. Adam stood there with a stupid grin on his face. Had he heard the words she'd voiced out loud? She heaved her arm back and threw the dustcloth at him. It bounced benignly off his chest, and he caught it. "Y–you shouldn't sneak up on people like that."

His grin grew bigger. "I wasn't sneaking, I was looking for you."

She pivoted away and moved some things around on the desk. He crossed the room, and his hands lightly grasped her shoulders, then he turned her to face him. Crossing her arms over her chest, she ducked her head and refused to look at him. What must he be thinking?

"Look at me, Hannah."

"No."

"Did you mean what you said or was it just a slip of the tongue?"

When she didn't respond, Adam reached out with two fingers and lifted her chin. Though her head came up, she refused to raise her eyes to his.

"Hannah, don't be embarrassed. It warmed my heart to hear those words fall from your lovely mouth."

After a long moment, she dared to peek up at him through her lashes. He truly sounded as delighted as his smile indicated.

"Listen to me. I *love* you." Adam cupped her cheeks with his hand, and she couldn't resist closing her eyes and leaning in to his caress. "There's no use fighting it. I've tried but I can't deny the truth. I know I've only known you a week, but I love you with all my heart. Dare I hope what I heard you say was the truth? Do you—can you—feel the same for me?" The hope in his beautiful blue eyes dissolved her resolve to be upset with him.

"You know I do."

Adam's whole face brightened with a huge grin. Hannah smiled in response to his boyish enthusiasm. He pulled her into his embrace, and she leaned her head up as his lips found hers. All too soon, he pulled away, but this time he held on to her, cuddling her against his chest.

"I never knew it could feel so good to love someone," Adam whispered against her lips. His breath carried the scent of the coffee he'd recently drunk.

Thoughts of betrayal to Jamie and his displeasure with her behavior invaded her happiness. With a heavy sigh, she leaned her cheek against Adam's warm chest, and his heart raced beneath her ear. Adam's hand left her waist, and tingles coursed down her spine as he slowly caressed her back.

After a moment of enjoying their closeness, she pulled herself free of his embrace, feeling the need to put some distance between her and Adam.

"Is something wrong?"

She hated the concern that stole the happiness from his gaze. "There's something we need to talk about."

"Fine, but first I want to hear you say it again."

"Say what?" she asked, knowing good and well what he wanted to hear.

"Hannah, please, I need to hear the words. . .to know you meant it."

She tilted her head back, looked deeply into his eyes, and flashed him a dazzling smile. "I love you, Adam. . .whoever you really are."

"What if I'm some horrible person?" he asked hesitantly, then looked away.

Hannah cupped his cheeks with her hands and forced his gaze back. "It matters not. It's you I love and not who or what you are, though I can't believe there's anything all that dreadful in your past."

Adam's grip tightened on her waist. "I love you also, Hannah. So much, it hurts."

"Me, too, but we must talk about some other things—important things," she said, with a measure of dread.

"All right then. Come on." He took her hand. "Let's go outside and walk for a while."

"Do you think it's safe?"

Adam shrugged. "I don't know, but I can't stand being cooped up inside any longer. We'll stick close to the trees and use them for cover." Hand in hand, they followed the creek as it wound its way across the heart of Reed Springs.

"I've been remembering some things."

Hannah looked up and caught Adam's gaze. "I'm pretty sure now that the brown-haired woman I keep seeing is my mother. I see her in a kitchen, wearing an apron, and she has flour all over her hands. The dream is so real, I can even smell her fresh bread. The man. . .I don't know. He could be my father, but he seems younger."

"Perhaps, he's your brother or a friend."

"It's possible. But there's more. . .something about some information."

"What kind of information?"

He shook his head. "I'm not sure, but I think I was supposed to deliver something to someone important—I just wish I could remember." He squeezed the bridge of his nose with his fingertips.

Hannah scooted closer, hooking her arm through his. "It's coming, Adam. Just give it some more time. You're beginning to remember."

"I'm just impatient. I know that there can't be anything serious between us until I figure out who I am."

"It's serious already, don't you think?"

He cocked his head and smiled, drawing his fingertips down her cheek. "Yes, my angel, but I mean I can't ask your father for your hand in marriage until I know."

Hannah's heart jolted, and she placed her hand on his chest. "You want to marry me? B—but what if you never remember?"

"One thing I do know is that I have a faith in God. I've caught myself praying on several occasions over the past few days, and that feels so right. I know I believe in the good Lord. I'm certain He brought us together, and I trust He will help me to remember my past so we can be together always."

"I'm so glad to hear you say that. I believe the same." Hannah's heart raced. She knew the time had come to share her secret, but she dreaded it fiercely. "My situation may be even more difficult for Him to work out than yours."

Hannah turned and walked a short distance away, summoning her courage. She finally turned back toward him. "You believe me when I say that I love you, don't you?"

"Yes, I do," he responded with a nod as he gazed deeply into her eyes. "But what's wrong?"

"Oh Adam," she whispered, as tears coursed down her cheek.

He walked to her, framed her face with his hands, and wiped her tears with his thumbs. "Shh. . .It'll be all right. Just tell me what is wrong, and we'll sort it all out."

"I don't see how." She twisted her hands. "Oh, I should have told you sooner. I. . .I'm promised in m—marriage to a man I hardly know anymore."

Chapter 13

As if weighted down with cannonballs, Adam's hands fell to his sides. He squeezed his eyes closed while his mind tried to absorb what Hannah had said. He moved away from her and leaned back against the tree, his hand covering his aching heart. Promised in marriage? How could she return his kisses and profess her love to him when she was pledged to another man?

It couldn't be true. This must be some kind of horrid prank.

Jolted back to the present, he realized Hannah had been calling his name. He looked up just in time to see her squeeze past him. Adam called to her and reached out, but grabbed only a handful of air. "Hannah. . .wait."

She ran toward the house. He pushed away from the tree he'd been leaning on and kicked into a run. Each quick step he took jarred his side, but he ignored the pain. In a matter of seconds, his long legs enabled him to catch up with her. He grabbed hold of her arm and jerked her to a stop.

"Stop—please." Holding his side with his free hand, he desperately fought to catch his breath. He leaned against the stair railing, sucking in sharp gasps, and he pulled Hannah into his arms. Her tears bled through his clean shirt and into his chest bindings. She put her arms around his waist and continued to sob.

"Shh. . . I told you—everything will work out." He held her securely in his embrace.

"I don't see how it can."

"I don't either, but I do know God wouldn't have brought us together like this if He didn't have a special plan for us." Adam brushed his hand down Hannah's back. "People don't fall in love when they first meet. It isn't normal. Trust me, angel. It will all work out."

Adam didn't know how long they stood there together, his arms wrapped securely around her, offering comfort, and he receiving comfort from her. He dashed a prayer to God, asking Him to work a miracle.

Hannah finally relaxed. "I'm so glad you know. I've been so afraid to tell you. At first it didn't matter, but each day as my love grew, I became more hesitant to mention it to you."

"Don't ever be afraid to tell me anything." Adam leaned his chin against Hannah's head. "It's better to know what you're up against—it's easier to fight it if you know." That sounded like good advice—if only he could believe it.

How could he fight an arranged marriage when he didn't know a thing about himself? He swallowed the lump in his throat. "Tell me about this man you're promised to."

Hannah pressed her cheek against his chest as if she needed a greater sense of security to broach the subject, and Adam tightened his grip on her, glad none of the servants were nearby. "You know how I told you that my family's closest friends live here. My father and Lucas Reed are old friends, as is my mother and Heather Reed. When I was born, Jamie showed a lot of interest in me. He carried me around and made toys for me, and our parents all thought it darling. Well, our mothers put their heads together and decided to arrange a marriage. It's Jamie, the eldest of the Reed sons, whom I'm promised to."

Jamie. Now he understood the significance of that name. "Why don't they live here?"

Hannah ducked her head. "It's a sad thing—Cooper, Jamie's younger brother, has disappeared from the college he attended in England. The Reeds sailed to England to see if they could track him down or find some clue as to what happened to him."

Adam's mind struggled to absorb all she'd said. He had to figure out a way to combat this unknown competitor. "So are they coming back here? Or are you just supposed to leave the home you love so much and live in the city you dislike? Or will he marry you and then just leave again?"

Hannah closed her eyes, as if his words hurt her. He pursed his lips, frustrated with the bitterness he'd allowed to seep into his voice.

"Didn't I tell you they were returning soon? That's why I'm getting the house ready. Everyone will return in the next few weeks to prepare for the. . . the wedding." She half-choked on the last words.

"So, you plan to marry a rich man?" Adam relaxed his hold on Hannah, but didn't release her. He didn't bother to hide his disappointment. How could he compete with a wealthy businessman and landowner? He had nothing to offer her—except himself.

"No, Adam." Hannah reached up and cupped his cheek with her hand. "You're the only man I want to marry."

Her sincerity touched him deep within, and his anger focused on the people who would force her to marry a man she didn't love. He reached out and touched a lock of hair that had escaped her cap. He rubbed the soft, golden strands between his fingertips. "Are you sure? You'd marry me not knowing anything about me?" A little laugh escaped his lips at the ridiculousness of his question, and he looked away. He didn't dare hope she'd answer yes. Women needed security, a place to establish roots.

She grabbed his upper arms and shook him, drawing his gaze back. "I know all I have to. You're a kind, gentle man who loves God, and you love me. What else do I need to know?"

"I can't even give you a last name," he whispered, his voice husky and his throat tight.

"You will, you'll see."

He gently set her back from him. He couldn't do it. It wasn't fair to her. "No, Hannah, I can't marry you until I know for sure. If I've done something illegal, I may have to go to jail, and I won't put you or your family through that kind of embarrassment."

"But I just said it doesn't matter to me." Her shoulders drooped, and her eyes held the confusion he knew her heart felt.

Adam wanted to pull her back into his arms, then run off and find a minister who could marry them right away. Instead, he crossed his arms over his chest. "But it does matter to me. I can't ask you to take my name until I know what it is. And there's the matter of your intended, who needs to be dealt with."

"How can you be so unreasonable? If you truly loved me, it wouldn't matter about your name." Hannah turned and stomped off. Then she stopped and spun back toward him, tears coursing down her cheeks. "How can you stand there and say you love me—want to marry me—but then say we can't be together. I don't understand. So you're going to reject me. . .again?"

He swallowed hard, hating that there was another valid reason for pushing her away, but he had to voice it. "What if. . ." He caught her wounded gaze and sent what he hoped was an apologetic look. "What if I'm already married?"

Her chin wobbled, and tears glimmered in her sad eyes. She turned and ambled away, looking utterly defeated.

He felt as if someone had stabbed him in the heart, but he didn't know what else to say, so he kept quiet and let her go. If he gave her time to collect her thoughts, maybe she'd come around and see that he was right. There were too many unsettled issues standing between them for them to consider a future together at this time. He walked out onto the piazza and leaned on the railing. The last twenty-four hours, his first active day since he'd acquired his injuries, had been exhausting—both emotionally and physically. Maybe if he gave Hannah some time alone, she wouldn't be so upset. He flicked an ant off the rail and heaved a heavy sigh.

Perhaps taking a walk in the gardens would help.

Probably not, but what else did he have to do?

He wandered through the gardens, enjoying the flowers' sweet scents and the feel of the sun on his face. He walked the paths, wondering the whole time if he was making a mistake where Hannah was concerned. But how could a gentleman—a man of honor—do any less?

He had to know his past before he could have a future with Hannah.

A horse's whinny pulled him out of the garden and toward the barn. He needed something physical to do, no matter how small. Perhaps he could groom a horse or two. As he approached the barn, he noticed Israel walking toward him leading a handsome dun. The animal limped slightly, and its front legs were scraped and bloody. What had happened to the poor creature?

Like a lightning flash, a blaze of recognition zigzagged across Adam's mind. A loud gasp escaped his lips. He could see the horse rolling toward him as clearly as if it were the day of the accident. That horse was the one he stole in Charleston so he could make his getaway. The very same horse that had fallen and rolled over him.

"Israel, where did you find that animal?"

"Down in the southernmost field. I done saw 'im two days ago, but he wouldn't let me get near till now."

Adam patted the horse's neck and walked to his other side, not surprised to see a slice in the animal's hide where the lead ball had grazed him. The roll the horse took had coated the injury with a layer of mud, which probably helped it to heal. "This is the horse I was riding the day I was injured." He moved to the front of the horse and stooped. "See here." He pointed to the animal's knees. "He stumbled and fell to his knees, and I flew over his head. Then the horse turned a flip, going down the hill, and rolled over me."

Israel shook his head. "The good Lord was'a watchin' over you, I'ma thinkin'."

Adam nodded his head. "I do believe you are right. Let's take this guy into the barn. He deserves a good meal and some tender loving care."

Israel put the horse in a stall, unsaddled him, and then gave him some fresh hay. While the horse ate, Adam combed its mane and tail, then brushed down the dun's hide. Tomorrow, he would take the horse to the creek and wash him off. The animal probably saved his life as much as Hannah had.

Somehow, he'd have to get the horse back to Charleston and to its owner. The saddle had B.R. engraved in the pommel. Perhaps the tavern owner would know whom it belonged to. Adam swallowed hard. A man could spend years imprisoned for horse stealing. He doubted the fervent need to get away from the men who sought to capture him would be considered much of an argument in the eyes of a judge. Just one more reason he shouldn't put too much hope into a future with Hannah.

❧

Hannah slumped in the buggy seat, exhausted from her physical labors and the mental and emotional turmoil of the day.

"Looks like some folks is at yo' place." Chesny held her hand over her brow to block the setting sun and sat up straight, looking past Simeon.

Hannah, too, looked toward her home. As the fiery orange orb of the sun ducked behind the large Madison barn, her gaze came to rest on a group of people moving in the shadows. She recognized her father's tall, stout form. "They're home! Hurry, Simeon!"

A few minutes later, the buggy pulled to a quick stop in the yard. Hannah didn't wait for help, but instead jumped out into the arms of her father. "How's my Hannah girl?" Richard Madison twirled her around in a circle as he'd done every time he returned home from a journey.

"I'm fine, Papa. How was Charleston? Did you bring me anything? Where's Mama?"

"Whoa now, slow down a bit. You sound just like you did when you were a girl." Her father pushed her back away from him, and his wide grin narrowed into a scrutinizing stare. "You look different. Did something happen while I was gone?"

"W–what do you mean?" Could it be true people could tell someone was in love just by the way they looked? Hannah steeled her features into what she hoped was a natural expression.

"I don't know." He shook his head and smiled. "I suppose my little girl's just growing up." Her father turned and said something to one of the workers as Michael approached.

"You've sure been keeping scarce lately, sis. I'd think you'd be over at Reed Springs enough when you marry that you wouldn't need to spend every day there now."

"Feeling a little neglected?" Hannah threw her arms around her brother's trim waist and looked up into his handsome, tanned face.

"Perhaps just a bit. You've been gone so much I was halfway surprised you didn't sleep over there, too." Michael grinned and tweaked the end of her nose.

She loved her brother and cherished his rare hugs, but her thoughts were on another man—a man whose arms she wished she could stay in the rest of her life.

Chapter 14

The next morning the whole Madison family was once again seated around the old wooden table in the dining room, enjoying a special breakfast of beefsteak, omelets, biscuits and gravy, and spiced apples. Hannah smiled to herself as she watched her father swirl his coffee around in his cup. It was a habit that she always enjoyed watching. She often teased him about swirling his coffee because he drank it black—it wasn't as if he was trying to mix it up.

Hannah squirmed as she realized her father was staring back at her, his expression unreadable. *He knows something he's not telling me. Could he possibly have found out about Adam?* Hannah's face tightened under his intense scrutiny, and she felt sure the color must have drained from her face.

"What in the world is wrong with you, sis?"

"What do you mean?" Hannah turned toward Michael.

"You look like you're about to take on the world. What's goin' on in that pretty little head of yours?" Michael teased.

"Nothing, I. . .uh. . .was thinking about some things, that's all."

"Well, you're about to have a few more things to think on, isn't that right, Caroline?" Her father smiled and looked over to her mother.

"Of course you are, dear." Her mother's countenance beamed as she reached into her pocket and pulled out a folded piece of paper. She waved the beige paper in Hannah's direction.

She scooted back in her chair and sat up straighter. "What is it?" she asked, feeling more than a little trepidation. The tablecloth, wadded into a hard ball in her fist, matched the tight lump suddenly forming in her throat.

"Why, it's a letter from my best friend, Heather Reed. She says they planned to leave England on April fifth to come back home. That was three weeks ago. They should be arriving any day now, and we'll be having a wedding." Her mother smiled as if all her dreams were coming true—and weren't they? Her dreams, not Hannah's.

Stomach churning at the news, Hannah fought for an acceptable response. She thought she and Adam would have plenty of time for him to remember who he was before her parents and the Reeds returned, but now it seemed that Jamie could show up at her doorstep any day and expect her to marry him. "Um. . .and what news has there been of Cooper? Did they find him?"

Her mother's smile dimmed. "Sadly, no. There has been no sign of him since the day he went cavorting with his two friends. None of them have been heard from since."

"But they don't want to postpone the wedding any longer," her papa said. "With Cooper's disappearance, it's all the more important that Jamie marry and father an heir."

Hannah stared at her plate, no longer hungry. Her papa made her sound like some kind of broodmare.

She couldn't help feeling a little sorry for Jamie. He was being herded to the altar every bit as much as she. Was he also having second thoughts?

An hour later, Hannah climbed out of the buggy and hurried to the secret room. She stepped through the doorway and called down the stairs, "Adam, where are you?"

"He ain't down there," Maisy called from the dining room. "He be out at the barn."

Hannah nodded her thanks and hurried back outside, passing Chesny. The woman just shook her head and went on inside. The creaking barn door grabbed Hannah's attention, and she stopped in her tracks. Adam stepped out of the building, and his haggard expression startled her. Something had happened. She raced to his side and put her hand on his arm. "Adam, are you sick?"

"Something like that," he sighed heavily, his voice filled with anguish. The pained expression on his face took her breath away. Dark shadows rested beneath his eyes. The teasing spark of love and playfulness normally centered in his blue gaze had faded to something that chilled Hannah all the way to her toes.

She threw her arms around his waist and held him tightly, feeling the thudding of his heart against her cheek. He barely put his limp arms around her, and he did not hug her back. As she pulled away and looked up at him, the anguished look in his face tore at her heart like a dull knife.

"What is it, Adam? Didn't you sleep? You look like you've been up all night."

"No. I didn't sleep at all." He ran his hand through his already disheveled hair.

"Why? Are you sick, then?"

Adam placed his hands on her upper arms and tightened his grip. "No. . .uh, yeah, I guess I am. Sick at heart. Hannah, look at me."

She couldn't for the life of her figure out what could have caused the tortured pain in her beloved's eyes. He took a deep breath and his words rushed out. "I've finally remembered my name—and everything else."

Hannah reached out, placing her hand on Adam's cheek. "Glory be, that's wonderful news!" She exhaled a tiny giggle. "I guess I shouldn't call you Adam anymore. So, go on with you. . .what's your real name?"

"It's—Reed."

"Reed?" The words left her mouth, whispered on waves of disbelief. She templed her fingers over her mouth.

"Yes, Hannah, and my mother is Heather Reed."

"I don't understand." She studied him, and the longer she did, the more she knew the truth. He had all the characteristics of the Reed men, save one. He had the black hair, the amazing blue eyes, but the dimples were missing. "You're not Jamie. And Cooper is dead. So, who are you?"

"Cooper isn't dead." His voice, though quiet, held an ominous tone.

Hannah's heart leaped to learn that her old friend might still be alive. "If he isn't dead, then where is he? His family has looked everywhere for him."

"Everywhere but at home." He squeezed his eyes shut for a moment and took a deep, shuddering breath. When he reopened them, Hannah felt icy shivers of apprehension racing down her spine.

"I'm not Jamie—I'm Cooper."

≈

"What?" Hannah felt her world spinning. She stared at him, trying to make sense of his words. Trying to determine if this handsome man standing before her could be the same person as the lanky youth who had left years ago with dreams of sailing the world. Her mind refused to believe. If he was Cooper, that meant she was engaged to his brother. "No, you're just not remembering correctly. How could you be Cooper? He's supposed to be in England."

He stood looking at the ground, shaking his head. A glazed look of despair had settled over his features. He glanced into her eyes, then looked away with a distant stare. His fingers toyed with a loose button on his shirt. "Hannah, I'm sorry. I know you're disappointed that I'm Cooper," he said in a harsh, choked voice. "Last night Israel found the horse I rode from Charleston. After I went to bed, I started piecing things together, and then all of a sudden, I remembered."

Hannah's head ached, and she struggled to sort things out in her murky mind. "B–but how did you get to America? Your parents are just now on their way back from searching for you over there."

His nostrils flared, and his eyes turned hard like ice. "Those men who attacked me were the same ones who kidnapped my two friends and me and forced us to work on a British ship. When it made port in Charleston, I managed to escape and brought proof that an upstanding Charleston businessman is actually a British spy. That's why those men sought to kill me. They must have thought my injuries from the fall off the horse mortal; otherwise, I've no doubt they would have put a lead ball through my heart."

Hannah pinched the bridge of her nose and pressed her eyes shut in an effort to stop the burning sensation. "So it's true then?" She opened her eyes and stared up into his sky blue eyes, and suddenly a memory of the two little boys she used to play with flashed through her mind. Both had black hair, but one had a smattering of freckles across the bridge of his nose and. . .the bluest eyes she had ever seen. . . . They were Cooper's eyes. The older boy who filled her memory was Jamie. The two boys looked very similar, but as her memory sharpened, she suddenly knew the truth—he *was* Cooper. She recognized the tiny scar on his cheekbone from the time he swung off a rope affixed to the barn rafter and fell, scraping his face.

As the reality of the situation finally sank in, Hannah's whole body started trembling, and tears gushed forth in a torrent down her cheeks. She swayed and reached for Cooper as her knees buckled. "No, it can't be true," she whispered. "I can't be in love with my fiancé's brother."

Cooper caught her and lifted her up into his strong arms. Hannah suspected his soft grunt was both physical and emotional pain. She buried her face in his shoulder as he carried her over to a pile of hay and sat down. Holding her on his lap, he pulled her securely against his chest. Hannah tightened her grip on Cooper's shirt. How desperately she needed to cling to him. Her anguish peaked to shatter her last shred of self-control. A raw, primitive grief overwhelmed her.

How could God do this to her?

To them?

Chapter 15

Minutes passed as they held each other in silent sorrow. Cooper hated to move, knowing this might well be the last time he held Hannah. He finally cleared his throat and whispered against Hannah's hair, now damp with his own tears, "Angel, it doesn't change how I feel about you. I still love you more than life itself."

After a few moments, Hannah gave him a tight squeeze and lifted her head. His gut wrenched at her puffy, splotched face. Her reddened, watery blue eyes gazed deeply into his. "I knew the first time I saw your beautiful blue eyes that there was something familiar about them. I don't know why I didn't recognize them sooner, Ada—uh, Cooper."

He offered a weak smile as she stroked his cheek with her soft hand. He loved the sound of his true name on her perfectly shaped lips. Cooper's gaze caressed her face, memorizing every inch of it, knowing the days ahead would be the hardest of his life.

"Do you know what today's date is?"

"What?" She wrinkled her brow. "Oh, uh. . .yes, it's April thirtieth. Why?"

"April thirtieth?" Cooper set Hannah back. He only had two days before the *Syrius*, a British frigate posing as a French warship, would set sail again and take his two friends and the other captive Americans with it.

Early this morning he'd gone to the field where he'd hidden the pouch with the stolen documents. He forked his fingers through his hair. Whom could he turn to for help? He'd been gone for so many years that he no longer knew what men his father trusted. Who was powerful enough to stop that ship from sailing? He turned back to face Hannah. "When is your father due back?"

She dabbed her puffy red nose with an embroidered handkerchief. "I came to tell you, but I didn't get the chance. My parents returned last night."

"I've got to talk to your father right away. I need to get to Charleston by tomorrow. There's a British ship that's anchored in the harbor."

Hannah gasped. "How is that possible?"

"Because it's disguised as a French vessel, and a number of Americans who have been abducted and forced to serve as sailors are onboard it. I was one of them. I've lost so much time because of my injuries that I've got to leave today. I must talk to your father, and I need to borrow a horse."

"Oh Coop." Hannah lightly touched his arm. "I knew in my heart that you weren't dead. We can take my buggy."

He shook his head. "I don't want you to go. Those men are still after me. They want the document I have proving what I'm saying is true."

Hannah clamped her hands to her waist. "You can't keep me from going home." Her tone held defiance as well as a subtle challenge.

He smiled at her spunk. Here was the woman he loved but could never have. He'd finally remembered why he knew what her sampler would say when completed: NEXT TO GOD, FAMILY IS MOST IMPORTANT. That motto had been drilled into him for as long as he could remember. He couldn't stand between his brother and the woman Jamie planned to marry. Cooper would sacrifice his dream so that Jamie could realize his.

He loved his brother as much as he loved Hannah. His father's own brother had hated him and nearly killed him. Lucas Reed had drilled into his sons that family comes first. Brother was loyal to brother—even if it meant sacrificing what he wanted most in this world.

He and Hannah would never have the chance to laugh together and to love each other completely. Tears burned his eyes, and he felt her loss already.

Hannah's eyes glimmered with unshed tears. "Oh Coop, what are we going to do?"

He shook his head. "I don't know, angel. I've prayed all night, ever since my memory came back. It was such a bittersweet event—to finally know who I am and yet to realize that the woman I'm in love with is promised in marriage to my own brother. The pain of it just about killed me."

Cooper ran his hand through his hair and paced back and forth in front of her.

"Let's go tell my parents what happened. Surely they'll understand."

He stopped pacing and turned toward Hannah. Her naiveté was both frustrating and enchanting. "Understand what? That you sheltered and tended a wounded stranger without any thought of your own safety? If I'd been a lesser man, I could have done horrible things to you. Are you going to tell them that you shaved me and doctored my injuries? I know it was all completely innocent, but do you honestly believe your parents will see it that way?"

Hannah's eyebrows shot upward. "You *were* injured and couldn't have hurt me if you wanted to."

Cooper couldn't hold back the bitter laugh. "Do you truly believe that? Don't you remember the day you found me in the barn when I grabbed your wrist and you couldn't pull away? And what about in the secret room when I thought you were one of my attackers, and I jerked you down into my lap? I could have overpowered you at any minute, Hannah. For a moment, when we were kissing that day, the thought actually ran through my mind. It scared me so much that I dropped you on the floor." Cooper rubbed the back of his neck. "Thank God nothing happened."

Hannah stalked toward him. "Why are you talking like this? I saved your life. There's nothing shameful about it. You would have died if I hadn't found you in the barn."

Cooper suddenly felt exhausted. What he had to tell her would drive a permanent wedge between them, but there was nothing else to be done. "Maybe it would have been for the best. I'll die bit by bit, every day, if you marry my brother."

"Stop it, Cooper," Hannah yelled. "I don't want to marry Jamie. You're the one I love." She crossed her arms over her chest. "You're scaring me."

Cooper knew the things he said had hurt Hannah, but it was the only way to make her understand the reality of the situation. "You know I said I'd marry you when I found out my true identity, but all that's changed now. I—I won't go against my own brother and steal his betrothed."

Her mouth dropped open, and she lifted her hand over her throat. Her eyes darkened with pain. "You don't mean that."

Cooper's throat ached from the thought of losing her. "Yes, I do. You're promised to Jamie. We can't go against the wishes of both our families. You have to marry my brother." He all but choked on the dreadful words. A sensation of complete loneliness and defeat engulfed him. This was his darkest hour, worse even than the day he was captured and thrown into that dark hole in the belly of that despised ship.

"I thought you loved me." Hannah's features contorted with shock and anger. Tears ran down her pale cheeks in rivers. "You're a liar! You probably said all those things just so I would take care of you and let you kiss me. How many other girls have you done that to? Oh—I hope I never see you again!" Hannah turned and ran around the side of the barn and out of sight.

Cooper stood unmoving, stunned to see his sweet angel ranting in a fit of hysteria. Had he made the wrong choice? It had taken all night to come to his decision. Wasn't his brother's happiness, as well as that of his mother and Hannah's parents, more important than his own?

"Wait, Hannah! You know I love you," Cooper yelled, suddenly sorry for pushing her away. She couldn't hear him. Hannah was already in the buggy, racing toward the horizon.

⁊

Boss watched the Madison girl drive away from the Reed house at a fast pace, and one corner of his mouth turned up. He spat out a chaw of tobacco and wiped his mouth on his sleeve before turning to his men. "See, I told you the kid would come here. Looks like that girl lied to us."

"Yeah, Boss, and it kinda looks like he ain't man enough t' handle her. I think she needs a real man."

Boss raised his hand as if he were going to smack Jeeter. "Shut up, Jeeter, and get on your horse. Sam, I'll keep an eye on the kid, and you two go catch up with the girl. Just maybe, we can use her as a bargaining chip."

᪵

Could there be any hope for the two of them now? As if he could see clear to heaven, Cooper stared up at the brilliant morning sky before he left for Madison Gardens. *Why did this have to happen, God? No matter what I do, I'll hurt someone I love.*

Cooper pressed his forehead, hoping to rub away the dull, aching pain embedded there. Though he wanted nothing more than to make things right with Hannah, he wouldn't. It was best that she understand that he couldn't go against his brother, no matter what. His father's twin brother had nearly destroyed the family because of his bitterness. Lucas Reed had raised his sons to love and respect one another and to always put the other before himself. He couldn't—he wouldn't take away from Jamie the woman he was to marry.

He saddled an old mare that Israel had called Honey and mounted. Before riding off, he took a long look at his family home. How could he have not recognized this place? How could he have forgotten that he was Cooper Reed, son of Lucas and Heather Reed, one of Charleston's most prominent couples?

When he left as a youth years ago to sail on his father's ship, he always knew he'd return one day, but now he didn't have that assurance. The best thing for everyone would be for him to disappear again. Perhaps he'd return to England and finish his education. Or perhaps he'd travel west and see some of the frontier. But first, he had to save his friends.

A short while later, he topped the tallest hill between the Reed and Madison plantations. Memories flooded back as Cooper rode up to the Madison's large house. He glanced at the big barn, shining bright with a fresh coat of white paint. He remembered playing there with Hannah, swinging on a rope, then jumping into a big pile of freshly cut hay. Hannah had sneezed and talked about the tiny specks of dust dancing on the rays of sunlight that sneaked in through cracks in the side of the barn. Fairies, she'd called them. Cooper smiled at the sweet memory.

Another image of him and Hannah hiding out in the hayloft while Jamie, Kit, and Michael searched for them rushed through his mind. His heart lurched as he remembered Hannah's sparkling eyes and mischievous grin the day she picked up an old, dried horse flop and lobbed it at Michael's head.

For a moment, Cooper wished he'd never regained his memory; then he and Hannah might have had a chance to be together. But who would have rescued his friends? He couldn't let them suffer, not as long as it was within his power to stop it, and besides, he would never have been satisfied not knowing the truth about himself. Yet now that he knew, how could he live with the pain of reality?

Cooper's thoughts drifted back to when Hannah had found him in the barn. It amazed him that he hadn't remembered her the first time he saw her. But then, she had changed—a lot. She had only been a slip of a girl about thirteen when he left. He could remember the tears in her eyes the day he rode away with his father.

He reined Honey to a stop in front of the Madisons' home. A tall, broad-shouldered man who looked to be in his early fifties, moseyed out the front door of the house. The man looked at him and touched the end of his hat. "Good day, stranger. Welcome to Madison Gardens."

"Mr. Madison?" Coop dismounted but didn't approach Hannah's father.

"Yes, I'm Richard Madison. Have we met before?"

"Yes sir, but it's been a long time. I'm Cooper Reed."

"Cooper?" The man's mouth fell open. "Well, I'll be a hog's uncle. We all thought you were dead." Richard jogged down the steps, clapped him on the shoulders, and looked him over. "What happened to you? Where have you been?" He yanked Cooper into a hug that made his sides ache. Richard stepped back and shook his head. "Your folks sure must be relieved to know you're all right." He looked past Cooper. "Where are they? Back at Reed Springs? Caroline had hoped your mother would stop by here first, but I suppose they were anxious to get home after being away for so long."

Cooper tied the horse to a hitching post. "I haven't seen my parents since they visited me several years ago in England. I just came from Reed Springs, and they aren't there."

Richard pursed his lips. "They'll be home soon. Caroline got a letter from your mother. So. . .what happened to you? Did you know your parents have been in England, searching for you?" He chuckled and shook his head. "Won't they get the surprise of their lives." Then he scowled. "You've worried your family, son. You should have let them know you were alive and in America."

"I couldn't, sir. I ran into some trouble." Cooper shook his head. "I was abducted along with some friends back in England and forced to work on a British ship the past six months. I have to get to Charleston. There's a British ship in the harbor that has Americans aboard who've been forced to work for the British. There's a Mr. Sutherland who poses as a local businessman."

"Poses?" Richard stiffened at the mention of the name. "I know Arlis Sutherland. His daughter was just here. She's a good friend of Hannah's. Your father and I have talked about Sutherland on more than one occasion. Always thought there was something nefarious about the man."

"Could I borrow a horse, sir? This one I took from home is too old to make the journey to Charleston." Cooper flicked his hand back toward Honey.

"Of course." Richard nodded.

"Thanks. You suppose you or Michael could ride with me? I had a run-in with some men. They were after this." Cooper handed Mr. Madison the document showing Arlis Sutherland had paid the three men for capturing any number of Americans and then forcing them into service on various British ships. "I figure they're still on the lookout for me."

Richard Madison adjusted his spectacles, studied the document, then looked off in the distance for a moment before his gaze returned to Cooper. "That's a good idea. I'll send Michael along with you, and you can take Johnny, one of my workers. He's a good shot."

Cooper followed Richard to the barn. His concern for Hannah clouded his reunion with his old buddy, Michael. During the hour it took to prepare the horses and stock up on food, water, and weapons, Cooper kept watching for Hannah, wishing she'd return home. He'd wanted nothing more than to charge after her, take her in his arms, and comfort her, but he had no right to do so. The deep, twisting pain knifed his insides again.

Hannah wasn't his to love.

She belonged to his brother.

Chapter 16

"Simeon, please pull over. I'd like a few moments to walk by the creek."

The buggy slowed, then stopped. Simeon hurried down from his seat and helped Hannah to step out.

"I won't be long. I just need some time to walk and think. In fact, you can go on back to Reed Springs and wait for Chesny. We're close enough to home that I can make it on my own from here." Hannah turned and walked toward the creek, eager to be alone.

"Miz Hannah, Chesny wouldn't be too happy if'n I was to leave you all alone."

"I'll be fine, Simeon."

He crossed his arms over his thin chest and leaned back against one of the buggy wheels. "You go on and take yo' walk, but I be waitin' right here when yo' done."

Hannah blew out a frustrated breath and nodded. He was just trying to protect her, and that should make her feel good, but it didn't. There was only one man she wanted watching over her other than her father, and that was Cooper. But it didn't look as if that would be happening.

Her lower lip quivered. She felt exhausted, as if every shred of hope had left her. Why did she have to be the one to find Cooper? She was content to marry Jamie and hadn't questioned her arranged marriage until Ruthie came and started asking her about it and then Cooper came and stole her heart. She could have gone ahead and married Jamie and been happy, even though she didn't love him. But now that she had experienced falling in love, how could she follow through with the wedding?

She swiped her burning eyes. Pebbles crunched against her shoes, and she stopped right at the water's edge. It lapped gently against the rocks, making a soft gurgling sound. If only she were as peaceful, but instead, a war raged inside her. Hannah picked up a rock and tossed it in, feeling a bit victorious for disturbing the quiet and creating concentric circles rippling through the water. She threw in another one.

Would her mother listen to reason if Hannah explained about her love for Cooper? No, her mother was tenacious—like an alligator with its prey. Once she snagged onto an idea, there was no changing her mind. The idea for Hannah and Jamie to wed had long ago taken root in her mother's plans—and those roots ran as deep as a hickory tree's. Even if she worked up her nerve to tell her mother, Cooper had made it clear that he wouldn't stand in the way of his brother's marriage—no matter what it cost him.

Fresh tears stung her eyes. She clamped her lips together, imprisoning a sob. *Dear God, is this my fault because I'm weak? I don't understand. Father, I don't know what to do.* She buried her face in her hands.

Hannah heard the sudden sound of boots scuffling on the pebbles behind her. Cooper! He'd come after her. She wiped the tears from her face and spun around. She sucked in a gasp, as a shiver of panic snaked down her spine. She stood face-to-face with two of the men who'd confronted her before.

The small man gawked at her like she was a huge steak he was ready to devour. He stepped forward, grabbing her upper arms.

"What are you doing? Let me go!" Twisting and jerking, she fought against the strong hands that held her captive. One of her arms broke free, but the other man grabbed hold of it.

The small, filthy man with rancid breath nestled up against her cheek, pricking her skin with his stubble. "Now you jes' hush up, missy, and stop yer strugglin'. Me and Sam's gonna take good care of you."

Sam. That name was familiar. Jerking her face away from his, she stared at the taller man and recognized his bushy mustache. "What do you want? My father will have your head if you don't let me go."

"Yer daddy don't scare us none, little lady," Sam growled.

"Maybe we can get the kid to swap this little gal fer that information he's got and get us a ransom out of ol' man Madison to boot." The sleazy man grinned and stroked his weak chin as if he were seeing hundreds of dollars coming his way.

Swap her? For the kid's information? What kid?

These were definitely the same men who were looking for Cooper, so he must be "the kid." Suddenly, it all made sense. They were searching for the documents he had that proved he'd been kidnapped. Somehow she had to warn him, but how could she get away from these ruffians? Simeon would help her, but if she cried out to him, her captors might shoot him. And what would they do to her? Her whole body started shaking as if she'd gotten lost in a blizzard.

"Relax, girl, nothin's gonna happen to you unless that Reed kid won't cooperate. We're just gonna take a little ride and get all of this sorted out." Sam motioned toward his horse with his head. "Get the rope, Jeeter."

Hannah clenched her eyes shut. A fear unlike any she'd ever known bore into the pit of her stomach. Her family would be distraught when she didn't return home before dark. They would all be out looking for her.

Jeeter let go of her, but Sam grabbed her around the waist with a grip as tight as iron shackles.

Moments later, the bony bandit returned with a rope. "Stick out yer hands, missy. I jes want t' be sure you don't wander off." He ogled her face as he wrapped the prickly rope around her wrists, and his beady eyes lingered on her lips, then his gaze roved down to her chest. He licked his lips and looked up at her with a wicked grin. Her heart stopped.

"Maybe me and you'll have some fun later on tonight."

A wave of nausea churned in Hannah's stomach. A measure of fear she'd never known clung to her like burrs on stockings. The world started swaying. Suddenly Sam scooped her up and tossed her onto the back of one of the horses. He took the other end of the rope that bound her hands and tied it to the saddle horn. Then he turned around to the other man. "Jeeter, you fool. You touch this gal, and I'll kill you myself."

"Aw, cain't a man have a little fun?"

"Not with this gal."

Hannah's hopes rose ever so slightly. Perhaps God had sent Sam to watch out for her. *Thank You, Lord, for protecting me from that vile man. Give me courage. Please, God, help me to figure out some way to escape, and protect Cooper from these men who mean to do him harm.*

A short while later, as they approached the Reeds' house, the leader of the trio of outlaws rode toward them. Hannah could tell by his expression that he wasn't in a pleasant mood.

"The kid lit out of here like the barn was on fire," he said, jerking his mount to a quick halt. "I followed him over to the Madisons'. He talked with ol' man Madison; then he and two others rode out like they was headed toward Charleston. C'mon, we gotta try and catch up to 'em."

He kicked his mount hard in the sides with his heels, and the big horse bolted forward. Jeeter rode off after him, leaving a dusty cloud in his wake. Hannah grabbed the saddle horn as Sam clucked to his horse.

That evening, they approached the outskirts of Charleston. Hoping for a chance to escape, Hannah stayed awake the whole day, waiting and watching for the perfect moment. They took back roads and trails, hugging groupings of trees that afforded cover. They rode into a part of Charleston that Hannah had never been to before.

"You two get her out of sight. I'm riding over to update Mr. S. on what all's happened." Boss rode off in another direction.

Sam and Jeeter stopped in a rank-smelling alley. Sam slid off the back of his horse, then pulled her down. He tugged her into a dirty building and shoved her into a small, dark room. Then he pulled a filthy kerchief from around his neck and gagged her.

"You keep quiet, or I'll let Jeeter in, you hear?"

Hannah nodded, fighting the urge to retch from the nasty cloth in her mouth. The door shut, taking the light with it, and she stood in the dark. All alone.

She backed up to a chair she'd noticed just before the door shut and lowered herself into it. The foul-smelling room must be used for storage. There were no windows, and she'd noticed a stack of crates along the far wall. But now, in the dark of night, she couldn't see a thing.

Desperate concern for Cooper buffeted her. She felt as if her prayers weren't reaching past the ceiling. Before long, exhaustion won out over her fear and discomfort, and Hannah turned sideways in the chair, laid her head against its back, and drifted off to sleep, dreaming of a daring rescue by the man she loved.

❧

The sensation of falling jolted Hannah awake. She shoved one leg forward and caught herself before she tumbled to the floor. Staring in the inky blackness, she shook her head, trying to get her sleep-laden mind to focus on her surroundings. The horrors of the evening came rushing back. What had her family done when she hadn't returned home? Were they out searching for her even now? Was Cooper?

Her heart ached at the very thought of him.

She might never see him again unless she got free of this place. The nasty neckerchief that had been crammed halfway down her throat to ensure her silence bit into the corners of her mouth. She lifted her hands and tried to work it free. Her shoulder muscles cramped from her wrists being bound so tightly that she could barely move.

Her nostrils flared as she labored to breathe through her nose. A strong odor assaulted her senses. At times she thought sure she wouldn't get enough air and would suffocate. Hannah leaned her head back against the rough chair and closed her eyes. *Relax. Panicking won't help.* Slowly, her breathing returned to a normal tempo.

As her physical struggles lessened, the events of the past two days came rushing back like a flash flood. She squeezed her eyes tightly shut as the familiar burning sensation returned. *Oh Adam. No, not Adam—he's Cooper Reed. Stubborn Cooper, who won't stand against his brother.*

If he loved her as much as he said, how could he refuse to put a halt to her wedding? Why did she have to fall in love with Cooper and not Jamie?

Hannah twisted her head sideways to wipe her tears on her shoulder. Was it only this morning that her world had suddenly collapsed?

❧

"You're knocking on the door of your own home?" Michael cast a sideways glance at Cooper.

"I haven't been home in over seven years. It doesn't seem right to enter without permission." With a tight fist, Cooper pounded on the door of his family's Charleston home again.

Darkness had set in, and the bells of St. Michael's church rang, heralding the nine o'clock hour. Several Negroes jogged down the street in their effort to get home before curfew. The latch jiggled and then the door opened, revealing a man about Cooper's age—a man he hadn't seen before. He had hoped for someone who knew him.

"May I help you, gentlemen?" The servant eyed Cooper and the other men, but his gaze latched on to Cooper. Did the man perchance notice his resemblance to his father?

"We need to see Lucas Reed, sir. Posthaste."

The servant's chin lifted. "Mr. Reed does not normally receive guests at this late hour."

"Well, he'll see us. This is his—"

Cooper elbowed Michael in the side. "Please tell him that Michael Madison, son of Richard Madison, is here to see him. I believe he will welcome the visit."

The servant obviously recognized the name even though he didn't seem to know Michael on sight. He nodded and held out his hand, indicating for them to enter. They did so, and the servant closed the door. "Please wait here, gentlemen."

Cooper covered his mouth to hide his yawn as he watched the doorman ascend the stairs. Was his old room still the same—the bed just as comfortable? He, Michael, and Johnny had ridden all day in order to arrive before dark, but before they could retire for the night, some serious business needed to be tended to.

Michael leaned sideways. "Why'd you punch me? I was just going to tell him you live here."

"They think me dead. I want my presence to be a surprise."

"Well, they're about to get one—a pleasant one, I would venture." Michael tugged Johnny forward. "Stand in front of Coop, and let's see how long before his father notices him."

Would his father even recognize him right off? He'd last seen his parents two years ago when they'd come to England to visit him, but he'd lost significant amounts of weight after being kidnapped and then injured. And they thought him dead. He could hardly hold back the grin threatening to burst out, knowing how stunned they would be to see him again. He would even be happy to see Jamie.

That thought killed his grin. He dearly loved his brother, but he couldn't be happy about Jamie's marriage to Hannah. If only his brother didn't love her and hadn't planned to marry her most of their lives. Coop had never told Jamie that he'd always secretly cared for the spunky girl who worked so hard to keep up with the boys she associated with.

His father exited the hallway and stopped on the upstairs landing, peering down at them. Coop scooted behind Johnny, finally allowing his smile to break forth. His father looked much the same as the last time he'd seen him, expect for having a bit more gray hair. The man was still tall and broad, in the shape of a man much younger than his actual age. It was his father's penchant for working hard that kept him looking so well.

"Michael." Lucas Reed lifted his hand in greeting, then jogged down the stairs with the stuffy servant following at a more subdued pace. "So good to see you again. How are your parents faring?"

"A pleasure to see you, too, sir, and my parents are well. They've been concerned about you." Michael shook hands with Cooper's father, then motioned toward Coop and Johnny. "We have some important business, sir. This is Johnny, one of our work hands."

Lucas shook hands with Johnny, then his gaze slid past the man to Cooper and back to Michael. Disappointment swelled within Coop, but then his father's gaze jerked back to him. He studied him with a hungered look, and Coop could see hope battling the fear to believe on his father's face.

He decided to put the poor man out of his misery. "It's good to see you again, Father."

Lucas Reed's blue eyes widened and blazed with delight. "Cooper? Is it really you, my son?"

"Aye sir, it is." His grin burst forth as he answered like his mother would have responded.

A joyous gasp spewed from his father's mouth, and then Coop was crushed in his strong arms. "Thank You, Lord, for returning my son."

Coop hugged his father and expressed his own thanks to his heavenly Father. There had been many days when he was slaving for twenty hours at a time when he wondered if he'd ever see his family again. His father finally set him back a few feet and devoured him with his moist eyes.

"We thought you were lost to us. Where have you been? Why didn't you send word that you were safe?"

"I couldn't, sir. I was abducted from London last fall and forced to serve on a British ship all these months."

The glint in his father's eyes hardened. "I knew something nefarious must have happened. There was no sign at all of you and your classmates. How is it you are here now?"

Cooper grinned, knowing his father would be proud. "We dropped anchor in Charleston Harbor, but all of us Americans and men from some other countries were locked below. They often locked me up alone because I had a tendency to sabotage things. I didn't serve all those years on your ships without learning a thing or two. After we docked, I recognized the bells of St. Michaels and knew I was home. I managed to escape."

"Well done, son." His father clapped him hard on the shoulder.

Cooper pulled the pouch from his waistband. "I also managed to find proof that a prominent American is in league with the British."

Lucas scowled. "Which American? Someone I know?"

"Have a look." He held the pouch out to his father.

Lucas pursed his lips, as if preparing himself to learn of the betrayal of a close friend. He unfolded the parchment, scanned it, and his frown deepened. "Why, this is treason!"

"And kidnapping, holding a person against his will, destroying American property, and so on and so forth." Cooper's delight in revealing this information to his father knew no bounds. If not for being abducted, he would have finished his education by now and may have well returned home. He'd be happily preparing for his brother's wedding and never have fallen in love with Hannah. He released a heavy sigh, not all that sorry about the latter, but it certainly would have made his life less complicated.

"We've not much time, Father. The *Syrius*, the British frigate I was on, is scheduled to leave tomorrow. We've got to save the others who are still held captive. I regret that I was unable to set them free before escaping. I had planned to get help and then go back for them, but I had an unforeseen accident." His fingers touched the scabbed-over wound on his head, drawing his father's gaze.

Lucas brushed Coop's hair back and studied the injury. "This is at least a week old. Where have you been since then?"

Michael snorted a laugh, and Cooper sent him a mock glare. "That's the ironic thing, Father. I was found out and chase was given. I managed to get almost home to Reed Springs when my horse gave out. I was thrown over his neck, hit my head, and then the horse rolled over me. I had amnesia and just regained my memory last night. It was Michael's sister who found me in our barn." He didn't speak Hannah's name—he couldn't for fear of giving himself away.

His father wrapped an arm around him and hugged his shoulders. "Praise be to God for watching over you. I can't tell you how grieved we've all been."

Movement upstairs drew Cooper's attention. Jamie stood at the top of the stairs, staring down.

"Come and greet our visitors, son. Your future brother-in-law has arrived."

Jamie trod down the stairs, his gaze focused on Michael. "Good to see you again."

The two men shook hands.

"So, how's that sister of yours?" Jamie asked.

Michael's gaze darted to Cooper, making his heart jump. Did Michael know? He hadn't said anything about caring for Hannah, but had she talked about him to her brother?

"Uh, she's well. She's been spending a lot of time at Reed Springs, getting it ready for your return."

Jamie smiled, turning Cooper's stomach. "Good. Soon enough it will be her home, too."

His father cleared his throat and introduced Johnny. "And of course you know this young man."

Jamie lifted his gaze to Cooper, and for the first time, Coop realized he'd grown taller than his brother by a good inch and a half. The same confusion crinkled his brother's brow; then his mouth dropped, and he glanced at his father. Lucas Reed smiled broadly and nodded. Delight spread across Jamie's face. "Cooper?"

He nodded. "Aye brother."

Jamie closed the distance between them and enveloped Cooper in a hug. "How is it you are here? Where have you been?"

Michael shook his head. "Why not send for your mother so we don't have to go through all this a third time?"

"An excellent idea." Lucas Reed grabbed Michael's shoulder and shook it. "I'll get her now. She will be so delighted." His long legs took the stairs three at a time.

Warmth flooded Coop's insides. He was finally home—with his family. Jamie shook him, regaining his attention. "It's so good to see you again, brother. You've arrived just in time for the wedding."

Chapter 17

A noise jerked Hannah awake again, and she was much relieved to see bright shafts of sunlight penetrating the dark room. The door opened and several men clomped in, each one looking at her. One man lit the two oil lamps hanging overhead, fully illuminating Hannah's prison for the first time since she'd arrived.

Squinting against the brightness, she slowly lifted her gaze up the length of a huge man wearing a tan coat who stood before her. He yanked down his gold vest, futilely attempting to cover his generous stomach. He doffed his black beaver hat and gave Hannah a smug smile. "Sam, untie the poor girl. Jeeter, go to the kitchen and get her some water or tea and something to eat. She must be half-starved." He smiled a grin she was certain he thought charming as Sam removed her bindings and the gag, but it sickened her stomach.

"I suggest you keep quiet, Miss Madison, unless you'd like to be gagged again." Sam walked across the room and deposited the ropes in a box.

Hannah slowly stretched her shoulders, trying to work out the stiffness. At the moment, she couldn't have screamed even if she'd been inclined to. She desperately needed some water. She rubbed her wrists, chafed with red rope burns. Glancing up, she surreptitiously studied the big man as she moved her tongue around, trying to work up some moisture in her dry mouth. She'd seen him before, but she couldn't remember where.

The door banged opened again and that weasel of a man returned, but this time he looked like an angel. In his hand, he carried a tin cup.

"Here's a cup of water. Lily's whipping up some grub fer the princess."

Hannah's gaze never left the cup. She licked her parched lips in anticipation. Jeeter handed it to her and turned, going back out the door. Though she wanted to gulp the cool water in one big swig, she sipped it slowly, using the extra moments to regain her composure. Anger over her abduction and concern for Cooper fueled her resolve to face the intimidating man head-on while her mind grappled for an escape plan. With a loud bang, she slammed the empty tin cup onto the table and smiled to herself when the big man jumped slightly.

"Who are you and what do you want with me?" She licked her lips to moisten them, wishing she had more water, but not wanting to lower herself to ask.

"I'm Arlis Sutherland, and I'm planning on making a little deal for myself. I'm going to trade you for some papers that were stolen from me," he said, as he lowered his enormous frame onto the chair across from her.

Hannah had a fleeting moment of pity for the poor chair as it creaked and groaned, but then his name registered, and she glanced up at him again. Ruthie's father? She'd only seen the imposing man a time or two, and even then, from a distance. Poor Ruthie. She shook her head in response to the man's comment. "Cooper will never make a deal like that. How could you possibly think you could ever get away with this kind of a scheme?"

"I've got a pretty good bargaining chip, wouldn't you say, Miss Madison?" Mr. Sutherland plopped his hat onto the table. He ran a hand through his thinning hair and gave her a tight-lipped smile. "It seems my men saw you in the arms of Mr. Reed. I figure he'd rather have his beautiful young woman back than a measly old piece of parchment."

Hannah's cheeks warmed at the thought of someone watching her and Cooper, but as her embarrassment ebbed, anger flooded in. She jumped to her feet so quickly her chair catapulted to the ground with a loud bang. Her legs threatened to buckle, and she grabbed the edge of the table for support. Leaning forward, she looked Arlis Sutherland in the eye. "You're nothin' but a lowdown coward to use a woman as a pawn. And you're dead wrong if you're think I'll let Cooper forfeit his information to you."

Mr. Sutherland didn't flinch at her tirade. The only indication that he'd even noticed was an uplifted eyebrow. "Sit down, Miss Madison, and I suggest you quiet down," he said as he lifted up the filthy neckerchief that had been in her mouth and twirled it around his plump fingers. He flicked a finger at Boss, who strode over, and pressed her back in her seat.

"You know, my dear, you're the one who is dead wrong. But at least you're not dead yet. And to tell the truth, there are things worse than death for a beautiful young lady like you." He rubbed his generous lips with a fat finger as he gazed at her.

Hannah shrank back in her seat, suddenly realizing how much danger she was in.

Jeeter bustled back into the room and set another cup of water and a plate of greasy food in front of her. Her mouth watered, but her mind refused to acknowledge that the stuff on the plate could actually be consumable.

"Mr. Sutherland," Jeeter said with a huff. "That Reed kid's in town. He's stayin' at his family's town home."

Cooper. Hannah's gaze switched to Jeeter. Cooper was in Charleston? *Keep him safe, Lord, and please help me.*

"Did he see you?" Mr. Sutherland asked.

"Naw, he was too busy stuffin' his face and talkin' to his folks."

Arlis Sutherland scowled. "I'm done for if Lucas Reed learns that I was involved in the kidnapping of his son. Perhaps it's time I cut my losses and return to England." He picked up his hat and twirled it on his finger. "But not before I get those documents back. Here's what we're going to do. . . ."

ҙ

Cooper stretched his arms and then patted his belly after the delicious meal the family cook had prepared. He dabbed his lips with a cloth napkin.

"Father shouldn't be gone long," Jamie said, from across the table. "He wanted to visit several men among the leadership of Charleston to decide what charges to bring against Mr. Sutherland and how they want to handle his arrest."

Cooper had hoped to go along with his father, but his mother wouldn't let him out of her sight. She sat beside him, reaching out and patting his arm every few minutes as if to check to see if he were real.

"I'm so thankful to our Lord for your return. We only got back from England yesterday. I wanted to stay and search for you longer, but we needed to get back for Jamie's wedding." She smiled at Jamie, then patted Cooper again. "And now we'll have the added delight of you being there as well. We planned to rest up a few days before returning to Reed Springs."

Cooper fiddled with his spoon. How could he attend that wedding, knowing the only woman he ever loved would be lost to him forever? Somehow he'd have to get out of going.

Michael shoved back his chair and stood. "Thank you for the fine meal, Mrs. Reed. If you don't mind, ma'am, Johnny and I will head to our rooms and let your family visit. I know it's been a long while since you've seen that scalawag." He winked at Cooper and grinned a smile so similar to Hannah's that it made Cooper's heart clench.

His mother nodded at Michael. "I can't thank you enough for accompanying Cooper home. We're forever in your debt."

"I do believe that lemon pudding you served erased any debts, ma'am." The two men left the room.

"It's good to see Michael again. Hard to believe he'll be family soon." Jamie lifted his cup of tea and took a sip.

Cooper grimaced. He didn't want to hear anything about wedding plans. They only emphasized how much he was sacrificing for his brother's happiness. He turned away, studying the room for any changes that had been made since he was last home. Other than two new paintings, everything was just as he remembered.

His mother turned in her chair, her brown eyes shining. Tufts of gray and brown hair stuck out from under her cap. Tiny lines creased the corner of her eyes. She was aging, but she was still beautiful.

"Tomorrow, we'll go out and get you fitted for a new coat and trousers. There's just barely enough time to have some clothes made before the wedding." She cocked her head and brushed a lock of hair from his forehead. "My boy is now a man. We've all missed you so much, and we feared you were dea—" She choked on the last word and turned away.

Jamie watched her with a concerned gaze. "I told you Coop was tough, Mum. I knew in my heart he wasn't gone." He shot a grin at Cooper.

Jamie had always been the perfect big brother. Yes, he sometimes was a tease but never in a cruel manner. He was always someone Coop looked up to. Jamie always stood up for him, and never let anyone bully him. He'd grown up to be a kind, responsible man, as far as Coop could tell. He'd make a good husband for Hannah. Cooper's stomach churned. If he couldn't have her himself, there was no other person in the world he'd want caring for her other than Jamie. At least he had that consolation.

"Why are you so down in the dumps, little brother?" Jamie's concerned blue eyes now focused on him.

Because I'm in love with your fiancée, he longed to shout. Instead, he shrugged. "Just tired, I suppose—and curious as to what Father is finding out."

"We'll know soon enough." Jamie's dark brows dipped. "It's difficult to believe Mr. Sutherland could be a British loyalist working right under our noses. Why, I do business with him on a regular basis." He pursed his lips tightly. "And to think he had my own brother locked up on one of his ships. It makes me want to—"

Their mother lifted a hand. "Remember, son, we're Christian folk. Your father and his associates will see that Mr. Sutherland is punished for his deeds, but we are to forgive."

Jamie shook his head. "How do you forgive someone for imprisoning your own son?"

"We do as God did. His Son was also imprisoned, but even Jesus forgave those who locked Him up and cruelly mistreated Him. We can do no less."

Jamie cast Coop an I'm-not-so-sure-I-can-do-that look. It warmed him that his brother would be so adamant in wanting retribution from the man who was responsible for Cooper's anguish, but his mother was right. He'd realized that no man could control life, other than in the choices he made. Life and death were in God's hands. There had been many times Coop thought he wouldn't see the light of day again, but God had brought him through, even when he didn't acknowledge God's hand in his life. "Mother is correct, Jamie. We must let go of our anger and desire for revenge. It only hurts us and those closest to us."

Jamie stared at him with his mouth partially open; then he smiled. "And when did you find God, little brother?"

"When I was locked up in a deep, dark hole, injured and alone." They didn't need to know that hole had been at Reed Springs and not onboard the *Syrius.* All that truly mattered was that he'd reconciled with God. Something he should have done many years ago.

The front door opened and shut, and all eyes turned toward the doorway. Coop's heart jumped when his father strode in, looking confident. His gaze latched onto Coop's and he nodded.

"All is taken care of. Members of the City Guard have been dispatched to arrest Arlis Sutherland." He pulled out his chair and dropped into it.

"What about the men still held captive?"

His mother waved to a servant, who silently stood in the corner by the dining room entrance. "Please bring Mr. Reed a hot cup of tea and a bowl of pudding." She turned her eyes to her husband. "And what of Mrs. Sutherland and Ruthie? All of this will be so hard on them."

Lucas Reed pursed his lips and shook his head. "I know not what will happen to them. I suppose they will return to England. Life will certainly be difficult if they choose to remain in Charleston."

"Yes, I'm sure it will."

Coop thought of the arrogant young woman he'd met the day Hannah found him. She would certainly be brought down from the high horse she was on. Being the daughter of a traitor would forever tarnish her life.

Coop listened to his family talk and studied each face. Once Jamie married Hannah, she would sit at the family's table. How could he endure that?

He clenched his jaw. He couldn't. And it wouldn't be fair to her to have him present. No, the best thing for everyone would be for him to leave again—the best for everyone, that is, but himself.

Chapter 18

I don't know why you think I need so many clothes, Mother." Cooper shook his head as he thought of all she had ordered for him at the four shops that they'd just visited. It was enough for three men.

"Because you are returning to society, and you have nothing but the clothes on your back."

"And those are mine." Jamie grinned widely.

Cooper couldn't very well explain he'd never use most of those clothes since he'd be leaving soon.

"Why don't we take luncheon at McCradys?" His mother tugged his arm, and he turned, allowing her to guide him toward the tavern well known for its fine food.

Cooper's forward progress halted when he came to a man leaning back in a chair. His crossed arms lay on his chest and his feet rested on the handrail, blocking the walkway. The man's face was hidden beneath his black hat.

"Excuse me, mister," Cooper said.

He pushed back his hat and looked up at him with a steely gaze.

Cooper took a step back, bumping into his brother. "That's one of the men who attacked me," he whispered over his shoulder to Jamie. Turning back to the man, Cooper's heart skipped a beat when he saw a gun pointed at his chest. His hand edged ever so slowly toward the knife hanging under his shirt.

His mother gasped, and she backed up, running into Jamie. "What do you want with us?"

The man with the droopy mustache jumped to his feet, ignoring Cooper's mother. "So you remember me, huh, kid?" His gaze dropped to Cooper's hand. "Git that hand away from that gun and keep 'em where I can see 'em."

"I don't have a gun," Coop said.

"Look. . ." Jamie set their mother behind him and stepped forward. "We don't want any trouble."

"Well, seems to me you've got it whether you want it or not," boomed a deep voice behind them.

Cooper spun around just as Jamie and their mother did. Two more men with guns had sneaked up behind them. Cooper glanced around but knew that no one had noticed their predicament.

"Let's just take a little walk that way." The biggest man said as he waved his gun toward the alley.

"What makes you think we'll go anywhere with you?" Jamie challenged. "There are people everywhere. Somebody will see you and know you're holding us against our will. The City Guard's office is just down the street."

The man sneered. "Go ahead and holler, but there's a pretty little gal that just might like to see y'all first."

Cooper felt the skin on his face tighten at the man's declaration.

"What girl is he talking about?" his mother asked, turning to gaze at him.

Cooper looked at her. He closed his eyes and sucked in a deep breath. *Oh God, take care of Hannah. This is all my fault. I shouldn't have let her ride off alone when she was so upset.* With resolve, he turned to Jamie. "They must have Hannah."

"Hannah? What does she have to do with this?" Jamie narrowed his eyes as he stared at Cooper. Though he wanted to slink away like a dog who'd stolen the steak off his master's plate, Cooper held his brother's gaze.

"So y'all coming or not?"

Jamie silently nodded, finally breaking his gaze. In unison, they turned in the direction the big man's gun waved and followed the man who had been sitting in the chair.

༄

Hannah jumped when the door banged open again. Her abductors had returned bringing some more people with them. She sighed. With a room full of captors, there'd be no chance for her escape.

The small room began to fill with people. One, two. . .five people walked in. Her breath caught in her throat as she recognized Cooper's lean form coming through the door. *No, Lord, not Cooper, too.* Sam held a gun to his back. Hannah looked up to meet Cooper's gaze, and she saw the regret encompassing his handsome face.

"Sit down," Arlis Sutherland ordered as he stood, his chair squeaking as if happy to be relieved of its monstrous burden. He motioned a hand to the only woman in the group, and as she stepped out from behind Cooper, Hannah realized it was her future mother-in-law, Heather Reed. She walked over and sat in the chair Mr. Sutherland had just occupied. Mrs. Reed offered Hannah a soft smile and reached out, grasping her hands. She was grateful for the silent support.

Cooper sat on the edge of the desk, next to Hannah. He subtly reached a hand behind her and briefly patted her back. Warmth traveled up her spine, and it took all the restraint she could muster not to jump into his arms.

Hannah glanced up, expecting to see Lucas Reed, but instead, her gaze collided with Jamie's. He walked over and stood behind her chair and his mother's. Heather glanced over her shoulder into Jamie Reed's eyes. He offered her a reassuring smile, then cast a peculiar glance in his brother's direction.

"Now, I want to know where my papers are." Mr. Sutherland smacked his meaty fist on the table near Heather Reed, and she jumped and leaned back, eyes wide.

"You're too late," Jamie told him, the timbre of his voice sounding much like Coop's.

"What do you mean?"

"My father and a number of his associates have already seen the information," Cooper said.

Ppfff! Sutherland exhaled a loud breath, which sounded to Hannah as if he practically strangled on it. "You're lying!"

"No, we're not. Evidently you haven't been home or you would have already been arrested." Cooper lifted his chin in the air. "So you see, you're too late. By now the captive sailors have been set free. You're a wanted man, Mr. Sutherland."

Ruthie's father stood glaring at him. Turbulent emotions flashed across his thick face, and his gray eyes darkened like angry thunderclouds. He turned his gaze on Hannah, and she became increasingly uneasy under his scrutiny. "Well, in that case, I may need a hostage to insure my safety. Sam, get the girl."

Hannah flinched at the icy tone of his voice. She felt the nauseating sinking of despair, and she bit her lip until it throbbed like her pulse. Feeling like a trapped animal, she looked at Cooper and then over to Jamie and Sam, who hadn't yet moved. Suddenly, Cooper jumped to his feet, but Jeeter jammed his pistol into his back and growled, "Sit down, sonny, 'fore I knock ya in the head with my gun like I did before."

Sam crossed the room in three steps and moved in Hannah's direction before a knock on the door halted him. He turned to Mr. Sutherland, who nodded for him to answer.

"Who's there?"

"It's me, Lily. Jeeter said I was to bring some more water and some whiskey."

Sam looked at Mr. Sutherland. He nodded again. Hannah thought Mr. Sutherland probably reasoned he needed a drink about now. She exhaled a sigh, glad for the short reprieve, and shot another prayer heavenward.

Sam opened the door just wide enough to slip his slim body through, then pulled the door shut behind him. Moments later, the door burst open. The room instantly filled with people with guns drawn. Jeeter's flintlock boomed behind her, and Hannah jerked her head down. The doorjamb splintered into tiny fragments just inches from her father's head. Jamie leaped from his chair. With the strength of youth behind him, he wrestled away the pistol Arlis Sutherland had just pulled from his waistband. As if blasted with a stick of dynamite, Cooper flew off the desk and knocked Jeeter to the floor. Boss cowered in the corner, eyes wide, anger battling with defeat. Several members of the City Guard strode over and quickly took Boss into custody.

Hannah massaged her ears with her fingertips and opened her mouth wide in hopes of clearing the ringing. The acrid odor of gunpowder stung her eyes. She looked over at Heather Reed. The older woman sat with her hands over her face. Wide brown eyes peered over her fingertips.

"Hello, Sutherland. Seems you have something that belongs to me," Richard Madison seethed through clenched teeth. He strode over and grabbed Sutherland by his cummerbund.

Michael stepped into the doorway with his gun ready and surveyed the scene. Buster slipped in behind him and went to stand protectively next to Hannah. He growled a low snarl and took a step toward Jeeter, who still wrestled with Cooper on the floor near Hannah's feet. Boots scraped against the wooden floor as the two men struggled. At the sight of the large dog's bared teeth near his face, Jeeter's spirit seemed to wither. In a matter of seconds, Cooper had the man on his feet with the gun now in his back.

"Well, Arlis, it looks to me like you're a bit outnumbered. What do you suppose we should do about it?" Hannah's father asked.

Arlis Sutherland scanned the room. The defeat registered on his face. "I fail to see that I have a say in the matter." He knocked his former business associate's hand off his cummerbund, and his large body hunkered down on the only empty chair in the room.

Richard Madison holstered his pistol and turned toward Hannah. "Are you all right, princess?"

Hannah jumped up and threw her arms around him. "Yes, Papa, but I was so scared for a while. I thought for sure they were going to take me away and I'd never see you again. How did you ever find me?"

"We had the good Lord's help, your mother's prayers, and a little bit of luck. Seems Jason Mayburn was riding out to talk to me about borrowing the services of my new bull. When he arrived, we were all half-crazy from looking for you. You'd been gone all day and it was getting dark and nobody had seen you. Mayburn mentioned that he passed three people, two men and a woman, on his way to Madison Gardens. He said the woman resembled you and didn't look too happy. So we packed up and made a beeline to town. Buster was the one that tracked you down once we got here. I guess you owe that ol' dog a big bone."

Hannah knelt down and gave Buster a big hug. He plastered a wet, sloppy kiss on her face. "Eeww!"

The tension broke around the room as everyone, except for the prisoners, started laughing. The City Guard members who'd been waiting outside, guarding Sam, left to escort the four men to jail.

"Richard, thank you so much for rescuing us." Mrs. Reed stood and hurried to his side. "I suppose you've heard that Cooper has been returned to us."

His smile stretched from ear to ear. "Yes, he borrowed a horse and my son."

"We can't thank you enough for your help." Mrs. Reed brushed the hair back from Hannah's face. "Are you all right, dear?"

Hannah smiled. "Yes, thank you."

"Well, I would imagine you'd like to get out of here."

She nodded. "That I would, most certainly. I'm famished."

Heather nodded to Jamie. "Wouldn't you care to escort your fiancée, son?"

Jamie slipped past Cooper. "Yes ma'am, I would."

Hannah darted a glance at Cooper, who matched her strained smile with his own weak one. Her heart skipped like a ricocheting lead ball.

"Might I have the pleasure?" Jamie stepped toward her, and she looked up at him with effort. He reached for his hat and seemed to realize it was gone. He turned and searched the floor.

"Looking for this?" Michael grinned as he handed Jamie a smashed black hat. Jamie took it and fluffed it and pressed it onto his thatch of dark hair. He turned back to Hannah and gave a smile so like Cooper's that Hannah wanted to cry.

"You've grown up to be quite a beauty, Miss Hannah."

She cleared her throat and felt her cheeks flush. She peeked around Jamie's arm and over at Cooper. He scowled at his brother's back, then shoved his hands to his hips, and his shoulders slumped as he stared at the floor. The aching in Hannah's heart became a fiery gnawing.

"We were headed over to McGrady's to dine. Might I have the pleasure of your company as we walk there?" Hannah forced her gaze away from the man she was in love with and turned her attention on the man she would be marrying. She nodded and hesitantly slipped her hand in the crook of his arm, flashing Cooper an apologetic glance. She knew he was just as displeased with the situation as she, but now wasn't the time for a confrontation.

"Heather, if you don't mind enduring my company until that rascally husband of yours can join us. . ." Hannah's father offered his arm to Mrs. Reed.

"It would be my pleasure, kind sir."

Hannah saw Michael flash a teasing grin at Cooper and offer him his arm. Cooper scowled at him and stalked out the door alone.

"What do you suppose has gotten into him?" Mrs. Reed asked.

Chapter 19

*T*his is my wedding day. Hannah exhaled a heavy sigh and stared out her bedroom window at the gray, dismal morning, which mirrored her emotions. The threat of a spring thunderstorm hung heavily in the air, every bit as foreboding as Hannah's feelings about today's event. This should have been the happiest day of her life, but she felt as if she were going to her own funeral rather than her wedding.

Cooper had avoided her ever since her rescue and his family's return to Reed Springs. Hannah knew he was hurting as much as she, but she also knew that she had to see him one last time. Once her decision was made, Hannah dressed hastily, hoping to get out of the house before her mother awoke. She pulled on a gown and tied a blue sash around the high waistline. Cooper had commented once that the ribbon brought out the color of her beautiful eyes. Her chin wobbled, and she let out a strangled gasp as tears blurred her vision. *I wonder if Jamie even knows the color of my eyes.*

Hannah collapsed on her bed and cried out loud to God. "Oh Lord, am I doing the right thing in honoring my parents' wishes and marrying Jamie? 'Delight thyself also in the Lord: and he shall give thee the desires of thine heart'—that's what Your Word says. I've been doin' my best to take delight in You. But how can I marry Jamie when I know my heart will always belong to Cooper?" She pulled a handkerchief from the dwindling stack she'd set on the table next to her bed the night before and blew her nose. "I tried to talk to Mama, but she insists she and Papa must not go back on their word to Jamie and his parents. Is that more important than their own daughter's happiness? Oh, it's all so confusing."

She allowed herself only a few moments to pour out her heart before God, then got up from her bed with resolve. If she was going to have any chance of getting away and seeing Cooper, she'd best get going now before everyone else got up. She put on her shoes and tiptoed as quietly as she could down the long hall. The clicking of her heels resonating against the wooden floor was deafening in her ears. If her shoes didn't give her away, surely the roar of her beating heart would.

Hannah tiptoed into the empty kitchen. Evidence that her mother was up and had already begun baking was everywhere. She sighed, thankful that her mother wasn't in the room just then. As she was relishing in the success of her escape, her mother came barreling in the back door, carrying a pail of eggs.

Hannah's heart sank all the way down to her toes.

"You're up early on your wedding day. I suppose you're a bit anxious." Her mother huffed a laugh and set the pail on the table. "I know I sure was the day I married your father."

Anxious, yes, but not in the same way her mother meant. "I want to go for a short walk before things get hopping around here."

"Taking a walk around your home for the last time before you marry is a grand idea. It's a good way to say good-bye to your past and to embrace your future. But then it's not like you won't be coming back often. It's only a brief walk from Reed Springs."

"I—I should go before time gets away from me."

The door banged again, and Chesny entered, carrying a pail of frothy milk. She cast a tight-lipped glance at Hannah. "Smile, child. It's yo' weddin' day!"

Was everyone against her?

Her mother nodded. "Jamie is a good man and handsome, too. He'll make you a fine husband."

Hannah gave the women a weak smile and ran out the door just in time to hide the tears that gushed forth again. Buster fell into step beside her, and she patted his big head, welcoming his company. The mile-long walk did little to calm her turbulent emotions. In the back of her mind, she could feel God's gentle encouragements. . . . *"Trust Me"*. . . . *"Trust Me."* But it was so hard to trust Him when there seemed to be no possible way out of her unwanted marriage.

As Hannah crested the last hill, the sun peeked through a break in the clouds on the horizon. Things were still quiet at Reed Springs. It looked as though everyone was still asleep, but she doubted that was true.

Hannah's eyes were glued to the house in hopes of catching Cooper alone. A movement in the corner of her eye drew her gaze to the opening barn door. Cooper walked out and looked around, as if he sensed her presence. Buster whined when he saw him.

She lifted two fingers to her mouth and blew out a whistle she'd perfected as a child, and her dog added a bark. Cooper's head jerked toward her, and their eyes met over the distance. He slowly raised his hand in acknowledgment, held it there for a moment, then disappeared back into the barn.

Heart plummeting all the way down to her boot tips, she turned back toward home. "Well, that's it, boy." She pressed Buster's head against her skirt, needing the love she knew he'd give her. Her lower lip trembled, and tears welled in her eyes. "Cooper won't talk with me."

She sighed a loud breath, determined to do what everyone expected of her, and continued walking. In a matter of hours, she'd be living at Reed Springs with Jamie, his parents. . .and Cooper. She shook that image from her mind. She had to put Cooper Reed out of her thoughts. It seemed that he had already done so with her. With resolve, she headed back to prepare for her wedding.

The *clip-clop* of quickly approaching hoofbeats stopped her dead in her tracks. She whirled around just as Cooper rode up on a gray horse that she hadn't seen before. The big animal nickered to her. . .and that was more than Cooper did. He jumped down to the ground and stood looking at her with a hard, unreadable expression on his handsome face.

She tried to hide her misery from his probing stare. Her newly found resolution melted in his presence. "Cooper—please—won't you do something to stop this?" Hannah reached out to touch his arm.

"There's nothing to be done." He stared at her with a hard, steely gaze. The blue eyes she loved so much now filled her with icy apprehension. "You want me to tell my own brother that I fell in love with the woman he's going to marry?"

"Yes!" That didn't sound so unreasonable to her.

"I—I can't. You don't understand how things are with us. Jamie and I are close. All our lives our father pounded into us that next to God, family is most important."

Hannah felt her heart shrivel as he recited the very words on her sampler—words she'd heard his father say.

"My father's brother nearly destroyed the whole family with his hate and vendetta to obliterate all that my father loved. I won't be like my uncle and cause a rift in my family—not even for you, angel. I can't do it."

The tiny spark of hope she'd managed to salvage was quickly stamped out. "But you're willing to destroy what we could have?"

Cooper looked at her through half-opened eyes. His pain-filled expression resembled someone's who'd been gut shot. "Hannah, I know I shouldn't say this, but I'll always love you. Nothing can destroy that." He looked away, his lips pressed tightly together, then he shook his head. "I'm sure I'll never marry, because no woman could ever replace you in my heart."

The ache in her heart became a fiery gnawing. "That's so easy for you to say." Hannah grabbed Cooper's upper arms and shook him with all her might. She wasn't ready to give in yet. "But what about me? You'd let me marry your brother, live in the same house, and sleep under the same roof as you, knowing that it's you I love and not him? Is that fair to Jamie?"

He heaved a sigh. "I'm leaving. . .after the wedding."

The anguish in his voice cut her to the quick. She couldn't bear the thought of never seeing him again—of being the one to drive him away from his close-knit family. "No, Cooper. . .please don't." She closed her eyes, utterly miserable, and tightened her grip on his arms to keep from falling from the weight of her despair.

When she finally reopened them, Hannah saw the tears Cooper had fought so hard against come rolling down his tan cheeks. "You're right. I can't stand the thought of you in Jamie's arms, much less sharing his bed—and me in the adjoining room. It would kill us both. Don't you see? Leaving is the only way."

"We could go away together."

"No, angel, I can't take you from your home—your family. I know how awful that can be. Besides, you know we'd be miserable if we did that." Cooper closed his eyes and shook his head. The agony on his handsome face ripped Hannah's heart in two.

"You know, it's really odd. Jamie was always the one who had to have his hands in every aspect of the shipping business, just like Father. I loved sailing, but what I'd learned during my years at sea was that I truly loved the land. I went to England to finish my education with the idea of coming back to the plantation and improving its output—of trying new things. Jamie prefers city life to living here. I'd hoped Reed Springs might be my inheritance while Jamie got the Charleston house and the shipping business." He shoved his hands to his hips, and his shoulders hunched forward.

"So, that's it then. You're not goin' to do a thing to stop this?" she squeaked, as a suffocating sensation tightened her throat.

"I won't go against my brother. I love him too much."

Hannah covered her face with trembling hands and gave vent to the agony of her loss. "I—I guess you love him more than me then." She sobbed a strangled gasp and turned away, no longer able to look on his handsome face.

☙

Hannah's anguished plea tore at every part of his being. Cooper had gone over and over the whole situation in his head. He'd prayed for days and still had no answer. "*Trust Me*" was the message that kept coming to his mind. And he was trying to trust God. . .but there just seemed no way for this situation to turn out good for everyone.

"Hannah, please don't go like this," he said, his voice ragged.

She whipped around, throwing sharp blue daggers at him with her eyes. "Just how would you like me to be going?"

Cooper removed his tricorn and crunched the edges in his hand. He had to help her see how he felt. "I was hoping you would understand. You have two brothers. What if the situation was reversed? Could you walk in and steal Michael's intended away from him, knowing how much pain it would cause him?"

The struggle taking place on her beautiful face shredded his already battered heart. After a moment she dropped her gaze to the ground. "No, I don't suppose I could."

He lifted her chin with his finger. With the back of his hand, he wiped the tears blurring his vision, then he stood memorizing every inch of her lovely face for the last time. Tears flowed freely down both of their faces. Cooper expelled a savage groan and pulled her into his arms.

For the moment, nothing else existed. He clung to her, knowing it would be his last chance. After this moment they wouldn't belong to one another ever again.

After a few short moments, Cooper released his death grip on Hannah and tilted her face up to his. He cradled her head in his hands and his fingers entwined in her hair. "I'll love you forever, my sweet angel." He leaned down and sealed their destiny with a final kiss as their lips and tears mingled together.

All too soon, he pulled back. "Good-bye, my love, my angel." He stroked her golden tresses for the final time, then released her so fast that she stumbled. He picked his hat off the ground where he had dropped it and slapped it back onto his head. Quickly, he turned, jumped on his horse, and rode away before he changed his mind.

At least Jamie would be happy, though he would never know the sacrifice that Cooper had made.

❧

Feeling more miserable than she ever had in her twenty years, Hannah turned and slowly walked back home. Lifting the skirt of her dress, she dried her tears. It was time she prepared to become the wife of Jamie Reed.

Chapter 20

The wedding was to take place at noon in the grassy area north of the Madisons' house, weather permitting. The menacing, gray storm clouds had threatened to release their bounty but so far had not followed through.

Hannah held up her small mirror and tried to see how her mother's wedding dress looked on her. They had taken it up in the bust and sides and let out the hem a full two inches. She despised the tightly laced corset she had to wear in order to fit into the gown's clinging bodice that tapered down to her waist. The corset made it hard to breathe and required her to stand up so much straighter than she had to when wearing her looser-fitting, high-waisted gowns. But she had to admit the royal blue dress with ecru lace trim was truly beautiful and the narrow cut made her look much slimmer.

She set the mirror on the dresser and walked over to the small window in her bedroom. Jamie and his mother were riding over the ridge in a buggy and heading toward the house, with his father riding alongside on his horse.

"Lord, I want to do Your will and to please You. Help me to be a good wife to Jamie. Perhaps in time, I'll grow to love him. I truly hope I do, for his sake. I'm going to trust You. . . trust that You have good things planned for me. Please ease this horrible pain in my heart, and take care of Cooper."

Hannah opened the large Madison family Bible and ran her finger over the page that held her family tree. After today, Jamie's name would be entered onto it next to hers. She let out a sigh and flipped the pages to Proverbs 3:5 and began reading. " 'Trust in the Lord with all thine heart; and lean not unto thine own understanding. In all thy ways acknowledge him, and he shall direct thy paths.' Amen, Lord. That is my prayer."

"Aren't you the pretty one? Look what I have for your hair," said her mother as she burst into the room and proudly held up a chain of tiny purple violets.

"They're very pretty."

Her mother had already arranged Hannah's hair in loose curls on the back of her head with shorter curls framing her face and now placed the floral chain on her head. Hannah picked up the mirror and stared at her reflection again. The dainty flowers added a touch of femininity. "I hope Jamie will like them."

"Jamie will be so proud of you, my sweet girl, but I'll dearly miss seeing you each morning."

"As you said before, I won't be all that far away. I'm sure I'll see you most days."

Her mother patted the bed. "Come and sit beside me for a moment."

Hannah lowered herself down next to her mother. Carefully she straightened her dress, knowing the warm, moist air would instantly cause wrinkles if she sat on it wrong.

Her mother reached for her hand. "I'm so proud of you, my dear. I've looked forward to this day almost since the day you were born. Heather came to visit me a few days later and brought the boys. Jamie begged to hold you and wouldn't take no for an answer. It was so out of character for him that Heather and I joked about you two getting married when you grew up, and before long, it became our dream. I'm so happy I lived to see this day. My own mother died before I married, and I so wished she could have been at my wedding."

Hannah was dumbfounded. Her mother had never told her that. She was destined almost from the day she was born to be Jamie's wife. This path had been laid out her whole life. She had only to follow it and everything would work out. She had to believe that.

Her mother squeezed her hand. "I saw Jamie arriving before I came in. I suppose it's time we were heading to the parlor to await the signal for the wedding to begin."

Footsteps came their way down the hall, and they both looked up. Jane appeared in the doorway. Hannah smiled at her sister.

"I've finished feeding the children and put them down for their naps. Jamie is here, and everyone is assembled." Jane crossed the room and reached for Hannah's hand, pulling her to her feet. "And don't you look lovely. Mama's dress fits you so much better than it did me."

"That's not true. I'm too tall to do it justice."

"It looked lovely on both of you, so enough of that talk. Let's be going." Her mother extended her hand toward the doorway.

Jane clapped her hands, a smile lighting her face. "Oh, did I tell you that the minister from town brought his brother? He'll be playing his violin as you march in. Won't it be so grand to have music at the wedding!"

"Yes, it's wonderful." Hannah tried to work up some enthusiasm for her sister's and mother's sake.

Jane waved them from the room. "We'd best be going."

Hannah nodded and her mother took her in her arms. As they parted, Mama wiped a tear off Hannah's cheek.

"I always cry at weddings, too." Her mother smiled and patted Hannah's cheek. "Time to be going, dear."

Taking a calming breath, Hannah followed her mother down the hall. *Go ahead and cry, Mama, and so will I, but we're not crying for the same reason.*

Moments later, Hannah peeked out the front door and surveyed the small crowd of guests gathered around the garden entrance. Her father strode proudly toward her, a big smile on his face. Michael, deep in an animated conversation with Jamie, flung his arms out to the side. Chesny stood with the other family servants in the shade of a huge pine tree, her hands also moving quickly as she conversed with Maisy and Leta. The minister's wife stood next to Heather Reed, who also took advantage of the shade. But where was Cooper? As much as Hannah wanted him to be there, she wondered if it might be easier if he weren't.

"Are you ready to be married, daughter?" Richard Madison bellowed proudly.

"Yes, Father." *But not to the man of my choosing—not to the man who stole my heart.*

He held out his elbow to her. "Then grab hold, and let's go get you married."

Together they walked arm in arm across the porch and down the steps. Mama followed, happily humming behind them. Hannah could faintly hear the violin playing, but most of the sweet music floated away on the stiff breeze. Everyone smiled as they moved toward them. Everyone, except Cooper. Dressed in his dark church clothes and leaning against a tall oak tree, he looked as handsome as she'd ever seen him. His black tricorn was pulled down low, hiding his eyes, and his arms were crossed stiffly. The toe of his boot stirred up tiny clouds of dust that quickly floated away on the wind.

As they came closer to the small cluster of people, Jamie walked away from Michael and went to stand in front of the minister. Cooper pushed away from the tree and walked over, standing a few yards away, to the right of Michael. Hannah glanced in his direction, but his head remained downcast.

She felt her father handing her off to Jamie, and she trembled as he took her hand. Hannah looked into the lightly tanned face of the man who would soon be her husband. His Reed-blue eyes held a mischievous glint that gave her pause.

Numbness filled her whole being. The minister was saying something about the sanctity of marriage. . .leaving your father and mother and cleaving to one another. Then he said, "If any of you know cause, or just impediment, why these two persons should not be joined together in holy matrimony, please speak up now or forever hold your peace."

Except for the birds mocking her with their cheerful songs and the trees rustling in the breeze, all was quiet. Hannah glanced over her shoulder and saw Cooper standing with his hands on his hips, squirming. When he looked up and held her gaze, a tiny spark of hope flickered deep within her. His dark brows knitted together, and Hannah watched the rise and fall of his chest as he seemed to be wrestling with his thoughts.

I love you. Hannah hoped Cooper could read the silent message in her gaze. A blazing light ignited in his blue eyes. Like a tiny flame sparking a prairie fire, suddenly his countenance changed from despair to resolve. He straightened and walked toward her.

Oh please, Lord, let it be.

Cooper stopped behind her, and the heat from his body sent goose bumps racing up her arms. "I object, Reverend."

Hannah dared to breathe again. Tears of joy blurred her vision when Cooper pushed his way between her and Jamie, ripping her hand away from Jamie's.

"I tried," he whispered, "but I just can't let you go, angel."

A cry of relief broke from her lips, and tears cascaded down her cheeks. For the first time in days, Hannah reveled in the joy of Cooper's love.

"Um-hum." The sound of Jamie clearing his throat jolted Hannah back to reality. She clung to Cooper's hand and glanced up at his brother. Even though her heart burst with joy, she desperately hoped he wouldn't be hurt. Immense relief flooded her to see his big grin. Jamie slapped Cooper on the shoulder. "It's about time you came to your senses, little brother."

Richard Madison marched up to them. "Just what is the meaning of all this?"

"Well, sir, it seems my little brother just about made the biggest mistake of his life," Jamie said.

"What mistake?" Lucas Reed roared.

"Don't know why you couldn't see it, Father." Jamie interrupted. "You and Mother were so busy tryin' to marry me off to Hannah that you were blind to the fact that she doesn't love me. She's in love with Cooper."

"How can she be in love with Cooper? She hasn't seen him since she was young." Heather Reed rose from her chair and stood next to Jamie.

"Well, Mum," Jamie said, "it seems that my little brother stole my intended right out from under my nose."

Clinging to Cooper's strong hand with both of hers, Hannah dared a glance at Jamie's face. He looked as relieved as she felt. Had he, too, been forced into this near-marriage? She'd thought he wanted to marry her, but perhaps he was just as apprehensive. She thought sure her heart would explode any second with sheer joy.

"Would somebody explain what is going on here?" Lucas Reed yelled.

Hannah felt the warmth of Jamie's hand on her shoulder and saw that his other hand clung to Cooper's shoulder. "It's quite simple, sir. Hannah almost married the wrong Reed brother. She loves Cooper, and she should marry him, not me."

Mrs. Reed stepped forward. "Cooper Reed, what is the meaning of this? How could you do such a horrible thing to your brother?" she cried.

Hannah held her breath, hoping that Heather Reed would keep her temper under control.

Before Cooper could respond, Jamie jumped back into the discussion.

"Don't you see, Mother? It makes good sense. You said yourself that Cooper hasn't been himself ever since we came back to Reed Springs. You said he was moping around like a lovesick puppy."

"Aye, I did. I thought he was pinin' away for some lassie back in England, but he had never mentioned a fondness for a young woman before."

Hannah's father turned a bewildered look toward Michael. "Just what do you know about all this?"

"I don't know how you and Mother couldn't see it. The two of them have been moping around ever since Jamie showed up. Haven't you seen the way they look at each other? I got curious the day Cooper and I rode to Charleston. I wondered why he was wearing my clothes. Then I put two and two together and realized that Hannah must have been taking care of him. No wonder she couldn't get over to Reed Springs fast enough each morning."

"It's true." Cooper smiled down at her and rubbed the scar on his forehead. "Hannah saved my life when she found me in the barn. I couldn't have lasted much longer."

Lucas Reed stepped forward. "This is all my fault. I strove too hard to make my boys close after what happened between Marcus and me. I see now that Cooper couldn't speak his mind for fear of hurting his brother." He turned to face his sons. "Forgive me if I went too far in establishing the family as most important."

Cooper smiled. "I forgive you, Father."

"Me, too." Jamie wrapped his arms around his father's and brother's shoulders.

Hannah's father turned to her. "Is it true? Are you in love with Cooper?"

"Oh yes, sir. So much that I thought I would die without him." She shot Cooper a hesitant smile.

"Cooper Reed," Hannah's father bellowed, "just how did this happen? How could you steal my daughter's heart right out from under my nose?"

"It's a long story, sir, and I'm afraid it's my heart that *she* kidnapped," Cooper said, smiling completely for the first time in days.

❧

A short while later, Cooper and Hannah had replayed the whole story. Jamie still stood with his hands on their shoulders, offering silent support.

"So you see, sir, your daughter saved my life. I'd be dead right now if she hadn't come along and taken care of me."

Hannah smiled openly at the man she loved. He stood in front of her father just as bold as you please. The pride she felt that Cooper had the gumption to stand up to her father's inquisition was equaled only by her love for him.

"And do you love her as Jamie says?" Father asked, his hands fisted on his hips.

"Yes sir, I love her with all my heart. I've been so distraught at the thought of losing her I was certain I would shrivel up and die. If you have no objections, Mr. Madison, I'd like to ask you for your daughter's hand in marriage." Cooper's gaze shot toward Jamie. "That is if my brother is willing to relinquish his claim to her."

Jamie pursed his lips and ducked his head, then looked around at those crowded around him. "This is probably my own fault. I should have put a halt to this sham engagement years ago."

His mother gasped and held her hand to her mouth, and Jamie sent her an affectionate smile. "I'm sorry to ruin your plans, Mum. I thought I could go along and would grow to love Hannah. I've always been fond of her, you know."

The melancholy smile he gave Hannah made her stomach swirl. The last thing she wanted was to hurt him.

"But I don't love her—not as Cooper obviously does. They deserve a chance at happiness—a chance to be together. I only hope that one day I'll find a woman who cherishes me as much as Hannah does Coop."

Hope coursed through Hannah's veins, caressing her like warm milk on a cold night. Her dream might actually be realized. Her pleading eyes held her father's, and she saw him weighing all that he had just heard. He turned around and looked at the shocked expression on his wife's face. Then he turned and looked at the same bewilderment on Heather Reed's face. "Well, does anybody have any objections to Cooper and Hannah getting married?"

Nobody uttered a sound. The dark clouds suddenly parted, and long fingers of bright sunshine illuminated the area, sending golden rays of sunlight blasting straight into Hannah's heart.

"All right then, I guess we have a wedding to finish—or rather—start!"

"Take good care of her, little brother." Jamie gently squeezed Hannah's shoulder.

Hannah fell into Cooper's arms with a squeal. "*Trust Me,*" the Lord had said. As Coop enveloped her in his strong arms, she marveled at the way God had worked everything out. She had been willing to give up her dream, but God had resurrected it in a way she never thought possible.

꒰ꙮ꒱

Cooper held Hannah tightly in his embrace, ignoring the gawking crowd of grinning spectators. "So, Hannah Caroline Madison," he whispered in her ear, "would you like to be *my* wife?"

"Oh yes, my love," she whispered. Tears—happy tears, he suspected—ran down her soft cheeks. "I can hardly wait."

Cooper leaned down and placed his lips on Hannah's as all the pain and despondency he'd felt the past few days and weeks melted away.

"Hey," Michael yelled, "the preacher hasn't reached the kissing part yet!"

Cooper pulled back, temporarily interrupting their kiss. Hannah's wide, enthusiastic grin echoed his. The laughter around them softened as they pulled apart and turned toward the front.

The minister scratched his chin, and he shook his head as if he were trying to recover from the shocking chain of events. He took a long look at the crowd and then opened his Bible. "I'll begin reading from the second chapter of Genesis. 'But for Adam there was not found an help meet for him. And the Lord God caused a deep sleep to fall upon Adam, and he slept: and he took one of his ribs, and closed up the flesh instead thereof; And the rib, which the Lord God had taken from man, made he a woman, and brought her unto the man.'"

Cooper looked down at Hannah's astonished expression and knew it mirrored his. God had taken Adam—Cooper in this instance—amnesia, cracked ribs, and all, and used them to bring to him the woman who would become his wife today. He smiled at his angel and turned back to the minister, anxious to begin his married life.

DUELING
HEARTS

Dedication

This book is dedicated to Barbour and the staff who work there. I wouldn't have a writing career if not for Barbour, and I will always be grateful to Becky Germany for buying that first novella and the ones that followed and then later for acquiring my first trade fiction series. Thank you, Tracie Peterson, for seeing something good in my writing and purchasing my first four Heartsong books and to Joanne Simmons for buying the next seven. Thanks also to the folks behind the scenes who work so diligently to put out a good product.

Chapter 1

Charleston, South Carolina
1848

Who is that lovely black-eyed Susan hiding behind the potted plants?" Reed Bishop nodded his head toward the corner of the large ballroom where a dark-haired nymph leaned against the wall, head down.

Damian squinted, staring past the stringed quartet, and shrugged. "She's a pretty thing, although that yellow dress of hers is rather shabby." He lifted his glass and sipped the punch, eyeing the young woman with disdain.

"Hmm... Maybe the gown looks shabby because her loveliness outshines it."

Damian sputtered then started coughing. When he regained his composure, he glanced at Reed with glistening eyes. "Are you turning poetic?"

Reed looked away, not wanting his friend to think he was besotted. He stared at the woman for another long moment then tugged his gaze toward the colorful line of dancers sashaying to the lively music.

"Why don't you ask her to dance?"

Reed shrugged. He probably would, but he didn't want Damian thinking it had been his idea.

"How did you manage to sit this round out, anyway? All the ladies have been chasing after you, anxious to catch your eye before you leave town."

Reed pursed his lips. "Mother pulled me aside to introduce me to an old friend, and the music had already started when we finished talking."

"Well, if I were you, I'd have snagged one of them gals anyhow."

"I can't say I don't enjoy the attention, but I feel kind of like a treed coon at times."

Damian grinned. "If you feel that way now, just wait until you return from college as a surgeon."

Huffing a laugh, Reed failed to see the lure. "Most surgeons don't have two half dimes to rub together."

His friend nudged Reed in the arm and winked. "Most surgeons aren't the grandson of Cooper Reed and half owner of Reed Shipping, and most don't own a plantation as large and prosperous as Reed Springs." Damian shook his head. "Why do you insist on sailing off to the wilds of Scotland when you have a thriving business to run here?"

Shifting his gaze back to the sprite in the corner, Reed shrugged. He hated it when one of his friends pointed out his family's wealth. He had the fortune—and oft times, misfortune—to be born into a wealthy family, but he didn't want people befriending him for that reason alone. Damian was his best friend, but he had never understood Reed's interest in science and didn't want him going away for several years. There was no point trudging through that muck again.

"I'm halfway surprised that your mother didn't keep you at home today, seeing as how you set sail in the morning. Is she still trying to get you to change your mind?"

He watched Dudley Brown approach the young woman in the yellow dress. "Yes, she doesn't understand my love for science and my preference to become a surgeon rather than running the plantation."

"You're her only son. It's expected you'd follow in your father's footsteps."

"My cousin is better suited to run Reed Shipping—and he has the desire."

Dudley Brown placed one hand on the wall to the right of the woman's shoulder and leaned toward her. The sprite's eyes widened, and her head swiveled back and forth like a weather vane in a thunderstorm. Reed grinned, glad she had the sense to refuse a rascal like Dudley. What would she say if *he* asked her to take a spin with him? He took a step in her direction.

"Good luck!" Damian called out.

As he drew closer, Reed sensed there was something familiar about the girl. Her eyes—as dark as black coffee—widened when he stopped a proper distance away. Her thin eyebrows dipped, and her mouth puckered. Hardly the response Reed expected—even worse than when Dudley had approached her.

"Good afternoon. I hope you're having a nice time here."

"I was doin' fine till *you* arrived." She turned her head away and stared over the fronds of a small palm tree toward the open doors to the veranda.

Not used to being snubbed by a Southern woman, Reed was taken off guard. Had he offended her somehow? But how could that be possible when he didn't think he'd even met her before? He glanced back at Damian. His friend eyed him with obvious curiosity. Reed hated to fail, especially when a friend was watching. "Have we met previously?"

She stiffened, hiking up her chin and staring at him with those captivating eyes. Had he ever seen a fair-skinned woman with eyes the color of onyx before?

"I can't believe you'd ask me that," she snapped at him, like an alligator latching on to its dinner.

He grappled for a response, but before he could form a retort, she darted between the potted trees and ran out the door.

Damian hurried toward him. "The only other time I've ever seen a female run away from you was the time you kissed the preacher's daughter right after church last Easter. What in the world did you say to that girl?"

"Nothing." Reed's arms hung limp at his sides, and he held out his hands. "Nothing at all. She seemed to think she knew me, but I've never met her before."

"She must have confused you with someone else."

Reed shrugged. The venom she spat at him had purpose. He may not have known her, but he was certain she knew him.

Clapping him on the shoulder, Damian gave Reed a gentle shake. "Don't fret over her. There are plenty of other butterflies in the garden you can cast your net over."

"Ha! Who's waxing poetic now?"

His friend's hazel eyes twinkled, and his ears turned red. "My cup is empty. How about joining me for some more punch?"

Reed followed, but his gaze clung to the doorway where the confusing woman had fled. He'd never had a woman run away from him before—at least not one without a justifiable reason—and it intrigued him. Most times women competed for his attention, batting their long lashes at him and even pushing their friends out of the way to get closer to him. He knew he was handsome—and wealthy—and he had the striking blue eyes that many of the Reed men he'd descended from had—eyes that women found irresistible. All but this woman.

☙

Carina raced down the hall, hoping against hope that *he* didn't follow. Her stomach churned just to be standing so close to a Bishop. And to think she'd actually talked to him. Not that she'd been very pleasant.

But he had surprised her. She'd never imagined *he* would ask her to dance.

Clenching her fist, she swung her arms as she marched in a quite unlady-like fashion down the upstairs hall to the room she'd gotten dressed in earlier. Reed Bishop's blue eyes haunted her thoughts. And until she'd seen him up close, she hadn't realized how his thick hair resembled the color of her favorite cypress swing on her front porch. She'd be lying if she denied he was hand-some. Too bad that he knew it and used his charm to attract females. Every other woman might beg him to dance and swoon at his feet, but she sure never would. Not ever.

She all but ran into the bedchamber where she had dressed earlier and dropped down onto the dressing table chair. She stared at her reflection in the mirror. Her hair, which she'd attempted to fashion into something pretty this morning, now listed to the left like a sinking ship. Yanking out the pins, she shook her head, and her locks tumbled past her shoulders, down her back. There was no point in trying to look like a lady. She failed miserably. Her dress looked like a worn-out slave's garment compared to the other gowns in the ballroom. Oh, why had she allowed Betsey to talk her into coming? She didn't belong here.

Tossing aside the finer travel bags stacked in the corner, she located her ragged satchel in the back, as if someone had been trying to hide it. Tugging hard, she pulled it free and fell back. She flung out her arm, whacking it against the tall post of the bed. Spinning sideways, she landed in a heap on the floor, with her skirt over her head.

In spite of everything, she started laughing. At least no one had seen her clumsy acrobatics. She pulled her skirt and petticoat off her face, and her gaze landed on a wide-eyed servant standing in the doorway.

The woman blinked several times then found her voice. "You. . .ah. . .be needin' some he'p, miz?"

Chapter 2

Reed was ready for the lengthy Virginia reel to be over so he could dance with a pretty girl and forget the sassy black-eyed Susan. His mind raced, searching every nook and cranny of his brain, trying to figure out why the woman had been so terse with him. He kept coming back to the same conclusion: She must have confused him with someone else, as Damian had suggested.

As the lovely ladies sidestepped past him on their way back to the front of the line where they'd meet their partners and then duck under the clasped hands of the lead couple, several of the unmarried women winked or smiled at him. Which one had he promised the next dance to?

The image of the female who had snubbed him entered his mind again. He wouldn't be content until he tracked her down and got the truth from her. He spun on his heel and strode toward the door where she'd exited the ballroom.

"Bishop! Ree' Bishop!"

Upon hearing his name shouted so rudely from across the room, Reed stopped and pivoted around. A ruckus to his right pulled his gaze back to the center of the room. The dancers skidded to a halt and looked around. Loud mumbles arose, and the couples in the center of the room stumbled aside as a man pushed his way through them. Many folks watched the man, but others turned and stared at Reed.

Damian hurried to his side. "Who is that?"

Reed shook his head, searching the crowd for his mother. He had no desire for her to be embarrassed in front of her friends by a man he must have upset somehow. The man staggered through the last of the dancers, and the music squeaked to a halt. The buzz of speculation filled the room like disturbed bees.

"Isn't that Johan Zimmer?" Damian asked. "Looks like he's chugged full."

Reed's gut twisted. He hadn't seen the Zimmers in years, in spite of the fact they were among his nearest neighbors. Not since. . .

Johan stopped three feet from Reed. "Yer fam'ly. . .they are c–cause of all our troubles." Johan swiped his sleeve across his mouth and took several quick steps back before he regained his balance, such as it was. Even from four feet away, Reed could smell the liquor on the man's breath. The Bishops and the Zimmers rarely socialized in the same circles. Johan was half a foot taller than Reed remembered but still as thin as a ship's ratline.

Damian glanced sideways at Reed, brows lifted. From across the room, Reed saw Mr. Hanover, the host of the ball, and several other men moving along the edge of the crowd toward them, probably thinking to stop a fight.

But a fight was the last thing Reed wanted. He'd thought the Zimmers' anger over what had happened had finally died down now that Karl Zimmer had been injured and had taken to his bed. Johan's father had been the one to stir up things when Reed's father was still alive, but since his death, the Zimmers had been quiet.

Damian stepped forward, his hand outstretched. He laid it on Johan's shoulder. "This isn't the place for a personal squabble, Zimmer."

Sloughing off Damian's hand, Johan scowled and staggered sideways, sloshing the wine in his glass onto the floor. Miss Abigail DuPree, who stood on Johan's far side, squealed and back stepped, holding up the skirt of her pink gown. She frowned at him, then pivoted and pushed her way through the gawking crowd.

Oblivious, Johan held out his bony finger. "I d'mand justice. Your *fader*, he cheated my f–fader, out of wha' was righ'fully his."

Reed stiffened and closed the space between him and Johan. "That's a lie, and you know it, as well as everyone else in this room."

Johan jerked as if he'd been slapped, splashing red wine onto his white shirt. "You have in–in–insulted a Zimmer for the las' time, Ree' Bishop." Johan tucked his wine under his arm, spilling the last of the liquid. He struggled to pull a glove from his waistband—a glove that looked closer to gray than white. Finally gaining hold, he yanked out the glove and slapped it to the ground at Reed's feet. "I ch–challenge you to a d–duel."

Gasps rippled across the room. Reed clenched his jaw. The dueling *Code of Honor* stated that a gentleman should never challenge another gentleman to a duel in public. That this man had, further insulted Reed.

Mr. Hanover drew up beside him. "You gentlemen take this disagreement outside. I'll not have dissension in my home."

"I apologize for this disturbance, sir," Reed said.

Mr. Hanover gave him a long, hard stare then nodded. Spinning on his heel, Reed glanced at the door where the woman in the faded yellow dress had fled. Maybe he'd see her later and could question her then.

He strode out the open double doors, past the silent, gawking string quartet, and onto the piazza. He clenched his fist as he passed several strolling couples out to the lawn and waited. Why, after years of silence, would Johan Zimmer choose today to once again accuse his father? Would these verbal attacks never end? His family had lost far more than the Zimmers when that cargo ship sank in a storm seven years ago. Johan couldn't have been more than ten years old then, so what had stirred him up to feel the need to force a duel?

With hands on hips, Reed watched Johan stumble down the stairs, nearly falling to his knees before righting himself. He searched for Reed, then his gaze latched onto him, and he proceeded forward, with a crowd of curious spectators following.

Reed had no desire to duel Johan. It would hardly be a fair battle anyway, with the man more than half drunk. But his own honor—and more so, his father's—had been insulted in front of their closest friends and business associates. To back down would belittle him in the eyes of the many men present who had dealings with Reed Shipping. And how would his mother look upon his participation? He heaved a loud sigh. There was no way he could win this ordeal.

He expected to see his mother leading the spectators. She would call a halt to the duel if she had it in her power—and profoundly embarrass him in the process. If he was fortunate, prior to Johan's disturbance she had left the ballroom to take an afternoon respite as some of the older women had and was not yet aware of the situation. He ran his hand through his hair. He should have stayed home and finished packing, but no, he had to have one last day of enjoyment before facing years of study.

Johan tottered to a stop several feet away and glared at him.

Damian hurried past him to Reed's side. "I'll serve as your second."

Reed leaned toward him. "I can't duel him in the condition he's in."

"People will think you're a coward if you don't. Besides, you don't have to shoot the man—just fire off to his side. Then his honor should be satisfied."

"And what if he shoots me?"

"Look at him. He couldn't hit the broad side of a clipper ship if he was ten paces away. How do you expect him to hit you?"

"Maybe he'll miss and shoot you instead."

Damian's eyes widened and he grinned, but Reed could see that his comment had shaken his friend. "Maybe I'll just go stand behind that tree over there."

Reed chuckled in spite of everything.

"Johan doesn't have the guts to go through with a duel," Damian said.

Tucker Marlow squeezed through the crowd and jogged toward Reed, a wooden box held tight under his arm. The man had supervised more duels in Charleston than anyone Reed knew.

Damian stepped back, and Marlow stopped where he'd been standing.

"Come over here, Mr. Zimmer." Tucker waved his fingers, beaconing Reed's accuser to join them.

Johan stumbled forward, his eyes dropping to the box. Uncertainty flickered in his eyes before his gaze hardened. Johan had always been a quiet boy, from the little Reed could remember about him. His father, though, had been vocal about his perceived wrong, in spite of the fact that everyone knew sending a shipload of cargo across the ocean was always a gamble. Reed's father might have owned the ship with Zimmer's harvest onboard, but it was hardly his fault the vessel had sunk in a storm.

Tucker cleared his throat. "Mr. Hanover has been kind enough to lend us the use of his dueling pistols, unless you prefer to use swords." He turned slightly to face Johan. "Mr. Zimmer, according to *The Code of Honor*, penned by our former governor John Lyde Wilson, you may apologize and walk away from this duel with your honor intact. Do you wish to offer Mr. Bishop an apology?"

Reed prayed the man had the sense to express regret for the way he'd slandered the Bishop family name and Reed's father. He had no desire to duel a drunken man.

Tugging at one earlobe, Johan glanced at Reed then at the crowd of spectators. He scowled. "He c–called me a liar, and his fader was a—a cheat. It's time those B–Bishops paid for ruinin' us."

Heaving a sigh, Reed turned to his second. "I thought you said he didn't have the backbone to go through with this duel."

Damian waved his hand in the air. "I doubt he even knows how to shoot. He's always been a milksop."

"Maybe *I* should just apologize." A myriad of thoughts raced through Reed's mind. If he offered an apology for the things that had happened in the past, would Johan be satisfied? His honor restored? The Zimmers had blamed the Bishops for their misfortune for as long as Reed could remember. But apologizing for something he had no part of stuck in his craw. Expressing regret was difficult enough for a man when he was the guilty party. Besides, he was from a long line of patriots and backing down had never been an option.

He stood straighter and eyed the scrolling inscription etched on the box of dueling pistols. Reed didn't doubt his own skill with a pistol, and dueling was a commonly accepted form of settling disputes among Southern gentlemen, but was he ready to risk his life for the sake of his pride?

"Don't back down, Bishop. Everyone'll think you're yellow."

Reed glanced over his shoulder at Grady Howard, one of his future college classmates. Had the man actually read his thoughts?

Beside Grady stood another half dozen men his age from wealthy families of the South, all of whom were leaving on the ship with him tomorrow. If he apologized now, they would all think him a coward. His reputation would be in shambles, and his classmates would make the years in Scotland miserable. There was no option left, but to continue. He turned his attention on his opponent and shook his head. "My family's honor has been ground into the dirt one time too many. It ends here. Today."

Johan's lips puckered, and his bloodshot eyes narrowed. "You Bishops don't know wha' honor is." He waved a hand at Tucker. "Get on with it."

"Do you have a second?" Tucker asked.

Johan looked around, as if hunting a friend. A man Reed didn't recognize stepped forward. "I'll be his second."

"Very well," Tucker said. He opened the box of dueling pistols and motioned for Reed's and Johan's seconds to step forward. "Mr. Bishop, as the wronged party, your second may choose first." Damian eyed the identical weapons then selected one. Both seconds loaded powder and ball; then each returned to his principal's side.

Reed eyed the pistol—a beautiful Henry Le Page creation with a walnut stock and a chrome-and-satin barrel. "Let me see it."

Damian handed over the pistol. Reed held it in his left hand, testing its weight, liking the feel of it in his hand. The firearm was a fine weapon and would serve him well.

Damian patted Reed's shoulder then took back the pistol. "I sure hope you come out the winner. I'd hate to lose my best friend. Having you go away for years is bad enough."

Reed swallowed the lump building in his throat. He could actually die today—and at just nineteen, dying was not something he'd wasted much time thinking about. Should he be the loser and perish, his mother would be shocked and deeply saddened that her only child was gone. They might not agree on many things, but he knew she loved him.

Tucker closed the pistol box and stepped forward. "Gentlemen, if you two will stand back-to-back, we'll get this thing over with."

Suddenly stiff and somber, Johan turned around and faced the other direction. Reed stalked over and stood behind him, the pistol in his hand shaking. He forced his fist to hold steady and inhaled a deep breath.

"All right, then, I will begin counting. You will both take a step in the opposite direction on each count I call out; then on number eight, you will turn and fire. God be with you both and may He vindicate the man in the right."

A trickle of sweat ran down Reed's temple. Off to his right, he recognized the chirp of a brown-headed nuthatch that flittered among the limbs of a tall pine tree. The bird's cheery squeaking was in dramatic contrast to the solemn event taking place on the massive lawn. The midafternoon sun struggled to peek through the gray clouds overhead, as if it, too, wanted to watch the events. In a paddock to his right, a dozen horses grazed peacefully on thick, green grass, and on the left, most of the spectators stood a respectable distance away. He couldn't help wondering which man they were cheering for. His family was well respected, but there were always those who despised them for their wealth and success.

"One."

Reed hesitated a moment then stepped forward when he felt Johan do so. He had only wanted to have an enjoyable day before he left America. Why couldn't Johan have kept silent?

"Two."

His whole body jarred as he paced forward. He swallowed the lump building in his throat. What a waste his life had been. His parents had coddled him and let him have his way much of the time when he was young. He'd grown into a young man who liked getting what he wanted.

"Three."

Five more steps to death, maiming, or vindication. But vindicating what? Would winning the duel actually restore honor to either man? Maybe in the eyes of those attending, but would it put an end to the Zimmers' accusations?

"Four."

Reed could no longer hear his opponent's heavy breathing. Was the man more sure of his abilities than he looked? A better shot than his reputation claimed him to be? Or maybe he was only pretending to be drunk. Reed clenched his jaw. He wasn't ready to die.

"Five."

Up to this point, he'd lived mostly for fun and for doing scientific research. He had preferred spending time in a tavern with his friends to working on the estate or at the shipping yard on the harbor that his father half owned. He remembered attending church when he was younger, but like his close friends, he hadn't seen a need for God or religion. He looked up at the sky. Would he stand face-to-face with God today?

"Six."

No, he wasn't ready. He had too much life to live. He'd finally settled on a career that sounded halfway interesting. He couldn't die today. He'd never become a doctor. And yet, how could he become a doctor knowing he'd killed or maimed a neighbor?

"Seven."

If he allowed Johan the first shot, he could well die without ever firing his pistol. He pursed his lips. He couldn't kill the man; that much he knew. When he turned, he would delay firing and allow Johan the first shot; then he'd place a shot close enough to look real. If he perished, so be it, but at least he'd die with a clear conscience, knowing he hadn't taken advantage of a drunken man.

"Eight. Fire at will."

Chapter 3

Carina stood on the expansive front porch of the Hanover home, waiting for the groom to locate her carriage and driver. She was so ready to head home. She never should have come. If only Betsey hadn't refashioned one of her mother's old gowns and encouraged her that attending today's ball would help her to get to know her neighbors better. But the slave woman was mistaken. The fine ladies of Charleston had made little to no effort to get to know her. They'd taken one look at her dress and stuck their rich noses up in the air. She was not a native of Charleston or even America. How could she ever hope to fit in with the local society?

No matter. She didn't need their friendship.

Leaning against a tall porch pillar, she studied the perfectly manicured lawn. The road leading up to the main entrance of her family's home looked like a forest compared to the Hanover's well-trimmed lawn and gardens. Farther away, dozens of palmettos lined both sides of the drive, making an inviting first view of the Hanover home. If she had forty-eight hours in a day, maybe hers could look as nice. At least she was able to file away several ideas for the day when she could squeeze out time to garden.

The door behind her opened, and Miss Elizabeth Hanover and two friends exited. They cast her an odd glance then sat in the rockers along the parlor window. Carina watched them out of the corner of her eye. All three were probably only a year or two younger than she. What would it be like to be friends with girls her own age? But then, those spoiled rich girls had nothing in common with her.

The young women giggled, and Elizabeth caught Carina's gaze. "I'm surprised to see you out here, considering what's happening out back."

Carina jerked her gaze away. Her cheeks warmed at the thought that the women had caught her staring at them. She glanced down the long drive, but her carriage still wasn't in sight. Then her mind latched onto what Elizabeth had said, and she turned back to face her. "What's going on out yonder?"

Elizabeth's blond brows lifted, and she glanced at her friends. "You mean you truly don't know?"

Carina shook her head.

"Oh dear." The woman to Elizabeth's right lifted her fingertips to her lips.

Apprehension skittered up Carina's spine like ants climbing a tree. "What is it? And why would I be concerned?"

251

Elizabeth stood and walked toward her. "Your brother created quite a disturbance on the dance floor."

Scowling, Carina couldn't for the life of her imagine her highly introverted brother asking a woman to dance. He didn't even know how to dance, as far as she knew. Why, she had barely managed to get him to attend. She narrowed her eyes, not sure whether to believe the uppity woman or not. "What kind of disturbance?"

The woman in the lavender dress jumped up from her rocker and hurried to Elizabeth's side. "I thought it was so exciting. That Reed Bishop, he's so handsome and collected."

Carina's heart jolted. Hearing Reed Bishop's name mentioned in conjunction with her brother was not a good thing.

"We're not talking about Reed, Amanda." Elizabeth tossed her head, and her blond ringlets bounced. She narrowed her eyes at Carina. "Your brother was drunk. He shouted across the ballroom, slandering Reed's father and disrupting the dance."

Carina felt the blood drain from her face. "What else happened?"

"Oh, Reed took it rather well, but your brother wouldn't listen and challenged him to a duel."

Carina gasped. "Today? Here?"

Both women nodded, but Elizabeth responded. "Yes, Reed leaves tomorrow to attend the Royal College of Physicians and Surgeons in Glasgow and will be gone several years. It had to be today."

Dropping her satchel, Carina picked up her skirts and raced across the porch and around the side of the house, her heart pounding. Her kindhearted brother knew little about weapons. He had no need for them since he couldn't stand to even squash a spider and thought hunting was cruel. He wouldn't even eat meat. Reed Bishop had been hunting all his life. She knew because she'd spied on him when she was younger. He was an expert shot and a man who had no heart. Her sweet brother was no match.

From the elevated porch, she could see across the wide, open lawn surrounded with pine trees on two sides, where many of the guests stood, watching the event. Farther past them, two men were already pacing away from one another. "No, no, no!"

She jogged down the steps, heedless of the heads turning her way. She had to stop this senseless battle.

With the crowd thinner along the edges, Carina squeezed her way past the wealthiest members of Charleston's society—past men and women dressed in their finery. Why would so many people, women especially, care to watch two men shooting at each other? Had they no sense of decency?

She had almost reached the edge of the crowd when she heard the counting. "Six."

Relief almost slowed her steps. She wasn't too late. Didn't the count go to ten? "Move out of the way." She tried to go around, but the crowd was pressed up against a row of thick hedges that lined the side of the garden. Pushing between two giants, she heard the count of seven. "Let me pass. Please!"

One man glanced down and turned enough that she could squeeze past him. Finally she had a clear view of her brother and that horrible Reed Bishop.

"Eight. Fire at will."

"Nooo!" Carina screamed. She rushed toward her brother, but someone grabbed her from behind, jerking her backward. "Let me go! Please!"

The hands held firm.

ð

Reed spun around, holding his pistol in front of him. Johan stumbled around, waving his firearm in the air. Reed slowly lowered his. How could he shoot a man who couldn't even stand up straight?

To his left, a woman's scream pierced the air. Johan's pistol exploded. A moment later, Reed's left arm erupted with burning pain. He jumped, and his own pistol fired. He grabbed his arm and looked down. A slit had been sliced through the sleeve of his dress coat, and the camel-colored fabric was stained with crimson along the tear.

"Good show, Reed. How bad are you wounded?"

Shaken from his stupor, Reed stared at Damian. "I think he just winged me."

"Well, it looks like you did more than that to him."

Reed's gaze jerked back to where Johan had been standing. Remorse surged through him like a tidal wave. He'd shot Johan? He must have fired the gun when he jumped after getting shot. Johan lay on the ground, a mass of red covering his torso. A woman in a dark blue dress rushed to his side and fell to her knees in the grass. Shame gutted Reed. What had he done? "I wasn't going to shoot."

"Well you did, and you've been vindicated. Your honor is restored." Damian pried the pistol from his fingers. "Let me return this, and we'll get out of here before that wife of Johan's makes a scene."

Reed didn't feel very honorable. He didn't even know Johan had a wife. The crowd of spectators surged forward. Men clapped his uninjured shoulder, offering him their congratulations.

"Well done, Bishop."

"That's fine shooting."

"Expert marksmanship."

The praises floated around Reed's head like pesky flies. He had to get out of there before he was sick. Pushing through the crowd, he ignored the pain throbbing in his arm. He'd shot a man—and that man could die because of him. How could he become a doctor now that he had a man's blood on his hands?

Chapter 4

Tanglewood Plantation, South Carolina
1852

Carina eyed the six slaves who stood by the wagon with their heads hanging down. Each clung to a burlap bag that held all of their belongings. She swallowed the aching lump building in her throat. They were healthy and better dressed than most slaves she'd seen in Charleston, and she knew each one by name, knew how long they'd lived at Tanglewood. Leasing them out was one of the hardest things she'd ever done, but she had to have income, and she had few options left. Tears burned her eyes, and she forced them away lest Mr. Davies see her crying and attempt to take advantage of her.

Most folks didn't give a hoot about their slaves and thought of them only as property, but to Carina, they were her friends—people she'd grown fond of and felt it her duty to watch over. But she'd failed them, and choosing who to lease to work in Charleston and who to keep was almost more than she could bear. By leasing this half dozen for a short while, she hoped to hang on to Tanglewood so that they would one day be able to return. Tonight, when she was alone in her bed, she'd cry at the unfairness of it all.

Lifting her head, she held out the slaves' papers then waited for Mr. Davies to look over them. "You promised you'd do right by them, and I'll trust you're a man of your word."

He grunted but merely continued perusing the papers. "Where's your daddy? And why ain't he out here tendin' to this business?"

Carina worked hard not to flinch. If Mr. Davies knew that her fader had taken to his bed over a year ago, he'd offer her half what she knew the slaves were worth. "I am the one handling this sale. Are we doing business or not?"

He rolled up the papers then studied her with narrowed eyes. "Looks like ever'thing is in order here." He smacked the roll against his palm. "Why not just sell them to me? I'll give you one thousand dollars for the lot of them."

Unable to hold back her gasp, she straightened her back and narrowed her gaze. "You'll not be taking advantage of me, Mr. Davies. Jesse alone is worth that much. If you're not interested in leasing them, you can take your business elsewhere."

He worked his mouth as if chewing on a slice of jerky. Rubbing his whiskery jaw with the back of his hand, he glared at her through unusually small eyes the color of swamp water. "You drive a hard bargain, Miss Zimmer. Perhaps we could barter a deal that would benefit us both."

Her fader had warned her that Mr. Davies was a shrewd businessman, but she wouldn't allow him to ramrod her. "What kind of deal?"

His lazy gaze drifted down her body, lingering at the most inappropriate places. She shifted from one foot to the other, fighting the desire to flee to the creek and wash off. She pulled a small pistol from her skirt pocket and crossed her arms, holding up the weapon with her shooting hand, her message clear. "I'll take two hundred dollars per month with the first two months up front as you promised or nothing. Make up your mind. I've got work waiting."

He muttered a half snarl, half laugh, then shook his head. "I'll give you one hundred fifty dollars per month and not a half cent more."

Carina's heart sank. She longed to keep her workers. Without them, the few slaves she had left would find it very difficult to manage everything that needed done around Tanglewood. But if she didn't get the money to pay the mortgage, she'd lose the land that she'd given her heart and soul for. She simply had to make this bargain today. She would never be able to work up her nerve to lease her people again. Her fader had taught her that sometimes the best way to seal a deal was to walk away. "Then good day to you, sir."

She turned her back to Mr. Davies and strode toward her servants.

Mr. Davies uttered a curse. "Now just hold your horses, missy. They said you was hardheaded, but I didn't believe it."

Who had said she was hardheaded? She turned back to face the despicable man, not at all liking that people had been talking about her.

"All right, I'll give you one hundred eighty dollars."

"The price is two hundred dollars. And you're getting a bargain."

He heaved a heavy sigh and shook his head. "All right. Two hundred dollars. But don't expect me to be coming around again to pay. You can come to Charleston to collect your payment."

Carina almost smiled at the relief she felt, in spite of knowing she'd have to travel so far to collect her money each month. Her fingers tingled as she watched him count out the bills and coins. She could pay the taxes and two mortgage payments, purchase some much-needed supplies and also seed for next spring's planting. And maybe now she could afford to hire a doctor from town to help her fader.

She kept the pistol in sight, counting the money as Mr. Davies did. He held it out like a man giving away his last dollar. She snatched it before he could change his mind. "Remember, it says in our agreement that you'll treat my people fairly, feed them well, and not beat them."

His thick lips tilted to one side, putting her in mind of a snarling wolf that had been in one too many fights. "They ain't *your people* for the time bein'. They belong to me now."

Her stomach clenched. Had she made a mistake? What other choice did she have? She'd already sold as much land as she could part with and still have a decent harvest. Fighting back more tears, she walked past each of the six Negroes who had served her so faithfully. "Thank you for your service here. I hope that this will be a temporary situation. Please work as hard for Mr. Davies as you would for me." She wanted to add *so he'll treat you well*, but she feared it wasn't true.

The four women in the group sniffled and offered her sympathetic glances before ducking their heads again. The two men didn't look up. She knew they understood she had no other choice, but they were frightened and filled with uncertainty about their futures.

Mr. Davies flicked his hand at the man who drove the big buckboard. "Isaac, get them Negroes on up in the back of that there wagon."

At Mr. Davies's harsh command, Carina spun around and hurried toward the house, the money in her hand feeling like thirty pieces of silver. She picked up her pace and jogged up the steps. She ran into the house, slammed the front door, and dashed up the stairs with tears racing down her cheeks. She'd always secretly hoped to set her slaves free one day. Buying, selling, and leasing was for produce and livestock, not people, and yet she was as guilty as the men she despised. Hunger and desperation drove people to do things they wouldn't normally do.

In her bedroom, she hid the money in a false bottom drawer in her dressing table then fell on her bed, exhausted and heartbroken. She despised crying, but her tears flowed like a swollen river cresting its banks, and she couldn't do a thing about it.

Would the day ever come when she had someone to lean on?

She was so tired of being strong.

❧

A fog parted, and Carina strolled along the banks of the river. She should be working, she was certain, but the peacefulness beckoned her. The water swished and splashed gently against the rocks lining the bank, in tune with the songbirds in the thick greenery above her. Across the river, a huge alligator sunned itself in the warm afternoon. They were massive creatures, those 'gators, with few cares in the world except finding something to eat and avoiding hunters who'd kill them for their hide. Would this one end up a pair of boots on some wealthy planter's feet?

She sat on a sun-kissed stone and rested her elbows on her knees, chin in her hand. Here, away from her fader's glare and verbal rantings, she could be the young woman she dreamed of—one whose only worries were which dress she would wear to the ball next week or in what manner she'd style her hair or which of the young men she wanted to marry.

"May I have this next dance, miss?" The handsome man's blue eyes gleamed.

Carina glanced down, pretending to be shy but inwardly delighted. *"Of course you may."* She put her hand in his big, capable one then waltzed around the room. No worries, only her and the man, so tall. . .so comely. A suitor to win her affections?

No, not a suitor at all. The dancer turned into Johan. Sweet, gentle Johan.

The music suddenly changed. The soft harmonies fled as a harsh clanging bullied them away.

Bang! Bang!

Loud horns replaced the lyrical flute. Drums drowned out the violin.

No, not drums.

Pistols.

The stench of gunpowder instead of the sweet scent of flowers.

Blood. Johan's blood.

Her brother fell, his lifeblood draining from the wound in his belly. Carina screamed.

"Miz C'rina, wake up. I done knocked on yo' door, but you didn't answer. You's having another one of them dreams."

A hand jiggled her shoulder, and Carina opened her eyes. Her room took shape as she blinked away the sleepiness weighing down her eyelids. Sweat dampened her shirtwaist, her hair, and the right side of her face where it had lain against her hand. Her head ached, and her eyes felt as if she'd washed them out with saltwater.

Etta stood over her, concern etching the girl's black eyes. Her frizzy hair refused to stay hidden under her red scarf, instead sticking out everywhere, giving her a whimsical look that fit her flighty personality.

Carina's heart still pounded from reliving that horrid day. Sunlight from the west flooded her room, reminding her it was afternoon, not morning. She had no cause to be in bed this time of day, and realizing that Etta of all people had found her so, irritated her. "Is something wrong?"

"Oh! Silly me. I done forgot." Etta straightened and lifted her fingers to her mouth. "Daddy said Abel hurt his leg out in the fields. He done sent Enoch over to the neighbors to see if'n Thomas can come and doctah him."

Carina's heart jolted. She couldn't lose a worker now that she'd leased out so many. "How bad is it?"

Etta shrugged and spun around, holding out her skirts and studying her reflection in the mirror. She swung back and forth, as if dancing.

"Etta!"

"Oh, uh. . .bad, I s'pose. Enoch, he was ridin' Comet."

It must be serious if Woodson allowed Enoch to take their fastest horse. Carina slid off the side of the bed, glanced at her own reflection, and winced. A large red circle resided where her hand had pressed against her cheek. Her hair wasn't much better than Etta's, but what did it matter? No one would see her except her people. "Go find your mama and tell her I said to bring the basket of medicines and bandages to the quarters."

"Yes'm." Etta yawned and strolled out of the room as if she hadn't a care in the world.

"Hurry!"

Etta jumped at Carina's loud bark and scurried down the hall and around the corner. Carina glanced down at her wrinkled skirt then fled the stuffy room. She could worry about her clothing later. Right now, she had to make sure Abel was all right. If anything happened to the jolly old man, she didn't know what she'd do. He was about the only person who could tug a smile from her solemn face.

As she passed by her fader's room, she slowed her steps and peeked in. The drapes were drawn, per his request, leaving the room hot and dusky. How could he stand it?

She tiptoed past the open door, glad that he was resting quietly. The way her emotions were today, she didn't know if she could endure another tongue-lashing from him, and once he learned the drastic step she'd taken today, one was sure to be coming. Maybe she just wouldn't tell him.

❧

Reed stood on the piazza overlooking the Reed Springs gardens. Scotland had been an experience he wouldn't have traded for anything, but it wasn't home, and nothing could compare to walking the halls of a home that had been in his family for generations. The garden had changed little in the three-odd years he'd been gone. Still perfectly manicured, like a beautiful woman dressed in her finery on her way to a ball. An artist's canvas of colors spread out before him—the vivid green of the grass and the palmettos lining the path to the dock; the blue of the Ashley River reflecting the sky; and the purples, yellows, and pinks of his mother's favorite flowers and shrubs. He'd be hard-pressed to explain to anyone how good it felt to be home again.

A knock sounded at his bedroom door; then it opened and his mother peeked in. "I heard you walking about. Are you decent yet?"

He chuckled. He'd been *decent* for more than two years now, ever since he met his Savior and dedicated his life to serving God. "Yes, Mother. Come on in."

Susan Bishop glided into his room, not looking a day older than when he'd left America. Though forty-four, she was still lovely. Her pecan-colored hair had yielded to gray along her hairline, but her face still had a rosy glow. Her brown eyes sparkled, revealing her delight at having him home again. She paused and glanced behind her, motioning to someone.

Penny, a new servant he'd met when he returned home yesterday, shuffled through the door, carrying a tray laden with breakfast foods. Reed hurried over to the table where he'd deposited his doctor's bag last evening and moved it to his bed. The tray clunked as Penny set it down.

"We didn't wait breakfast, since I knew you'd be exhausted from your travels and would most likely sleep late." His mother turned to the servant. "Thank you, Penny, you may go."

Penny curtsied then scurried from the room.

"I wasn't sure if you still drank coffee or if you've reverted back to the ways of your English ancestors and now drink mostly tea."

"Either one is fine, Mother."

She swatted her hand through the air. "I declare, what is this *Mother* bit? I've missed being called *Mama* for the past few years."

Reed lifted up one of the silver domes, revealing a bowl of porridge with a circle of melted yellow butter forming a pool in the center. He set the lid back down and peeked at another hidden delight. Two thick slices of ham lay nestled beside an omelet. His mouth watered. "You don't know how much I missed our fine Southern food, Mother."

Her thin brows lifted. "Mother?"

Reed shrugged and grinned. "Don't you think *Mama* is a bit childish for a man of twenty-three?"

She hiked her chin and straightened to her full five-foot-four height. "I do not, at least when we are home." She pulled out a chair. "Sit. Eat."

"Yes, Mama." He chuckled. "But only if you'll join me."

She nodded, her delight evident in her soft smile. She poured them both a cup of coffee, adding milk and sugar to hers.

Reed didn't know where to start first. A trio of tempting pastries formed a triangle on one plate, but it was the lure of the ham that pulled him the strongest. When was the last time he'd eaten meat and been certain what creature it came from? He loved Scotland and the Scots, but they sure ate some disgusting things.

"What was that shudder for? Is something not to your liking?" She reached to take away his plate of ham and eggs.

He grabbed it and lifted it out of her reach, grinning playfully at her. "Ah-ah. I'm not done with that yet, Mama." When she placed her hands back in her lap, he put his plate back on the table. "That shudder was because I was remembering some of the 'delicacies' we were encouraged to eat in Scotland."

His mother's eyebrows lifted. "Such as?"

"The worst of the lot was haggis." He couldn't help shuddering again. The one and only time he ate it, he'd spent the rest of the evening outside, retching. "It's a nasty-tasting dish of sheep's innards cooked in a sheep's stomach, and usually served with neeps and tatties."

His mother's eyes widened. "It all sounds so foreign. Haggis? Neets and tatties?"

"Neeps." He paused for a sip of coffee, closing his eyes as he relished its strong flavor. "Mmm...delicious." He took another long sip then bit off a hunk of ham. "Actually, the neeps were tolerable. They're some kind of mashed yellow turnips, and tatties are simply potatoes."

"Oh, I don't suppose I thought much about the food you were eating. I was more concerned that you were working too hard at your studies and then later in that infirmary. I prayed so hard that you wouldn't catch some horrid disease."

Reed reached over and patted her hand. "You needn't have worried. The Lord took care of me, even before I served Him."

Her broad smile warmed his heart.

"I can't tell you how it thrills me to hear you talking about our Lord. For so long I worried that you might not turn out well—and look at you now." She pulled her hand out from under his and laid it on top, squeezing his. "Are you content with your decision to become a doctor?"

He nodded. "Yes. I have no regrets."

Reed winced the moment the words left his mouth. He did have a regret—one that still haunted his dreams on occasion.

"What's wrong?"

He hung his head, trying to put from his mind that terrible day—the day he killed a man.

"You're remembering that duel, aren't you?"

He nodded, not all that surprised at his mother's perception.

"That was a long time ago, son. Fretting over it won't change anything. God has forgiven you, and you need to forgive yourself."

Glancing up, he didn't try to hide the pain he felt. "Just how do I do that? I'm a doctor—dedicated to helping people—but I shot my neighbor."

"Have you never lost a patient to death?"

Reed clenched his jaw. "Of course I have. But it's not the same." He stood and strode out onto the piazza. Leaning on the railing, he hung his head. He'd lost more patients than he could count. Medicine was a science, not a cure-all.

"It's not that much different. You had no malicious desire to inflict harm when you shot Johan Zimmer, did you?"

He shook his head. "I only sought to restore honor to Father and our family name, which Zimmer slandered in public. I should have just walked away and refused to fight."

His mother blew out a heavy sigh. "I don't condone dueling, by any means, but to have refused when Johan challenged you would have affected your standing in our community. There are plenty who think dueling is a barbaric way to settle people's differences—me included—but there are many others who'd refuse to do business with Reed Shipping if you'd said no. Things are slowly changing, thankfully. There's talk of initiating legislation to abolish dueling."

"That's a good thing then."

Reed dreaded the day when he'd have to face the Zimmers. Apologizing hardly seemed the proper thing to do given that so much time had passed, and even mentioning the deed was likely to cause hurt. But wouldn't just seeing him have the same effect on the Zimmers? He'd wrestled over and over with the idea of not returning to Charleston—about traveling out West, where no one knew what he'd done, but how could he do that to his mother after she'd waited so long for his return? He'd just have to face the Zimmers when the time came. "Do we still have the same neighbors?"

"Yes." His mother nodded. "Your cousins Seth and Emily Madison still live at Madison Gardens, at least when they're not in Charleston so he can run Reed Shipping." She gasped and turned toward him, touching his sleeve. "Did I write to you that Emily is with child? Now that you're home, you can deliver her baby."

Reed pursed his lips and shook his head. Though he wondered about the Madisons—had even received two letters from Seth—his mother had failed to discern the real meaning of his question about their neighbors. "Don't you think that would be a little awkward? Considering that I've known both Seth and Emily most of my life."

"Oh, pshaw. You're a doctor, and I'm sure Em would be thrilled to have an educated man tend her instead of a midwife."

He wasn't so sure, but voicing his opinion wouldn't change his mother's.

"And I guess you want to know—the Zimmers still own Tanglewood, although there is much less of it than when Karl first bought it."

"Tanglewood?"

"Yes. Didn't I write and tell you that's what Carina finally named it?"

He searched his mind but knew she hadn't. The fact that the German family hadn't named their estate had been fodder at gatherings for as long as they'd lived here. "No."

His mother's chest rose and fell as she sighed. "It's a fitting name for the place now. With Karl bedridden and Jo—uh. . ." She glanced up with a worried gaze.

"It's all right. You can say his name."

"Well, Carina has had her hands full hanging on to the place. I bought some land from her even though we didn't really need it."

Carina. He'd always liked that name, but he'd rarely seen the girl it belonged to. Before the ship sank with Karl's whole harvest aboard, he'd ridden over a time or two with his father. The small, dark-haired girl shied away from visitors, but he'd watched her from the window while their fathers conducted business. She was always herding Johan around. He was only an inch or two shorter than her then, but there was no doubt who ran the roost. A little female chick. Pretty, if his memory served him well.

"I feel so sorry for her. She never does anything but work. Never attends the balls or social events around here or in Charleston. I don't believe the poor girl knows how to have fun. Bless her heart."

In spite of the heaviness of the topic, Reed smiled. He'd missed hearing his mother's smooth Southern accent after listening to the hard-to-understand Scottish burr for so long.

Quick steps thumped down the hallway, stopping at his door. He and his mother turned in unison.

"Miz Bishop, pardon me, but Enoch from the Zimmers' is at the door. He say one of them's workers is hurt and can he fetch Thomas back to tend him?"

"Of course—"

"No! I'll go."

Reed's mother sucked in a breath and grabbed his arm. "See that Enoch has a drink if he's thirsty, Penny." When the maid had gone, his mother gave him a stern look.

"What?" He strode across the room and opened his bag, knowing already that everything was in order.

"You know that most of the Reeds before us and then us Bishops have never owned slaves, but the Zimmers do. I'm not prejudiced, but many people around here would think less of you for tending to an injured slave. Are you certain you want to walk down that path? It could end your career as a doctor before it even begins."

"I pledged to care for any hurting person, no matter the color of his skin." He snapped the bag shut and reached for his frock coat. He was far less concerned about what people thought about him than he was worried about encountering a member of the Zimmer family. But he couldn't allow a man to suffer because the situation was awkward for him.

His mother nodded and smiled. "I'm happy to hear you say that, son. But just remember, things change slowly in the South. People here are steeped in tradition."

"I know, Mama. Now, I must go."

"All right. I'll gather some things and have Charley drive me over. Maybe there's something I can do to help. I can at least keep Carina company. She cares so much about her slaves that she's bound to be upset."

Reed strode from the room, thinking it ironic that Carina cared for her *slaves*. If she cared so much, she'd set them free.

Chapter 5

Abel's groans tore at Carina's heart long before she reached the slave quarters. She'd had the elderly man's house built closest to the barn, hoping to save him a few steps each day. Why had he been working in the fields? Woodson had been instructed to give Abel only simple jobs like repairing harnesses, grooming the horses, and feeding livestock. She wanted him to feel useful, but she didn't want him out sweating in the hot sun. As odd as the situation was, he'd become her mentor and a friend, and she didn't want to lose him.

Little Sammy leaned against the door frame, staring inside. Tears streamed down his dark cheeks, but he didn't utter a sound. When he saw her, he ran to her, burying his face in her skirts. Carina patted his back and hugged him; then she stooped down. "Your mama is bringing bandages. I'd like you to go see if she needs help. Then I have a special job for you, if you're up to it."

Torn bits of leaves clung here and there to his curly black hair, as if he'd shredded a handful and tossed them in the air over his head. She plucked out the larger ones.

Sammy swiped his eyes with the back of his hands and stared up at her with watery eyes. "I's a man. I can do anythin', Miz Zimmer." The thin seven-year-old stood straight like a soldier then leaned over and wiped his damp cheek on his shoulder.

Smiling, Carina hoped to put the boy at ease and make him feel useful while getting him out from underfoot. "I need someone who can wait out front and tell Enoch and Thomas where we are. Can you do that?"

"Yes'm." He smiled then darted past her, his thumping bare feet pounding across the dirt path.

Stopping outside Abel's house, Carina stood beside the open door, half afraid to peek in. What if the injury were serious? Would he die?

She nibbled on the knuckle of her index finger, wishing there was someone else who could handle this crisis, but she had long ago learned that if she didn't do the tending, it wouldn't get done. Lowering her hand and straightening her spine, she stepped inside. "How is he, Woodson?"

Betsey's husband glanced up and gave a brief shake of his head. Chester, the other field hand, stood at the end of the bed, shifting from foot to foot.

Soft moans rose up from the lone bed. Abel lay in the shadows, his hand holding tight to the edge of the mattress. His right leg was bent like a stick snapped in two so unnaturally at the midcalf, but as far as she could tell, the wound hadn't pierced his skin. She despised seeing him suffering and chastised herself for worrying earlier about losing another worker when her good friend lay writhing in pain. People would look down on her if they knew that some of her father's slaves were her best friends. It was because of them that she found the strength to go on each day.

"Ches'er, go fetch me two fresh boards 'bout a foot-and-half long, and git some bandages from Betsey." The low timbre of Woodson's deep voice kicked Chester into action.

He hurried past Woodson, nearly running into her. His eyes widened; then he ducked his head. "Pardon, Miz 'Rina."

"That's all right. I snuck in quiet-like. I already have Betsey gathering the bandages."

Chester's eyes shone with unshed tears, and his lower lip quivered. "It were my fault, Miz 'Rina. I done left a spade out in the field. We was ready to come in, and Abel said he'd fetch the spade." His shoulders drooped and he shook his head. "Ol' Abel, he done stepped in a hole we hain't filled in yet. His leg snapped like a fox's in a trap." He made claws with his fingers then clapped his hands together.

Carina shuddered at the vivid demonstration. "It's all right, Chester. I know Abel doesn't blame you, and neither do I. Accidents happen." She knew the man's fears stemmed from her father's past harsh treatment. He would have beaten Chester severely not just for causing another worker to be injured but simply because he'd left a tool out in the weather. She believed in treating the slaves with kindness and received their loyalty for it.

Woodson cleared his throat and scowled at the younger man. Chester cast another glance at Abel then hurried out to do Woodson's bidding.

"What can I do to help?"

"Ain't nothin' to be done till I get some supplies, unless you want to snitch some of yo' daddy's whiskey to ease Abel's pain."

Carina despised drinking, and her fader had strict rules about not letting slaves have whiskey. He just didn't want to share, but in this one thing, she agreed. Liquor weakened people to where they couldn't function or think straight. It emboldened them to do things they wouldn't normally do. But it would ease Abel's pain. Could she sneak a small amount for Abel's sake without her fader noticing?

"I can try." She hurried outside, feeling guilty that she was relieved to have a task to do so she wouldn't have to witness Abel's suffering any longer. Poor old man.

She cut through the barn and scanned the area to make sure the horses were all right; then she lifted up her skirt and jogged toward the house. The door to the kitchen flew open and banged against the side of the building. Betsey hustled out the door onto the whistling walk and hurried toward her.

"How's Abel? He be dead?"

Carina smiled. Betsey always expected the worse. "No, but he's in a lot of pain. Woodson wants me to sneak some of Fader's whiskey for him."

Betsey's eyes widened. "That be dangerous, even fo' you."

She nodded. "I know. I'll be careful—and quiet. Where's Etta? I don't want her down at the cabins, blubbering and upsetting Abel."

"I know. She be in the kitchen peelin' taters for supper."

"All right. I'm heading in the house and will be back in a few minutes. I hope."

Betsey tightened her lips then turned toward the barn and shuffled away, as fast as her wide body could travel.

Carina wiped her feet on the faded carpet runner just inside the side door. The poor thing was as sad as the rest of the house. She remembered the day it arrived on a wagon her father had driven from Charleston. Her mama had been so excited and had done a little jig in the yard, looping arms with Carina and swinging her around. Those had been happy days.

But happy days rarely occurred anymore. She didn't have time for them—nor lollygagging and dreaming about the past.

She tiptoed up the stairs, trying to step lightly so as to not put her full weight on the steps and make them squeak. Pausing at the entrance to her fader's room, she exhaled a soft sigh to see he was still sleeping—and that he'd rolled over so his back would be to her. If not for Abel's dire need, she'd never attempt such a feat.

Walking on her toes, she crept across the room, following the lone sliver of sunlight that defied the thick drapes. It led almost directly to the round drum table that held a tray with a single bottle and glass. Glancing sideways, she held her breath as she reached for the bottle.

Her fader snorted then rolled onto his back and scratched his chest through his nightshirt. Carina froze. All except for her trembling hand.

"Hey there, girl. What's that you're doing?"

8

The warm breeze brushing Reed's cheeks as his horse galloped down the road confirmed that he was truly home. No more chilly days and frigid nights trying to keep warm in a drafty room. No more twenty-hour days working in a smelly infirmary filled with the sick and dying. No more odd Scottish food.

He much preferred helping people one-on-one—and tasty Southern cuisine.

As his horse approached the turnoff to Tanglewood, Reed slowed his mount to a trot. If he hadn't known where the entrance to the plantation was, he would have missed it. The quarter-mile drive was overgrown with trees with dead and broken limbs, shrubs that looked as if they were fighting one another to see which could get to the far side of the road first, and vines that battled the shrubs. An abundance of weeds with colorful flowers rose up between the wheel tracks in their effort to erase all evidence of human life.

Karl Zimmer must be terribly ill to allow his home to remain in such a state of disrepair. A shaft of guilt stabbed Reed. If he hadn't killed Johan in that duel, would Tanglewood be in such a dilapidated condition?

He nudged his mount into a gallop again. No amount of remorse could bring back the young man, and Reed had poured out enough remorse over the past few years to fill an ocean. He was a different man from that arrogant youth he'd once been. God had changed him, and now God was giving him a chance to help the Zimmers.

A young boy sat on the steps to the main entrance of the house. He jumped up and waved at Reed, his arms flapping like a bird not yet old enough to fly. Guiding his horse over to the child, he scanned the house and yard. It was in the same condition as the drive. Chipped paint curled up on the side of the house, like a beggar woman's tattered skirt, revealing a dingy gray petticoat.

"You come to he'p Abel? They's over at his cabin." The boy jumped off the top step and loped toward the barn.

Reed reined his horse to the left and followed. Instead of going into the faded barn, the boy skirted around it, sliding to a halt outside a small cabin.

"In there." The boy's thin finger disappeared behind the doorjamb.

Reed dismounted and held out the reins. "You think you could walk my horse and then get him a drink?"

A wide grin tugged at the boy's cheeks. Reed couldn't help noticing the child's spiked lashes. Had he been upset over the injured man or something else?

He untied his medical bag from the back of his saddle then ducked through the doorway. His eyes adjusted to the dimmer light as a moan rose up from across the small room. A tall, broad-shouldered man turned away from the bed and stared at Reed, as did a shorter and much wider woman. Neither said a word but stared at him as if he were an apparition. A dark stain covered the white of the man's shirt.

"I'm Dr. Reed Bishop. Can you tell me what's wrong with this man?"

The couple eyed one another. The woman's brows lifted, but the man gave a quick shake of his head. They kept their heads down as was the way of most slaves, but the tall man cleared his throat. "I reckon you be lookin' for Massa Zimmer. He up at the big house."

Karl Zimmer had been bedridden for a while—that was common knowledge. "Has he taken a turn for the worse?"

"Nah sir. He be the same."

"Then I'll see to this man first. What's his name?"

The man's head jerked up, his eyes wide. "We ain't never had no real doctah tend any of us."

The woman's dark eyes brimmed with hope. "He be Abel, and his leg be broke."

The tall man shushed her and scowled. "Miz Zimmer, she done sent for someone already."

Reed heaved a sigh. He knew discrimination ran both directions at times, but would they stand in the way of his helping their friend just because he was white? "I know. Enoch came to my home—Reed Springs. I've just returned from Scotland, where I was educated at the Royal College of Physicians and Surgeons of Glasgow. I'm quite capable of tending your friend."

"Let the doctah be." A weak voice rose up from the bed, and the tall man turned and glanced down.

Reed got his first look at his patient—an older man. He was within his right to step forward and start assessing the injured party, but he waited. For some reason, he wanted the tall man's approval. Finally, Woodson nodded and stepped back.

Stooping down, Reed lifted Abel's wrist and checked his pulse. Weak but steady. He scanned the slave's length, narrowing in on the ripped pants and crooked leg. At least as best he could tell in the dim lighting, the broken bone wasn't protruding through the skin. *Thank You, Lord, for that.* "I need more light. Do you have a lantern?"

Woodson shook his head. "Massa Zimmer, he don't allow no fires near the barn."

Reed pursed his lips. He didn't like the idea of moving Abel, but he had to see well if he was going to help him. He held his bag out to the woman, who took it with lifted brows. "Woodson, I need you to lift that end of the mattress while I hoist this end. We'll take Abel outside where I have proper lighting."

Woodson hesitated.

"Go on, git hold of the bed." The old man swiped his hand in the air; then it dropped back to his side.

In less than a minute, they had Abel situated outside under the shade of an apple tree. The old man groaned but never cried out. Reed hated that moving his patient caused him additional pain, but it was necessary. He quickly assessed the man's injuries—a severely fractured leg, but that seemed the extent of it. Standing, Reed motioned to the two servants to come to him. "I need a bucket of water," he said to Woodson.

Nodding, Woodson jogged away. Reed turned to the woman. "Do you have any paperboard and some starch?"

Betsey's eyes rolled upward as she considered his question. Then she nodded so hard her jowls jiggled. "Yes suh. I know just where some be." She turned and cupped her mouth with her hands. "Sammyyy! C'mere, boy."

A short while later, once all the supplies had been gathered, Reed dispensed a dose of laudanum and sent more prayers heavenward, asking God to help

Abel endure setting the leg and the splinting procedure. Finally, he stood and surveyed his handiwork. Not too bad at all.

Betsey wiped Abel's brow with a damp cloth and cooed to him. "You be all right soon enough. Mm-huh, you will."

Reed washed the starch mixture off his hands in the bucket of fresh water that Woodson had brought him then dried his hands with a clean towel. He offered Woodson and Betsey a smile. "With good fortune and God's healing hand, Abel should recover use of his leg, as long as he stays off of it for the next month, giving it time to heal well. Take special care that he not move his leg until the starch mixture hardens. Could take the rest of the day. You can give him a dose of laudanum for the pain." Reed showed Betsey how much to dispense. "But be careful that you don't give him too much. Mix it in a cup of willow bark tea if he finds it too distasteful." At the sound of quick footsteps, he turned, flinging the towel over his shoulder.

The young boy, Sammy, who'd been tending his horse, ran toward him. He skidded to a halt, his eyes wide when his gaze dropped to the splint on the old man's leg. "How come Abel's leg done turned all white?"

"That be a splint," Betsey said. "It'll make Abel's leg better."

"How?"

Betsey shrugged. "Ask the doctah."

The boy spun toward Reed, but his eyes shot past him, just as Reed heard the soft swish of fabric. His heart jolted. A woman jogged toward him—a thin woman with enough curves to spark his interest, dressed in a faded brown skirt and off-white shirtwaist. He lifted his gaze to her face, and something hit him hard in the gut. Dark hair shoved up in a haphazard bun tilted to one side, and enticing wisps curled around her lightly tanned cheeks that would be an embarrassment to most Southern women. Eyes as mysterious as the ebony sky on a starless night stared down at Abel while her brow puckered to a V. Why was she so familiar?

Her gaze jerked up to Reed's and her enticing eyes went wide. She blinked several times, then her face scrunched like a grape left too long in the sun. "What are *you* doing here?"

A grin tugged at Reed's mouth. So much for Southern hospitality. That was hardly the thank-you he'd expected for risking his reputation to help her slave—at least he assumed Abel belonged to this intriguing woman.

That sense of knowing her—of seeing her before—flickered in his mind then exploded like a flame to whale oil. She was the black-eyed Susan from the ball—the same ball where he'd dueled Johan Zimmer. "And just who are *you?*"

She pursed her lips up to one side, then whisked around him as if he were of no more consequence than an old fence post. She stooped next to the old man. "How are you doing?"

The boy bounced on his toes and tugged on the woman's faded skirt. "Miz Zimmer, that doctah done put a cocoon on Abel's leg."

Zimmer? His vixen was Carina Zimmer? How could he have not known? He stepped back, staggering under the weight of this revelation. No wonder she'd refused to dance with him all those years ago at the ball.

She straightened and then marched toward him, her eyes slatted. "Who authorized you to treat my worker?"

Reed opened his mouth, but her reaction stunned him to silence. Any other Southern woman would graciously thank him for treating her slave, although she may well turn her back afterward and rant about how disgraceful a thing she thought it was. But not this woman. She didn't give a hoot about tradition but faced him head-on—and in spite of her rudeness, he couldn't help admiring her candor.

"I did not give you permission to be on my property, nor did I authorize you to treat one of my people. I want you to leave." She stamped her foot. "Now!"

Betsey hurried around behind Miss Zimmer, shoving Reed's instruments into his bag. He winced at the harsh treatment of the brand-new utensils that he hadn't had a chance to properly clean yet. The slave woman waddled over and held out his bag to him, the gratitude in her eyes palpable. He offered her a gentle smile and nodded his understanding, but the grin soon withered in the face of Miss Zimmer's anger.

"Well, are you leaving?"

"Miz Zimmer," Betsey said. "He done he'ped Abel out. He say that thing on Abel's leg will he'p it to heal better and make it stronger. Can't I at least offer him some pie and tea?"

Miss Zimmer scorched her maid with a glare then turned her incendiary gaze back on him. He should go. Although he hated to leave his patient so soon, he'd done all he needed to do for now. "Make sure Abel stays in bed for the next few weeks, and give him that dose of laudanum like I explained earlier. No walking or standing until I give permission. Woodson, let's get Abel back inside where he'll be more comfortable."

"We don't need help from a *Bishop*." Miss Zimmer nudged her chin toward the trail, her meaning evident.

Reed strode forward, stopping a few feet in front of her, and met her eye for eye. She had to tilt back her head to keep her glare locked onto his. He'd never noticed before the extraordinary length of her ebony lashes or that her eyes were so black the pupil and iris all but melded together. A strip of paler skin at the base of her neck moved as she swallowed hard—the only indication that he had any effect on her. He longed to slide his finger across her skin and see if it was as soft as he expected. He stepped back, and swallowed, too. "I'll. . .uh . . .be back tomorrow—to check on my patient." He nodded to Woodson and

Betsey then marched around Miss Zimmer and strode past the barn. Now where had that boy put his horse?

"Don't come back, Bishop." Miss Zimmer's harsh words snapped at his heels like a pesky terrier. "We Zimmers tend our own."

Chapter 6

Reed marched back to the front of the barn, searched for his horse, and found him roped to a post near the water trough. Emotions battered him from all sides, like a rudderless ship tossed about on stormy waters. Anger swelled, but as it receded, guilt gnawed at him. Carina Zimmer had a right to be angry at him for all the pain he'd caused, but that didn't mean she could deny her servants proper medical treatment, especially when there were precious few surgeons willing to treat slaves.

He tossed the blanket onto the horse's back then set the saddle down and cinched it. His mother had ordered the saddle specially made with leather straps to hold his medical bag, but Reed didn't bother attaching it. Mounting in one swift movement, he just wanted to get away before he stormed back and said something to that irritating woman that he might regret.

The trail that led back to the road didn't just look shabby now. Instead it sent a message: Stay away. Ride on past, and don't stop here. You're not welcome.

He drew in a breath through his nose and exhaled. What kind of life had Miss Zimmer lived that would make her so closed off and bitter? He thought of the differences in the two neighboring estates. Reed Springs was probably five times larger and kept in immaculate condition. His estate radiated life, prosperity, and openness, while Tanglewood represented failure, struggles, and death.

A motion in front of him caught his eye. A buggy turned the corner and approached, carrying his mother, and behind it rode the Zimmers' man, Enoch. Miss Zimmer was in no mood for visiting, and he wasn't about to let that snippety woman lambast his well-meaning, kindhearted mother.

The buggy slowed and stopped. Reed didn't recognize the driver—a young man of about thirteen—but there was something familiar about him. Hadn't his mother said the boy's name was Charley?

His mother tilted back her head and peered out from under the brim of her bonnet. A wide blue ribbon, the color of the sea, wrapped around the hat and was tied in a huge bow beneath her chin. His mother always did love her bonnets. She smiled, and he remembered all the lonely nights in Scotland when he'd longed to see her face again. Nobody except for his heavenly Father loved him like his mother. "Are you finished already, son? The injury must not have been as bad as Enoch indicated."

"The man's leg was fractured. I splinted it."

His mother lifted her gloved fingertips to her lips. "Oh, the poor dear. When you come back to check on the man, you can bring Carina some of my willow bark tea. That will ease the pain some."

"Miss Zimmer isn't receptive to receiving help from us Bishops. It's best you just turn around and head back home, Mother."

She pinched her lips as if tasting something sour then shook her head. "No, Carina is just upset at seeing you again after what you did, but she'll let me help her."

Reed stiffened. "After what *I* did?"

His mother glanced at the youth beside her. "You know."

Leaning forward, he met her gaze. "That was all Johan's doing. I had no intention of shooting him."

The boy's eyes widened, and he glanced at Reed's midsection, as if looking for a weapon.

"But you did, and it cost Carina her brother. Surely you can understand how seeing you again is upsetting her. She just needs time."

He raised his hands in surrender. "You should have stopped me from coming over if you knew that to be the case."

A gentle smile lifted her lips. "There's no stopping you when you've made up your mind."

※

Reed stood on the piazza and watched a rabbit hopping from one spot in the lustrous grass to another. It paused, lifted up its head, and looked around, then dipped its head and came up chewing. It hopped to another spot and did the dance all over again. Such a serene scene.

A yawn slipped out. He leaned his weight against the railing and looked to the east, where the Zimmer plantation resided two miles away. Had Abel slept any better than Reed? Was that stubborn Miss Zimmer up yet? It was common knowledge that many Southern belles stayed up late at night when the temperatures were cooler then slept late into the morning, but he couldn't imagine Carina Zimmer enjoying such luxuries.

He sipped his lukewarm tea, trying to decide whether to ride over to Tanglewood or not. The doctor in him felt the need to check on his patient, but he also ought to honor Miss Zimmer's request to stay off her land.

Long lashes and fiery eyes had invaded his dreams the night before. He heard her screams over and over as her brother fell to the ground, bleeding. He saw the blood on the man's shirt as he all but ran from the scene. Rubbing his arm where Johan's shot had grazed it, he relived that horrible day. He hadn't wanted to shoot but had reacted and accidentally pulled the trigger. Intentional or not, the result was the same. A young man had died at his hand.

A knock sounded on his bedroom door. He turned and padded into the room, noticing a young Negro servant waiting in the hall. Her yellow dress reminded him of the one that Miss Zimmer had worn at the ball, except the fabric of this dress was stiff with newness and vivid in color. Why would such a thing sadden him?

He lifted his brows. "Yes? Tansy, isn't it?"

The young woman nodded but kept her head down, revealing the floral pattern of her multicolored head scarf. "Miz Bishop wants to know if'n you is gonna eat breakfast downstairs with her or in yo' room."

"Tell her I'll be right down."

Tansy gave a quick shake of her head, a brief curtsy, and scurried away. Reed grinned. His being home had set on edge the newer staff, although those servants who had been around most of his life seemed delighted to have him home again.

He dropped into a rococo side chair, pulled on his boots, then jogged down the stairs. His mother was already seated, sipping her tea. Her gaze snapped to his as he crossed the room, and she smiled warmly. "Good morning, son."

She stared at him as if unable to tear her gaze away. "I'm still getting used to your being home. Sometimes I declare it must be a dream. I missed you so much." She blinked her eyes as if to stem tears.

"So did I." He cleared the tightness from his throat, pulled out the chair at the head of the table, and sat.

"You missed yourself?" She giggled and covered her mouth.

"What? Oh." Reed grinned. "No, Mama, I missed you."

She hid her smile with a sip of tea. Tiny lines crinkled in the corner of her eyes. Sparse webs of gray spread from her temple back to where they disappeared among the darker strands of her hair, which had been plaited, curled, and pinned perfectly on the back of her head. His mother's hair lay flat against her head, and not a single strand dared to poke up its head for fear of being snipped off. Such a contrast to Miss Zimmer, whose hair reminded him of the fuzzy-haired Scottish sheep.

His mother tapped her fingernail against her saucer, making a tiny clinking sound. "What are your plans now that you've returned home?"

Reed stared into his teacup. He'd contemplated the same thing many times. Should he move to Charleston and set up a practice or remain on the plantation where he'd have less opportunity to tend the sick and injured but would be near his mother? "I honestly don't know."

"I'm sure you want to serve as a surgeon, but I'd love to see you take over the operations of the plantation. It is your inheritance, after all."

Reed pursed his lips. The plantation had always been the one bone of contention between his mother and him, ever since his father passed on. He loved his home, but becoming a planter had never been his dream. All his life he'd cared for injured animals. Training to be a surgeon had been the realization of his biggest dream. "Harley seems to have things under his control. Reed

Springs has fared well these years I've been gone, hasn't it?"

She nodded, but it was obvious that his response didn't please her. "That's true, but Harley is just a hired man, not an actual owner."

Reed caught his mother's gaze. Her brown eyes conveyed the turmoil going on inside her. Why couldn't she understand his need to ease people's suffering and mend their wounds? Why must the plantation always come between them? "You asked what I intended to do, Mother." He broke her gaze, unable to see the hurt in hers, and stared out the open window. "I'd like to find a spot of land closer to the main road and build a clinic."

She sucked in a breath but didn't say anything.

Could she not see that even this was a compromise for him? If he lived in Charleston or another town, he'd see a number of patients daily. By living at Reed Springs, he'd be close to her and could share most meals, but he'd never have the patient traffic he would in a city.

Footsteps sounded in the entry, and the footman cleared his throat. The man held a silver tray with a missive on it in one hand. Reed's mother slowly turned her head as if it were an effort. Knowing he disappointed her weighted down Reed's shoulders as if he were carrying a hundred-pound sack of rice.

"What is it, Jarrod?"

"A letter has arrived for Mr. Bishop, ma'am."

Reed's gaze jerked to the silver tray. Had the invitations to balls already begun to arrive? He had dreaded attending one, ever since the duel.

"You may bring it to Reed."

The footman nodded and strode forward, stopping on Reed's left. He held out the tray, Reed took the sealed note, and the footman left the room. A scrolling Z had been pressed into the wax seal. He searched his mind, trying to think of a friend or acquaintance whose last name started with a Z, but nothing came to mind.

"Well, are you going to stare at that note all morning?"

Reed slid his index finger under the flap and popped the wax seal loose. The terse note chilled him as much as if he'd fallen in the river in midwinter.

"What does it say? Bad news, from the look on your face."

He scanned the message again. Surely he'd misread it:

I challenge Reed Bishop to a duel at dawn, two days hence, at the dock at Tanglewood.

Carina Zimmer

Chapter 7

Reed hunkered low as the wind and horse's mane whipped his face. The animal's hooves thundered down the dirt road toward Tanglewood. He had decided to abide by Miss Zimmer's wishes and stay off her land, but her ridiculous challenge had changed his mind. Had the woman no sense at all?

Who would care for her father or her plantation or her slaves if something happened to her? Did she honestly think she had a chance shooting against a man who was an expert shot?

Not that he liked shooting, but his father had taken pride in his natural ability. It never mattered to his father that it cut Reed to the quick to kill an animal they needed for food. The family had to survive, his father always said, and a man had to provide for his family. He was much relieved when Harley had suggested raising beef. Reed had always made sure to be in Charleston or away some other place when it was time for slaughtering. He didn't want to seem lily-livered, but he couldn't bear to witness such an event.

His mount galloped down the lane toward the Zimmer home. He'd say his piece to Miss Carina Zimmer, check on his patient, then leave this run-down joke of a plantation.

As he neared the house, he reined in his horse and dismounted while the gelding was still walking. He dropped the reins, knowing the animal wouldn't go far, and climbed the steps two at a time. Reed pounded on the front door so hard it hurt his fist. When no answer came, he rapped on it with his other hand, just a bit more gently.

The door finally jerked open, and Betsey stood there with wide eyes. "Great day in the morning!" She glanced over her shoulder then back at him. "What you doin' here, Doctah Boss?"

Reed's anger dimmed at her uncouth greeting. And Dr. Boss? Where had she come up with that nomenclature? He shook off any traces of humor and reminded himself of Miss Zimmer's challenge. "I need to see your mistress."

Betsey's head swiveled back and forth. "Huh-uh. No, you don't."

Reed lifted a brow, more than a little surprised that Betsey would correct a visitor. A smidgen of fear passed through the slave's eyes, sending instant regret coursing through him.

"Miss Zimmer, she don't want to see you, sir. You bein' a Bishop an' all."

"I can't help who I am. I need to speak with her."

Betsey pressed her lips together and peeked behind her again. The heavyset woman shifted from foot to foot, obviously uncertain as to what to do.

Reed decided to let her off the hook. "I'll go check on Abel. Maybe you could let Miss Zimmer know that I'm here and would like to talk to her."

She bobbed her head up and down, her relief evident. "I can do that, sir. Mmm-hmm, I can."

He spun around and crossed the yard, having no doubt that once Carina Zimmer learned he was there, she'd come to chase him away like a hound dog after a rat. He wished he hadn't run off in such a rush and had thought to grab his medical bag.

Reed halted at the open door of Abel's cabin. Knocking at a slave's door felt odd, but barging on in didn't sit right with him either. He stood staring at the opening a moment then looked around for Woodson. At this hour, the man was most likely out in the fields. No one else was around either. Reed sighed.

"C'mon on in, whoever is out there." Abel's faint voice drifted out the door.

Reed stepped inside. "How are you doing today?"

"Better'n yesterday." Abel chuckled then groaned.

Smiling, Reed crossed over to the man's bedside. He checked his pulse—strong enough—and felt the man's forehead. Thank the good Lord there was no fever. "How is the pain?"

"Well, it's there, but not so bad if'n I swallow that nasty med'cine."

Feeling more confident that the man would survive, Reed relaxed. He checked to make sure the splint had hardened as he'd hoped. "Just make sure that you stay off that leg. No standing or working for a while."

Abel pursed his lips. "I can sit and mend tack and stuff. Maybe make some nails."

Reed shook his head. "Not this week. I want you flat on your back. I'll check again in a few days, and if you're still doing well, we'll try sitting you up. You'll probably be dizzy as long as you're taking the laudanum, but you need it until the pain in your leg dulls."

Abel scowled.

"I'll talk with Miss Zimmer to make sure she understands why it's important that she not push you to work more than I say you can."

The old man's gaze shot to his. "Miz 'Rina, she won't hardly let me work the ways things were. A man's gotta work, Doctah Boss."

Reed tried not to smile at the second use of the odd nickname. One of the slaves must have referred to him by that name, and the others had picked up on it. He squatted down to be on Abel's level. "A man needs to be able to walk to do most chores. You can best serve Miss Zimmer by getting well, and if you want to walk again, you need to follow my instructions."

Abel worked his mouth as if to say something but simply nodded. He yawned and closed his eyes. Reed stood and tiptoed out of the warm cabin.

The cooler breeze instantly refreshed him. He glanced down the row of ten slave cabins, noting that of all the buildings he'd seen so far at Tanglewood, surprisingly they were in the best condition. The wood had not yet faded completely, and though they were not as nice as the two-room cabins with lofts that the Reed Springs servants lived in, they were by far better than most slave quarters. Few that he'd seen on other plantations even had furniture. It would seem that Miss Zimmer took better care of her slaves than she did herself. In spite of her challenge to a duel, that thought elevated his opinion of her. He still didn't agree with owning slaves, but hers were healthy, well fed, and well cared for. Quite the dichotomy.

He strode back past the barn, where several slats had fallen loose and lay on the ground. The odor of manure and hay emanated from the building. He picked up a board and studied it. The plank was still of fair quality and could be reused if a man had a nail and hammer.

His horse grazed contentedly near the paddock, and since no one was about, Reed walked into the barn and looked around. This place was not neat and orderly as his barn was. Instead of the tools being hung up in a tack room, racks, shovels, and hay forks lay dumped together in a heap. A few bridles hung by nails on one wall, and just two saddles set on lopsided racks.

The compact gray horse stuck its pretty head over the stall gate and whickered to him. He crossed over to it and scratched its head. "Well. . .good morning."

The horse nudged his hand as if asking for more attention. He ran his gaze along its shoulder, back, and rump. Other than being on the thin side and having its right front cannon wrapped, the animal looked fairly healthy.

"What are you doing to my horse?"

He spun around at the harsh feminine voice. Miss Zimmer stomped toward him, wearing the same outfit as yesterday—faded white blouse, worn skirt, and a scowl.

Reed raised his hands in surrender. "Just looking at her. She's a fine animal. An Arabian, I'm guessing. Though I've only seen a few of them."

Miss Zimmer's expression softened as her gaze shifted from him to her horse. Why should that bother him?

She shook her head and walked toward him. "No, Lulu is a Morgan."

His gaze swiveled back to the animal. Compact and sturdy with strong limbs, arched neck, and an expressive face. "I should have recognized her breed. My father had several Morgans back when he used to harness race. Though I don't ever remember seeing a gray one."

"They're not as common as bays, blacks, or chestnuts, but I think she's much prettier."

Reed caught Miss Zimmer's gaze, intrigued with her dark eyes. "Mmm. . . lovely."

She blinked, her cheeks grew crimson, then she scowled and stepped back. "Why are you here again? Our duel is tomorrow."

"No, it is not."

Her brow crinkled a moment; then her expression grew serious. "Yes, it is."

Reed stepped closer. "No. It is not. I refuse to participate in another duel, especially one against a woman."

Her eyelids narrowed to a mere slit; her nostrils flared. The crimson on her face now wasn't from embarrassment. She spun away from him, flinging a light floral scent in his direction. Her hair, though unruly in its loose bun that threatened to unwind at any moment, looked clean and shiny. Her clothing was another thing—shabby, just like her property. Now that he thought about it, Betsey's dress was newer than her mistress's. He longed to take Miss Zimmer to Charleston—to see her dress like any other plantation mistress—but he'd have to hog-tie her to get her there. He closed his eyes and shook his head. How could he be attracted to this woman? She wanted him dead—and she wanted to be the one to pull the trigger.

"What's wrong? Are you ill?"

The unexpected compassion in her voice took him by surprise. He longed to make peace with her. "Yes, in a manner. I'm sick of this feud. Can't we set it aside and be friends? We are not our fathers. I'm sorry that your father lost his harvest and had financial troubles because our ship sank. But have you ever considered that we lost an expensive ship and a portion of our harvest, too?"

She blinked, a confused look crossing her face; then her gaze hardened. "But you didn't lose a brother."

He glanced down at the ground. "I never had one to lose, but my only sister died shortly after her birth."

Her mouth gaped open, but she wasn't ready to give up the fight. Her pert chin lifted. "I demand that you give me the satisfaction to right the wrong you did when you shot my brother. I expect you to be at the dock tomorrow at dawn. And no need to bring a second. We will deal with one another directly."

She spun around, not waiting for his response. Did she actually think he would duel with her? He marched after her.

"I'm not battling pistols with you."

Flinging out her arms, she pivoted as gracefully as a belle at a ball. "*Ja*, you will—or I'll come to your home and hunt you down."

He stared at her a long moment. Wishing things were different wouldn't change how they actually were. "I believe you would. But are you willing to shoot me in cold blood? Because I will not fire at you."

Her lips puckered and a myriad of expressions dashed across her pretty face. She tramped right up to him, stopping so close that if he as much as twitched he'd touch her. Tilting her head back, she glared up at him, nostrils flaring like a wild filly. The warmth of her breath feathered his face. If he leaned forward a few inches, he could steal a kiss. He almost smiled at the thought but worked hard to keep his expression somber.

"You Bishops are responsible for everything bad that has ever happened to us. I never even wanted to come to this country in the first place, but my fader had to have his way. My mother died as a result, now Fader is wasting away and doing nothing but sleeping and drinking, and Johan is lost to me. You'd be doing me a favor by shooting me, Mr. Bishop."

"Well, I won't. You can be sure of it. And I won't be at the dock tomorrow morn."

&

Carina couldn't believe that Reed Bishop actually had showed up at the dock, after the adamant way he staunchly said he wouldn't. Her fader sure didn't think he had the nerve to face her in a duel, but this wasn't the first time he'd been wrong. The shimmering morning sun, peering over the horizon like a beacon lighting the way, silhouetted Mr. Bishop as he walked his horse along the banks of the Ashley River, in no apparent hurry to arrive at his destination. Part of her hoped that he wouldn't come. She hadn't been thinking clearly when she'd challenged him, but pride and stubbornness would not allow her to withdraw. What would happen to Tanglewood—to her people, her fader—if she was to perish in this duel? Of course, being a surgeon and a fine shot, Mr. Bishop could choose to wound her in a nonvital spot, then patch her up and go on his way, his satisfaction intact. But would she be satisfied?

No, that wouldn't do at all. She had too much work to do to be bedridden with a wound. She'd just have to shoot him first. Swallowing hard, she paced the damp grass, the hem of her skirts growing wetter by the second. Could she actually shoot him?

Wasn't that why she'd practiced over and over, all these years? Why she had become an expert shot? To extract vengeance on the man who had killed her brother? The man whose family had started her father's downhill spiral.

Betsey's warning—a verse from the Bible—rang clear in her mind, *"Avenge not yourselves, but rather give place unto wrath: for it is written, Vengeance is mine; I will repay, saith the Lord."* She glanced down at the box of dueling pistols she'd borrowed from her fader's collection, uncertainty battling the desire for revenge.

She should never have told Betsey about the duel, but she had to let someone know—in case things went the wrong way. The woman had pitched a conniption fit, telling her what a fool she was for sending that written challenge and how good a man Doctah Boss was and how he'd helped Abel when no other white surgeon would have come near him with a ten-foot pole.

A chickadee called out a tune in the trees to the left, drawing her attention. She turned away from Mr. Bishop, who had dismounted and was walking her way. Was she wrong? All night she'd wrestled with her decision. Who else was there to stand up and demand satisfaction for the way her family had been wronged?

Forgive and forget, that's what Betsey said.

But for as long as she could remember, her fader had blamed Frank Bishop for his financial demise and later Reed Bishop for killing his only son and heir.

Carina's lip quivered. After all she'd done to keep the plantation going, her fader never once recognized her efforts or mentioned her as being his only heir. It was always her brother. What would happen when her fader died?

She huffed a harsh laugh. Maybe she would die today, and then maybe he'd bemoan her passing, but she doubted it. No matter how hard she worked, she could never gain his approval. Karl Zimmer had always been a demanding man, and being bedridden hadn't changed a thing. The only good she'd done was to help her slaves live a better life. At least they would be sad if she did not survive.

She had to see this thing through. If she lived, so be it, and if not, then her worries would be over. She spun around and marched toward Reed Bishop.

Like a pesky fly buzzing around her head, she heard Betsey's warning. *"You ain't ready to die. You ain't made things right with the good Lord."* She waved her hand in front of her face as if to drive away the taunting, but she just succeeded in gaining Mr. Bishop's attention. She lifted her chin. "I'm glad to see you actually showed up."

He removed his hat and held it in his hands. His brown hair, the color of one of Betsey's sweetgrass baskets, curled slightly in an enticing manner. Would it be soft to touch or stiff like Lulu's mane? His brow creased, but even so, he was still a handsome man. "Are you truly glad?"

The sad expression in his vivid blue eyes gave her pause, not to mention his unexpected question. Did it bother him to think she wanted him dead? And did she really? "I. . .uh. . .of course. One can't participate in a duel by oneself."

He sniffed a laugh and gave her a tight-lipped smile of resignation. She hadn't expected him to be sad. Did he truly think he would perish today?

She stiffened her back, opened the box of pistols, and held it out to him. "Choose your weapon, sir."

His eyes lifted to hers. "You actually mean to follow through with this ridiculous contest?"

Tilting her head back, she gazed into his eyes. If she killed him, she'd never again see those beautiful eyes. And his mother—the only neighbor who had reached out to her—would be heartbroken and never forgive her. It pained her to think of Susan grieving for her son. Until this moment, she had only thought that killing Reed Bishop would take away the pain of Johan's loss, but two wrongs didn't make a right. She would have to be satisfied with just wounding him. She grimaced but nodded. "I do. You took my beloved brother from me, not to mention our family's fortune."

He slapped his hat back on his head and shoved his hands to his hips. He cut a fine figure in his tan frock coat, gold brocade waistcoat, and dark brown trousers tucked into his boots. "I've already explained about what happened between our fathers. Losing a shipment to weather or thieves is an unfortunate incident that too often occurs when merchants do business. As for your brother, he challenged me. It wasn't the other way around."

"Johan was a quiet, gentle soul. He never fought anyone and preferred gaining book knowledge to physical pursuits." She blinked and stepped back, feeling as if she couldn't breathe. She'd heard rumors whispered about that Johan had been the one to issue the challenge to duel, but she'd never believed it. And she didn't believe it now. "That's impossible. Johan would never do such a thing."

"Ha!" Mr. Bishop tossed his hands out to his side. "You were there. Did you not hear him? Your brother was drunk, Miss Zimmer. The liquor in his system must have emboldened him."

Several thoughts dashed across her mind. Her father complaining that some of his liquor was missing just before the duel. Of smelling the foul stench on Johan that day he'd been shot. Was it possible he'd drunk himself into a stupor that empowered him to do something so completely out of character? She shook her head. "No, I don't believe you."

He hung his head as if disappointed in her and kicked a stone, sending it spiraling toward the riverbank. Why should that bother her? He heaved a loud sigh and looked up, his gaze pleading. "I was leaving the day after that ball. I was on my way to become a surgeon—a man who heals people. Why would I challenge a man to a duel that might end his life? I'm a man of healing, Miss Zimmer, not hurting."

"But you hurt my brother. You *killed* him."

"I never meant to. I wasn't even going to fire at him, but when his lead ball hit my arm, I jumped and my finger pulled the trigger by accident."

"Ha!" Carina barked a laugh. "You expect me to believe that the shot that killed my brother was an accident?"

He nodded. "Yes, because it was."

Reed Bishop looked so sincere she almost believed him. If she hadn't known without a doubt that Johan could never do such a thing, she might have been swayed. But the truth was Reed Bishop had killed the only family member who loved her. She'd been less than two when their mother had died giving birth to Johan. For as long as she could remember, she'd helped take care of him. And now he was gone.

She lifted the pistols again. "Choose your weapon, and do it now."

Mr. Bishop stared at her, a muscle twitching in his clean-shaven jaw. His gaze dropped to the guns, and after a long moment, he selected one. He loaded the weapon then waited while she set down the box and finished loading hers.

"I have one favor to ask, Miss Zimmer."

Carina's heart jumped. What could he possibly want from her? "What's that?"

The muscles in his jaw flexed, and he blew a long breath from his nose. He caught her gaze, sending her stomach into spasms.

"If I perish, promise me that you'll see to it that my mother is well cared for. I don't want her to suffer because she has no one special in her life who loves her like I do."

She narrowed her eyes. Was this merely a ploy for her sympathy? Did he not know that she had lived the last four years grieving, angry, and plotting revenge as his mother would if he died today? Yet thinking of Susan Bishop having to endure such agony made her stomach ache. Watching over his mother was the least she could do, not that his mother would want to have anything to do with her after the duel if her son died at her hand. She nodded. "I promise. Now, walk ten paces then turn and fire."

He stared at her, nothing moving but his lashes and a muscle in his jaw. "As you wish, Miss Zimmer. Take your best shot, and I hope and pray that it relieves you of the terrible burden you're carrying."

Chapter 8

Stubborn, mulish woman—beautiful woman.

Did she honestly believe he could shoot her?

She didn't know him very well if she believed that.

In truth, she barely knew him at all.

He counted to ten in his head as he walked back toward his horse. He hadn't thought Miss Zimmer would actually go through with the duel, or he would have left the roan in a better place where he couldn't accidentally catch a lead ball fired by an incompetent shooter. He had no real fear that Miss Zimmer would actually hit him, yet knowing that he'd never intended to shoot Johan either left him a bit uneasy.

He wouldn't shoot her, no matter what. He couldn't live with himself if he damaged her lovely flesh or caused her pain. But he *had* inflicted pain—the deep, grieving pain of loss. He knew how it felt because he still missed his father, even though they were often at odds with one another.

He reached number ten in his count and turned. Carina Zimmer had already turned and pointed her pistol at him. Never once in the times he'd relived that duel with her brother had he ever dreamed he'd find himself in such a predicament. He caught her gaze and fired his pistol into the air, knowing that doing so violated code duello's rules for proper dueling. But there was hardly anything proper in a pistol battle with a woman.

Her mouth dropped open then snapped shut. She turned slightly sideways and aimed her pistol at him like a professional shootist might. A bead of sweat ran down his cheek as he lowered his weapon to his side. He had assumed Miss Zimmer didn't know how to shoot—a bad assumption on his part if her stance was any indication. Standing firm, he met her gaze for gaze. She held steady but didn't fire. *Father, watch over me. Keep Mother in the shelter of Your arms should I perish today.*

His opponent's pistol lowered, but she jerked it back up.

It wobbled.

She steadied it again and took aim. His heart pounded a frantic beat like it had the first time he performed a surgery. He took a deep breath and turned sideways as she had, making himself a smaller target. He didn't plan on making things any easier for her. His medical bag was on his horse, so if she didn't inflict too serious a wound, he might be able to treat himself.

Suddenly her pistol shimmied and fell to her side. She dropped it and hunched over, crying out a sob that went clear to his soul. He wasn't sure whether to shout a hallelujah, hurry to his horse and hightail it home, or wait. He doubted Miss Zimmer would be happy that he'd witnessed her collapse.

He took a step toward her. He couldn't just walk away and leave her all alone in her misery. Besides, she might get a sudden urge of boldness and shoot him in the back. He took another step and then another. Her soft sobs tore at his gut. *Comfort her, Lord.*

The next instant, he felt as if God had told *him* to comfort her. He stopped in front of her, but she seemed not to see him. He lifted his arms, stepped forward, and wrapped them around her. She stiffened for a moment then fell against his chest, crying more than he'd ever witnessed a woman cry.

"You're all right. Don't fret," Reed cooed to her. He muttered prayers heavenward and patted her back. He longed to help her, to make her life easier, if only she'd let him. But he was probably the last person she'd accept assistance from. *Show me what to do, Lord.*

She clutched his shirt and leaned into his chest. His heart ached for her. She had so much responsibility on her slight shoulders. He thought of his mother and how she had run the plantation for so many years, all on her own. How was she able to keep things running so smoothly, but Miss Zimmer wasn't? He had it within his power now to make life easier for his mother. Guilt gnawed at him like a rat in a bag of grain.

Reed longed to lean his cheek against the top of Carina's head, but he resisted. He might be unable to deny a growing desire to know her better, but he didn't harbor any false hopes that she felt the same. Was she even aware that he held her in his arms?

❧

Carina stiffened. What was she doing enfolded in Reed Bishop's arms?

She couldn't shoot him, especially after he discharged his pistol in the air and stood still, waiting for her shot. How could he be so gallant in the face of death? How could the arms of her mortal enemy feel so safe? So good? So comforting?

When was the last time someone other than Betsey had hugged her? Reassured her? And why was he doing so when she'd come within a hair's length of shooting him?

He was still her nemesis. And she had a death grip on his waistcoat.

She released it suddenly and stepped back. His arms loosened but didn't let her go, as if he enjoyed holding her. She kept her gaze on the ground, too embarrassed to look up. "Please, let me go."

"I'd prefer not to."

Her gaze lifted to his of its own accord, and the tenderness in his eyes took her breath away. Was he merely attempting to use kindness to get her to forget about the duel? Their feud?

She stiffened her back and hiked her chin. "Turn loose of me, Mr. Bishop."

He heaved a sigh that washed across her face and dropped his arms so fast that she wobbled and had to grasp his arm to steady herself. Now that she was adrift from him, the loneliness rushed back. How could she betray her family by taking comfort from her enemy? Why did he of all people have to be her one adversary?

She turned her back to him and wiped her face with her sleeve. How could she ever face him again?

She couldn't.

Carina bent, picked up her pistol, and discharged it toward the river. Mr. Bishop jumped at the loud blast. He must have thought she could actually go through with shooting him—and that saddened her. But what else should she expect after the way she'd treated him?

Making a wide arc, she passed by him and retrieved the pistol case and his weapon, which lay on the damp ground where he'd dropped it. She would clean the weapons later. Right now she merely wanted to collect them and make a quick retreat back home.

She felt his eyes on her, but she couldn't face him again. The way he'd stood there, patiently waiting for her to kill or maim him, had completely disarmed her. Had stolen her anger and hatred. She'd come to the river expecting to die or at least to be injured, but he had willingly become the scapegoat, and she didn't know how to handle that.

She'd been angry for so long that she didn't know what to do, so she merely headed for home.

Maybe tomorrow when the duel wasn't so fresh in her mind, she'd round up her anger and feel normal again.

❧

Reed hated to see her go, looking so dejected and alone. He doubted he'd ever forget how good it felt to hold her in his arms. She wasn't the first woman he'd hugged, but with the exception of his mother, she was the only one since he'd given his heart to God. Holding the sobbing Miss Zimmer had filled an empty place in him that those teasing, painted women from the taverns he used to frequent never could.

He felt as if she'd taken a part of him with her, and he wouldn't be whole again until he was with her. He released a loud sigh.

What in the world was wrong with him? He was pining for a woman who hated him—a woman who'd nearly sent him to his Maker.

He shook his head and strode toward his horse. He mounted but had no desire to move on. How did one go from expecting to be dead to living out the rest of the day as if nothing had happened?

His horse nibbled at the ankle-high grass and meandered just so that if Reed lifted his head, he could see Miss Zimmer hightailing it back home. What was she thinking? Had this duel settled anything?

"Please, Lord, make it so. Relieve Miss Zimmer of the heavy burden that she's carrying. Help her to forgive me."

He sat praying and enjoying the serene setting. Water swished softly through the tall marsh grass, and a trio of turtles sunned themselves on a large, flat rock near the bank. Yellow butterflies flittered from one wildflower to another. Cypress trees with their knobby roots, flowering dogwoods, and mossy oaks lined the edges of the river. This was a place so filled with life.

Reed heaved another sigh and reined his mount toward home. Now that he was going to live another day or so, he needed to hire someone to build his office. He'd ask Harley, since it was a sore spot with his mother.

He reined the roan to a halt just outside the barn and dismounted. The same young man who'd driven his mother to Tanglewood hurried out to receive the horse.

Reed unfastened his medical bag and nodded his thanks to the youth. "Make sure to brush him down and give him some oats."

"Yes sir, Mistah Reed. I always do. Caesar, he's a good horse."

Charley led the gelding into the barn, and Reed followed him. He walked from stall to stall, studying the horses. He was going to need one of his own since he'd be staying at the plantation, and though Caesar was a decent horse, Reed found his particular gait uncomfortable. He wasn't ready to relegate himself to a buggy that doctors so commonly drove. A good saddle horse would do him well. "Which of these is the best horse for riding long distances?"

Charley crinkled up his nose. "Well, sir, I don't rightly know, beings as how I ain't never rode one very far."

Reed pursed his lips. He should have thought about that. A Negro—free or slave—riding along on a fine horse was bound to be stopped and most likely harassed. If he didn't have the proper papers, he could be in trouble. "Which one does Harley ride most often?"

"That'd be Pete. He's the big dun that stays in that third stall over there." Charley pointed across the barn.

Reed thanked him and strode up to the house. The more he thought about it, the more he liked the idea of buying a horse of his own. Maybe he could talk his mother into going to Charleston for a few days to shop while he searched for a good horse. He smacked his riding gloves against his palm, liking the idea more and more. That would also give him the opportunity to research and locate a carpenter to design and build his office.

As he passed through the gardens, his stomach growled, reminding him that he hadn't yet eaten breakfast. He left before Cook had anything prepared this morning, not that he had much appetite given the circumstances. Now he was starving and ready for just about anything Cook could dish up.

He had a lot to be thankful for. He was still alive, as was Miss Zimmer, and both unharmed. Maybe things today had put in motion the end of the troubles between his family and the Zimmers. He'd held Carina in his arms and knew one thing for certain: For some odd reason, he liked her. More than liked her. He was attracted to her like he'd never been to any other woman.

The big question, however, remained: What was he going to do about that?

Chapter 9

"Carina! Amos!"

At her fader's sudden cry, Carina tossed down her hairbrush and ran down the hall. What would he say when she told him that Amos was no longer here, and neither were five other of their slaves? She'd managed not to tell him by simply avoiding him and staying busy away from the house. But it was bedtime, and he knew she'd be home. There was no evading him this time.

She skidded to a halt on the wood floor just outside his bedroom door. Her hand lifted to her nose at the sour odor emanating from the room. "Ja, Fader, what is it you need?"

"Where's Amos? He missed giving me a bath yesterday. I got sick today and retched all over myself. The stench is unbearable. Where is that boy?"

"Didn't Betsey clean you up and give you a fresh nightshirt?"

He swatted his hand through the air. "I don't want that woman near me. She scrubs so hard she could rub smooth the back of an alligator."

Carina grinned. There was truth in that statement. Until she was old enough to wash herself, she'd just resigned herself to having red skin from Betsey's scrubbing during her weekly bath time. Her smile faded as she remembered her dilemma. "I can have Enoch or Woodson come up and give you a bucket bath."

"Woodson! He's not a house servant. Why, his hands are as rough as oak bark. Send Amos to me, and do it quick."

Her fader crossed his arms and glared at her. Carina swallowed hard. She'd made a decision for the welfare of all, and now she'd have to face the consequences. If she ever hoped to inherit Tanglewood—and there was nothing she wanted more, save the welfare of her servants—she had to prove to her fader that she was capable. She sucked in a strengthening breath and straightened her back. "Amos isn't here. He's gone."

"Gone!" Her fader bolted upright off the stack of pillows he'd been reclining on. "Did he go and run off? Who'd you hire to find him?" He scooted to the side of the bed and swung his legs over the edge, more nimbly than she'd seen him move in months.

She rushed to his side, uncertain if he could stand if he tried. How long had it been since he'd left his bed? She reached out to halt him. "Now, Fader, you are in no condition to get up."

He raised his elbow and shoved her back so hard she stumbled. She stepped on the hem of her skirt and fell on her backside, the fabric beneath her ripping. Tears pooled, but she forced them away. This was her only decent skirt.

Her fader scowled at her. For too long, she'd let him intimidate her and order her around as if she were one of his workers. She was his daughter—and the only reason he still had a home. She gathered her tattered skirts and ragged dignity and stood.

She pierced her fader with a glare. "Amos did not run away. I leased him and five other of our people to Mr. Davies for six months."

The left side of his face puckered up. "Lease? Zimmers don't lease their slaves. I'll be the laughingstock of Charleston."

She feared he was already ill-thought of by most of the people who knew him. Before he took ill, he was never kind. He took anything he could take and never gave an inch. Many times she wished he had died instead of her mother or Johan. She hung her head at the insensitive thought. What kind of daughter was she?

Her fader scooted back into bed, launching a rank odor her way. He certainly needed a bath. "Tomorrow, you will go to Davies's business and tell him the deal is off. Bring back our slaves, you hear me?"

She hiked her chin. "I can't do that. Mr. Davies and I signed a contract. We need the money for the mortgage payment and supplies. For seed. We can manage without the extra help and will save food by having less mouths to feed during this difficult time."

Karl Zimmer's face grew as red as the borscht he loved so much. "I'm still the owner of this plantation. What makes you think you can do whatever you please?"

Carina winced. Her legs trembled, but she knew she had to stay the course and not back down. Her fader never respected anyone who caved to his hollering. "You're no longer physically able to run this plantation. I've done what I had to and made choices only after considerable thought and discussion with Betsey and Woodson."

"Discussion! With slaves?" He grabbed one of his pillows and lobbed it at her. "Slaves don't know squat. You can't discuss with them. That just shows you aren't fit to run this place."

"Neither are you." She nearly gasped out loud at her disrespectfulness. Never had she stood up to her fader before. "Someone has to make the decisions around here, and I'm the only one who can. You drink yourself half to death every day. A drunken man can't run a plantation." She took a step back, shocked at her tirade and half-afraid of what he would do to her. Thank the Lord he wasn't able to walk.

His face grew crimson, and he sputtered. "I don't know why Johan had to die instead of you." He reached under a pillow and pulled out one of his empty bottles and flung it at her.

Carina spun sideways and ducked, but she wasn't fast enough. The spiraling bottle crashed into her forehead, sending pain ratcheting through her. Her fader's face blurred then all turned black.

❧

Reed never thought he'd ever want to throttle another man, but if not for the fact that he was a God-fearing man, he was certain he would have laid his hands on Karl Zimmer—ill or not. How could a father be so cruel as to throw a heavy bottle at his daughter's head?

He tied off the last suture and snipped it.

"Is Miz 'Rina gonna be all right?" Betsey wrung her thick hands together and watched him from the far side of the bed.

"I hope so. I'll certainly do all I can to help her." He poured a generous amount of brandy over the wound to clean it then placed a square of cloth over it and wrapped Carina's head to hold it snug. He was grateful that she hadn't awakened during the suturing procedure, but the longer she was unconscious, the more concerned he became. *Please, Father, let her be all right. Heal her, Lord.*

He breathed in a long breath and straightened, rubbing the small of his back. He'd done all he knew to do. Now she was in God's hands. Reed turned down the lantern, knowing Carina would most likely be sensitive to light when she awoke since she had a head wound.

Betsey waddled around the bed and pulled a side chair from a desk across the room and dragged it toward him. She set it next to the bed. "You sit, Doctah Boss, and I'll go fetch you some tea and a slice of my buttermilk pie."

He smiled. "That sounds wonderful. It's been awhile since I ate anything."

Reed settled in, planning to stay until he knew Carina was faring well. The frayed curtains danced on the light breeze, while tree frogs, crickets, and other insects serenaded the moon as it made its way across the night sky. He laid his head against the ladder-back chair and closed his eyes, reliving the moment Enoch had come to his door and said that Miss Zimmer had been injured.

His first thought was of the dueling pistols, but he quickly cast that aside and asked Enoch what had happened. Reed clenched his back teeth, angered again at the unfair circumstances Carina was forced to endure. And a good measure of her suffering was his fault.

He longed to be her friend, to help her, but he doubted she'd be receptive. He slid his hand down her forearm to her slender wrist and checked her pulse. Breathing a sigh of relief, he boldly slid his hand into hers and held it. Hers was small, though not soft like his mother's, but rather callused, and her nails were chipped, rough. What kind of work had she done to earn those calluses? Reed pursed his lips, hesitated a moment, then placed a kiss on her index finger. Some way, somehow, he would make things easier for her.

Releasing her hand, he sat back and placed one hand over his chest. He'd do well to remember his patient's vendetta. She would not be happy to awaken and find him in her bedchamber, even with Betsey present, too. He rested his elbows on his knees and stared at the floor. He'd give Carina until he finished his tea and pie. If she hadn't awakened by then, he'd use smelling salts, but he preferred that a patient come to on their own.

Standing, he stretched and walked to the window, gazing out at the near-full moon. If his presence upset her, he'd go downstairs and supervise her from there. His mind whirled with ideas as to what he could do to help her. She was a neighbor and injured. He now had a legitimate excuse to come to her home and help out. Neighbors helped neighbors during times of trouble.

Once Carina was out of the woods, he'd put together a team of his servants and start clearing her drive. Maybe if it was more inviting, other neighbors would feel compelled to stop by for a visit.

A rustling sounded behind him, and he turned, checking Carina. Betsey shuffled through the door, carrying a tray with a huge slice of pie, a teapot, cup, and a small sugar bowl and creamer. She set the load on top of the desk and blew out a loud sigh. "I declare, those steps get taller and taller ever' day."

Reed's stomach growled in response to the sweet scent of the pie, and a warm cup of tea might help him to relax. But he doubted it. He wouldn't truly relax until Carina opened her eyes and yelled at him to leave. He smiled at that thought.

Betsey chuckled low and deep as she poured his tea. "Guess that pie arrived just in time."

He crossed the room and claimed the pie, cutting into it, then savoring the sweet flavor. "This is delicious. With desserts like this, I don't know how Miss Zimmer stays so thin."

"Hmpf." The colored woman crossed her arms across her ample bosom and plopped back down in the chair on the far side of the bed. "That's because she don't eat nuthin'."

"And why is that?" Though thinner than most women he knew, she seemed healthy enough. She'd never been faint or ill in his presence. In fact, she'd always had plenty of gumption and fortitude, enough to chase him off her land if need be. He couldn't help smiling as he remembered her ordering him off her land. No sir, Miss Carina Zimmer sure didn't lack fortitude and determination.

"I think she don't eat so we have more food." Betsey shook her head. "I fuss and fret, but nothing I can do will make Miz 'Rina eat another bite once she decides she's done."

"Maybe she'll eat if the doctor orders her to."

"And maybe she'll hop out of that bed and chase you off with her shotgun again."

Reed grinned and shook his head. "You're a sassy thing—you know it."

"I know." Betsey smiled and ducked her head. He doubted she'd ever talked to Mr. Zimmer so freely.

Reed finished his pie then downed his tea. He checked Carina's pulse again then paced the room for several minutes.

"Walkin' a hole in the carpet ain't gonna make her wake up no faster."

He sat back down and crossed one leg over his knee. His foot jiggled and he tapped the leg of the chair with his index finger. His gaze traveled around the room. The only furniture was the bed, desk, two chairs, and a commode with a chipped pitcher sitting in a ceramic bowl. Three pegs hung on the wall—one was empty, one held the shirtwaist he'd seen Carina wear several times, and the other held a faded brown dress with small yellow flowers. The sparseness of the room and her wardrobe put him to shame.

Betsey hummed a tune under her breath while she stitched up a tear in the ugly skirt Carina always wore.

"Why doesn't she have more clothing?"

Betsey's brows lifted in a manner that told him he'd overstepped his bounds. She glanced at her sleeping mistress then back at him. "Ever' time we get new fabric, Miz 'Rina, she says it has to go to someone else 'cause they needs it worse'n her, but that ain't the truth. She won't let me make her a new dress or skirt. She just wears this nasty old thing."

"What if the doctor ordered it burned for the sake of her health?"

Betsey smiled widely. "I like how you think, Doctah Boss, but there ain't nuthin' to replace this with." She held up the sad-looking skirt.

"Maybe my mother could help."

The slave woman pressed her lips together and shook her head. "Miz 'Rina, she don't like to accept he'p from others. She gots to do ever'thing herself."

Reed's admiration for the stubborn, independent woman kept rising. She placed her slaves before herself, worked her fingers to the bone to keep Tanglewood running while also tending an ailing father. "What exactly is wrong with Mr. Zimmer?"

Betsey lifted one shoulder then dropped it back down. "Don't rightly know. He took to his bed after a sickness over a year ago and nevah got up again—at least not when nobody is lookin'."

Leaning forward on his arms, Reed glanced at Carina again then focused on her maid. "You're saying he can get out of bed when he wants to?"

"I'm not sayin' nuthin'." She pressed her lips together and shook her head then glanced at the door and leaned toward Reed. "Just that he don't treat his daughter good. She works from sunup to past dark ever' day, and he don't lift a hand to he'p. He just moans and groans, drinks that liquor all day, and pines away for that no-good son of his. Would be better for all if he just up and died."

"I should check on him while I'm here."

Betsey's eyes went wide and she waved her hand in the air. "Oh no, sir, he wouldn't like that none. He hates Bishops even more'n Miz 'Rina."

Reed ducked his head, not wanting her to see how her words had wounded him. He didn't want Carina to hate him. He wanted to be her friend. *Please, Lord, soften her heart toward me. Make her willing to let me help her.*

He considered his plan again. Those limbs that hung over the drive were dangerous. If one was to fall when someone was riding under them, a person could get killed or seriously injured. First thing when he returned home, he would set his plan into action.

Chapter 10

Carina fought the darkness, searching for the voice that called to her. Where was she? Why was the fog so thick?

A strip of light appeared in the distance, and she clawed her way toward it, though it pained her eyes fiercely. And her head—the pressure, the pain—was a horse sitting on it?

"Come on, Carina, wake up."

Someone squeezed her hand. The touch felt odd—unfamiliar, but welcoming. Reassuring.

"That's it, come on."

Now her hand was encased between two big, warm hands, guiding, leading her across the dark abyss to the light. To him.

She blinked and saw Betsey stand and hurry toward her. Glancing up, she recognized the cracked plaster of her bedroom ceiling—a large, spiderlike web creeping across the ceiling and down the walls. Why was she in bed in the middle of the day? What had happened?

Lifting her hand, she found the reason for the pressure in her head. A tightly wrapped bandage. "Off. Hurts."

A gentle hand pulled hers back. "Sorry, but the bandage needs to stay on for a few days. You've had an accident, and you have an inch-long gash that I had to suture."

Carina scowled and turned toward the man's voice. Brilliant blue eyes laced with concern stared down at her. Reed Bishop's eyes. What was he doing in her room?

She pushed up in the bed, causing pain to radiate through her head, then clutched her forehead, unable to hold back a groan.

Mr. Bishop stood. "I'll give her some laudanum for the pain. Would you mind bringing some more hot water, Betsey? We can mix it with some tea."

Nodding, the maid rose and hurried to the doorway. "Etta! Bring up some hot water."

"Ow, don't holler." Carina squeezed her eyes shut, partly because of the pain and partly so she didn't have to look at *him*.

The doctor picked up her wrist and held on to it. "Good. Your pulse is steady and strong. Tell me how you're feeling. Is there anything you want?"

She wanted him to hold her hand again, to coo those soft words of encouragement again, and to tell her everything would be fine. But it wouldn't. Never.

Last night had proven that no matter how hard she worked or what she did, she could never replace her brother. That she could never earn her fader's approval. How would she find the strength to go on? Maybe it would have been better if she'd never awakened.

"What's wrong? Is the pain severe?"

"Why do you care?" She pulled the light quilt up to her neck. "Why are you here?"

"Betsey sent for me when you were injured, and I came right away. A head wound is nothing to take lightly."

She didn't want to be beholden to him. She couldn't pay him for his services. Turning her face to the wall, she spoke what she felt he wanted to hear. "Well, you've treated me, so now you're free to go."

"I'm the doctor, Miss Zimmer. I'll be the one who decides when to take my leave."

Inwardly, she was glad that he didn't back down, but she knew she shouldn't be. Why would he of all people be the one to comfort her—to make her feel better? She should be angry still, but she was just too tired. She'd lost her will to fight. Her heavy eyelids weighed too much, and she couldn't resist the pull of sleep. Maybe when she awakened, she would discover this was all a bad dream.

❧

Reed paced the piazza and stared across the front lawn—a weed patch, actually—and down the drive. Clearing all the debris and getting this place looking decent again would take many men and a lot of muscle. He didn't mind helping a neighbor in need—it was the way of life in the South—but what was one to do when said neighbor didn't want help?

A grin tugged at his lips. He was the doctor and could order Miss Zimmer to stay in bed for several days, which she should anyway. If he got together a large enough crew and recruited help from his cousin, just maybe they could get the drive cleared before the obstinate woman found out.

He contemplated the distance. Would she be able to hear them working? If they started at the entrance near the main road first and worked their way toward the house, they could probably get most of the job done before she caught wind of it. He rapped his palms on the porch railing, liking the idea more and more. Might be a good idea to mention it to Woodson so he didn't come after them with an ax.

The door opened, and his mother stepped out. She'd arrived early, right after the breakfast hour, with a basket of fragrant goodies on her arm.

He nodded to her. "Are you satisfied Miss Zimmer will live?"

Grinning, she wrapped her arm around his waist. "I never had a doubt, not when she had the care of such a fine doctor."

Her praise warmed his heart. Even though her greatest desire was for him to be a planter as his father had been, she still had the grace to encourage him in his dream.

"I'm not so sure she'll be able to live down her embarrassment of you being in her room and seeing her in her nightgown though." She glanced up at him with a stern look. "You didn't help Betsey get her changed out of her dress, did you?"

"I'm a doctor, Mother. Things like that don't affect me."

She studied his face. "Don't be telling me whoppers, son."

He grinned and lifted his gaze to see Sammy zigzagging along the side of the barn, chasing butterflies. "I did not help with that. Etta assisted her mother in getting Miss Zimmer into her nightgown."

"Well, I'm relieved to know you still have some sense of decency."

He enjoyed the playful banter but was glad he'd skirted the truth. Seeing capable Carina lying there bleeding and unconscious had just about been his undoing. Would she despise him all over again because she'd have a scar where he'd stitched her wound? It would have been far worse and taken much longer to heal if he hadn't sutured the gaping injury.

"She'll be fine, son, though her dignity may be fragile for a bit, especially when you're around. Carina doesn't like people helping her."

"And why is that?"

She turned to face him and crossed her arms. "She's had to be strong, independent, all her life. She lost her mother at such a young age and had a younger brother who looked up to her all his life. Her father uprooted them from their home and brought them here. Karl never should have become a planter. His trade was watchmaking, but he had lofty visions of leaving Boston to live in a warmer climate and grow crops. Karl never had the fortitude nor the proper knowledge to run a large plantation, and he wasn't willing to learn from his neighbors when they offered sage advice."

"Karl? You know him well enough to refer to him by his first name?"

She pursed her lips and nodded. "Yes. Your father befriended him when he first moved here. I came with him a few times because I felt sorry for Karl's motherless children, but I didn't like how he looked at me when your father's gaze was occupied elsewhere."

Reed narrowed his gaze. The more he heard about Karl Zimmer, the less he liked. "I should check on him, but Betsey doesn't think he'd be receptive."

"It would be a good thing if you tried."

He nodded, knowing the doctor in him really gave him no choice. He'd check on both Mr. Zimmer and Abel before leaving today. Sammy gave up chasing butterflies and hunkered down like a bobcat, trailing a yellow cat into the barn. In the paddock on the far side of the barn, Lulu ambled along, stretching her head below the lowest rail in search of grass on the other side.

"I've made a couple of decisions. I plan to buy a good horse and also to hire a carpenter to build a clinic near the road."

His mother's chin lifted slightly. "It's good you've decided what you want to do." Her words belied what she truly felt.

"I thought I'd have a bell installed that could be rung to alert me when someone had arrived at the clinic. That way I can be at home when I'm not needed there."

Her head jerked toward him, her gaze hopeful. "Does that mean you intend to oversee the plantation, too?"

After learning of Carina's sacrifices for her home, how could he do less? He hadn't considered how much of a burden it must have been for his mother to make all the decisions of the plantation by herself. "Yes, Mama. I'm sorry for not seeing how much of a burden that was on you sooner."

She smiled and leaned her head against his shoulder. Her silence and the way she hugged his arm spoke volumes. For far too long he'd played around and had fun with his friends. It was time he stepped up and became the man of his home.

But when he thought of his home, it seemed incomplete. Something was missing. His mother hadn't pressed him, but he knew for certain that she'd been scouring the community in search of just the right woman for him to marry. She would expect him to give her an heir before too long. Was he ready for marriage and fatherhood?

His thoughts drifted back to Carina. Dared he hope she could ever come to have feelings for him?

God could work mighty miracles, but he was afraid to believe that even the good Lord could effect such a drastic change in Miss Zimmer's heart.

❧

For days, a ceaseless pounding had assaulted Carina's head. Only at night did it lessen. She hated being abed for so long when so many things needed attending, but when she'd tried to rise, her vision blurred and swam around the room. Betsey and Etta had delivered meal after meal and stuffed her like a roasted hen with broth, bread, and porridge for the past three days. Though she rarely ate much at most mealtimes, she was hankering for something more substantial. A thick beef or venison steak sounded more to her liking than broth.

With her puny breakfast over, she was bound and determined to get out of bed. She sat up, glad that the awful dizziness seemed to have passed. Scooting sideways, she dangled her legs over the side of the bed and waited. When nothing happened, she eased off the side and stood. Her legs trembled from lack of use, and the dull pain in her head intensified. But the pounding she'd heard now sounded as if it were coming from outside. She inched toward the window, hoping her legs wouldn't give out, and she finally latched onto the frame. Her limbs were more wobbly than a newborn filly's.

She peered outside, past the barn, looking for Woodson and Enoch. What could they be doing to make so much noise? As far as she could tell, neither man was working in the field. A loud crack, like an explosion, sounded off to the southwest, and she spun her head in that direction. From her viewpoint, she could only see the part of the drive closest to the house. The noise sounded farther away. Could it be coming from the Bishop plantation?

She had to know, even if she had to walk across the hall to find out.

"Jes' what do you think yo're doin', missy?" Betsey stood in the doorway, filling the whole opening. Her chest rose and fell at a frantic pace, as it always did right after she'd climbed the stairs.

"It's time I was up. There's plenty of work that needs doing." Her talk was bold, but she glanced back at the chair, needing to sit before she collapsed. She didn't want Betsey to see her weakness.

"Either you sit down or get back in the bed." Pushing past Carina, Betsey hurried to the desk, pulled out the chair, then gave her a no-nonsense glare.

Trying to fool Betsey was a waste of time. She grabbed hold of the chair's back, while her maid took hold of her other arm and helped her down. "Sometimes I wonder who's the boss around here."

"There's a new boss around these days." Grinning, Betsey crossed to the bed and yanked off the sheets. "These could use a good washin'."

"I could use a good washing." Carina grinned. "And what did you mean about there being a *new* boss? Are you talking about Woodson? Or you?"

Betsey mumbled something about uppity white folks, but Carina knew she was only teasing. "We'd best get you washed up. Mrs. Bishop, she done told me she'd come back to visit midmornin'."

Carina didn't miss how her maid had avoided her question, but she simply didn't have the energy to pursue an answer. And Susan was returning. Her first inclination was to decline the visit, but in truth, she had enjoyed her time with Mr. Bishop's mother yesterday, and she'd even found Susan's reading of the scriptures a comfort. It was Susan's son who set her on edge. She glanced down at her hand and rubbed her fingers together. The man she'd attempted to kill had turned around and doctored her, comforted her, and caressed her hand. She'd treated him so horribly, yet one would never have known by the way he'd acted. Was it merely the doctor in him that was able to push aside a personal offense to so meticulously care for the very person who'd inflicted the pain? Or was there more to it?

Betsey grabbed the pitcher off the commode. "I'll be back with some hot water, so you just sit there and don't do nuthin'. If you need somethin', holler for me or Etta—she be downstairs dustin'." Turning, she bustled out the door, mumbling something about "that girl" under her breath.

Carina laid her head back against the chair and concentrated on the look she remembered in Dr. Bishop's caring gaze. He had seemed worried, as if he truly cared about her. But how could that be possible? Hadn't he shown the same compassion for Abel?

She stood and walked back to the window, feeling a bit stronger. Susan had told her how much her son had changed in the time he'd been gone. How becoming a Christian had changed him from a selfish, spoiled boy to a gentle, caring man. Leaning her head against the window frame, she wondered if that was true. Was Susan just a proud mother, overemphasizing her son's positive traits?

Betsey's labored footsteps plodded down the hall in her direction. Could she talk to her about Dr. Bishop? She heaved a sigh. Probably not. Her maid had fallen in love with him the day he splinted Abel's leg, and now Betsey's feelings had surely grown like bread dough on a warm day since he'd taken such good care of her.

Rather than dreading her next encounter with Reed Bishop, she looked forward to it. Was there any hope they might become friends? Was she willing to turn loose of her bitterness to make that happen?

Even if she did, how could he ever forget how she had treated him?

And what about Johan? Could it possibly be true her brother had started the duel?

She shook her head. She didn't have a prayer of a chance that a Zimmer and a Bishop could ever make peace.

Chapter 11

Reed wiped the sweat from his eyes. The scene playing out before him made him proud to be a Southerner. He'd put out the call—that Carina Zimmer had been injured—and people from most of the neighboring plantations had either come to help or sent a crew of workers. Along with the dozen men he'd rounded up from Reed Springs, the total numbered more than twenty-five at last count. Saws swished, hoes whacked, and the colored folks serenaded everyone with soul-touching spirituals.

A bevy of the females, both white and Negro, had set up camp under a huge live oak and a batch of stew was simmering over a campfire. A couple of men had set up tables in the shade for them, and several other ladies were setting out cups of cider and water for the meal. Women who weren't cooking sat on a blanket talking and sewing. This was more than a chance to help a hurting neighbor; it was an opportunity for community—for friends and even some family—to spend time together.

The difference they'd made was astounding. Dead limbs had been removed and cut up for firewood, which Enoch had been hauling up to the house. All the vines that had tangled around trees and begun to choke the life out of them were gone, shrubs trimmed or removed. Why, the next time he rode over to Tanglewood, he might accidentally ride right past the entrance because it looked so different.

Carina needed a sign with her plantation's name on it, and he could make one. He wondered what she would say when she saw what they had done. Would she be happy—or angry?

Reed's cousin caught his eye and waved. Seth pulled a bandanna from his waistband and swiped his face as Reed approached. "Taking a break already?"

"Already!" Seth gazed up at the sky. "By my calculations, it's almost quitting time."

Reed's stomach growled, as if in agreement. He gazed past the last of the workers to the final curve in the road. Once they rounded that point, anyone at the house could see them. He was somewhat surprised that Carina hadn't come stomping down the road with her shotgun, ordering them off her property.

"What's wrong? You look nervous."

Shrugging, Reed turned back to his cousin. "Just wondering what Miss Zimmer will say to all this."

Seth frowned. "How could she not be pleased?"

Reed walked ahead three feet, picked up a large stick, and tossed it in the back of the rubbish wagon. "It's a difficult situation. She hasn't had anyone to rely on and has managed to run the plantation and care for her ailing father all by herself."

"What's wrong with her father?"

Shrugging, Reed stared back at the house. "I tried to examine Mr. Zimmer, but he just lambasted me and sent me from his room. I have my suspicions that it may just be the drink that is incapacitating him—that and his bad attitude about all things."

"Hmm. . .I see what you mean. Must be hard for Miss Zimmer to live here alone and never see other people."

Reed nodded. "If I have my way about it, I plan on changing that."

Seth's green eyes twinkled. "Do I detect a blossoming romance?"

"Ha!" Reed barked such a loud laugh that several people turned to see what was so funny. "If there was such a thing, it would be decidedly one-sided." He lifted his hat and fanned his sweaty face. His gaze followed a man with a scruffy beard and ragged, loose-fitting clothes as he wandered along the edge of the work area closest to the food tables.

"What do you make of him?" He nodded with his chin toward the man.

Seth shook his head. "Never saw him before. Must work for another planter."

Reed continued watching the man. He'd done little work today, although if one weren't watching too closely it wouldn't have been noticed. The man ambled along, picking up a vine or twig here and there, his gaze continually flicking back to the food table, where the women almost had the meal ready. Reed's mouth watered.

And where was his mother? She'd promised to come down and help oversee the food preparations. Even as the thought fled his mind, he saw her walking down the road, a basket over her arm with Betsey and Etta close behind her. She looked every bit the mistress of the plantation. He was partly relieved Miss Zimmer hadn't come, too, but on the other hand, he was anxious to see her again. Excited to show her what her neighbors had accomplished. Wary to see her reaction. Would life with Miss Zimmer always be a constant ebb and flow of emotions and desires?

He walked out to greet his mother and relieved her of her basket. He nodded to Betsey and Etta. "How's my patient today?"

Betsey shook her head. "Fussy. Grumblin' to get up. Don't know how much longer I can keep her down."

"Are you sure she can't start moving around some—maybe leave her room? She's about to go crazier than a chicken in a rain barrel." His mother glanced up at him and smiled. She might be sweet, but she was a Southern lady and had no reservations about using her feminine wiles to sway him to her side.

He hadn't seen Carina in two days, so he needed to check on her anyway. "I'll stop by when we're done here and assess how she is doing."

"Mind that you wash up first." His mother's gaze ran down his dirty shirt and trousers. The shine that had been on his boots this morning was buried under a layer of dust. He wasn't in much of a state to go visiting, but then he wasn't going to impress a lady, but rather to check on a patient.

Seth slugged his arm. "Hey, look over there."

Reed turned and glanced in the direction his cousin pointed. The thin man with the scruffy beard they'd discussed earlier grabbed a whole loaf of bread and shoved it into his satchel. He glanced right and left, slid over to another table near a tree, and leaned on it, while his gaze darted all over. Reed looked back at Seth so the man wouldn't see him staring. "Is he doing what I think?"

"Look!" His mother gasped. "Why—that man is stealing that slab of ham!" She waved her hand in the air as if trying to flag down a runaway wagon. "Somebody, hey! Stop that man."

"C'mon." Reed yanked on Seth's shirt. If the skinny man they'd seen earlier was hungry, all he had to do was tell somebody, and they'd willingly give him food. But to steal it, that was something that couldn't be tolerated. He kicked up his pace, but the thief darted into the wooded area surrounding the swamp. With Seth on his heels, Reed dodged in and out of tree after tree, but the wiry man knew just which way to go to elude him. Finally Reed stopped and leaned over, resting his hands on his knees as he struggled to catch a breath.

As his breathing slowed and the thundering in his ears subsided, all he could hear was Seth's loud breaths beside him and the normal sounds of the swamp—the swish of the Spanish moss on the gentle breeze in the trees overhead, a loud splash in the pond's inky water to his right. Songbirds serenaded the treetops, insects hummed, and a chorus of frogs joined the symphony.

Swamp grass, a myriad of trees and bushes met his gaze, but not a person other than his cousin. How had that man just disappeared?

"He's gone. Let's head back. I'm starving."

Reed nodded. "Just let me wash off in the pond." Stooping beside the bank, he searched the area near the shore, making sure no gators were hovering close by. He wouldn't be the first man surprised by one of those big creatures lurking just under the surface of the water. He dipped in his hands and swished them around, washing the day's grime off.

Seth nudged Reed's backside with his leg. "Watch out for the swamp monster." He chuckled.

Reed finished splashing water on his face then rinsed his hands. As a doctor, he preferred being cleaner and washing his hands more frequently than most men did. He stood and shook his damp hair on Seth. "You need a bath, cousin. You're pungent."

"Hey!" Seth gave him a playful push.

They headed back, neither talking. Reed thought about how they'd played as kids around the swamp at Reed Springs and also neighboring Madison Gardens, where Seth had grown up. He hadn't thought of the swamp monster in years. Those had been fun times.

"I guess we need to ask around and see who that fellow works for. Maybe they'll know where he's run off to."

Reed nodded his agreement as they broke through the tree line. The four planters from the surrounding plantations who'd been helping all day headed his way.

"Looks like that thief got away." Mason Dugger stared past Reed as if waiting for the man to walk out of the woods.

"He seemed to know the swamp area quite well, and he was fast." Reed looked from man to man. "Which one of you does he work for?"

Each of the planters cast accusing glances at one another. Finally Peter Reynolds shook his head. "Not me. Never saw him before."

The others followed suit, each denying having hired the man. Had the thief been hiding in the woods and taken advantage of the situation? Had he heard about the gathering and come to help in order to eat? Not that he'd been all that much help. Reed rubbed the back of his neck, not liking Carina being so defenseless in that big house without a man close by to help if needed. Of course, Betsey would probably come running and wallop an intruder with her iron skillet—if she could catch him.

"What's so funny? Is there something you're not telling us?" Seth stared at Reed like he'd taken leave of his senses.

Sobering, he shook his head. "I just had a thought. I'm concerned about both the Zimmers being injured and no able-bodied man in the house, should the thief decide to break in."

John Bowman grunted. "She can get one of her slaves to stay on the porch and keep watch all night." He turned and sauntered back to the food tables, where people had started filling their plates. As if the issue had been settled, the others also turned and headed back to their meal, all except for Seth and William Dean, a newcomer to the area. Dean was a hard worker—a widower with two children, Reed had heard, even though the man was only a few years older than Reed.

He scanned the area and located Woodson and Enoch, still loading wood into the wagon. What his friends didn't know was that Carina only had one other male servant besides those two. She was down to a bare minimum of workers and couldn't afford to have one of them stay up all night keeping watch. Sammy would volunteer, he was certain, but it wasn't likely the boy could stay awake all night, and besides, he'd be precious little help when confronted by a grown man on a mission.

"That Mrs. Zimmer must be a widow, huh?"

Reed's gaze jerked back to Mr. Dean. The widower would probably be considered a handsome man to most women with his blond hair and brown eyes. He was about the same six-foot-tall height as Reed, but the planter was much broader in the shoulders. Didn't women prefer men with big shoulders? He straightened and glanced at Seth, who shrugged and grinned. "Why do you ask, Mr. Dean?"

He swatted his hand in the air. "Call me Will or Willy. Aren't you the new doctor? Sure glad to have one closer than Charleston."

Reed nodded, relaxing under the man's welcoming smile. His straight, white teeth would probably be another factor in his favor with females. Reed touched the end of his front tooth with his tongue, the tooth that was missing a corner from when he fell and smacked his face on Cook's worktable, years ago.

Will nodded. "And I believe in being straight with folks. I've got me a young boy and girl who need a mama. I'm looking to marry again. Don't much care for being alone." His gaze searched the crowd and landed in the area where Reed's mother was passing out slices of bread to the men in line. "She's a fine-looking woman, although a bit older than I expected. You think she's open to marrying again?"

Reed clenched his jaw. Surely Will must be looking at someone other than his mother.

Seth turned with obvious curiosity in the direction Will was looking. "Which lady are you talking about?"

Will smiled widely and pointed straight at Reed's mother. "That one there in the pretty purple dress with the brownish hair. Hat tied under her chin with the big bow. Isn't that Mrs. Zimmer? I saw her walking from the house with two of her servants."

Seth sputtered and doubled over. "Ho, ho! That's hilarious."

Reed narrowed his eyes.

Will looked at Seth as if he'd turned green and grown six horns. "What's so funny? I need a wife, and it doesn't matter to me if she's a bit older, as long as she'd be kind to my children. Nothing humorous about it."

"A *bit* older?" Reed ground out between clenched teeth.

Will swung around and took another look. "Well, maybe a tad more than a bit, but she's still a fine-looking woman. How old do you reckon she is? Thirty-two, maybe?"

Seth slapped his leg and laughed so hard tears ran down his cheeks. Will blinked, obviously confused, while the people closest to them turned to see what was going on.

"That woman is not interested in getting married."

Will's chin lifted slightly. "How do you know? Have you already approached her?"

Seth roared with laughter and fell down to his knees. He cackled like an old hen then snorted and gasped for a breath.

Will shook his head. "What—is—so—funny?"

Reed wanted to be angry, but the humor of the situation overpowered his irritation with the misguided man. "That is not *Miss* Zimmer. That woman you're admiring is my mother."

Seth snorted and managed to get up on his knees. His cheeks were wet with his tears. "Yeah, and she's twenty years your senior."

Will looked at Reed. "Oh." Then he glanced down at Seth. "Oh." Suddenly he puffed up, his cheeks the color of the filling of Mrs. Bowman's cherry pie. He nodded at Reed. "My apologies. I should probably be getting back to my children. Left 'em with their mammy." He slapped his hat back onto his head and marched to his horse, stiff and proud.

Seth continued to chuckle. Reed nudged him with the toe of his boot. "Not a word of this to Mother, you hear me?"

Seth pressed his lips together, but he was still laughing, if his bouncing shoulders were any indication.

Reed held out his hand for his cousin, and Seth took it, allowing Reed to help him up. Seth wiped his eyes and grinned. "I wish you could have seen your face. I don't know though. Were you upset because he confused your mama for Miss Zimmer, or because Will is looking to marry and isn't too picky?" Seth glanced over his shoulder to where one could see a corner of the upstairs of the Zimmer home; then he caught Reed's gaze. "You know that you just confirmed to Dean that Miss Zimmer isn't married, don't you? When you emphasized she was a miss." He smacked Reed on the shoulder. "Don't dawdle too long. If you've got designs on Miss Zimmer, cousin, I wouldn't wait long to tell her."

Reed's jaw dropped as Seth strode toward the tables. How did he know that Reed liked Carina, when he barely knew it himself? He glanced in the direction of the house. Maybe he should stay a night or two to make sure things were all right. Tomorrow his men and Carina's could finish the drive's manicure project. Then maybe he'd take her for a short buggy ride and show her what all her neighbors had done.

He just hoped she wouldn't be so upset that she'd pull out her pistol again and fire it at him this time.

Chapter 12

Carina was going to shoot Reed Bishop. She'd hoped this could be a new beginning between her and the doctor, not to mention a chance to finally get out of the house, but the day had suddenly plummeted downhill like a runaway buggy. He hadn't even noticed that she was wearing the new skirt his mother had helped her sew the past few days from some unused fabric she had stuffed in a wardrobe.

She stared at her trees—chopped, sawed, and whittled back into submission. The horrid vines that had threatened to choke the life out of her bushes and trees were gone. There were even wheel tracks pressing down the weeds in the road. It looked nice, actually. In fact, she couldn't remember when it had ever looked so orderly.

"Well?" Reed nudged her shoulder with his, a proud twinkle in his eye. "You going to say anything?"

She faced him on the seat—the very narrow seat. His cheek was less than a foot from hers. She swallowed. "Part of me is furious. How could you do such a thing without my knowledge, and how did you get it done so fast?"

"Had some help."

"You must have had a whole lot of help. Who was it?"

He pulled in his lips and looked off to the side, giving her a moment to study him. His cheeks had a pleasing tan, not the pale color of so many businessmen from the city. His nose was straight and just the right size—not too big or too small. Today his clothes were dirty from his physical labors, not spotless as on most occasions. She actually preferred this more casual look. His hair hung down to his shoulders, damp and curling from a recent washing. She exhaled a sigh. Why did they always have to be at odds with one another?

He turned back to her, his eyes pleading for understanding. "I. . .uh. . .told some. . .uh. . .neighbors about your being injured and how you needed some help."

"What!" She shot to her feet, conking her head on the top of the buggy. Rubbing the sore spot, she glared down at him. "I do not need help, Dr. Bishop. I've told you before that Zimmers take care of themselves. Who was it who helped, anyway?"

"Sit down before you fall off the buggy, please." He gently tugged on her arm.

She did as asked, but only because standing there with her neck bent so awkwardly due to the low roof made her head hurt. Folding her hands and clenching them, she listened as he rattled off a list of her neighbors who had come and helped clear her long drive. Her ire grew with each name that fell from his lips.

So many names. So many people to be beholden to. How could she possible pay them all back?

Now she understood what all the pounding had been about. It hadn't been her head at all—well, maybe some of it was at first, but not later. Even her fader had fussed about it, according to Betsey, but he merely drank more and spent the past few days in a stupor.

Carina allowed her gaze to wander down the closely cropped drive. It actually did look very nice. Maybe they could plant some flowers along the side of the road, but then that would require a lot more labor and someone to locate the plants and then water them. She sighed. Always more work.

"Tell me what you're thinking. Are you upset?"

The gentleness in his voice drew her, made her want to cast aside all her worries and trust him. But how could she ever truly trust a Bishop?

"Yes, I'm upset. Just think how many people I'm indebted to now—and I don't even know some of them. How could I ever repay them?"

He turned slightly in the seat, knocking his knees against her. "They don't expect repayment. They did it to help an injured neighbor."

"Why? Why now, when no one ever offered to help before?"

"Everyone needs help sometimes. Help from family. Help from friends, and help from God."

"You're avoiding my question, Dr. Bishop. Why help me? Why now?"

"Because I put out word that there was a need."

She glanced down at her hands. "Therein lies the truth. They came because *you* asked. You—a Bishop, descendant of the Reeds who helped establish Charleston and have lived in the area for more than one hundred years, so the story goes. It had nothing to do with me or my father."

His arm slipped around behind her, resting lightly on the seat, almost an open invitation for her to scoot up close to him, but she didn't move. Could barely breathe.

"That's just the way of the South. Neighbors help neighbors. I realize it's harder for you to understand since you're not native to here, but accept their assistance and desire to help and be grateful that they did. I nearly got lost in those mangy trees and shrubs every time I rode home. Thought for sure one of these days a vine was going to shoot out, trip up my horse, and drag me into the swamp, never to be heard from again."

She giggled at the ridiculous image he painted. Glancing up at him, her smile fled. The intensity in his eyes stole her breath. He reached up and smoothed a lock of hair behind her ear, so gentle, so different from her own father's cruel touch. She ducked her head and turned away.

Think of Johan. Think of all Fader had been through she thought to herself. She couldn't allow herself to get close to this man. Her fader would never allow her to marry a Bishop.

She shook her head. Marry? Where had that thought come from?

"I'm sorry you're not happy. I just wanted to help you."

"No, don't misunderstand. I do like the changes." She stared down the road then over her shoulder back toward the house, taking in everything. All trees and shrubs within three feet of either side of the road had been cut back or removed. Several piles of debris were placed every hundred feet or so.

"I've talked with Woodson, and he will burn those rubbish heaps tomorrow or the day after, depending on the winds. We were late finishing today, and folks needed to head home to tend to chores."

She nodded, amazed at the difference. "It looks very nice. I just. . ."

"Don't make things more than they are."

Her irritation fueled. He had no idea what it was like to be shunned. Not a single neighbor other than his mother had ever come to visit her. Not even after Johan died. She blinked back tears. "I appreciate your efforts, but those good people did this for you, not me. They don't even know me."

His arm lowered onto her shoulders and rested there, as light as a feather. "I think you're wrong. If they could get to know you, you'd see that. Why not get out and attend some of the local social events? Come to church when the itinerate pastor visits each month?"

She shook her head. Tanglewood was her private sanctuary. The only safe place. She didn't want to leave it. "I can't."

"Yes, you can." His arm tightened. "You can go with Mother and me."

She shook her head. He'd never understand what it was like to be the daughter of a man people despised—a man who had cheated his neighbors to benefit himself. A man who never forgot a wrong done to him. "Please, take me back home."

His heavy sigh sluiced guilt through her. He removed his arm and jiggled the reins, turning the horse back toward the house. He'd only been trying to help. She held her hands in her lap, wishing more than anything that things could be different.

"I'll be gone for the next few days."

His statement and the lifeless way it was uttered dug a hole in her heart. Why couldn't he understand? She had no way to repay anyone. Keeping the plantation running and growing enough food to feed her small crew along with caring for her fader took all her time and energy.

"I'm going to Charleston to purchase a horse and hire someone to build a clinic for me. Is there anything you need from there? I'd be happy to get it."

His offer to help was generous, all things considered. Generous, just like him. She had hated him for so long that she still had trouble reconciling the kindhearted Dr. Bishop with the scoundrel she knew he'd been when he was younger. The lout who killed her brother.

He pulled the buggy to a stop, set the brake, and climbed out, then turned and held out his hands to her. Swallowing back her nervousness at touching him, she forced herself to move and stood, taking care not to bang her head again. She placed her hands on his shoulders, and he gently lifted her to the ground. When he didn't release her right away, she glanced up. Those eyes, so intense, so blue, seemed to look clear into her soul. What did he see? A woman who wished things could be different? A woman who was sorry for all that had happened between their families?

He let go and stepped back. "You may get up and move about the house now, but don't do any physical labor. If you start feeling dizzy, sit or lie down. And have Betsey change your bandage in a few days."

She hated the professionalism in his voice and the dullness of his eyes, as a man who'd lost all hope. What had he hoped to gain from her? Why hadn't he just stayed away? Stayed in Scotland?

Knowing him to be the sweet man he was now only made things so much more difficult. Just think of how he'd cut Johan's life short. Had her brother been here all these years, her life would not have been so hard. "Thank you for all you've done, Dr. Bishop. If you could be so kind as to provide me with a list of the people who worked on the drive, I would appreciate it. I'd like to pen them a thank-you note."

He gave a terse nod and held out his hand, helping her up the stairs. He opened the door for her. "I'll check on Abel before leaving. If he feels up to it, he can sit now and do simple tasks like polishing tack. Nothing that requires walking yet."

She nodded. "I understand."

"Another thing. Betsey has probably mentioned this by now, but there was a vagrant down where we were working. He stole some food then ran off into the swamp."

Carina's heart leaped. "Do you think he might come here?"

He pressed his lips together and shrugged. "I'm hoping he was just hungry and has moved on, but it might be a good idea to post a night guard for the next week or so."

That meant she'd be short another servant. She could hardly expect a man to stay up most of the night then work all day. But neither could she risk their safety or that of her property. She couldn't afford to lose so much as a shovel or a spoon. Crossing her arms, she ran her palms up and down her outer arms as she searched the fields and then the area around the barn. Was someone spying on them even now?

He lifted his gaze past her to the stairs leading to the second floor. "One more thing you should know, I attempted to examine your father yesterday, but he wanted nothing to do with me."

"Can you blame him?" She stiffened at the unexpected harshness in her voice. She hadn't meant to sound so bitter.

His lips pressed tightly together, a wounded look in his eyes. He ducked his head. "No, I don't suppose I can. My family has done nothing but cause him—and you—trouble. Please accept my sincere apologies, Miss Zimmer." He slapped his hat on his head, spun around, and jogged down the stairs, taking Carina's heart with him.

≈

Stubborn, mulish woman—beautiful woman.

Why couldn't she acknowledge what was happening between them? He knew she felt something, because her whole demeanor had changed. Her true anger had dissipated only to be replaced with a false, forced anger, as if she needed to hold on to it or lose her identity. If she liked him at all, why did she keep pushing him away? Had he completely misread her interest?

He'd almost kissed her in the buggy. What a mistake that would have been. He smacked the reins on the horse's back, and the animal jumped and leaped forward. Getting away from the beguiling Miss Zimmer was probably the smartest thing he could do. She wasn't some wounded animal he'd found out in a field or the barn, but a living, breathing person. He couldn't fix all her problems, and trying to wasn't God's will for his life. He was a doctor—and he needed a clinic.

He turned off the main road onto the quarter-mile drive that took him home, slowed, and studied the landscape. A beautiful valley spread before him with a backdrop of trees that hugged the river. This was the perfect spot for his clinic. Close to the main road, yet far enough away that the dust stirred up by travelers wouldn't drift into the windows. Maybe closer to the river would be better, so that he'd have quicker access to fresh water.

He tapped his lip and glanced around the field. Finally he nodded. "This is it."

Chapter 13

Carina sat in the rocker on the front porch, watching the smoke from the debris piles slowly change from black to gray. Thankfully, the wind had blown it away from the house all day.

Sammy raced around the corner and didn't stop until he reached the porch. He climbed up onto the railing instead of using the stairs and sucked in a breath, his dark eyes shining. "Daddy says to tell you that there's the last of the piles."

"Thank you for telling me." She wrinkled her nose. "You smell like you've been standing downwind of them."

He nodded. "I played in the smoke. Pretended I was an Indian." He jumped to the ground. "Daddy says I should go see to Abel. See if'n he needs somethun'." He loped away as fast as he'd come.

She shook her head, wishing she had his energy. Just two years past twenty and she was already tired. Maybe she just hadn't fully recovered from her injuries yet. But her discouragement was more than physical. Her heart ached. It probably would never heal, not after her fader's harsh words and treatment. She shelled the last of the peas in the bowl on her lap, blinking back unwanted tears. *Why couldn't you have died instead of Johan?*

Betsey banged her way out the front door. "You done shellin' those peas yet?"

She held up the bowl and gave her maid a proud smile. "All done."

"Took you 'bout as long as it does Etta."

Carina lifted her brows and couldn't resist teasing. "I've been injured."

"Hmpf. Ain't nuthin' wrong with yo' fingers." She stared off toward the road. "Guess Sammy and Woodson'll stink to high heaven when they gets home. Gonna have to go dunk 'em in the river."

Carina smiled. From what she'd heard from Sammy, the menfolk went for a swim most warm evenings. She wished she had that liberty, but she was always afraid of an alligator inviting her for dinner or someone seeing her. And lately, she kept getting the feeling she was being watched. Her gaze traveled around the yard, the barn, the paddock, and back to the road. Maybe her head wound was the cause of her insecurity of late.

"Sure do miss Doctah Boss, don't you?"

Jerking her head sideways, she stared up at her maid. "Why do you call him that?"

Betsey shrugged. "It just seems fittin', is all."

"He's not your boss, you know."

She harrumphed again. "Ain't nobody 'cept'n you be my boss—you and the good Lord and maybe Woodson. Sometimes."

Carina chuckled. "It's good you included your husband, although you and I both know he's not the boss of the family."

Betsey gave her a stern look. "Now don't you be tellin' him that. What he don't know won't hurt him."

Laying her head back against the rocker, Carina smiled. She hadn't smiled since Dr. Bishop left two days ago. She hoped he didn't come back. It would be the easiest thing for them both—and for her heart, for she feared he'd unwittingly staked a claim on it. But that could never be. Her fader would never allow it.

"What's got you so down in the dumps?"

Carina twisted her mouth up to one side, unsure how much to tell Betsey. Her maid was the only person she could really talk to, other than Abel, and there were only certain things they could discuss. Susan had started coming around more often, though, but she could hardly talk to the doctor's mother about him.

"Go on and admit it. You miss him, too."

"Who?"

Betsey gave Carina's chair a shove, setting it into motion. "You know who."

She shook her head. "It could never work. Fader would never allow it."

"Yo' daddy ain't gonna be alive forever, now is he? You best be considerin' the future before you find it arrived and done left you behind."

Some days it seemed as if her fader would live forever. He was too cranky to die. She winced at the sliver of guilt that pricked her for even thinking such a thing. "How is he? I haven't seen him since the accident." She had no desire to see him.

"That weren't no accident. He threw that bottle on purpose, and you know it."

"I shouldn't have stood up to him. He doesn't like people doing that."

"He don't like much of anythin', if'n you ask me."

"Don't be mean."

Betsey pulled over the other rocker and sat down. "Yo' daddy is the mean one. He needs to find God, just like you do. I keep tellin' you that you don't have to bear all yo' burdens alone. God can he'p."

Carina closed her eyes, dreading another lecture about God. "Why would He help me now, when He's never done it before?"

"Hmpf. You don't know what He done and what He ain't done. How do you know He ain't already he'ped you?"

Carina jumped up. Was it too much to hope for a little peace and quiet on her own front porch? "He didn't help when Mother died, and He didn't save Johan."

"Yo' mama, she had a weak heart, child. And it's a blessin' that she didn't have to live all these years with yo' daddy, him being a mean ol' curmudgeon and all."

Pacing to the end of the porch, she saw Woodson walking up the road with another man, one who was leading a horse. Her heart jumped, and she narrowed her gaze. Could Reed have returned already?

" 'Tain't the doctah. His shoulders is too big."

Disappointment pressed down on her in spite of her decision to avoid Reed Bishop. "I wonder who it is."

"Don't know. I'd best get these peas a-cookin'. I'll check back in a few minutes, in case you want tea or coffee for yo' guest."

"He's not my guest."

"Well, he sure ain't come to see me." The door banged again.

Carina smiled at her maid's sassiness. Though it didn't always sound like it, Betsey respected her—she knew that. Carina actually enjoyed her maid's cheekiness and how it livened up her monotonous life. She watched the two men. The fact that the white man walked side by side with Woodson spoke volumes about him. So many white men forced their slaves to lag behind them.

They drew up to the porch, and the stranger removed his hat and smiled. "Ma'am, I'm William Dean. I bought the farm about four miles down the road. Used to be the Marshal place."

Carina nodded a greeting, thankful that Woodson did not leave her alone with Mr. Dean. Was he just being neighborly—whatever that was—or was there something he wanted? Should she ask him to sit? She tightened her hands on the porch rail. For a woman who lived in the South, her social skills were terribly lacking. "Nice to meet you, Mr. Dean. I'm Carina Zimmer."

Laugh lines crinkled in the corners of his brown eyes. His straw-colored hair hung thick and a bit shaggy. Betsey was correct about his shoulders being wider than the doctor's, although they were nowhere near as inviting to cry on. She ground her back teeth together. *Stop thinking about him.*

"How can I help you, Mr. Dean?"

He glanced at Woodson, then down at the ground. Carina glanced past her visitor to her servant. "Maybe you could water Mr. Dean's horse for him?"

Woodson gave a brief nod. She knew he understood her desire for him to stay close enough to keep an eye on things but far enough away to give them some privacy.

"That would be nice. Thank you." Mr. Dean handed off the reins.

"Would you care for some refreshment?"

He glanced at the front door then back at her. "If it wouldn't be too much trouble, ma'am. I could use a drink of water. That smoke kind of sticks to your throat after a while."

She invited him to have a seat then stuck her head in the doorway and called for Etta. After a long moment, the girl sashayed toward her. "Etta, I have a guest. Could you please bring us some tea, a glass of water, and some of your mama's shortbread?"

The girl's eyes went wide, but she nodded. "Yes'm."

Having guests was a rare occasion at Tanglewood, and she suspected both Etta and her mother would be listening near the door before too long. Stepping back outside, she reclaimed the rocker on the opposite side of the porch, leaving a more than respectable distance between her and Mr. Dean.

His gaze shifted toward the house, and Carina's eyes followed. She grimaced, realizing for the first time in a long while how sad her home must look to others. The place needed a fresh coat of milk paint, but when was she supposed to find the time for that?

"I moved here from Virginia a few months back," he said, curling the brim of his worn planter's hat. "Abigail Marshal was my great-aunt. She didn't have children, so when she died, she left the place to me."

Carina nodded, not sure why he was confessing all this to her.

A soft smile tilted his lips. "I've got me the most darling two young'uns you've ever laid eyes on. Clifton is five, and Lucy is just three. She's got her mama's blue eyes." A crease darkened his brow, as if his comment disturbed him for some reason.

Blue eyes—that put her in mind of a certain man she was trying hard to forget. She guided her thoughts in a different direction, trying to think of something neighborly to say. "We also moved here from the North when I was a girl. How is your wife adapting to living in the South?"

He frowned, making Carina wonder what she'd said that bothered him. Maybe his wife didn't like it here. Footsteps sounded, and Betsey carried a heavily laden tray outside, her gaze shifting straight to Mr. Dean. She set the tray down on a small table on the far side of his chair. Carina blew out a breath, hoping her maid would be nosy and stay close. And if she was going to be a proper hostess, she probably should move close enough that she could actually reach the tea. She rose, and Mr. Dean shot to his feet so fast that Betsey gasped and jumped back clear against the porch railing, her eyes wide and her hand on her heart.

Carina couldn't help the giggle that slipped out. She rarely saw her maid move so fast.

Mr. Dean's ears turned beet red. "Sorry for frightening you, ma'am."

Betsey's surprise at the apology addressed directly to her was obvious probably only to Carina. "No never mind. Have a seat, sir, and I'll po' you some tea." She cast a confused glance at Carina.

"I was just going to change chairs, so that I could serve the tea."

Betsey hiked her chin. "I do the servin' here. You just sit back down and talk to yo' guest."

If Mr. Dean thought her maid's bossiness odd, he didn't reveal it in his expression. He waited for her to sit then did so himself. Nice as he was, she was ready for this visit to be over. Having him here somehow seemed a betrayal of Dr. Bishop, not that that made a bit of sense to her. She looked across the yard to see if Woodson had finished watering Mr. Dean's horse.

Betsey handed Mr. Dean a glass of water, then poured the tea into cups. She added a spoon of sugar and a few drops of cream, just as Carina preferred it, and carried it to her. Blocking her guest's view with her body, her maid's brows lifted then waggled up and down. Carina waved a hand of dismissal, hoping Mr. Dean didn't notice. Betsey merely wandered back to the far side of the table. "What would you like in yo' tea, sir?"

"Oh, uh. . .just sugar." His gaze swiveled back to Carina. "Um. . .you asked about my wife, ma'am." His lips pressed into a thin line. "She passed on just over a year ago."

"Oh I'm sorry." Carina didn't know what else to say. She had no experience in friendly conversation and had already made one faux pas.

He shook his head and smiled. "It's all right. You had no way of knowing." His gaze darted to Betsey then back to Carina. He set the glass down and leaned toward her. "I know this is going to sound rash, but I came here with a purpose, Miss Zimmer. You have a. . ." His gaze darted around the yard. "Uh. . . a fine plantation, ma'am."

Carina tried hard to ignore his phony use of *fine*, found it difficult. Did he think she'd sell him her land? Didn't he say he just got a farm?

He ran his hand through his thick hair and stood, paced past her to the end of the porch, then turned. "I don't need more land, Miss Zimmer. I'm a widower—a widower who desperately needs a wife."

Chapter 14

Reed's gaze traveled down Market Street, taking in the changes since he was last in town. "I was so anxious to get back to Reed Springs—to be home and to see Mother when I first returned from Scotland—that I didn't even notice the changes here."

Damian nodded. "New buildings shoot up around here faster than storms blow in off the sea." He snapped his fingers. "Oh hey, the city has plans to build a new customs house straight up ahead on the other side of East Bay Street."

Reed looked down the long street to the far end where East Bay Street intersected it. "Isn't that mostly marshland?"

"At the moment. They plan to fill it in."

Shaking his head, Reed said, "It's amazing what men can do when they put their heads together."

Damian clapped Reed's shoulder. "Speaking of what men can do, congratulations on becoming a doctor."

"Thank you. I can't say I enjoyed every minute of my studies and working long hours at the infirmary, but learning so much about the human anatomy, how to aid it in healing, and how to mend lacerations and fractured bones. . . well, it was fascinating."

Grinning, Damian shook his head. "You always did like tending injured animals."

"True, and remember that time you cut your arm and wouldn't let your mother care for it?"

"Right. I wanted my good friend Dr. Reed to see to my wounds."

Reed chuckled. "You're fortunate you didn't die from a blood disease."

Both men stepped to the side, tipped their hats, and allowed a trio of women to pass by, then resumed walking side by side. Street vendors hawked their wares, pedestrians walked along the other side of the street, some casually strolling, others striding with purpose. He loved coming to Charleston, partaking of all it had to offer, but his home was Reed Springs, and until this very moment, Reed had never realized the truth of that.

"You can't imagine my surprise to look up from my desk and see you standing in my office. I didn't even realize you had returned."

"Did you not get my last letter?"

Damian harrumphed. "Which letter would that be? The one I got in 1849 or the one in 1851?"

Reed felt his ears grow warm. "I was very busy, and besides, I don't remember receiving more than a handful of letters from you either." He nudged his friend with his elbow. "Whatever happened between you and that gal you wrote me about who you met on that trip to Boston? What was her name? Melanie?"

Holding up his index finger, Damian waited while a carriage of giggling young girls drove past them. "*Melody*, and she's sweet music to my soul."

Rolling his eyes, Reed said, "And you once accused me of waxing poetic, if I remember correctly."

His friend slowed his pace then turned in the open door of a café. "This is the place I was telling you about earlier."

Reed sniffed the fragrant air. Pastries were fresh from the oven if he wasn't mistaken. "If the food tastes as good as it smells, we're in for a treat."

"Trust me, my friend, it does. I eat here frequently."

They took a table near the front window, which allowed Reed to watch the people coming and going. Charleston was so different from Glasgow. He studied the café, from its tall walls of dark wood to its small tables. "So, what's tasty here?"

"I like their chicken and dumplings."

"Sounds good to me. What happened between you and this Melody?"

Damian had always smiled more than anyone Reed had ever met, but the smile that revealed his somewhat crooked teeth now was the biggest one he'd seen on his friend.

Reed lifted his brows. "Good news, from the looks of it."

Damian clapped Reed on the forearm and leaned toward him. "I know you'll find this hard to believe, considering the frisky colt I used to be, but I'm now a happily married man."

Reed's mouth dropped open, and he stared at his friend, hardly able to believe what he was hearing. *Damian* and *marriage* were not two words he'd ever have used together in a sentence.

Chuckling, his friend shook his head. "I knew the news would bamboozle you. But there's more."

Reed blinked. "How can there be more? You have two wives?"

A young woman stopped at their table and rattled off the list of items available. Damian ordered for them both while Reed sat back in his chair and studied his friend. There was definitely a maturity that hadn't been present before. Why, his old buddy didn't so much as wink at the winsome waitress.

When she walked away to wait on another table, Reed leaned forward. "What else is there?"

"I'm going to be a father come this summer."

Completely stymied, he fell back against his chair. "Uh. . .congratulations."

"Hey, hey." Damian chuckled. "That's about the same response I had." He tugged at his collar. "A bit hard to take it all in, isn't it?"

Reed nodded. "True, but you seem happy and more settled than I've ever seen."

"I am settled. Very happy and very settled. Can hardly believe I'm going to be a father though. All that's a bit scary."

"You'll do fine, I'm sure."

Damian leaned toward him. "And you'll deliver the baby, right?"

All manner of thoughts assailed him—of the numerous women he'd seen die as a result of childbirth, of the infants who had died. The last thing he wanted was something like that to come between him and his best friend. "I. . .uh. . . am honored you'd want me, but I don't plan to practice in Charleston. There are plenty of doctors here already."

Scowling, Damian pursed his lips and stared out the window. "Where then? Will you move to a smaller town or travel out West?"

"No, I've just hired two men to build a clinic at Reed Springs, up near the main road. That way I can stay close to Mother."

"Ah, I see. She's still trying to get you to run the plantation, eh, and you're still trying to avoid it." His friend caught his eye. "Might be easier to steer clear if you don't live there."

The hum of conversation and clatter of forks against plates surrounded him, as he struggled to put his thoughts to words. "I'm not trying to steer clear of my responsibility. That's part of the reason I decided to settle there—so I can be near Mother and oversee things at Reed Springs and treat the people in the area. They need a doctor."

"I don't like the fact that you aren't going to be here to deliver my child, but I see the wisdom in your choice. So, have you had any patients yet?"

He nodded, his thoughts shooting straight as a lead ball to Carina. Had she missed him? Or was she glad that he was no longer coming around? "Actually, yes. I splinted a man's fractured leg and sutured a woman's forehead." *A very beautiful, spirited woman.*

Damian crossed his arms on the table, leaning forward with an intense stare; then he pointed his index finger at Reed. "What's that look I just saw?"

"What look?"

"That goofy kind of grin that I saw in the mirror for the first few months after I fell in love."

How did one answer such a question? Was his attraction to Carina so obvious?

"What woman did you sew up? Was she unmarried?"

Reed did not want to have this conversation. Damian would take a tiny thread of information and run with it. "Just a neighbor. That's all."

Damian's eyes rolled up as if he were searching his mind, trying to remember all the people who lived near him. After a moment he looked at him again. "What woman?"

"No one in particular."

"Well, does she have a name?"

Reed nodded and watched a wagon loaded with feed sacks pass by. WOOSTER GRAINARY—with an *i*, rather than the correct spelling of *Granary*—had been painted on the side of the vehicle.

Damian cleared his throat. "Well? The more you draw this out, the more interested I'm getting. Must be a very special lady."

He glanced at his friend. "It was Carina Zimmer."

Scowling, Damian tapped the table. "Zimmer." Suddenly his eyes widened. "Any relation to Johan Zimmer?"

Pursing his lips, Reed nodded. "His sister."

Damian fell back against his chair, looking stupefied. "Well, that certainly was unexpected. And how did that go?"

Reed sniffed a sarcastic laugh. "She sent me a letter, challenging me to a duel." He conveyed all that had happened, including his growing attraction to a woman who despised him. He needed to talk to another man, especially one who had gone through this whole falling-in-love-and-getting-married thing.

"Wow. That's some story, my friend."

"Yes, it is, but what should I do about her?"

Damian's brows lifted. "What do you *want* to do?"

"I don't know."

"I guess you need to figure that out. You mentioned in one of your letters that you became a believer in Christ. Have you prayed about your relationship with Miss Zimmer?" He waved his hand in the air. "I mean, with all that's gone on in your past, I'd think you'd need a word from God before pursuing her."

The waitress bustled over and set a basket of sliced bread in the center of the table. She hurried back to the counter then returned with two plates of steaming chicken and dumplings. While his friend was distracted with his food, Reed marveled at how wise he seemed to have grown—from a joking hooligan to a married man and soon-to-be father. And when had *God* become a word Damian was so comfortable with?

Picking up his fork, he stirred his food. He'd prayed about Carina, hadn't he? Yes, he was certain he had, but not nearly enough. He took a bite of dumplings, closing his eyes as he savored the salty dish. One thing was for certain, if I-never-take-anything-serious Damian could find a woman, get married, and be happy, so could he.

❧

Carina paced the hallway just outside her fader's door. She'd put off seeing him for as long as she dared. The last thing she wanted to do was to make him angry again. Taking a bolstering breath, she peered inside and found him sitting up in bed, staring out the window.

He noticed her and turned her way, frowning. His normal expression. "Well, what do you want? What have you sold off now? The back half of my house?"

His house. Not theirs, just his. She ducked her head, wondering why she even felt the need to come visit him. "I just. . .umm. . .thought I'd see if there was anything you needed."

"Hmpf. It's about time." He lifted his head, and his scowl deepened. "What's that thing on your head?"

She lifted her hand, touching the cloth tied around her forehead. "A bandage."

"Why? What did you do?"

Carina stared at him with disbelief. "You honestly don't remember?"

He shook his head.

"You walloped her with a bottle, that's what." Betsey bustled through the door, arms crossed over her bosom. Carina had been so worried about seeing her fader that she never even heard her maid's approach—and that wasn't something easy to miss.

"I did no such thing." He turned his fiery gaze toward Carina. "Why didn't you sell off that yappy woman instead of Amos? Why do you let her tell such lies against your own fader?"

Most of her life she'd been afraid of her fader, yet she'd wanted his approval. But Betsey had been the one to hold her when she fell down, to encourage her, to teach her right from wrong. Betsey had loved her when her own fader felt nothing but disdain. Carina lifted her head. If he threw another bottle at her, so be it. "Because it's the truth. You got angry and threw a bottle at me."

"Lies! Get out! Both of you. Out of my sight." He grabbed a pillow and pitched it at her.

Betsey hurried out the door. Carina caught the pillow and held it to her chest. She might have found the nerve to stand up to her fader, but his rejection still hurt. A parent shouldn't hate a child for no reason. "From now on, I'll have one of the men bring up your meals."

The look he shot her could have curdled fresh milk. "Get me another bottle of whiskey."

Carina walked over to the sofa and laid the pillow on it. This topic was bound to come up sooner or later, so it might as well be now while she was feeling so bold. "There isn't any left."

"What! Why not?"

"Because there's no money with which to purchase it."

He snatched up the empty bottle hidden among his quilts and hugged it. "Sell something else. A horse. A cow. Another slave."

"No, Fader. I will not sell something we need just to fuel your habit. You will have to learn to live without it, as I have learned to do without so many things I need." She spun on her heel, unwilling to argue with him.

"Carina! Carina! You get back here!"

She hiked her skirts and hurried downstairs. If she could have done so with her ears covered, she would have.

"I'll sell that woman, you hear me, girl?"

Carina sniffed, trying valiantly to hold back her tears. She didn't want him to have the power to upset her. She needed to be stronger than him. When she reached the bottom stairs, Betsey was there. Carina fell into her big arms and was squashed against her maid's chest. Then the tears fell.

"It'll be all right, sweet child. Yo' Betsey is here."

"I'll never be able to please him."

"Nobody can, sweet thing. He's got a world of hurt all bottled up inside him, and it spews forth whenever an'body goes near him, just like a mad critter. It ain't no fault of yo's. That man, he needs the Lord Jesus in his heart."

She was so tired of being strong, of being the one in charge. She endured Betsey's jiggling, because next to being in Reed Bishop's arms, there was no place more comforting. "What would I do without you?"

"Hmpf. I don't know, child, but ol' Betsey, she ain't always gonna be here. That's why you gots to learn to take yo' burdens to the Lord. He be the only One who'll always be there for you."

Carina closed her eyes, too exhausted to argue. *Are You really there, God? If what Betsey says is true—that You'll always be there for me—show me. Show me that You're real. Somehow. Some way.*

Chapter 15

Carina guided Lulu around the far edge of the largest of her three crop fields. Her fader once grew tobacco here, but the rich soil was now divided into sections of turnips, peas, carrots, and brown potatoes, which waved their greenery in the warm breeze as if greeting her. Soon she would need to plant sweet potatoes and okra. She hadn't yet decided if she'd made a mistake to switch crops and grow vegetables, but she couldn't abide smoking and had quickly grown uncomfortable supporting selling tobacco, even though there was money to be made in such a crop. A smile tugged at her lips as she remembered something her mother had said: "If God had wanted people to smoke, He would have made their nose turn up like a smokestack."

That statement always set her fader off on a tirade of how her mother didn't appreciate all his hard work to put food on the table and a roof over their heads. Carina never understood that argument, because it was their slaves who labored, not him. He merely told the overseer what to do, as far as she'd been able to tell; then he'd visit in his study with friends, drinking, smoking, and playing games of chance. Her mother had never succeeded in getting him to stop smoking in the house, but at least Carina had. That was one thing she was proud of. When he first became bedridden, he'd fallen asleep smoking one night, and if she hadn't checked on him as she was heading to bed, the whole house might have burned down instead of just the quilt being damaged. After that she'd refused to buy him cigars, and he was forced to quit smoking. Now that she'd refused to buy him liquor, would he become even more difficult to live with?

She rubbed her eyes and yawned. Several times through the night, she'd woken up to the crackling of glass breaking—a drinking glass or a vase he'd thrown against the wall—and to his cries for liquor to ease his pain. Was she wrong to refuse him? Was he in real pain, or was that just an excuse to get his way?

Sometimes she felt as if she were the parent and he the child.

She made a clicking sound and tapped her heels against Lulu's back, and the mare started walking again. Her injured leg had healed well and no longer seemed to bother her, but for now, Carina would keep her to a slow gait. She adjusted the skirt of her only dress to hide the calf that peeked out from under her petticoat, a dress that had extra-full skirts that allowed her to ride astride and still keep her legs from showing.

The rapid *tap-tap-tap* of a woodpecker echoed across the open field, providing a sharp contrast to the slower whacks of Chester's ax as he chopped firewood for Betsey's stove. The early morning fog had burned off, revealing a clear sky almost as brilliant as Dr. Bishop's eyes. She circled around the far side of the field, checking for weeds and dryness, then crossed over the ditch that connected to the Ashley River—a ditch her fader had ordered dug years ago to make watering the fields easier. One of the wisest decisions he'd ever made.

Woodson and Enoch were crouched down, plucking weeds from around tiny melon sprouts. Her mouth watered at the thought of the juicy fruit that always tasted refreshing on a hot day. Woodson stood and sauntered toward her. She reined Lulu to a stop and waited.

"Seedlin's is lookin' good."

She nodded. "Yes, they are. I'm sure hoping for a nice crop this year."

He nodded. "I'm askin' the good Lord for His blessing on your land, too."

"Thank you. That's kind of you."

The tall, thin man shook his head. "No, Miz 'Rina, it's a selfish prayer. I likes to eat as good as any person, and my Betsey, she needs plenty of them good vege'bles to keep her happy and cookin' up a storm." He grinned and winked at her.

Carina chuckled. "That's true, but I do thank you anyway." She nodded to the left. "Speaking of vegetables, looks like some of our greens are ready to be picked. Can you get to that before lunch, so I can let Betsey know to expect them?"

"Yes'm, we can do that. I'd best get back to work, or Enoch'll get ahead of me. We's racin' to see who can weed our section the fastest."

"Go on then." She smiled her thanks, and he nodded, then ambled back to where he had been working. Woodson never seemed in a hurry, but he was a hard worker and managed to keep the other men productive. She was blessed to have such loyal people working for her.

Blessed. That wasn't a word she'd often used. Her life had been so hard. Was it true, as Betsey had said, that her burdens would be lighter if she had faith in God? She tilted her head back, lifted the brim of her sun hat, and gazed up at the sky. *Are You truly up there, God?*

No answer came, but her thoughts turned to a scripture she'd read in her mother's Bible the night before. Something about God blessing her land if she humbled herself and prayed.

Betsey had told her many times that she should open her heart to her heavenly Fader. To trust Him and rely on Him to lighten her burdens. That He was a Fader of love, patience, and peace.

But she'd never had a loving fader. Wouldn't even know what one was if not for watching Woodson with Sammy and Etta all these years. He was firm but playful. Teaching and patient. He hugged them. Teased them. Loved them.

She was jealous of a slave.

And yet those slaves were her true family. They cared for her.

Her gaze lifted to the sky. She wanted to believe there was a greater power at work in the world. One who cared about people. One who cared about her. "Help me, God. Show me that You are real."

❧

Carina rode into the yard and discovered a buggy near the paddock. A pair of feet hung over the backseat—the napping driver, she suspected. Her gaze shot to the house then down at her old work dress. She swiped her eyes, damp from tears that had come as she beseeched God to help her.

Sammy left Chester's side, where he'd been stacking wood, and raced toward her. "Mama says to tell you that Mizzes Bishop be here and fo' you to get on inside in a hurry."

She slid to the ground and tossed him Lulu's reins. No need to tell him to take care of her beloved horse. Untying her bonnet, she hurried around to the far side of the house and peeked into the kitchen that set back a hundred feet or so from the main building. Stomach-teasing odors emanated from the room, but her maid was not there. Etta sat on a stool on the far side of Betsey's worktable, staring off into space. "Where's your mama?"

The girl jumped and snatched up the sampler she'd been working on for as long as Carina could remember. "You scared the wits out of me, Miz 'Rina. Made me mess up my stitchin'."

Pursing her lips, Carina resisted shaking her head. "Where's Betsey?"

"In the parlor, seein' to Mizzes Bishop. That Doctah Boss's mama is real nice."

She nodded her agreement then jogged to the back door, hung up her hat, and gazed in the mirror of the hall tree. Her cheeks were red and her unruly hair damp and curling in all the wrong directions. She licked her hands and attempted to smooth it down, but to no avail. Would it be terribly rude to just wear her hat in the house? No, Betsey would never let her get away with that.

With a deep sigh, she hurried to the parlor, stopping just outside the entrance. Susan Bishop sat on the sofa, sipping tea and talking to Betsey. Carina's heart flip-flopped. Had the doctor come with his mother? Abel had made no mention of him when she stopped to visit with him a few minutes ago. She leaned forward just enough to see that he wasn't in the room. Disappointment warred with relief. She didn't know what to say to him when she next saw him, and she knew she would before too long. Her hand lifted to the sutures in her forehead. Would it hurt when he removed them?

"The candy is quite tasty. Hard—made of cooked molasses, brown sugar, and butter that is boiled for a half hour or so. Then you add a quart of parched and shelled groundnuts, pour the mixture in a shallow tin, and allow it to cool, so my friend from up north in Baltimore said. You break off a piece small enough to fit easily in your mouth," Susan said. "So tasty. Oh, and imagine this. . .she found the recipe in *The Carolina Housewife*. Isn't that ironic."

Betsey nodded, looking mesmerized, although Carina wondered if she knew what *ironic* meant. It was little wonder Susan's son had no qualms about treating a black man, when his mother, the epitome of a plantation mistress, didn't mind conversing with a slave and even treated her as an equal.

"That sounds mighty fine. Bet my Sammy and Miz 'Rina would like that." Betsey glanced past Susan, noticed Carina, and stood. "Speakin' of her, here she be."

Susan's warm smile helped settle Carina's unease. "What a pleasure to have you visit again." Carina took the seat Betsey had vacated, her mind begging to ask about Reed. Was he back from Charleston? Did he find the horse he wanted? Did he think about her while he was gone?

"How is your head doing, dear? Does it still pain you?"

She shook her head. "No ma'am. Not so much." Carina glanced down, noticing the dirt under her fingernails from when she'd walked the fields and plucked some weeds earlier. She slipped them under the folds of her skirt, which now seemed ridiculously abundant, hoping Susan wouldn't notice. Reed's mother always appeared perfect. Her hair was immaculate, in spite of the fact she'd ridden over in the buggy. Her dress, a beautiful royal blue and light blue, didn't so much as have a wrinkle. Why, she doubted the woman ever sweated. "And. . .um. . .how have you been?"

"Perfectly fine, thank you. Especially now that Reed is back."

Carina realized too late that she'd reacted to the mention of the doctor, and there was little doubt Susan had noticed. Her lips turned up in a gentle smile; her brown eyes twinkled.

"I'm hoping he will come and remove these sutures. They pinch at times."

Susan's smile dimmed. "I'm sure he will. He's just a bit distracted at the moment. The men he hired to build his clinic returned from Charleston with him, and they are at this very moment laying the foundation. Reed was there watching when I passed by on my way here. His enthusiasm is as contagious as the plague."

She couldn't help smiling, just imagining him out there planning where to put his surgical table, how he'd arrange his medicines and his instruments. He was a good doctor, caring and gentle.

Susan cocked her head. "You like him, don't you, dear?"

She lifted her hands to her warm cheeks, knowing they gave her away. "I. . . uh. . ."

"It's all right. I didn't mean to embarrass you."

Susan's hopeful smile sent prickles of guilt racing down Carina's spine. She leaned forward, clasping her hands together. "Please don't misunderstand me. I do like your son, but there can be nothing between us other than friendship. My fader would never allow it."

"Fathers have a way of changing their minds when it comes to their daughters. Mine was completely opposed to my marrying Frank at first. I think it's because he knew we'd be spending so much time out at the plantation, and he would miss me. But it all worked out."

Carina shook her head. "My fader will never yield. In fact, if he knows I want something, he's even more adamant against it." The truth of the matter hurt her deep within. Susan had a father who loved her so much he didn't want to lose her. She blinked back tears.

"What's wrong, dear? I'm sorry if I upset you." Susan stood and rushed to her side, resting her hand on Carina's shoulder. "Tell me, dear. What is it?"

She pressed her lips together and shook her head. Even though she longed to share her doubts, to explain how her father mistreated her, what would it accomplish? Nobody could understand. "I would have to speak ill of my fader to explain it."

Susan squatted down and caught Carina's gaze. "It's admirable that you don't want to talk about him, but sometimes it does a soul good to share your problems with another person. It doesn't have to be me, but I do encourage you to find someone you're comfortable talking with. I've found that it helps ease your burden." She pushed on the armrests and slowly stood. "Oh, my knees aren't as flexible as they used to be."

Carina jumped up to steady her. "Are you all right?"

"I'm fine, but I do believe I'll be applying some of that liniment my son prescribed when I return home. I took a fall down the stairs once when I was younger and twisted my left knee. It's never been quite the same."

"I'm relieved to know you have a flaw." Carina gasped and covered her mouth. "Oh my. That didn't come out quite right."

Susan's shoulders jiggled; then she laughed aloud. "I'm far from flawless. Just ask my son."

Smiling back, she tried to relax, grateful that Susan was not as quick to take up an offense as her fader was.

"Would you mind if we walked a bit? I tend to get stiff if I sit too long."

"Of course not." Carina held out her palm. "After you."

Susan stopped at the front door and donned her lovely bonnet. Carina had rarely ever seen one quite so fancy with its lace and ribbons. She decided to leave her ragged straw hat hanging.

Betsey entered the back door and hurried toward them. "You ain't leavin' already? I was hopin' Miz 'Rina might invite you to stay fo' lunch."

If Susan was repulsed by the maid's impertinence in offering an invitation instead of Carina, she didn't show it. "Why, thank you so much. I would love to stay sometime, but Reed is expecting me home in time to dine with him. If I don't return on time, he's likely to come looking for me." She laid her fingertip across her lips, eyes gleaming. "Then again, maybe I should stay."

Was Reed Bishop's mother playing matchmaker? Surely Carina had mistaken her meaning. Why would she possibly encourage a union of her highly sought-after son with a woman who had so little to offer?

Chuckling, Susan laid her hand on Carina's forearm. "I'm only teasing, dear. Don't get in a panic."

"Miz 'Rina can send you an invitation to come next week, and maybe you can bring Doctah Boss with you." Betsey lifted her chin slightly, as if not yet ready to concede defeat.

Widening her eyes, Carina shot her a glance, urging her to hush. It was a good thing she didn't have company very often, because she'd probably be in a constant state of embarrassment.

"I'd like that, and I'm sure Reed would, too."

Carina couldn't help wondering if the two women were in cahoots with each other. Maybe she'd just let Susan and Betsey dine with the doctor while she made herself scarce.

"Oh, before I forget, I need to give you something." Susan reached for her handbag that lay on the hall tree bench, opened it, and pulled out a cream-colored paper that had been rolled up like a scroll and tied with a lavender ribbon. "This is for you."

Her mouth went dry as she reached for the paper. What could Susan have needed to write her that couldn't be spoken face-to-face? Her index finger slid over the embossed stationer's mark that indicated the fine quality of the paper.

"Go ahead. Open it," Susan prodded.

She glanced at Betsey, who nodded her eager encouragement. With dread, Carina untied the ribbon and unrolled the paper to reveal a fancy script:

To Miss Carina Zimmer,
   Mrs. Frank R. Bishop requests the honor of your presence at a ball to be given in honor of her son's return home and his achievement as a surgeon.

Carina couldn't read any further. A ball. She hadn't been to a ball since. . .

"Now don't start fretting, dear." Susan offered a heartening smile. "I realize that you haven't been to many social events of late, but where better to start than my home? You won't have far to travel, and it will give you the chance to personally thank your neighbors who did such a lovely job on your drive."

Carina glanced at Betsey, who lifted her brows, her eyes wide, and eagerly nodded. No help there.

How could she face all those people? She had nothing to wear. She couldn't possibly agree, no matter how much it might disappoint Susan. "I—"

A thump sounded on the porch, then the front door flew open. Sammy burst in, eyes wide and tears streaming down his cheeks. He grasped hold of her skirt and gazed up at her. "Miz 'Rina! Some man done took Lulu!"

Chapter 16

Reed walked the foundation of his clinic. Would the four-room structure be large enough? He'd have a room where family members could wait, a private examination room that could double as his surgical room, and two separate areas for male and female patients. He stood with his hands on his hips and glanced heavenward. "Well, Lord, what do You think?"

One of the workers looked up. "Pardon?"

"Oh, nothing." Reed waved his hand in the air. They must think him odd, but he was sure they wouldn't mention it if they did.

The sound of pounding hoofbeats drew his attention to the road. His mother's buggy careened toward the side of the road, straightened, then began to slow. Reed ran toward it. Where was his mother? Had something happened to her?

Charlie jumped from the seat the moment the buggy stopped and met him. "Yo' mama sent me. There's been a theft at the Zimmers'. A horse and some food."

"Is Mother still there? Was anyone hurt?" *Is Carina all right?* he wanted to ask.

"Everyone's fine. Mrs. Bishop's the one that sent me. Says for you to get some men and ride the line between here and Tanglewood. It was a skinny white man that done the stealin'."

Reed's jaw clenched. It had to be the same man who had stolen food last week when they worked on the drive. He nodded his thanks. "Go back to the Zimmers' and stay there with Mother until I get there. I don't want her on the road if there's a dangerous man about. Tell Miss Zimmer I said it would be a good idea to arm herself and her workers."

Charley nodded. "Chester is stayin' 'round the house. Them other two men is followin' the tracks."

Reed hurried to Caesar and mounted. He wished now that he'd taken time to search for a better horse, but since the carpenters had been available, he'd been anxious to get back so they could get started. He galloped Caesar to the house, ran inside, and retrieved his Sharps rifle from his gun cabinet in the study.

Jarrod crept into the room with a fireplace poker in hand. "When I saw the door left open, sir, I thought we had an intruder."

"Ironic you should mention that. There's been another theft at the Zimmers', and word is he's headed this way. I'm headed out to search for him. Please alert some of our men to help with the search, and pass the word for the women and children to gather in a safe place."

Jarrod nodded. "Right away, sir."

Reed rushed outside and mounted. He prayed that the Lord would help him find the thief and that he would not get injured. A doctor needed to be healthy to take care of others.

Thuds from the horse's hooves echoed below the new bridge that had recently been built over the creek that paralleled their drive for a short way. The old gazebo needed replacing soon, too. Maybe that could be next on the carpenter's list. He rode past the pasture that held several dozen, fine-quality brood mares with newborn foals. How odd it was that the thief chose to steal one of the Zimmers' few horses when Reed Springs had an abundance of them. Maybe the thief avoided his place because of the numerous workers.

For close to an hour, he searched the acres of farmland, the groves of trees that hugged the river, and the woodlands that remained unused. He hadn't yet spotted either of Carina's men, and he'd almost reached the border between his land and hers. Slowing the horse, he listened for the sound of humans. Nothing but nature's chorus met his ears. The thrum of insects. A hawk screeching high overhead. Squirrels chattering in a nearby tree. A horse's whinny off in the distance.

Caesar lifted his head and pricked his ears forward, looking off to the right. Reed stared in the same direction. Had the animal heard something, or was he just listening for the other horse to whinny again? Could that have been Lulu?

A loud cry echoed through the trees. His horse pawed the ground and whickered. Something wasn't quite right, and Caesar sensed it. Reed turned him toward the noise, keeping his rifle ready. The horse plodded forward. Reed kept his ears attuned to the sounds around him, listening hard for anything out of the ordinary.

A short while later, he rode down a hill, and something white flapping in the trees across the field caught his eye. A woman's petticoat?

He reined Caesar around to the right, using the underskirt for cover. About fifty feet away, he slid out of the saddle. A shrill, catlike squeal halted his steps, and he lifted his rifle in case he needed it as his gaze searched the trees. Caesar jerked his head up and shied sideways, then trotted off. Reed lunged at him but missed. He spun back around. The petticoat lay on the ground, and he stood facing the thief he'd chased the week before—a thief who now held a gun on him.

"No! Don't shoot!" A woman who sat on the ground leaning back against a tree held up her palm toward Reed, then just as quickly lowered it to her swollen abdomen. "Oh help me, Johnny."

The man glanced over his shoulder, his indecision obvious. Reed took a chance and lowered his rifle. He couldn't risk shooting with the woman lying so close to the man. If the thief shot him, so be it. "I'm a doctor. I can help."

The thief eyed him as if weighing his measure then nodded and tossed his gun to the ground. "Isn't loaded anyway."

Reed hurried to the woman's side and squatted. "Are you having birth pains, ma'am, or some other ache?"

She rolled her green eyes. "How should I know? This is my first baby."

He reached for her arm then paused. "May I?"

She frowned. Sweat beaded on her forehead, and her auburn hair hung damp. "May you what? Are you a real doctor?"

Reed smiled, hoping to reassure her. "May I take your pulse? And yes, I'm a real doctor—a surgeon, actually."

"What's a pulse? And I don't want no cuttin' on me." Her gaze lifted behind. "Johnny?"

The thief lowered himself to the ground beside the woman and took her hand. Reed glanced at him, noticing immediately how thin he was up close. "Are you ill?"

Johnny shook his head and looked away.

"He don't eat enough," the woman said. "He's been giving me most of the food because of the baby."

Reed's opinion of the man elevated somewhat, although thievery was never the answer for not having something to eat. Johnny looked to be close to his own age, and though about the same height, he was about half of Reed's weight.

"Oh, oh! The pain's comin' again. Help me."

She reached out to Reed. He grasped her wrist and checked her pulse, relieved to find it strong. Though on the thin side also, she didn't have sunken eyes and hollow cheeks like Johnny. He took her hand and waited for her pains to subside, and when they did, she let go of him, laid her head against the tree, and closed her eyes. "What's your name, ma'am?"

"Millie. Millie Jones."

"My name is Dr. Bishop."

Johnny's dull eyes popped open, and he stared at Reed. His shaggy beard touched his chest and held pieces of grass on one side as if he'd slept on the ground.

"We need to get your wife out of these woods. Can you take my rifle off a ways and fire it into the sky? There are other men nearby who can help us."

Johnny didn't move but glanced from Reed to Millie. In light of the fact he'd sacrificed the little food he had for his wife, Reed doubted the man would run off. So why the hesitation?

"Look," Reed said, "I know you're the man who took that food last week, and I'm guessing you are also the thief who stole food and a horse from Tangle-wood today, but none of that matters now. You're about to be a father. Do you want your child born out here in the woods?"

He pursed his lips, lowered his gaze, and shook his head. Finally he rose and trudged to the rifle. Millie yelped when he fired into the air.

❧

"Do you see anyone yet?" Carina called to Sammy, who stood in the open window of the barn loft.

"Not yet." The boy shook his head.

"Be careful up there. We don't want you breaking your leg like Abel." Sighing, Carina walked back to the porch where Susan sat in one of the rockers, mending a pair of Sammy's pants. "What do you think is taking so long?"

"Maybe they had trouble getting the buggy through the trees. Didn't Enoch say Reed found that couple in the woods?"

"Yes. Do you think I should check the room again?"

Susan smiled. "I doubt anything's changed since you last checked it."

"I don't suppose so." Carina sat on the top step and rested her cheeks in her hands. She wasn't sure if she was more nervous about housing strangers in her home or seeing Reed again. What would she say to him? Would he still look at her with those beautiful eyes as if she were someone special? No one had ever looked at her like that, except maybe her mother, but she had died so long ago Carina could barely remember her.

Why hadn't Reed taken the couple to his home? It would be far quieter there, and the couple wouldn't have to endure her father's curses, moans, and retching. But then again, maybe that would work in her favor, and they wouldn't stay long. She twisted her hands together. What a gracious hostess she was.

"Stop your fretting, dear. Everything will work out."

Carina nodded, hoping Susan was right. Closing her eyes, she muttered the prayer she'd started repeating several times a day. *Help me, Lord. Give me strength.*

"Hey! Someone's a-comin'!" Sammy bounced up and down, far too close to the window's edge.

She jumped up. "You scoot back, right now. You hear me?"

He did, and then she noticed he wasn't looking in the direction she'd expected, but rather down the drive. She walked away from the house and lifted her hand over her eyes.

Susan came off the porch and joined her. "I thought they'd come from the other direction."

"Me, too." A sour feeling settled in the pit of Carina's stomach as the wagon drew nearer. "That's not your buggy."

"Why, isn't that Mr. Dean?" Susan asked. "Oh, and look, he has his children with him." She started forward toward the wagon.

Carina followed, knowing for certain Susan wouldn't be so happy when she learned about Mr. Dean's last visit.

Reed exhaled a huge sigh when the Zimmers' kitchen and then the big house came into view. Mrs. Jones was going to deliver her child within the hour—he was as certain as one could be without examining her. Unlike Carina, who preferred to keep her problems to herself, his patient had moaned and groaned the whole way, grumbling about every bump and jiggle. Her poor husband had sat up front next to Woodson, who drove the vehicle. Johnny had been slouched down with his hat covering his face most of the way. Reed wasn't certain if his odd behavior was due to his sad state of health, to avoid acknowledging his wife's complaints, or just because he was relieved to have help for her. He'd stayed off to himself once Woodson and Enoch arrived, then had disappeared until they left to fetch the wagon, and returned with Lulu.

"Oh, is this buggy ever gonna stop? Just kill me now and get it over with."

Reed couldn't help chuckling. "I know you're uncomfortable, Mrs. Jones, but I'm not about to let you die. Not if I can help it."

"I just want this over."

He glanced at the buildings again. Just a few more minutes, then they could get her into the house and into a bed. "What do you plan to name the baby?"

"Depends on if it's a girl or boy."

"Uh. . .yes, I suppose it does. And what if it's a girl?"

Millie shook her head. "Johnny don't want no girl. Said his papa wasn't never partial to girls neither. I reckon we'll call him after his papa, Johnny."

"Won't that be confusing?"

She shrugged then grimaced and latched onto Reed's arm so hard he wondered if he'd be able to use it if needed. "Oh. . .somebody help me."

The buggy pulled to a stop, and Reed jumped down. Johnny slid off, and his knees buckled. Reed grabbed him. "Whoa there, hang on."

Footsteps sounded behind him, and he glanced over his shoulder, expecting to see Carina, but Will Dean met his gaze. Reed paused. What was *he* doing here?

"Need some help, Doc?"

He didn't have time now to analyze the situation. "Can you help this man upstairs so he can lie down?"

Will nodded and took Johnny's arm, all but dragging him toward the porch. "Where should I put him?"

"Ask Miss Zimmer." Reed hated ordering the man to initiate conversation with Carina, but he had no choice.

"Follow me, Mr. Dean," she said.

Reed's gaze snapped to hers, met, and held, like a ship tethered to its dock. Then she slipped away into the house, with his mother following.

Woodson hopped down and stood beside Reed, waiting for orders. "Help me get Mrs. Jones inside."

A short while later, with Mrs. Jones more comfortable in bed and Johnny lying on a cot facing the wall, Reed relaxed just a hair. Betsey had recruited Woodson to lug up a pot of hot water, while Etta collected some cloths and towels for the birthing. Carina stood in the hall, staring at Millie Jones. He longed to talk to her but knew the infant's birth was imminent.

Footsteps sounded in the hall; then his mother stepped around Carina and looked at her. "I talked with Mr. Dean and invited him to come another day when things were less hectic."

He couldn't tell if that was good news to Carina or not. He remembered the man stating how he was looking for a wife and inquiring after her. Had they come to an agreement already?

"Ay-yi-yi! I'm dying, I tell you."

"Reed," his mother called in a tone that always grabbed his attention. "Tend to your patient."

How could he tell her that he felt too awkward with Carina standing there watching? And Mrs. Jones hardly needed a crowd. "Mother, could you assist me?"

"Certainly, son. Just tell me what to do." She crossed to his side.

Carina's wounded stare nearly tore his heart out.

"Mr. Jones is badly in need of something to eat. Would you mind seeing if Betsey could make some broth? I fear it's been so long since he's eaten well that he won't be able to tolerate much."

She nodded then disappeared down the hall.

Mrs. Jones's wails made even her husband jump, but he was either too tired or too scared to look up from his bed.

Chapter 17

He didn't want her there. He'd asked his mother to help him, not her. Carina's chin quivered.

She hurried past her fader's door. He was the last person she wanted to see.

"Carina! What is all that caterwauling?"

She stopped. Sighed. He had a right to know what was happening. *Give me strength, Lord.*

She spun around and entered his room, stopping just inside the door. "I'm sorry for the disturbance, Fader. Dr. Bishop found a woman who is about to give birth, and he brought her here."

He pushed up from his pillows, scowling. "Why here? Why didn't he take that noisy—"

"Fader!"

Puckering up like an old turnip, he glared at her, and she glared back. At least he didn't have any bottles to lob at her.

"Why didn't the doctor take that woman to his own house? Doesn't he know there's an invalid here trying to rest?"

"The woman is very close to delivering, and our place was much closer. I will shut your door if it's bothering you so much."

"Fine. But I want them gone first chance they get. We aren't running a hotel here, and we've had to sell off our slaves just to eat."

"Leased, Fader. They will be returned to us when the contract expires." She glanced around his room, checking it. Betsey or Etta must have opened his window because it had been closed earlier. The nightshirt he'd worn the past few days lay in a heap on the floor at the foot of the bed. How odd that someone would have left it there and not placed it in the laundry pile. "Well, I need to be going. Do you want anything else?"

"Just some peace and quiet." He crossed his arms, and she took a good look at him. He'd aged a lot lately. His hair was white, not the light blond it used to be, and his dark eyes looked dull. He'd lost weight. "And my whiskey."

"I'm sorry, but we're out, and I don't intend to buy any more." She backed out, pulling the door shut. As she walked down the stairs with Mrs. Jones's loud grunts following her, she realized that her fader hadn't been as mean as in the past. Maybe her prayers were finally working.

She thought about how Reed had chased her from the room. Well, maybe some of them were working.

Reed stood at the top of the stairs and listened to Carina down below, rattling off a list of things that needed doing today: laundry, the meal items that needed fixing, how Etta was to stay upstairs and work just in case he needed something. Betsey confirmed she had the items for the meals, then Carina walked to the front of the house. He stepped back, not wanting her to see him, but she exited out the front door, never even casting a glance his way.

From the window on the landing, he watched her stride with purpose out to the barn, wearing an old dress with skirts big enough to hide a horse under. She entered the shadows and out of his view. He blew out a sigh.

"So, what are you going to do about her, son?"

He spun around. "Who? Is something wrong with Mrs. Jones?"

"For a surgeon, sometimes you're not too smart. I'm talking about Carina."

He swallowed hard and tried not to look surprised. His mother always was perceptive. "I don't know. It seems like whenever I try to get close to her, she backs away. I'm not sure she doesn't still despise me." Voicing the thought that had chased him all week hurt more than he expected.

"I don't believe that's true." She laid her hand on his arm. "She's had a rough life, son, still does for that matter. She doesn't know how to depend on anyone but herself."

"So, how do I get her to trust me? She doesn't believe that Johan started that duel. She blames me for his death, and rightly so."

Her lips turned up in a sympathetic smile. "Give her a little time. She's been reading the Bible, and I believe God is drawing her near."

"I'm afraid I don't have a whole lot of time, not with Mr. Dean coming around." Reed turned back and looked out the window. Carina rode out of the barn on Lulu's back—riding astride. His mouth fell open. Would that woman never cease to surprise him?

"My stars."

His mother chuckled. "Carina's not exactly representative of your average Southern woman, is she?"

Reed had to smile. "No, she is not. That's for certain."

"Who's that out there?" a deep voice called from the room across from the one the Joneses were staying in.

His mother lifted her brows. "I'll check on Mrs. Jones and the baby and leave that old bear to you."

"What would the good ladies of your society club think if they heard such talk, Mother?" Though he pretended to be astonished at her name-calling, Reed couldn't help chuckling.

His mother winked and lifted her index finger to her lips. "Shh. . ."

He faced the door, steeling himself for the lambasting he knew was coming, and peered in. "It is I, Dr. Bishop. May I come in, sir?"

"What are you doing in my house again?"

"I delivered a baby last night."

"Oh, yeah. Carina told me there was strangers staying here."

He lifted his chin, and as the light from the open window illuminated his face, Reed could see the severe yellow cast to his chin. He stepped closer, wanting to look at the man's eyes. "How long has your skin been so yellow?"

"What!" He raised his arm and slid back the sleeve and stared at his skin. "What do you mean? Looks fine to me."

"Hmm...look at me, please." When he lifted his head with a haughty glower, Reed lifted one of the man's eyelids, unhappy to see the yellowing there also. "May I see your tongue?"

Mr. Zimmer surprised Reed by complying. "You're thinner than when I last saw you. How's your appetite?"

He fell back against his pillows as if just that small effort exhausted him. "Don't have one."

Reed had seen a number of patients at the infirmary in Glasgow with the same symptoms, and not a one of them got better. This was not news that Carina needed to hear. She already had far too many burdens on her thin shoulders already.

"Say, can you get me some liquor? This ache in my gut hurts me something fierce." He crossed his arms over his thin chest. "That closefisted daughter of mine refuses to buy me any."

"I'm afraid I can't do that, sir. That's between you and your daughter."

Mr. Zimmer's head snapped up. "You Bishops never did do a thing to help a Zimmer. Get out of my room."

Reed moved off the side of the bed and stood. "I'm sorry you feel that way. I was hoping to talk to you about Carina."

"What about her?"

He hadn't planned out what to say if he ever got to talk to Carina's father. He still wasn't completely sure of his feelings—just that he had them—and they were strong. But God had opened an unexpected door, so he would step through. "I have feelings for her."

Karl Zimmer wrinkled up like a prune and muttered a curse. "Over my dead body. No Bishop will ever marry my daughter."

⁂

Carina rushed up the steps. She'd forgotten her sun hat, which she'd left in her room yesterday. Her fader's harsh words gushed out the door, stabbing her heart. She'd been right. His animosity toward the Bishops was as strong today as ever. He would never allow her to marry Reed. She spun around, her heart breaking, and rushed down the stairs. She never should have gotten her hopes up.

Chapter 18

Carina held Millie's baby in her arms, watching the quiet little boy doze. Tufts of blond hair stuck up like duckling fuzz. "What did you name him?"

With her eyes never leaving her baby's face, she replied, "Jonathon Carl Jones."

"Karl?" Carina's gaze zipped to Millie's. "That's my fader's name. Will you spell it with a *C* or a *K*?"

One side of Millie's mouth cocked upward, and she shrugged. "I've only ever seen it spelled with a *C*."

"*K*. It's a *K*," Mr. Jones mumbled from the other side of the bed.

Carina and Millie looked at each other, brows lifted. Then they giggled. Millie's husband hadn't said a thing until that moment, as far as she knew.

"Come and see your son, Johnny. He's so sweet. He's got your nose, I believe."

"Not now. I'm tired."

Millie shrugged, but her disappointment was evident. Carina handed the baby back to his mother. "Will you call him Johnny like his father?"

"We haven't really talked much about that yet. I was thinking about maybe calling him J.J." She glanced over at her husband. "Is that all right, Johnny?"

He shrugged but didn't comment. The man was horribly thin. Susan had told her what Reed had conveyed to her—that he'd nearly starved himself to save his wife and baby. Knowing the lengths he'd gone to—even stealing to keep them alive—had washed away any uncertainties she had about them staying with her. Maybe when Johnny got better, he'd be willing to help out around the plantation, and maybe she could find some way to pay him a small salary, though she had no idea how she'd do that.

"I'd best get back to work now. If you need anything, just holler."

Carina slipped down the hall into her room and shut the door. She pressed her skirts against her flat stomach. Would she ever marry? Would she ever know what it was like to carry a man's child? In that moment, as if someone had illuminated a dark room, she knew the truth. The only man's child she wished to carry was Reed's.

But that could never be.

❧

Reed strode into the music room and dropped into a chair. His mother halted the song she was playing beautifully and smiled.

337

"The walls are up on two of the clinic's rooms already."

"So why aren't you happy?"

Reed shrugged. He knew, but he had yet to tell her.

She rose and glided toward him, perfectly presentable, even though the breakfast hour had barely passed. "Is it Carina?"

"I don't know what to do, Mother. I approached her father, but he said he would never approve a marriage between us."

She cocked one brow. "Marriage? You actually asked him that?"

Reed thought back a moment. "No, but I told him I had feelings for her."

"Hmm. . .the Bible does tell children to honor their fathers."

He opened his mouth to protest, but she held up her palm.

"Hear me out before you say anything." She took the chair next to his and turned toward him. "Give this over to the good Lord. If it's His will for you to marry Carina, trust Him to work it all out."

"You make it sound so simple."

"Well, frankly, it is. Either you trust God with your life and trust Him to help you through the problems in your life, or you don't."

Reed gave her a melancholy smile, for that was all his hurting heart could manufacture. "How did you get to be so wise?"

"Old age, I'm afraid. You'll be wise, too, once you start turning gray headed."

"Some days I feel like I already am." He straightened in his chair, knowing what he had to say next would please her immensely. "I've been praying, Mother, and doing some thinking, and you're right."

"Wonderful! What am I right about?" Her brown eyes glimmered.

"About me and the plantation. I've realized that I need to step up and do my duty as part owner of Reed Springs. God showed me that I need to embrace my inheritance. After what happened at the duel, I felt I didn't deserve all of this. I wasted much of my youth, and being a surgeon, making my own way, was penance."

"Oh Reed. All of this is a gift, just like God's love. You can never earn it, because it's already yours."

He smiled. "I know that now, Mother."

"Mama. . ."

He uttered a mock sigh and shook his head. "I'm happy to say, *Mama*, that as of today, you've been relieved of your duties."

"What duties?"

"All of them. Everything having to do with the plantation. I'm ready to take my place as planter—but I also intend to be a surgeon."

"Hmm. . ." She tapped her index finger against her lips. "Let me get this right. You plan to select all the meals for each day, and see that the maids dust behind the lamps, and oversee the spring cleaning and the hanging of netting on the beds?"

He sat back in his chair. "Uh. . .no. I'll leave those and the other household duties to you. How about this: Anything inside you tend to, and outside duties will belong to me."

"That sounds wonderful, son." She hopped up. "Come with me."

He rose and followed. "Where are we going?"

"Outside."

He rolled his eyes at Jarrod as they passed him on their way out the back door. "Why are we going outside?"

"So I can show you how to hang up the laundry."

❧

If not for her heart breaking like an egg crushed under Woodson's big foot, everything else in Carina's life would have seemed as close to perfect as it could get. The crops were healthy and growing well. Her fader still grumbled but not so much as before when he'd been drinking. Baby J.J. and his mother were doing well, and she'd even seen Johnny outside at a distance, though the man seemed so shy that he wouldn't talk to anyone but his wife. At least he had Millie, and she seemed happy and contented.

She finished brushing Lulu and leaned her head against the mare's warm side. *Thank You, Lord, for giving her back to me.*

After giving her mare a final pat, she wandered back to the slave cabins to see Abel. She'd noticed him sitting outside under a tree when she rode back from checking the fields. He waved and flashed her that big, toothy grin she loved.

"Mornin', missy."

"Good morning, although it's getting closer to noon."

Abel pushed back his hat and looked up. "That it is. No wonder my belly's ticklin' my innards."

Carina chuckled. Abel had a way of making her laugh. "Would you like me to get something for you to eat?"

"Nah, I can wait a spell. Oh, oh!" He snatched up a long, narrow stick from off the ground and worked it down into the splint from the top side, then tugged it up and down. His eyes looked up, and a contented grin replaced his agitated look. "Ahh. . .that sure feels good. This ol' leg is about to itch off."

"Have you asked the doctor about that?" Just mentioning Reed made her miss him anew. She hung her head, wishing there was a way to change things.

"Ain't seen him since the day he delivered that baby. What was that—ten days or so?"

"Eleven."

"Not that nobody's countin'."

She glanced up but didn't smile, realizing she'd been doing exactly that. Pining for what she couldn't have was making her miserable.

"You needs to give yo' burden to the Lord, missy. You don't have to carry it yo'self."

"I'm trying, honestly. But it's so hard at times."

"I know it is, but don't you think it was hard on God when He let His Son die for the sins of this world? Ain't nuthin' that's worth anything that don't cost us something."

She'd recently read in the New Testament about how Jesus had willingly died on the cross to set man free from the bondage of sin. She thought of Millie's sweet baby and how hard it would be for her to sacrifice her child. Carina shook her head. It would be unbearable to watch your child suffer. How much more must it have been for God, who could have merely uttered a word or even a whisper and made all of His Son's suffering on the cross stop.

How small and petty her worries seemed in the light of Christ's sacrifice.

"Thank you, Abel. You sure are wise."

She made her way past the barn but paused when she saw the wagon in the yard. "Oh no. Not again." This was the third time since the day Johnny and Millie had arrived that William Dean had come to visit, and each time was just before the noon meal.

She was in no mood to see him again. He was a nice enough man—and his children were sweet—but she had no desire to marry him. How was she going to get that across to him?

Carina spun around and hurried past the barn. Abel's brows lifted when she came his way again, but she turned right and darted behind the barn. Lifting her skirts, she climbed into the paddock and hunkered down, hoping the fence rails might give her some cover. Comet whickered and walked her way. "No!" She swatted her hand in the air. His head jerked up, but he didn't take the hint and slowly wandered in her direction. Not wasting any more time on the gelding, she looked for Mr. Dean, and when she didn't see him, she made a mad dash toward the side of the house.

Etta sat outside the kitchen and saw her coming. "Wha'cha doin', Miz 'Rina?" she called out loudly.

"Shhh. . ." Carina held her finger to her lips.

Etta glanced around, eyes wide. "What's wrong? How come we gotta be quiet?"

Heaving a sigh, Carina straightened. What was the point of sneaking around when you had Etta to announce your presence?

As she crept in the back door, she thought she heard the front door close. Could she be so fortunate? She tiptoed past the stairway leading to the second floor and into the parlor, where she peeked out the front window. Sure enough, Mr. Dean was climbing into his wagon. He stood there a minute, hands on hips, and slowly turned in a half circle. Was he looking for her?

He turned back toward the front of the house, and she jumped sideways, out of view. Holding her breath, she listened for the jingle of harnesses, and then finally let the air from her lungs.

"What in the world are you doin' standing in the corner, child?"

Carina jumped. How could a woman as large as Betsey be so quiet when she wanted to be?

"I ain't seen you doin' that since. . .well. . .can't say as I ever have."

"You scared me."

"What are you up to?" Her maid narrowed her eyes. "Hiding. Mmm-hmm. From that nice Mr. Dean. Shame on you."

Yes, he was nice, but he wasn't Reed Bishop, and she didn't want to give the man any false hopes.

"Well, never you mind. Yo' daddy's wantin' to see you. That lawyer man was here whilst you was out checkin' the fields." Betsey's wide grin reached from ear to ear. "So get on up there. I'm dyin' to hear the good news."

Had he finally changed his will to make her his heir? Dare she hope? But what else could her fader want? He never asked for her, not unless he wanted to try again to get her to buy him some whiskey, but even those requests had come less often of late. Standing outside his door, she braced herself. In spite of Betsey's optimism, she had a feeling she wouldn't like what he was going to say.

She rapped on his door then pushed it open. The room was darker than usual with all but one of the curtains shut tight. The stench and the heat were nearly unbearable. How did he stand it? She swallowed hard. "You wanted to see me?"

"I did. Here." He flung a half-curled piece of parchment paper at her.

Unrolling it, she tilted it toward the light and read the heading. LAST WILL AND TESTAMENT.

She sucked in a breath and glanced at her fader. This was it. He must have changed his mind. Why else would he have her read his will? Her gaze dropped back to the paper, and she scanned the information. Her heart stopped.

I will my complete estate to my son, Johan Karl Zimmer, and in the event of his death to his legal heirs.

"I don't understand. Why would you leave everything to a son who is dead?"

Her fader's eyes gazed past her, to the right.

"Because he isn't dead."

She spun around, hand on her chest, at the sound of a man's voice coming from the corner. Johnny stepped out of the shadows, wearing a shirt that had belonged to her brother, a shirt that hung far too loose on his skeletal frame. He had shaved and washed his hair. He resembled someone, but who? She shoved the thought away. "What are you doing in Fader's room?"

A smirk lifted his lips on one side. "You don't even recognize your own brother? You disappoint me, Carina."

"Johan?" She studied his features. He had matured and looked far different. He'd always been thin, but his cheeks had never been hollow. When he reached up and tugged on his ear, she knew it was him. "How is it you're alive? You died."

"I'm sorry, but it is me."

She didn't know whether to run and embrace the brother she'd missed so much or not. He made no move to come to her. In fact, he seemed colder than she remembered. Distant. How could she have not known him when she first saw him? "Now I know why you never let anyone see your face."

He shrugged, and the tiniest of grins pulled at one side of his mouth. A fire lit in her stomach. The brother she loved so much was home—back from the grave. God had truly worked a miracle for her. She stepped toward him. "Don't I get a hug? Remember how you used to fall into my skirts and embrace my legs?"

He frowned, looking much like her fader, who remained oddly quiet. "Let's wait until you've heard everything and see if you still want one."

She reached back and grabbed hold of the footboard again. What could that mean? "At least explain how it is that you're alive."

That grin again, as if he had pulled something off on everyone. "I was never hurt as bad as you assumed."

"But I saw the blood."

"What you saw was a red wine stain and *some* blood."

Behind her, her fader chuckled, as if he'd been part of the ruse.

She concentrated hard, trying to remember that awful day. Was it possible? She'd been so distraught. Could she have missed such a thing? All she remembered was the blood. How pale he'd looked. How much pain he'd been in. "You tricked me?"

It must be true, for here he was. She lifted her gaze to his face, longing to touch him, to make certain she wasn't dreaming. "So why did you disappear? Where have you been?"

A muscle twitched in his jaw, and he scowled again. "What happened is that I fainted, Carina. I was so afraid when I shot Reed Bishop in the arm and he raised that pistol to shoot me, I simply fainted. He winged my side as I fell." He stared at the ground and shook his head. "All I'd ever been was a weakling who'd hung on his sister's skirts. I was too embarrassed to face anyone after that. I had to get away from here—get away from *you*."

"Me?" A searing pain lanced her heart. Johan despised her as much as their fader did? "I—I don't understand. All I did was care for you—love you."

He huffed a haughty laugh. "Of course you don't. You smothered me. You were always the strong one, so strong that I never had a chance. Like the bigger baby bird that forces the smaller one from the nest."

His words blistered a spot deep within that her fader had never been able to reach. The boy she'd loved so much hated her, and she still didn't understand why. She loved him as much as a mother loved her own child. She hung her head, wanting just to flee the room.

"I had an interesting visitor a short while ago," her fader said, his voice as haughty as her brother's. "Mr. Dean, a fine man if I do say so, has asked to marry you, and I've agreed."

"No!" She clutched the bed frame with both hands. "You can't. I don't love him."

"Ha! What does that matter?"

She tightened her grip on the wood bars, trying hard to stay upright. "Why? All I ever did was take care of this place. To make sure we kept our land when you took to your bed. I've worked dawn to dusk to make sure we all have food to eat. Why are you doing this?"

He sat up, his eyes cold. "Because you sought to replace me. Thought you could run this place on your own, and look at it. You've sold three-fourths of our land."

It was only one-fourth, but she didn't have the strength to correct him. She was losing the one thing she held dear: Tanglewood.

"You sold my slaves and pocketed the money and refused to buy me whiskey. You chased my only son and heir away and made friends with my mortal enemy. It's not one thing, it's many that you've done. Now do you understand?"

He didn't want an answer. His mind was made up.

"Tanglewood belongs to your brother now. Pack up your things and prepare to leave. Mr. Dean will be by to collect you at noon tomorrow."

Numb. Cold. As if her blood had thickened, Carina could hardly move. She forced herself to turn, keeping one hand on the bed frame. Lifting her gaze to Johan, she hoped to see a speck of the boy she'd cherished, but he was not there. He'd been replaced by a coldhearted imposter. His arms were crossed over his thin chest, and the look on his face said *checkmate*.

Somehow she made it to the hall. Millie's door was open, and she was bent over the bed, talking to her son. How ironic that Carina had placed them in the room that had been Johan's. She realized that the woman she was staring at was her sister-in-law. The baby was her nephew. But she knew in her heart that he would never know her.

Tears filled her eyes and overflowed. She sucked in a sob. Millie turned, giving her a curious stare. She stood and smiled, started to come to her. In that moment, Carina was certain that she didn't know of her husband's deception.

She raced down the hall, ignoring Millie's calls, turned into her room, and locked the door. Sliding down to the floor, the floodgates burst. She had lost everything.

Reed.

Her family.

Her home.

But most of all, the slaves—her dear friends.

Now she fully understood what it must feel like to be a slave, torn asunder from all that one loved.

343

Chapter 19

"Let's call off this whole thing, Mother." Reed buttoned his Highland frock coat, knowing his request would not be granted. His mother had invited half of Charleston to tonight's ball, while he had no desire to see a soul.

"You know it's too late. And seeing all your friends and our business associates will be good for you. Maybe it will pull you out of your melancholy."

She was wrong. He paced to the window and looked down on the carriages coming up the drive like ants to a picnic. Several servants were directing the guests where to park. How would he make it through this long afternoon and evening? He'd be expected to smile and dance. How could he make merry when his heart was shattered?

The woman he loved was married.

Why hadn't he acted sooner? Tried again to reason with her stubborn father?

He'd gone to check on his patients two days ago—to tell Carina he loved her, but she was already gone. Gone with William Dean. Reed clamped down on his back teeth. Hadn't she known his heart? Why had she been in such a hurry to marry?

She must have had feelings for Will. That was the only answer he could come up with.

"Come, now. We must greet our guests."

He clung to the window ledge. *Help me get through this night, Lord. Then help me through tomorrow. And the next day. My heart is empty. Deflated.*

His mother tugged on his arm. "Come. You're the host tonight."

He hung his head. "I can't. Go without me."

She raised her arms, cupping his cheeks with her warm hands. "Look at me, Reed."

He managed to do as she asked, but even that took effort.

"Now, listen to me. You have to trust God. You can't give up."

"I don't know how to go on without her. She was the brave one. The one with heart."

"What you say about Carina is true, but don't cut yourself short. You're a talented, godly man with a heart of gold. God has plans for you, but if you wallow in self-pity, you'll be worthless to Him." She gave him a gentle shake. "You've got to trust Him. Do you understand?"

He closed his eyes, letting the truth of her words soak in. Since he had lost

Carina, he'd all but walked away from God. His hurt had kept him away. *I'm sorry, Father. Please forgive me. Strengthen me.* "I hear you, Mother."

"Good, and it's *Mama*. Now let's go."

❧

She didn't want to come, but William had insisted—been quietly adamant and unrelenting—so unlike him.

How could she face Reed? Face all the others who had to be whispering about her. And what if Johan and Millie came? Surely Susan wouldn't have invited them, and yet they were her neighbors now.

She'd dawdled so long that they'd missed the meal, but she didn't care. That just meant less time at Reed Springs. She stood against one wall, attempting to hide behind a trio of plants. She had only seen Reed a time or two when he passed by dancing with a pretty woman, but each time it had been a different woman. Did he ever think of her these days?

The fast-paced music of the Cally polka slowed and the musicians shifted to a slower-paced waltz. That was one more dance completed. A few more minutes until they could leave.

"Excuse me, ma'am, but could I have this dance?"

Reed. Carina sucked in a sharp breath, afraid to move. How could she say yes? How could she touch him? Be so close as to feel his breath on her cheek? To look into his eyes? She kept her head down and shook it. "I'm sorry. I can't."

"Why, would your *husband* object?"

The bitterness in his voice drew up her head. "Husband?"

Reed's gaze hardened to a smoky blue. "Will's not here tonight? Surely you didn't come without an escort. Why, that would be as scandalous as riding a horse astride."

Why was he deliberately trying to provoke her? "I—"

She couldn't stand there and not touch him. Not see the fire ignite in his gaze when he looked at her. This Reed Bishop was not a man she knew. Pivoting sideways, she darted between two of the plants and raced outside. Unlike the last dreadful ball she'd attended, this one took place on the second floor of the Reed home. She ran onto the piazza and found herself trapped with no place to go. At least she didn't have to look at him. She gazed out on the beautiful garden below. The azaleas flamed bright pink, red, and white, while a myriad of other flowers turned their faces to the sun that would soon be setting.

Her heart pounded at the deliberate footsteps slowly coming her way. What did he want her to say? That she was sorry for what her fader had said to him? He had no idea how truly sorry she was.

He blew out a heavy sigh. "I'm sorry, Carina. I so wanted things to be different."

She blinked her eyes, trying hard to keep from crying. Her throat ached.

What torture this was.

"Have you nothing to say?"

From the corner of her eye, she saw him rub the arm that had been wounded in the duel. At that moment she realized how she'd wronged him. "I'm so sorry, Reed."

"For what?"

She had to look at him when she apologized. She owed him that much. Lifting her gaze to his, her heart clenched. There was so much pain it nearly buckled her knees. "I'm sorry for blaming you for Johan's death. I'm sure you've heard by now that he's alive and well and living at Tanglewood."

"Yes, I did, but I don't know whether to congratulate you or offer condolences."

She had to smile at that. "Considering all that's happened, I'd say condolences is probably the correct choice."

His hands lifted to her upper arms. The light breeze lifted his hair then dropped it. "What did happen?"

"What have you heard?"

"Not much. When I rode over to check on Abel, he was the only one I saw, and he didn't say much. Just that nothing was the same with you gone."

Her lower lip quivered. "I miss them all so much." She lost the battle against her tears.

His gaze softened. "I didn't mean to make you cry." He lifted his thumbs, and ever so softly wiped her tears with them.

The music drifted out the open doors, as if calling them to take part. Reed's finger slid up her temple and lifted her hair, revealing the row of sutures. "I need to come by and take those out, probably this week. Do you think your husband would mind?"

Hadn't he said that before? "I don't have a husband."

His hand stilled, as did his breathing. His eyes dropped to hers. "What about Will?"

She shook her head. "We aren't married yet."

"But you're living at his place."

"But I'm not living *with* him."

Reed stepped closer. "Then where?"

She ducked her head. Will had agreed only as long as she didn't tell anyone, but she couldn't hurt Reed further by lying to him. She shrugged and offered a weak smile. "He fixed up one of the old slave cabins on his farm. He doesn't own any slaves, so I have the whole place to myself."

Reed closed his eyes as if the thought pained him, but the next words out of his mouth shocked her. "Thank You, Lord!"

She pulled away. "You're happy I'm living like a slave? Not that it's all that bad where I am."

He instantly sobered. "No, I'm not happy about that at all. Why *are* you living there?"

"You're serious. You really don't know?"

He shook his head. "I rode over to Tanglewood, ready to defy your father and to confess how much I love you, but Johan said that you had married Will Dean. I can't really tell you what happened after that. All I knew was I'd lost you."

Carina held her breath. Dare she believe it possible? "Do you really? Love me?"

He cupped her cheeks and touched her forehead to his. "With all my heart. Don't marry Will. Please, Carina. I don't know how to go on with my life if you're not in it, by my side. I need your strength."

She sucked back a sob and fell into his arms. Abel had been right when he'd told her to trust God to work things out. Carina felt as if she'd finally come home. Home in Reed Bishop's arms. He pulled back and gazed on her face, all the love he felt flowing from his amazing eyes—eyes she hoped their children would one day have.

He leaned down, touching his lips to hers, sealing his pledge of love.

A woman cleared her throat, and Carina jumped back from Reed.

"Mother?"

"I see you two have reconciled things." Susan smiled. "Are you having a good time?"

Carina glanced at Reed, whose ears had flamed as red as her heart.

"Yes, Mother, we're having a fabulous time."

"Wonderful. I just wanted to let you know that Mr. Dean has returned home."

Reed blinked. "What do you mean?"

Susan's head lifted, a smug smile on her pretty face. "He and I had a discussion the other day when I delivered the gown to Carina. I let him know that she was spoken for, even if she didn't know it yet."

"Mother!"

If Carina had any doubts that Reed knew of his mother's talk with Will, the forcefulness in the single word drove it away.

Susan held up her palm, as if to silence her son. "You may thank me later, Reed. Right now a certain young lady awaits your attention." She turned back to the door.

"Mother!"

Glancing over her shoulder, she tossed them a satisfied grin.

"It's *Mama*—to both of you."

JOIN
US
ONLINE!

Christian Fiction for Women

*Christian Fiction for Women is your online home
for the latest in Christian fiction.*

Check us out online for:

- Giveaways
- Recipes
- Info about Upcoming Releases
- Book Trailers
- News and More!

Find Christian Fiction for Women at Your Favorite Social Media Site:

 Search "Christian Fiction for Women"

 @fictionforwomen